$100

THE SWISS AFFAIR

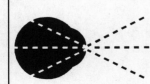

This Large Print Book carries the
Seal of Approval of N.A.V.H.

THE SWISS AFFAIR

EMYLIA HALL

THORNDIKE PRESS
A part of Gale, Cengage Learning

GALE
CENGAGE Learning®

Farmington Hills, Mich • San Francisco • New York • Waterville, Maine
Meriden, Conn • Mason, Ohio • Chicago

GALE
CENGAGE Learning®

LIBRARY OF CONGRESS CATALOGING-IN-PUBLICATION DATA

Hall, Emylia, 1978–
    The Swiss affair / by Emylia Hall. — Large print edition.
        pages cm—(Thorndike press large print basic)
    ISBN 978-1-4104-7052-2 (hardcover) — ISBN 1-4104-7052-0 (hardcover)
    1. Friends—Fiction. 2. Lausanne (Switzerland)—Fiction. 3. Large type books. I. Title.
PR6108.A4825S95 2014
823'.92—dc23   2014011336

Published in 2014 by arrangement with Harlequin Books, S. A.

Printed in Mexico
1 2 3 4 5 6 7 18 17 16 15 14

For Bobby

PROLOGUE

Before Hadley, there was Lausanne. Before Kristina and Jacques and Joel, there was still Lausanne. Their presence in the city was only passing; the lake did not burst its banks, no mountainsides were sent crumbling and no shutters broke from immaculate buildings to go clattering to the ground. Yet between the striding bridges and the turreted apartment blocks, the tree-lined streets and the looping parks, they played out their trysts and tragedies. Through it all, Lausanne remained unaltered, but the same could not be said for the lives of the people who lived there.

It was Hadley's second year of university, and she was spending it abroad, in Switzerland. *La Suisse.* Her idea of the place had belonged to cartoons — cuckoo clocks and soupy cheese, triangular chocolate and cool neutrality — but then she'd looked in a guidebook and seen the words *Swiss Rivi-*

era. She'd read about Lausanne, a city of vertical streets, rising spires and tumbling rooftops. She'd seen a picture of Lac Léman, shining like a polished mirror, with the serrated edges of Les Dents du Midi and Mont Blanc rising behind. There were palm trees and vineyards and palatial hotels with striped awnings that flapped in the breeze. Lausanne seemed possessed of a quiet glamour, discreet but with a rippling undercurrent, *un frisson.* Hadley had only been too happy to leave her university back home, with its huddled, squat buildings that were gray as elephant hide, boys who smelled of yesterday's beer, and girls who twittered like birds on a line. She'd imagined herself in this new Swiss landscape and had been in its grip from the very beginning.

Until the end of her days, she would probably always be able to picture the lakeside bathed in September sun, the clutches of international students sitting on the steps by the marina, laughing at the fountain spray, shielding the light from their eyes. At the start of the academic year Lausanne was always full of such types — slipshod groups who were yet to find their way, united by little more than being aliens, in the same place at the same time. If only someone had

10

taken them each by the hand, said *you are in a place of dreams but tread carefully. And look after one another.*

She would probably always remember the Hôtel Le Nouveau Monde, its delicate bulk like a glamorous but portly *femme d'un certain age.* Her heart would flutter, as it forever did, for there would be something about the place that would draw her still. She'd think of the gold-and-primrose dining room, the delicate squares of chocolate resting on the saucers of coffee cups and Hugo Bézier rolling a cigar between nimble fingers, his creased smile glinting through his cognac glass. He'd told her once that it was her very greenness that had attracted him in the beginning. How she'd stood so upright, looking somehow poised for flight. And it was true, for she'd been light as a butterfly as she'd danced into her new life, and she'd shed her old one as easily as a chrysalis. How cocooned, how gray, how very dull it had felt in comparison.

At the time she'd felt quite certain that her future lay in Lausanne, and, despite all the things that happened, she supposed she was still right. For it was just as Joel Wilson had said in his very first lecture, as he'd appropriated the words of Ernest Hemingway in a loose Californian drawl, *there is never*

11

any end to Lausanne. He had told them that, after their year, each of their memories would be completely different, that was how it was with Lausanne, just as it was with Paris. With hindsight she wondered if perhaps he'd been trying to prepare them, to warn them that Lausanne wasn't the kind of city to take its place among their memories with obedience and grace. Rather it would permeate everything that came afterward, and all of them, including him, would return to it again and again in their minds. They wouldn't be able to help themselves. Joel couldn't have known what lay ahead at that point, but it was almost as if he had. His light eyes clouding as he'd turned his back on the lecture group and stared from the window at the sliver of lake that lay beyond.

Hadley's year abroad was always going to be a love story. When you long to feel another's beating heart pushed close to your own, you don't think about those same hearts one day breaking; nor the splinters that will run beneath your skin, prickling and burning for the longest time. But this is a story about more than heartbreak. It's about an old man sitting at a typewriter, his fingers darting over the keys as a young girl watches in complicit quiet. It is about a city, a place at once fairy tale and reality-bitten, glorious and imperfect, sun-soaked and winter-whipped. More than anything, it is a story about old lives ending and new lives beginning, and it turns on the sweetest of moments, when two perfect strangers chance upon one another, and instead of letting the day blow them past, they pause. They turn. They speak. The story starts.

CHAPTER 1

Hadley Dunn was in Switzerland by accident, really. She'd never imagined that she could study abroad, thinking it was only for fast-tongued linguists, or almond-eyed Parisian pin-ups, the kind of girls who smoked cigarettes through pouted lips and drank their coffee black. Yet one moment, on a featureless February day, the idea came to her. She might have dismissed it as an idle daydream, but it planted itself with inexplicable solidity and continued to grow.

She had arrived for her seminar early and noticed someone flicking through a brochure for L'Institut Vaudois before class. It was Carla, a girl with a brisk bob and studious oblongs for glasses. She'd talked over Hadley in the last lecture, interrupting her as she'd tried to get to the bottom of the professor's obtuse requests for further reading.

"Are we paired with Lausanne, then?"

Hadley asked, as she took the seat next to her.

"Paired? This isn't a school exchange. There's an understanding between our two universities and the English departments. They'll swap a student, just one a year. And it's pronounced 'Low-zan' not 'Law-sahn.' "

"*Low-zan.* Why only one?"

Carla shrugged, and her mouth pursed.

"No idea, but I can't imagine many people will apply. Switzerland's a really expensive place to live."

"Oh, is it in Switzerland? Cool. Can I see?" asked Hadley, leaning over so that she could get a better look. The picture showed an important-looking building made of glass and chrome, set before a lawn that was neat as a bowling green and fell all the way to the edge of a great lake.

"Don't you live at home still?" said Carla.

"Yes," said Hadley.

Behind the building ran a band of spiked mountains. They were ice-white against the blue of the sky, and looked as though someone had painted them in as an after-thought, a flash of inspiration from a stage-hand. Hadley took the brochure from Carla and inspected it closer. Surely no university in the world could be ringed by views like that.

16

"So, this is just your nearest university? You didn't choose it, as such?"

Hadley finally tore herself from the page and looked up.

"Of course I chose it," she said. "Anyway, what does that have to do with anything?"

As her school friends had headed north and south, east and west, Hadley had stayed where she was. She'd enrolled at her local university, only a short bus ride from where she lived with her parents and little brother in Tonridge. Sam had arrived unexpectedly four years earlier, a bundle of sweetness, hilarity and unending demands. Her mum's laughter lines ran deeper than ever these days, and her dad's hair had turned a heavily seasoned salt-and-pepper. If she'd left home, they would have felt her absence acutely. Who would have shifted the peas on Sam's plate so that they made a smiley face, or helped start a snail farm in the bottom of a bucket? Not to mention all the babysitting. When Hadley read the letters from her far-flung friends, she saw between the lines. For all the tales of late-night fun, skipped lectures, easy love and easier lust, there were stacks of unwashed dishes in communal sinks, inane conversation over squares of toast, and life lived in an all-seeing goldfish bowl; she told herself these weren't the things to tempt her away from home in the name of supposed freedom, and most of the time she believed it.

"I'm just saying," said Carla, "you have to be adventurous to study abroad."

"It'd be an amazing adventure."

"And it doesn't suit everyone."

Hadley suppressed a smile. "You mean it wouldn't suit me?" she said.

She might not have yearned for a wider world, but that didn't mean she never wondered about it. She observed the other students, the ones who drove themselves to campus at the start of term, their backseats loaded with bent lamps and potted palms, or walked from the train station, weighted by rucksacks, arms still tanned from some foreign adventure; these people seemed to blow in from another world entirely, and they struck her as curious. They seemed to be already fully formed, passing effortlessly from school, through university and then into the rest of their freewheeling lives. Beside them, Hadley felt the novice, her lack of experience as glaring as a white sheet. She had an easy faith, however, that exciting things would happen to her one day. And when that day came, she'd be ready.

Behind her glasses Carla's eyes were mud-brown and unblinking. She didn't answer Hadley's question; instead she gave a prim little smile and clicked her fingers for the brochure. Hadley stared at her. She opened her mouth to say something, then closed it again. She handed the brochure back reluctantly, and Carla returned it to her bag. The professor, a crowlike man who always smelled of egg sandwiches and old coffee, sloped into the room and fumbled with his briefcase at the front of the class. Hadley opened a can of Coke and settled back into her seat. He began to talk about the Victorians and the Industrial Revolution, but she was hardly listening. She was thinking about the mountains, and what it would be like to live so close to them, and whether they'd make any sound at all, because how could something that massive loom silently? Wouldn't there be cracks and whispers and whistling winds? Would you grow used to it, that stolid, eternal presence, and carry on with life as if it was ordinary? A different kind of ordinary, but ordinary nonetheless. More likely you'd spend all day gazing skyward, happy as a mayfly.

A week later, just as the department secretary was counting the last of the applications to study abroad, Hadley tossed hers into the pile.

"The deadline was 5:00 p.m., I'm afraid," she said, glancing up. Her expression was unreadable. The shutters were drawn over her eyes.

"Seriously?" said Hadley. "But it's only half past."

"Rules are rules."

Hadley sank her head onto the counter-top. The secretary shifted her cup of tea and carried on flicking through the paperwork, first extracting her form as though it were a weed.

"It's just, I've spent the last week deciding if I wanted to apply or not," Hadley said, "I never thought anything could be so exciting and terrifying at the same time."

In front of her the papers were still being shuffled, stacks of neat handwriting, no doubt full of professions of suitability and promises of exceptional academic achievement. Carla had been wrong about no one wanting to apply.

"I thought that there was no way I could afford it," she said, "but then I found out that there were grants available, so that made me rethink everything." Hadley laid her hand on the secretary's arm and felt her flinch beneath her light touch. "Please," she went on, "I mean, I suddenly realized that I really do want to go. I probably won't get picked, but I want to at least try. I filled out the form as quickly as I could. Look, the Wite-Out is still drying."

There was a moment's silence. Along the hall, doors were slamming, signaling the end of the day.

"What if I just slip it in to the pile?" said Hadley. "We can pretend it's been there all along."

"Oh, quickly, then," the secretary said without looking up.

Hadley flung her arms up and leaned over the counter, offering a messy sort of hug.

The older lady stayed as stiff as a rod. "Don't make me change my mind," she said.

Three weeks later Hadley received a letter, of no more than four or five typewritten lines, telling her that her application had been successful. It took a moment for the news to sink in. Just like that, she'd swapped a year at home for a year abroad. A path had been laid out for her, and she had been happy enough staying on it; would so sudden and dramatic a swerve change the course of Fate? She didn't rush to accept her place. She wondered if she'd been right to want it.

It was her mum who finally convinced her

to go. They were washing up together one night after dinner when Hadley stopped and stared out the kitchen window. The view was of the house next door, line after line of perfect brickwork. The pointed tops of a wooden fence broke the rhythm at neat intervals. Her mum squeezed her hand.

"Sorry, I was miles away," said Hadley, with a smile. She returned her attention to the dirty dishes.

"We never want to hold you back," her mum said.

"But you don't. . . ." she began.

"Hadley, look at me. Sometimes I don't know what your dad and I would have done without you. But Sam starts school in September. Everything changes."

"I know. I've thought about that."

"There's a whole world out there," she said, looking into her eyes with pearly intent. "Perhaps it's time to take it. Take it with both hands, and don't regret anything for a minute."

Sometimes it turned out that people delivered their most important words when they were wearing splattered aprons, their hands awash with soapsuds.

At the airport her mum pressed her into a tight hug, her hair snarling in Hadley's earrings, their tears switching cheeks. Sam handed her a scribbled drawing of a stick girl and a roly-poly snowman with a string of podgy mountains in the background; Hadley dropped a kiss on it before folding it carefully away. Her dad insisted on carrying her cases, wanting to be useful until the last. He promised that they would save up for a visit in the summer, at which point Hadley's mum broke into a song from *The Sound of Music*. Thereafter followed a deliberately chirpy argument about whether the film was set in Austria or Switzerland, and Hadley's dad admitted to a crush on Julie Andrews. In the end the last boarding call for Geneva rattled over the speakers, and she knew she had to go. She turned one last time to catch her family waving vigorously. She had the distinct feeling that she was breaking some small thing, a binding thread that would stretch tauter and tauter until it gave up, just because it had to. She waved and waved, then pelted for the plane.

Once in her seat, Hadley took a breath and sank back into the silence of the skies. She turned the name *Lausanne* over and over, and it rolled across her tongue like a new kiss. It was her secret city, for hardly anyone had heard of it. Even Carla had admitted as much at the end of term, as she'd wished Hadley *bon voyage* with surprising grace. Then she had ruined it, in one deft move. "All I can think," she said, "is that perhaps it's not as nice as it looks."

It was late afternoon, and the September sun was still burning brightly, filling the train carriage with summer's last light. From Geneva to Lausanne the railway tracks followed the length of Lac Léman's shore. Hadley caught flashes of glistening water and saw the purple outlines of mountains rising behind. To the other side were sweeping vineyards and fields of swollen pumpkins. Now and again she saw a boxy château with closed shutters and high gates, and hillsides peppered with chalets, their pointed roofs and wooden verandas making them look like children's toys.

She regarded her fellow passengers with interest; a young backpacker with a scraggy beard was peeling an apple with a penknife; an elderly lady with a fallen beehive was sitting with a bat-eared bulldog curled in her lap; two suited business types, with the same dark sheen to their hair and their shoes, were hiding behind their newspapers. However fleeting, these were the people of her new life, and she felt drawn to each one of them. She was already gathering everything she saw, like a collector of curiosities who finds even the ordinary to be notable.

After less than an hour, the train rolled into Lausanne's station. Hadley stared at the white letters set on a blue sign. *Lausanne.* She had been here so many times before, if only in her imagination, that when the moment came she almost forgot to get off. She started, scrambled for her case and jumped down onto the platform. With impeccable punctuality the guard blew his whistle, and Hadley turned to watch the departing train. She imagined it continuing along the lake's shore, whipping into the mountains, spinning ever closer to the Italian border for it was bound for Milano Centrale. Other places that perhaps one day she would visit, too. She glanced again at the sign beside her, *Lausanne.* Already the name was more than just a collection of letters. She felt a prickle of anticipation, swiftly followed by a woollier, less distinct feeling. It was the sense that as long as she stayed just where she was, at the threshold of new experience, all would remain glorious. Nothing would ever be ruined.

The city was sizzling in the lingering heat of summer. Hadley dutifully wore the padded jacket that had been a parting gift from her parents, and it swaddled her, making perspiration dot her brow. She resolved to buy a chicer mackintosh for the autumn, the neatly belted kind the two women were wearing who passed her in the station forecourt. They'd clattered across the marbled floor, their lips moving prettily as they said words like *vraiment, absolument,* exclaiming and reasserting with panache. There was something about the French language, words were never just words; they seemed to change the air around them.

On her head, Hadley wore a knitted beret. It was another gift from her parents, but closer to the mark this time. *Just like one of those film stars!* her mum had cried as Hadley had tried it on. She'd twirled the shorter pieces of her hair so they'd clung to her cheeks in sculpted fashion. "I might get it cut," she'd said, *"c'est plus chic, comme ça."* She'd braved the hairdresser on the high street, with a picture torn from a magazine clasped in her hand. It had been the girl from the film *Breathless — À Bout de Souffle.* When she'd gotten home, Sam had thrown himself on the floor laughing and said she looked like a boy. But she'd felt light and mischievous. It was a haircut to cause trouble in, and to smile about it afterward.

Just inside the station there was a kiosk

for the tourist office, and Hadley helped herself to some leaflets and maps as a woman with a delicately tied silk scarf looked on. Her case was heavy, and her coat, even tucked under her arm, was hot, but it felt important to walk through the city that first day. Despite her bagful of pamphlets for attractions and complimentary brochures, she wasn't a tourist. A tourist would get on the wrong bus or fall into an overpriced taxi. She had the address of her new home scrawled on a piece of paper in her pocket — *Les Ormes.* It meant The Elms, a name that might have conjured up nursing homes and retirement parks in another setting, but in Lausanne seemed touched with glamour.

Hadley took a quick seat at one of the café tables just outside the station, brushing aside the vestiges of hasty departures, half-empty coffee cups and balled paper napkins, and unfolded her map. She studied it, sketching a route through the city. She glanced up to check the street name on the opposite building, looking past the fluttering flags and green bursts of formally planted trees. A lost soul with a crushed tin of beer rocked on his heels, watching her. She stood up, ignoring the line of taxicabs and their lolling, cigarette-flicking drivers.

She tied her unwieldy coat through the loops of her rucksack, took hold of her suitcase and set off.

Hadley had no possible reference point for a place like Lausanne. She'd holidayed with her family among the dunes of a wind-blown French campsite, and spent a week in the white heat of a Spanish apartment complex, but she'd never before been plunged into the depths of a continental city. She had only been to London twice, let alone anywhere else. The last time was to celebrate with friends after their exams; she'd kissed a boy beneath the Bermondsey railway arches, and lost her sandal to the tracks as she'd leaped aboard the last tube train. Lausanne was entirely undiscovered, as rare and intoxicating as new love.

From the station a narrow, pedestrian street appeared to point directly upward. Hadley took it, hefting her case along behind her. The area had the slightly down-at-heel air of so many station districts, all fast food and cheap boutiques, but now and again side roads spun away, appearing tree-lined and paraded with elegant villas.

After a panting climb, she emerged at the base of a grand square. She inhaled its air of dignified bustle, and immediately stood a little straighter. People were everywhere, walking with snappy direction, and despite the last fling of summer, they were dressed soberly, in creams and grays and camels and chocolates and blacks. Hadley fell into step with them and soon found herself in the winding streets of the Vieille Ville, the old town, with its opulent boutiques and extravagant patisseries with enticing displays. There was every temptation to stop and look and go in, bite into the end of an éclair and run her finger through a pan of just-cooled chocolate, but she kept on, her desires buttoned. As she turned up another hill, she checked her map and saw that she was at the bottom of the long, looping road that led up to Les Ormes. She'd been walking for half an hour, and a blister had begun to snarl at her heel. She could feel her top sticking to the small of her back and the trickle of perspiration that ran between her breasts. She could see already that Lausanne was too elegant a place to be disheveled in; the locals were uniformly cool and unflustered, so Hadley paused, collected herself and did her best to appear the same.

At last she came upon the approach road for Les Ormes. The accommodation office had said that the residence was built into the hillside, and that each room had a balcony. At the time, that had sounded romantic and picturesque. In front of her was a flat gray block that had none of the Vieille Ville beauty, nor the grandeur of the city center; its facade was as welcoming as a prison. The name Les Ormes was etched on the wall in black letters, and she stared at it. The main entrance didn't present itself obviously, and she went the wrong way at first, ending up by a bank of bins and a scrub of grass. She turned and walked back again. A side door banged, and two dark-haired girls swung out, chattering in something that sounded like Spanish. The door slammed shut and locked again before Hadley could catch it with her foot.

"*Excusez-moi?*" she called after them.

"*Si?*" They turned to her.

"This is Les Ormes, right? How do I get in?"

They grinned and pointed around the other side of the building. She fell into step with them.

"You know, when I first saw it, I was sort of hoping it wasn't," she said.

Hadley knew that she should probably have been trying to speak in French, for it was to be their common language for the year, but in the moment her scant knowledge deserted her. She wanted to explain that she had imagined something different,

30

she didn't know what exactly, just something more *Swiss*. But before she could work out how to say it, they nodded in the direction of a side alley, then left her, their torrent of talk barely faltering.

Trying not to feel deflated, Hadley walked around the corner and came upon the main entrance. There was a nondescript stretch of pebbled concrete, a set of bicycle racks and, without a doubt, the most beautiful view that she had ever seen. She dropped her case and rushed to the wall. Leaning forward on the flats of her hands, she stared out over the city. The cathedral reached for the sky with five points, and a castle perched in the middle of the twisting streets, as perfect as a chess piece. Turn-of-the-century apartment buildings, majestic and comely and pouting with balconies, sat alongside pastel-painted low-rises. Beyond the tumbling rooftops lay the dazzling water of Lac Léman with the French Alps like a concertina behind, spike after spike after spike, and almost close enough to touch. With her lips breaking into an incredulous smile, Hadley experienced a sensation more potent than wonder or admiration, or the already forgotten worry that reality might tarnish the dream. She'd felt it on the train, again as she walked through the city. And now, with the whole of Lausanne at her feet and a hillside breeze catching her hair, she felt it more keenly than ever. There was an extraordinary sense of promise pervading everything.

CHAPTER 2

It is sometimes said that the first night you spend in a new place sets the tone for all that is to come. In the beginning, Hadley might not have wanted to believe such a thing, but as the evening rolled on, it became a brighter, more hopeful prospect.

She was in an Irish pub set two streets back from the lakeside, in the company of an American, an Italian and another British girl. "Mulligan's" was the kind of place that seemed filled with packs of strays, bound only by the loosest of ties, conference attendees and indifferent work colleagues from international companies, their camaraderie masquerading in quick rounds of drinks. Hadley and her companions sat at the rear, crowded around a table meant for two. They drank bottled beer and asked each other to repeat things above the roar of the jukebox. She didn't think any one of them was having a particularly good time, but they were committed now. When Bruno had suggested a drink back in the kitchen of Les Ormes, they'd all agreed, displaying the eagerness of people who were only recently thrown together and were yet to identify one another's faults.

Chase, Bruno and Jenny all lived on her corridor at Les Ormes. Hadley had met them soon after she'd arrived, in the communal kitchen at the end of the hall.

She had just unpacked her bag in her room, and her few belongings were now in place; her toothbrush stuck out of a bleary glass cup, her clothes were hanging in a brown wardrobe that smelled of forgotten things, her books were stacked on a folding table that ran beneath the window. She'd glanced briskly in the mirror, run her fingers through her hair then set off to brave the kitchen.

"Hi," she said, pushing through the door. A girl sat at the table, propped on her elbows, her blond hair pulled back in a soft ponytail. She looked English; it was there in the familiar set to her cheeks. She rubbed her nose with the back of her hand; "hi," she said, "I'm Jenny," and then sneezed, a quickly stifled noise that sounded like a cork being pulled from a bottle. Opposite Jenny, a burly figure in a striped shirt and cream trousers was rocking back on a spindly chair. His hair was black and curly, and his cheeks were dusky with stubble. He swung back and forth with what he perhaps hoped was nonchalance. "And I'm Bruno," he said. Hadley smiled in acknowledgment, then glanced past him to the balcony, where a second boy was slouching in the doorway. He was willowy, with pale hair falling across his forehead and a small, indignant mouth. One hand held a coffee cup and the other a cigarette. He nodded at her briefly before turning his back to send a sequence of perfect smoke rings out over the railing and beyond.

"I just got here," Hadley said, to no one in particular but in the end alighting on Jenny.

"Oh, great, you're English, too, that's a relief," Jenny said, and smiled chummily.

"And you?" Hadley glanced across at Bruno, who was still rocking, the chair barely containing his bulk.

"Guess!"

"I'm not sure," she said, "Spain, maybe?"

He screwed up his face in mock disgust. *"Italia!"* he roared, pronouncing each syllable with great satisfaction. "But you wouldn't believe it, my mother's British, she's from London. I went to school there for three years, so my English is basically perfect. You know St. Alexander's, I suppose? Everyone always does."

"Not me," said Hadley, checking her desire to laugh. She considered whether to take a seat at the table with them or to walk out onto the balcony, ostensibly to admire the view but really to strike up a conversation with the slightly more interesting-looking boy and his smoke rings. Jenny bit her nails, Bruno swung on his chair.

"Wow, that view!" Hadley exclaimed, and went outside.

"Another Brit?" the boy said, glancing sideways at her.

"How can you tell?"

"Because I just heard you talking. There are so many of you here, I might as well have gone to Oxford."

"Oh, are there? I was hoping to get away from them myself. And you're American?" She resisted the temptation to add, *and why do you sound so cross?*

"New Jersey, through and through," he said.

He lit another cigarette and leaned on the railing. His shoulders stuck out like wings through the back of his T-shirt. His arms were long and faintly freckled.

"Do you like it here so far?" Hadley tried.

"I'm still deciding," he said.

Bruno had joined them on the balcony, and Jenny was behind him, her hands closing around a mug of tea.

"You can go skiing about an hour from here," Jenny said, her voice expressing little enthusiasm for the idea.

"Do you ski?" Hadley asked, wondering if she needed to rearrange her quickly forming picture of her.

"No," she said, "but people do."

"They certainly do," said the American boy.

"What was your name again?" Hadley asked him.

"It's Chase," he said.

"I suppose this block's full of lots of other students?" She attempted to disguise the urgency of her question. So far, communal living wasn't filling her with excitement.

"Some are still arriving," said Bruno. "The room next to you, Kristina Hartmann, she's not here yet."

"How do you know who she is?" Hadley asked.

"Haven't you noticed? Our names are on all of our doors," said Jenny. "I think it's creepy. Someone could come in off the street and find all the girls' rooms."

"We'll protect you, *bella*," said Bruno.

"Won't we, Chase?"

"Something like that," said Chase.

"I think we should all go to Mulligan's tonight," said Bruno. "Hadley, you want to come?"

"How do you know my name?" she said.

"He saw your door," said Jenny.

"But how did he know that was my room?"

"Lucky guess," said Bruno, with a wink.

"You look like a Hadley," said Chase.

"Does she?" said Jenny. "I wouldn't have the first idea what a Hadley was supposed to look like."

"And what's Mulligan's?" Hadley asked. "It doesn't sound very Swiss."

"It's not," said Jenny, "it's brilliant."

That first night Hadley thought they made a misshapen quartet. She learned that Jenny had left a boyfriend behind in England and was wondering whether to end things with him. "I have to be here for my course," she said in a flat and injured voice. "I never chose to come, so where does that leave me and Dave? Nowhere." Chase, meanwhile, saw Lausanne as just a pin in a map, with lines shooting out in every direction. He hankered after soaring passes in the Italian Alps, the sardine ports of southern France, the bell-shaped rooftops of Eastern Europe. Bruno's aim seemed simpler. He was content to just be. "It's the good life here," he said, *la vie est belle, n'est-ce pas?*" throwing his hands wide as he spoke. That night, Bruno shouldered his way to the bar time and time again, shrugging away their offers of money with gruff generosity. He had the thickset cheeks of a young aristocrat, and on his little finger he wore a signet ring like a rubbed penny. It seemed to Hadley that he didn't particularly evaluate any of them; he asked no questions nor even showed mild curiosity, as though it was enough that they were simply there, at his table.

As the others chattered away, Hadley was quiet that first night. It seemed inappropriate to proclaim this as the greatest adventure of her life. For the truth was, tucked in the back of the bar, with Bruno's leg pushing a little too close to her own, Chase's spiky stares and Jenny's forlorn hunch, it didn't particularly feel like it. Just before midnight, the others voted for a taxi back to Les Ormes. Hadley hesitated. That year in Switzerland, she had vowed to start doing things differently. She could feel the night breeze coming over the lake, and behind her were the city's steep black streets, inviting discovery. She waved Jenny, Chase and

Bruno off in their cab, explaining that she wanted to walk home, fanning away only the mildest of protests. The car whistled off, and she breathed in the Lausanne night in deep draughts. She was far from home, and no one really knew her; there was untold freedom in that.

Hadley walked toward the water. Across the lake, *en France,* the distant lights of Evian twinkled. Closer to shore, the waves slopped messily, and invisible masts chinked and rattled. She stepped outside of herself, wanting to appreciate the moment with all of its picturesque qualities. But instead she felt slightly uneasy; it was the expanse of darkness, the absence of people, the strangeness of it all. She decided to return by daylight and explore then. She turned and walked back toward Mulligan's, feeling just slightly defeated in her attempt as an adventurer. Through the smeared windows, she could see chairs stacked on tables and a cluster of stragglers at the bar.

"Excuse me."

She started at the voice. She turned around.

"I saw you with your friends inside. Are you okay, walking back on your own? It's late."

He was American, and he was a man. He

was probably somewhere in his late thirties, but he seemed the kind to have looked like a man his whole life. He was burly chested, with big shoulders and a square and muscled look. Leather jacketed. A little hard-boiled. A lick of black hair falling forward. She took all of this in with one seemingly casual glance.

"I'm fine," she said, "but thank you."

She didn't turn to go, not yet.

"Lausanne seems like a pretty safe city, but you never know," he said.

He rubbed the side of his chin as though he'd once had a beard. It seemed to Hadley a practiced, somehow naked sort of gesture.

"It's okay," she said, "I'll look both ways when I cross the road. I won't talk to strangers." She smiled and it was easy. "So, in that case, I guess I'd better go."

He lit a cigarette and nodded through a puff of smoke. She noticed his eyes then, and they were softer than she had thought. A liquid blue.

"Where are you from?"

"England."

"I can tell that. Whereabouts?"

"Somewhere in the middle."

"I spent a summer there once, years ago now. In Cambridge."

"Cambridge is beautiful," said Hadley.

"Yes, very," he said, looking directly at her in a way that didn't quite betray his thinking, "Now, tell me, what are you doing in an Irish bar on your first night? Not so very Swiss of you."

"How did you know it was my first night?"

"Second, then. Third at the most. But I'd put money on the first. You've got that look about you."

"I didn't choose it," she said, ignoring his last remark. "The people I was with did."

"You need to find some better people to show you around."

"Or," she said, "I'll just enjoy discovering it by myself. Anyway, why were you in there, then? If it was so bad? Maybe it's your first night, too?"

"Maybe." He smiled.

"I should go," she said. "Bye."

She began to walk away.

"Take it easy."

"What's that?" She turned back to him.

"I said 'take it easy.' "

"Okay, thanks. I will. You, too."

"That's very polite."

"Well, what do people usually say? I've never been told 'take it easy' before."

"What, never?"

Hadley shrugged. "Not that I can remember. It's not very British."

"Well, I'm honored to induct you."

"We should be speaking French, really."

"Au revoir, mademoiselle," he said, his smile crinkling.

"Au revoir, monsieur," she replied.

She walked away from him then, because it felt like the next thing to do. When she glanced behind her he was gone. Folded back into the dark city's fabric.

In the early hours of the following morning, Hadley was startled into wakefulness. She lay for a moment, twisted in her bedclothes, listening. Her room was almost entirely dark, with just thin slits of light where the blinds didn't meet. The noise came again. A rattling of a handle, the clacking of a key in a lock and a soft but audible string of curses in a language she didn't recognize. Hadley raised herself up on one elbow and listened. Perhaps it was Kristina Hartmann, taking the last unoccupied room on the corridor. She got out of bed and padded to her door.

Turning the handle, she poked her head out. Hadley's hair was a sleep-fuddled knot, and she wore striped pajamas that gave her a childish air. The girl in the corridor didn't hear the opening of her neighbor's door and continued to fumble at her own. Hadley took in her four dark leather cases that were

43

strewn across the hall, and her coat, a mackintosh like the ones she'd admired earlier, thrown down on the floor. The girl had golden hair that fell all the way to the middle of her back. An extravagantly patterned scarf was slipping from her shoulders. She ran an exasperated hand through her hair, whipping back a swath of it, and Hadley noticed her nails, painted in black cherry, and the smudge of a fading love bite on her neck. The girl turned suddenly and saw Hadley watching.

"Oh, did I wake you?"

Hadley wondered how she knew to speak to her in English. Her voice had a vague American lilt, and she looked the part with her tall, athletic build and bright looks, but there was another inflection that she couldn't quite identify.

"It's okay. Can't you get into your room?" asked Hadley.

"The bloody key they gave me won't do anything," she said, rattling it again in the lock. "It's useless. I guess I'll have to wake the porter. But he's probably awake already, wondering who's making all this ridiculous noise. Like you."

Hadley folded her arms across her chest, aware suddenly of her baggy trousers and ill-fitting top.

"I'm sorry," the girl said. "I feel terrible. I just want to get in my bloody room, I've been traveling all night."

The way she said *bloody* tickled Hadley. There was a whiff of the Home Counties about it. But despite her perfect language and accent, she was so far from English. Her cheekbones were high and slanted, giving her a powerful, feline look, while a mass of pale freckles dressed her down again and made her friendly. Everything about her seemed sophisticated — the linked gold chain at her neck, the shine of her smile, the perfume that Hadley caught the scent of even as she stood three feet from her. It was something smoky and daring.

"Let me try it for you," she said. "Mine's a bit sticky, too."

It opened on her second try.

"How did you do that?" the girl cried. "Amazing!"

Hadley helped her carry her cases in. She dragged the largest, catching her bare toe on its edge.

"I'm hopeless," the girl said cheerfully, throwing herself down on the bed. "What would I have done without you? What's your name?"

"Hadley Dunn," Hadley said. "I'm in the next room."

"And I'm Kristina." She held out her hand to shake, and Hadley took it, not sure if she'd ever shaken another girl's hand in greeting before. It felt formal and jaunty at the same time, and they smiled at one another. "So we're neighbors," Kristina said, "that's brilliant."

"I can't recognize your accent."

"Denmark."

"Oh, wow, really? I've never met anyone from Denmark. And how come you're arriving so late? Did your plane just get in?"

Kristina pulled up her sleeve to look at her tiny gold watch. It hung on her wrist as loosely as a bracelet. "Practically four o'clock in the morning," she said. "I was in Geneva and completely lost track of time. So what's it like here, then?"

Hadley didn't expect the first thing to come to mind to be the watery blue of the unknown American's eyes, and his crooked smile, and how thinking about those very things had sped her walk home through the city. She started to speak, but Kristina interrupted her.

"Don't answer now, Hadley, you must go back to bed. You can tell me what I missed in the morning. I'm really sorry for the disturbance."

"Oh, it was no disturbance," Hadley said.

46

She shivered, for it was cold in Kristina's room. She shrank smaller inside her pajamas and rolled on the balls of her feet. There was always time for friendships to develop, when fleeting first impressions could be replaced by more informed judgments, but within their brief meeting Kristina had somehow imprinted herself upon Hadley. She felt as if she were six years old again, on her back lawn, spotting a new friend through the fence posts, a relationship that could be sealed with the bite of a chocolate bar or a ride on the back of a bicycle.

"Maybe we could have breakfast together?" she suggested.

"I'd love that."

"After you've had a lie-in, of course."

"I hardly sleep as it is. I'll be up with the sun."

Hadley stifled a yawn. "Me, too. Good night, then."

"So nice meeting you, Hadley. Thank you again for saving me."

Back in her own room, Hadley walked over to her window. She lifted the blind a fraction and peeped out at the sleeping city. *"J'habite à Lausanne,"* she said. Then she went back to bed and fell asleep almost instantly, a smile at her lips.

That first night her dreams were twisted

versions of the evening's events, where insignificant details were switched around and made to matter. It was Kristina who appeared childlike and sleepy in baggy pajamas. It was the unknown American who unstuck the lock of her door. And it was Hadley's neck that was smudged with a love bite, a mark of honor that was already fading, as fragile as a butterfly's wing.

CHAPTER 3

Despite only a few hours of sleep Kristina rose early, just as she had said she would. She swung into the kitchen with her hair still wet from the shower, wafting scents of coconuts. Hadley saw how in the light of day her skin was sun-brown, and her hips pointed through the denim of her jeans. She might as well have stepped from the pages of a magazine. They made a pot of coffee together and spread rose-colored jam on neat roundels of baguette. Kristina laid a paper serviette across her knees and pressed a finger to each scattered crumb on the tabletop. She seemed delicate and reckless all at once.

"To our first morning," said Hadley, holding up her coffee. Kristina laughed and chinked cups with her, and it seemed more as if they were making a pact than a toast.

"And every morning after," Hadley added. "You know, I can't believe the others are ly-

49

ing in bed on a day like this." She and Kristina were sitting side by side, facing the view of the city. In the night, snow had fallen on the farthest peaks, and the thinnest slip of cloud streaked the sky. "I can't wait to get out there. Can't you feel it calling?"

"Maybe they're hungover."

"But you can be hungover anywhere. It's such a waste."

"Maybe they just know that they're here for the whole year. The city's going nowhere, Hadley."

"I want to make the most of every moment. I'll never have a first morning in Lausanne again. Never."

Kristina stood up and went over to the window. She threw it open, and the cool air danced in.

"There's a phrase in French, you know," she said, turning back to Hadley, "*Il faut profiter.* It means, 'make the most of it' or 'take advantage,' that sort of thing. But it's more than that. It's about really appreciating things, luxuriating in a moment. I barely know you, Hadley, but I can already tell that you're going to *profiter* the whole time you're here, because you want to."

Kristina's blithe conviction was catching.

"I love that," Hadley said, "I hope it's true."

"I know it is. So, there you go. French lesson number one. Now, shall we get out of here?"

"*Oui*. Let's *profiter.*"

They took the bus to L'Institut Vaudois to register and saw it together for the first time. The campus was all formal gardens and directional architecture, built on a hillside outside of the city. The lake was just discernible in the distance, the ever-present mountains forming a rim.

"I can't believe this place," said Hadley, throwing out her arms as she took it all in. She told Kristina about seeing the brochure that day last spring, as the snooty Carla had flicked through its pages. And how the reality looked exactly the same, better even.

"I never actually imagined I'd get here," she said. "It feels like a dream."

"We'd better make sure it's a good one, then," said Kristina, hooking her arm through Hadley's. They carried on down the walkway, Kristina tall and slender as a lily, the breeze taking hold of her hair and throwing it out behind her like a bride's train. Beside her, Hadley appeared skull-capped and impish.

Without ever having been to the campus, Kristina seemed to know her way about.

She crunched on an apple as she walked, tossing the core into a rhododendron bush with casual abandon, her rapid chatter never faltering. She was studying art history and already knew all the names of her professors. She talked about her love of the Romantics, foppish young men in billowing blouses who painted scenes of unrivaled beauty, and as she spoke, it was as though she knew the lives of the artists; as if she'd lain on a bed draped in silk and been rendered beautifully and from every angle. For a moment Hadley imagined being a tutor and having her in your class. She would be the one whose eyes you'd seek, whose papers you'd look forward to marking, whose tutorials would run longer than anyone else's.

"What's your favorite book in the whole world, Hadley?" she asked, alighting on a new subject with ease.

They were on a raised section of the walkway from which a broader band of lake was visible. It looked flat as a mirror, and invited reflection. Hadley thought about the question. Over the summer she had read Hemingway's *A Farewell to Arms,* in preparation for a course she wanted to take on American Literature. She'd finished reading it on the bus one day and had been so lost in the story that she'd missed her stop. Outside it had been raining, just as it had rained in the book, and as she'd cried at the last pages, the tears on her cheeks had exactly matched the drops as they'd run down the window. She told Kristina this.

"Hoary old Hemingway! Who'd have thought?"

"And it ends here in Lausanne. I didn't even know that when I started reading it. I couldn't believe it."

"Does it? That's romantic."

"It's not romantic, it's just very, very sad," she said, but Kristina was already on to the next thing. The campus café had presented itself, and soon they were inside, sitting among the deserted tables, eating chocolate-stuffed croissants and toasting their status as official students over shots of coffee.

"We have to go out and party tonight," said Kristina, setting her cup down with a clatter. "It's absolutely essential. *Faire la fête,* that's what the Swiss-French say."

"*Faire la fête,*" repeated Hadley, "that's got a nice ring to it. But the place we went to last night was terrible, it couldn't have been less Swiss."

"I know where we can go," said Kristina. "We'll just have to find people to buy all our drinks."

"Expensive?"

"But beautiful."

Early that evening, in the kitchen at Les
Ormes, they debated how the night might
be shaped. It was also the first time that the
others met Kristina. Bruno's eyes glazed
with lust, Chase looked as interested or as
uninterested as he seemed in meeting
anybody and Jenny almost appeared to back
away, as though Kristina's good looks made
her a suspicious sort of person. Kristina
suggested drinks at the Hôtel Le Nouveau
Monde, seconded by Hadley, but Jenny and
Bruno voted for Mulligan's again; they'd
latched on to it in the way that people
sometimes do in a strange and foreign city,
with over-familiarity and a delight in the
quick establishment of routine. Chase
wavered between the two groups, but in the
end Jenny caught his arm and pulled him
along with them, a gesture which brought
the start of a smile to the corner of his lips.
Nobody seemed to protest the split.

While it was a warm evening, one of the
last of days of summer, the distant mountains were hunched and glowering with the
suggestion of a storm to come. The air was
thick with thunder flies. Before they made it
to the lakeside, Hadley and Kristina found

a bar beneath the cathedral where tables were arranged on steps and the view was of a patchwork quilt of rooftops. They drank tall cocktails, their glasses stuffed with ice and lime quarters, and giggled over the waiter's manner of winking whenever he set down their drinks.

"I can't go on all year like this," said Hadley. "I'll be drunk and broke."

"It's my first night," said Kristina, "and only your second. We're celebrating. What is it, why are you grinning like that?"

Hadley shook her head. "I don't know, I feel half-mad. I'm happy, that's all. I'm really, really happy."

"Good. We like happy," said Kristina. "Happy is good." Her eyes glittered, and there was cocktail-sweet laughter at her lips. "Come on, let's head to the lake. The Hôtel Le Nouveau Monde is waiting for us." She delivered it in an exuberant French accent, and Hadley found herself repeating her words, like a charm.

They zipped across the road to the hooting of horns, narrowly dodging a soft-top sports car blasting French techno. When they eventually came upon the lake, the sun was just setting in a soft glare of pink and silver, the water mottled like the underside of a trout. For a moment they just stood and stared.

"God, it's beautiful," said Hadley.

"No," said Kristina, pulling her arm, "*that's* beautiful."

The Hôtel Le Nouveau Monde was wedding-cake white, laced with wrought-iron balconies and capped with tangerine awnings. On its roof the name stood out in letters four feet high, like the old-fashioned neon of Parisian rooftops, a touch of showmanship, in an otherwise discreet facade. Hadley could only imagine the sort of people who would stay in such a place — film stars, frivolous lovers, brilliantly spiky old dames burning through their children's inheritance. The building was so contained, so solid-looking, when really it should have been pulsing with the energy of all the interesting lives contained within; the flags ought to have been spinning on their poles, the shutters flapping.

"A good hotel is the most perfect thing in the world," said Kristina dreamily.

"I don't think I've ever really been in one," said Hadley.

"Well, let's change that."

"But it's so grand, we can't just wander in, can we?"

"Of course we can. There's always a bar."

"But look at what I'm wearing," she said.

Hadley had on one of her charity-shop finds, a skimpy cornflower-blue tea dress and an oversize man's cardigan that skimmed her thighs. On her feet she wore scuffed white sneakers. "They'll never let me in like this."

"They certainly will," said Kristina. "All we have to do is smile. And look like we belong."

"Well, the first part's easy," said Hadley.

The clientele of the Hôtel Le Nouveau Monde had the kind of confidence that Hadley presumed only came with great wealth, that feeling of never doubting that the world and everything in it was yours. Hadley and Kristina stood just inside the lobby bar and watched for a minute. A woman in a jet-black cocktail dress sat alone by the unmanned grand piano, cool as an Egyptian cat. A couple twined on a sofa, the warm shades of a lamp bringing out the matching red-gold tones in their hair. Kristina took Hadley's hand and led her into the next room where a jazz number was playing, low but definite. Giant gilt-edged mirrors made the room seem endless. The stools at the bar were taken by a group of men whose combined cologne hung like a cloud. Their cuffs moved to show the bulbous heads of expensive watches, and as they crossed their legs, the tips of their leather-soled shoes pointed. Hadley noticed how the men turned to look at Kristina with undisguised admiration.

"I'm not sure if this is my kind of place," she began to whisper, but Kristina was already moving toward the counter, where she was quickly swept upon by the attendant barflies.

"Hadley, what do you want to drink?" she called back over her shoulder, but a martini glass had already been thrust into Kristina's hand, and one of the men was tucking a cocktail umbrella into her hair. Hadley saw her tip her head back and laugh. She smiled and turned away, catching the eye of an elderly man who was sitting on his own at a table in the corner. Her smile stayed at her lips, and he returned it with one of his own.

"Up until about an hour ago they were still typical Swiss men," he said. "It's quite incredible to witness such a transformation firsthand. Your friend is the first to succumb to their well-oiled and somewhat brazen form of charm. Will you be the second, I wonder?"

His voice was low and sonorous, the most precise English, accented with French, and he spoke with exaggerated slowness, as

58

though he had all the time in the world.

Hadley shook her head. "Not my type," she said, still smiling.

"A good thing, too," he said, "I fear they'll be rather less fun when they return to their boardrooms in the morning. Their jollity is as permanent as the ice in their glass."

His tanned skin was smooth at the cheekbone, his eyes were brown and round as chestnuts, and his silvery hair was combed with precision; the effect was of extraordinary polish.

"How long have you been watching?" asked Hadley.

The old man nodded from side to side as though she'd made an astute observation.

"All my life, some would say. All my life."

He had the demeanour of a voyeur, for, despite seeming entirely at home in the hotel bar, there was an aura of distance about him. His eyes twinkled with a private amusement, a look that Hadley recognized straightaway.

"May I offer you a drink?" he said.

"Oh, no," said Hadley, "thanks, but I'll get my own."

"Here," he said, and proffered his drink. "Smell it. And tell me I can't tempt you."

Hadley took it from him. She bent her head and sniffed. "It smells strong," she said. "What is it?"

"One of the better cognacs I've ever tasted. And if you knew me at all, you'd understand that's quite a statement."

"I'm not really a cognac drinker."

"You look too young to be any kind of a drinker. How old are you girls these days? I'm out of practice."

"Well," said Hadley, "only speaking for myself, of course . . ."

"Mais oui . . ."

"I'm nineteen."

"Of course you are. A perfect age."

Hadley glanced back to see where Kristina was and saw her in the midst of the men at the bar. It was as if she were a rare flower that botanists had stumbled upon in the desert. They crowded around her, scarcely able to believe their find.

"Go on," said the old man. "Join them."

"I've actually no desire," said Hadley.

"That, I can scarcely believe."

"They're not interested in me, anyway."

"I scarcely believe that, either. What is your name?"

"Hadley."

"Hadley, I'm Hugo Bézier. And I'm enchanted. That's what we say in French. *Enchanté.* Much more romantic than 'pleased to meet you', don't you think?"

Hadley held out her hand to shake his, and he took it, suppressing a smile.

"In Switzerland it's conventional to swap three kisses," he said.

"What, even when we don't know each other?"

"I'd say especially when we don't know each other."

He seemed a genuine *Lausannois,* the first Swiss person she'd spoken to beyond the most basic of pleasantries. She wondered if he was staying at the hotel, one of those distinguished elderly residents she read about in books, the kind who lived out their last days in opulence, wearing velvet slippers to dinner and knowing all the waiters by name. She was just about to reply when she felt Kristina tugging at her arm.

"We're going swimming," she said, with glee. "And you're coming!"

"Swimming? Swimming, where?"

"In the lake! It was Philippe's idea. Hadley, he's crazy. You'll love him."

"Really?" said Hadley, doubting both assertions. "But we only just got here, I was about to have a drink. . . ."

She turned back to Hugo, but he was already getting to his feet. A fedora was on his head and he shrugged a camel-colored woolen coat over his shoulders.

"It's time for my beauty sleep," he said.

"What, no more cognac?" said Hadley.

He picked up his glass, of which there was half a centimeter remaining. He offered it to her.

"Dutch courage," he said. "Isn't that what you English would say? The water's a little cold at this time of night, if I remember."

Hadley tossed the drink back, her throat burning sweetly. Hugo Bézier was walking away before she could say thank you, or good-night, or anything else at all.

They didn't swim. It was one of those wild ideas, tossed with great bravado, which then fell with a whimper when the moment actually came. By the time they got to the water, the skies had broken and rain fell in giant drops. The three men made a great show of seeking shelter; they suggested more drinks, another bar, but the light had gone from the night. Hadley said she was happy to go home, Kristina agreed, and the others sulked back to their hotel. Hadley and Kristina strolled together in the rain, their bare legs slick, their hair hanging in tendrils.

"It still feels like summer here," said Hadley. "Even the rain's warm."

"You wait until the snow comes," said Kristina. "Enjoy this while it lasts. Winter will be amazing, though. I'll teach you to ski."

"Really? Would you?"

"Of course." She shrugged. "It's easy, and you'll love it. Hey, who was that old man? That's not your type, is it?"

"What? No!"

"A sugar daddy?"

"He was interesting. I liked him."

"Just very, very old."

They ducked under a bus stop and squeezed the rain from their hair. Hadley shivered, and Kristina threw an arm around her.

"I shouldn't even have been talking to those guys," she said with a slightly drunken hiccup. "Jacques would hate it."

"Who's Jacques?" said Hadley.

The bus came then, splashing through puddles and wheezing to a stop. They boarded, staggering into a seat as it quickly moved away again, narrowly avoiding treading on a miniature poodle that belonged to a sour-faced lady.

"Is it only midnight?" said Kristina. "It feels so much later."

"Is Jacques your boyfriend?"

"Oh, Jacques, Jacques . . . I can't even begin, Hadley. It's too long a story for a nice night like this."

She leaned her head on Hadley's shoulder, her spun-gold hair falling across her friend's damp cardigan, and closed her eyes. After a moment they flicked open again.

"What about your love life? Is it horrifically complicated?"

"I don't actually have one," said Hadley.

"You don't? But, you're beautiful."

"I'm really not."

"Well, you're lucky."

With that, she closed her eyes again and fell sweetly to sleep.

CHAPTER 4

Their first days in Lausanne passed in a blur of exploration. The students of Les Ormes were not quite visitors and not quite natives, so they circled the sights of the city and took road trips, they hunted out side-street bars and ate off *prix-fixe* menus in budget restaurants. Until the semester started they were at liberty, so Hadley, Kristina, Bruno, Chase and Jenny spent their time largely with each other. They had been thrown together, and somehow they stuck. Jenny, Bruno and Chase were a tightly knit trio, with Hadley and Kristina willingly on the peripheries.

Hadley had always had friends, loose formations shaped mostly by circumstance, girls she had trooped about with, sharing perfume and spilling laughter. But there had never been anyone quite like Kristina. Perhaps it was the combination, Kristina and Lausanne, Lausanne and Kristina.

Really, the two were inextricable, but there was something golden about her. When a new idea seized Kristina, her whole being appeared to glow. She believed in *il faut profiter* just as much as Hadley did. If they went for afternoon coffee, it would turn easily to sticky-rimmed cocktails and a dawn homecoming. A black-and-white film at the Arts Cinema, all stolen glances and brooding looks, would be followed with a garish romantic comedy and belly-stitching laughter. Even cooking a simple supper at Les Ormes felt like an adventure; they giggled as they wept over the chopping of onions, shared a spoon to taste their creations, swilled cheap wine as they leaned against the kitchen counter. As much as they spent their time together, Kristina didn't mention Jacques again. For all her openness, the way she linked arms with Hadley, offered her forkfuls of food from her plate, answered the door in the scantest slip of a towel, it seemed that on this one subject, she didn't want to be pressed. So Hadley left it alone. Sometimes, they would just sit on their balcony railings in one or the other's room, legs dangling as they looked out over the black-night city. Kristina would light a cigarette and hold it delicately between her finger and thumb, a precise and pretty smoker.

"Don't you feel like you could just jump?" Hadley said one night.

"I'm actually a little afraid of heights," Kristina said, shyly almost, as though she was sharing a secret.

"Really? You don't seem like you'd be afraid of anything. Kristina, look at it, all the buildings lit up, the lights at the edge of the lake, the mountains behind, going on forever and ever. I just want to dive in."

"You're the one who doesn't seem afraid of anything."

"Me? I don't think so. I'm afraid of everything. I was nervous about coming here."

"Why?"

"It felt like a risk. I'm not usually the risk-taking type."

"There's nothing risky about being in Lausanne, Hadley. It's just another city, another country."

"You would say that, you're . . . jet-set."

"Jet-set?" She snorted with laughter. "I don't think so. Anyway, we're both here, so that makes us the same. And we do dive in, every day we do."

"Of course we do. The city's ours." Hadley waved her hand, and her bracelet, a linked chain of silver stars, slipped from her wrist. She let out a cry, and Kristina reached to grab her, thinking it was Hadley who was falling. The bracelet had plummeted out of sight into the canopy of elm trees. They clung to one another, laughing.

"I loved that bracelet!" wailed Hadley.

"Oh, no, was it precious?"

"It was to me."

"Did a boy give it to you?"

"No, my mum."

"Oh, God, it wasn't an heirloom?"

"Not exactly. It was two pounds, from a car boot sale. Nobody's heirloom."

"You want to go and look for it?"

"We'll never find it. It'd be impossible."

"I don't mean in the dark, but in the morning."

"It's too steep, we'd practically need crampons and ropes. No, it's gone. It's okay, Kristina, it's gone."

"We'll get you a new one," said Kristina. "It was pretty. I noticed it the first day we met. It was made out of little silver stars, wasn't it?"

"They were all different sizes, and it looked kind of imperfect. That's what I liked about it."

"We should go to one of those *ateliers* by the cathedral. You could draw it, and I bet someone would be able to re-create it for you."

"I think it'd cost more than two pounds," said Hadley. "And it wouldn't be the same, anyway. No, it's lost. *Au revoir,* my *petit* bracelet."

With a last wistful look below, Hadley climbed down from the railing. She held out her hand to Kristina who took it and jumped down beside her, landing as lightly as a dancer.

When Hadley knocked for Kristina the next morning, she wasn't there. She breakfasted alone, for it was still too early for the others to rise. They had been in Lausanne for over a week now, and she was beginning to understand their rhythms; she and Kristina were the only ones who chose to get up before midday unless they had to. Hadley made coffee and sat cross-legged in a chair, watching the light on the water. It was especially silvery that morning, and mist trailed its edges. She was mesmerized and still waking. She didn't hear the door open and jumped as she felt a hand on her shoulder.

"God, you scared me." Hadley took in Kristina's heavy boots and jogging top, the blush of her cheeks and light sheen of perspiration on her brow. "You look . . .

odd. Have you been out already?"

"Since dawn, practically. I've been climbing. And scrambling. Little bit of sliding. I nearly gave up and then there it was, glinting at me."

Hadley's mouth dropped open. "You didn't . . ." she began.

Kristina opened her palm, and there it lay, a tiny heap of tangled silver stars.

The day before the semester started, Bruno proposed an excursion. It was dry and bright, and from the balconies at Les Ormes you could see all the way into the mountains. The waters of Lac Léman invited voyage and adventure. Bruno was the only one among them who had a car, and he suggested that they all drive into the hills. He took the wheel, with Chase beside him, and Hadley, Kristina and Jenny packed into the backseat. They ran along the lake road, cutting through vineyards and shoreline villages. They saw houses that seemed to climb on top of one another with haphazard arrangements of rooftop and gable, pushing ever closer to the deep water's edge. Chase popped a CD of hard rock into the player, and Bruno took the corners faster than ever. Hadley wound down the window and let the whipping air slap her cheeks until Jenny complained that her ears hurt and Kristina's bare arms were dotted with goose pimples. She closed it reluctantly.

Bruno drove them to an out-of-season ski town, where they strolled the leaf-blown streets and walked beneath the robotic structures of shutdown chairlifts. Jackets and scarves, unnecessary in the lowlands, were hurriedly pulled on. Soon, they all scattered, lured in different directions. Bruno hiked the steep stretch to a turreted hotel that clung to the edges of the high slopes. Jenny went to a gift shop, where she shook row after row of snow globes and chose a stuffed bear in lederhosen as a gift for a niece. Chase sat on a bench in the chalet-lined main street, sketching in the notebook he carried, looking distinctly urban in his navy parka. He curved an arm around his picture as Hadley passed. Kristina found a clothing boutique and twined real furs about her shoulders, turning in a mirror to admire herself as a white-haired assistant stooped and smiled. Hadley watched her for a while, then wandered off on her own, too. She bought a postcard with bent edges, a replica vintage picture. It showed a woman in a sporty pose, leaning on her skis. She wore a knitted sweater and had a red scarf tied jauntily at her neck.

71

Her face was turned to the sun, and an unending blue sky fell behind her.

Hadley wrote her card at a table in a bakery as a spinach tart wilted beside her and her hot chocolate formed a slippery skin. *Without the snow, it feels like we're here when we shouldn't be,* she wrote, *it feels like a privilege and a trespass.* She didn't know whom she was writing it for, not her parents, certainly. She tucked it into the pages of a book in her bag. She bought another card on her way out, showing a marmot, a mountain creature somewhere between a squirrel and a guinea pig, with jagged front teeth and a goofy grin. That one would be for them, she decided; her brother, Sam, would love it. She imagined it propped on their mantelpiece at home, beside the one she'd sent of Lac Léman. "Our daughter's spending the year abroad," they'd tell their visitors, with a puff of pride and only the smallest creak of sadness. Sam would stand on tiptoes to pull faces at the marmot.

A privilege and a trespass. Hadley turned over the words that had come to mind. She wondered if they were meant for more than this ski town, with its shuttered hotels and padlocked restaurants, suspended in the no-man's-land of autumn. What if it was the whole year abroad? She liked the feeling of having chosen to be somewhere, rather than it having chosen her, but Lausanne wasn't quite real to her yet. She felt like a child who had slipped through the gate of a secret garden; the grass underfoot was soft, she could hear all the birds singing, but she couldn't help looking over her shoulder, wondering if, at any moment, she'd be spotted, an interloper in paradise.

Kristina seemed to have no such qualms. She tripped about with a happy sense of entitlement. She'd told Hadley that she'd spent the summer on the French Riviera, from which Lausanne was a mere train ride away, one of those fast French trains you read about in the papers, that leaned close to the rushing ground, champagne corks popping in the restaurant car. Perhaps to Kristina, Lausanne was just another beauty spot in an already scenic life, between the painted Danish houses and palm-shaded terraces of Saint-Tropez.

Hadley liked the idea that whatever happened that year, Lausanne would remain hers. She would always be able to talk about "her year in Switzerland," and she'd feel like someone different then. Would her skin be sun-blushed golden? Her pose nonchalant and cultured? The seasoned Francophile, with a hatful of traveler's tales, and thanks to Kristina, a skier's swagger. Or would she be the same as she always was, just possessed of new memory, a perfectly contained world that she could take out and shake like a snow globe whenever she wanted. There would be something different. She already knew that much.

Later, they all regrouped in an inn on the fringes of the town and drank pale beer out of tall stem glasses. The interior was dark and smelled of age-old wood, and stag heads were mounted on the walls. The barman spoke Swiss-German, in a lilting dialect, and wore a felt hat tipped low over his eyes. They settled at a table by the window, and Hadley couldn't stop staring. The view extended down the valley, mist strung the tops of the evergreens and a torrent of river was just visible.

"Does anyone else feel as though they shouldn't be here?" she said, turning back to the others. "It's like we're skipping class."

"The semester doesn't start until tomorrow, Hadley," said Kristina.

"I know that, I mean, just being here, so far away from everything. It's like another world. Not just this place, but Switzerland. The fact that we're here at all."

"Tell me about it," said Jenny. "We're miles from anywhere. Dave might as well not exist. I hate it."

"You hate it?" Hadley was openmouthed.

"I don't mean I hate it *here*. I just hate the fact of it. He's in England, I'm here, it's pointless."

Chase shrugged. "You can always leave a place if you want. Or break up with your boyfriend. That, of course, is the other option."

"I'm not saying that. . . ." Jenny began in reply.

"Sounds to me like love's the problem here," said Bruno, holding up his glass. "So, here's to not being in love! Here's to freedom!" He waggled his glass for a toast, but the others were slow to oblige. "Chase? Come on!"

"Cheers," Chase said, chinking glasses. "To new beginnings."

Jenny smiled at him and gulped down her beer. Hadley glanced across at Kristina, but she was fiddling with her nails and didn't appear to be listening.

On the way back to the car, Kristina caught Hadley's elbow.

"What do you think Bruno meant when he said love's the problem?"

"I'm not sure he meant much at all," said Hadley. "Jenny's just missing her boyfriend, that's all. Or maybe she's not, and that's part of it, too."

They kicked through the crumpled brown leaves together, walking behind the rest of the group. The air had turned and had a chill in it now.

"But they're right," Kristina said. "It's a trap. A trap as much as a release."

"Why do you say that?" Hadley asked. Before she could ask, *Is it Jacques?* Kristina had quickened her pace and fallen into step with the others. Hadley was left wondering.

As soon as the semester began, Hadley and Kristina's timetables took them in different directions across campus. Kristina became swept up in crowds of other students, art history types with velvet jackets, half-moon glasses and consciously disheveled hair. Hadley's time was spent between the French language school, where internationals took classes on grammar and made cautious forays into French fiction, and the English department. At L'Institut Vaudois, if you chose to study English literature, all the teaching and course work was in the English language; so as well as a scattering of Swiss, there were a number of professors from the U.K. and America among the staff. On her first day in the corridors of the English department, Hadley saw a poster on a notice board saying that Professors Caroline Dubois and Joel Wilson would be hosting welcome drinks for students and faculty near the beginning of term. According to her timetable, she had Professor Wilson for American Literature, and her first lecture was that Friday. Hadley decided that she would see what the class was like before she committed to going to the drinks; she pictured everyone standing around stiffly, chewing peanuts solemnly and nursing plastic cups of wine.

She wandered along the corridor and saw another notice board, with a parade of photographs of every staff member. Hadley stopped beside it and tried to spot Professors Dubois and Wilson. She saw Caroline Dubois first. Her auburn hair was pulled back into a tightly coiled chignon, and her peach-colored blouse shone silkily. "Caroline Dubois, expert on the Romantics," it said beneath. Her look was too steely, not soft enough to be romantic, Hadley thought. It was always a disappointment when people's looks didn't match their interests. Hadley looked on along the line of pictures and was surprised to see a face she knew. Even without the spilling streetlight and the unexpected crackle of his voice, she recognized the American from her first night in

Lausanne. She remembered the plume of his cigarette smoke and the pale oceans of his eyes. *Joel Wilson.* "Specialism: Hemingway and the Lost Generation," it said. Hadley glanced left and right along the corridor, inexplicably feeling as though she had stumbled across something illicit. Satisfied that she was alone, she stepped closer and studied his picture.

Unlike Caroline Dubois, Joel Wilson matched every idea. His muscular frame was clearly delineated by his white T-shirt, and a lock of dark hair rolled across his forehead. His look dared the camera to take his picture. He perhaps wasn't immediately handsome, not to ordinary eyes, but he seemed to have conviction, a kind of strength, that made even this flattened print of him, this two dimensional likeness, difficult to resist. She wondered if, in class, he would recognize her as she'd recognized him. That first night he must have guessed her to be a newly arrived student, for she had been so obvious, hadn't she? Her loose band of friends, her roving eyes, her self-consciousness that had seemed to seep from every pore, a longing for experience that marked out all the green girls and boys. And yet there had been no distance between them, no line of authority marking the edges of their conversation. On the street they had seemed like equals, fairly matched, and all the while his identity had remained a mystery.

Hadley didn't have to wait very long, for Joel Wilson's first lecture was that Friday morning. Overnight the seasons had turned; it was a day that owed more to the approaching winter than to the last days of summer, but the air was still bright with sunshine and the sky a newly painted blue. Kristina had left early for class, and the others seemed to be sleeping in, so Hadley traveled to campus alone.

The bus ride took her along sweeping residential streets. She could see into passing windows, and she liked to imagine the people who lived inside those stately blocks. She pictured their elegant feet treading over the parquet floors, their arms throwing open the casement windows to greet the day. There would be old ladies whose hands creaked with the weight of costume jewelry, possessed of small dogs with peeping tongues. Young men, soulful and accomplished, their lives complete except for the love of an English girl. Her imagination always grew skittish at this point. Hadley didn't know what she wanted, only what she didn't. No more childish college boys, with their drinking contests and dirty sheets, their deodorant stains and ill-written lecture notes. No more disappointment served in a chipped mug the next morning, and goodbyes that tasted of toothpaste and stale lager.

She found herself wondering again about Kristina's mention of Jacques. She didn't seem like one-half of a long-distance couple; there weren't lengthy, teary telephone calls or piles of kiss-printed letters in her room. Nor did Kristina turn her head from the spry looks of Swiss boys. Hadley thought sometimes about raising the topic, saying his name out loud — *Jacques.* Surely it wouldn't be too much, just a conversation between two friends, both looking for reasons to say, *I know* and *me, too,* the spaces between their lives ever closing. But upon this one subject Kristina still stayed tight-lipped.

"If you talk about it, you'll lose it," Joel Wilson told them. "Hemingway always believed that, and I'm with him."

It was her first American Literature class, and she had taken a seat somewhere near the middle, beside a ferrety-looking boy with an earnest stack of books.

"I guess that makes this the shortest course at this college," he said, "and my job a whole lot easier."

Hadley laughed, and her pen skidded on the page. The boy beside her turned to stare, his brow peaking quizzically. Joel Wilson glanced Hadley's way, and she smiled in acknowledgment. He nodded briefly but perceptibly, in the way that you might if you were reminding yourself of something you already knew.

He had arrived five minutes late for his own lecture, shrugging his jacket from his shoulders on his way from the door, throwing his tattered briefcase at the lectern and narrowly missing it. He'd shoved his hands in the pockets of his jeans and grinned at them all, as the contents of his case lay scattered on the floor. "The land of clocks and watches, and still I'm late," he'd said, "what are you gonna do?" He was already unlike any of the teachers she'd had at school, and any of the lecturers in her first year at university. Hadley was on his side right from the beginning.

"Where shall we start?" he asked them, leaving beat pauses as though he was genuinely seeking their suggestions. "Here's an idea. Let's begin with the kind of attraction that can only end in misery. How does that

81

sound? A romance, whose only consumma-
tion will be one of failure." He looked
around the room as he spoke, and Hadley
twitched in her seat. "Do you think you can
handle that? Can your hearts bear the
breaking? Okay, then. Let's talk about *The
Sun Also Rises*."

Standing at the front of the class, Joel Wilson looked as if he knew a secret, and that
if you listened carefully enough, he'd let you
in on it. He had slides, and he clicked
through them at a rapid pace and with staccato rhythm. Some showed sections of type,
blown up and fuzzy at the edges. Some were
photographs, the dazzling red of a torero's
cape, the neat bob of a woman's head, sleek
as a boy, Hemingway himself, the thrust of
his chest, eyes like bullets. Joel, as he told
them to call him, was fast on his feet, spinning on his heel whenever he wanted to
make a point, almost seeming to pirouette
his way across the room. But when he
stopped still, the world appeared to stop
turning with him, and everybody held his
gaze. Hadley wrote frantically, without ever
looking down at the page for long. Later in
the library she would try to decipher these
notes and find it impossible. She would
write it all out again from memory, hearing
the thrum of Joel's voice in her head.

Especially the part where he talked about her.

"I've got a class list here," he said. "Stand up, please, Hadley Dunn."

Hadley felt her cheeks burn. She got up, knocking her pen to the floor as she did so. She couldn't remember swapping names with him on the street.

"You're Hadley?" he said. "I might have guessed. You're aware of your namesake, I take it?"

It had been her mum's idea but was not due to any literary enthusiasms, as Joel Wilson must have imagined. Hadley had been the name of the singer in a pub band that had been playing on the night her mum had first met her dad. This other Hadley, a girl with bare feet and hair to her waist, had walked onto the stage, the microphone squeaking, and sung of love won and lost, in a voice that thrilled and haunted with equal measure. The story went that after her song, James Dunn had made his own professions of love at first sight, whispering into Hadley's mum's ear as she'd stood in line for a drink at the bar. The girl packed up her guitar and went back into the night, stardust in her wake, as the soon-to-be Dunns fell into the sweetest kiss they'd ever known. She was the daughter of romantics, if not book lovers.

"Yes," she said, "I am."

"Then I'm pleased to have you in my class."

His gaze cut her clean in two. Joel clapped his hands together and dismissed them, throwing in a breezy reminder about the upcoming drinks party. Hadley liked the fact that he hadn't told the others his reason for singling her out, that Hadley was the name of Hemingway's first wife. It was as though he expected them all to know already. Or if they didn't, it didn't matter, anyway, because maybe you did lose things if you talked about them. As Hadley walked out of the room, she felt the eyes of some of her classmates on her. She fiddled with her scarf and affected nonchalance. She didn't dare look back to see if he was watching her, too, but she felt somehow that he probably was. It was just like before, when he'd stood and smiled on the dark street, lighting his cigarette before turning away. She walked away now as she'd walked away then, a new kick in her step that was only obvious to those who knew to look.

CHAPTER 5

In those early days and weeks, nights out would often last through till morning. Kristina and Hadley would come home in the pale pink dawn, sometimes accompanied by straggles of the others, a rambling Chase, a wan-cheeked Jenny, a lustrous Bruno. After one such night, Kristina and Hadley trailed back up the hill to Les Ormes, and there was serenity in the city's stillness. The clamor and hot press of the club they had left behind was like a muddled dream. As they walked, they both inhaled the morning air at exactly the same moment, then broke into crisscrossing laughter.

"It feels so good, doesn't it?" said Kristina. "I swear I don't get hangovers in Lausanne. The air's so . . . What's the word? *Restorative.*"

"People used to do that, didn't they? Go to a place to 'take the air.' I like that. It's so civilized."

"Maybe that's what we're doing here," said Kristina. "Taking the air. Recovering. Recuperating on the Swiss Riviera." She paused. "Hiding," she added.

Hadley thought of how the night before they'd danced through the fountains of the Ouchy waterfront, their jeans wet and slapping. How two boys had passed them in the library the next day and waved, calling *hey, fountain girls.*

"I don't think anyone could accuse us of hiding," said Hadley, with a snicker of a laugh. She caught Kristina's eye. "Definitely not."

"Maybe that's the trouble, then."

"Jacques?" she said, and it was the first time that she had mentioned him again.

Kristina made a small, exasperated noise and pulled her hair back into a ponytail. She spun it round her fingers and fixed it with a clip.

"Yes. No. I don't know," she said.

"Am I supposed to guess? Okay. He's your boyfriend back in Copenhagen. A childhood sweetheart. Only now you're here, and he's not, you're having second thoughts. Maybe like Jenny."

"Nothing like Jenny. And I don't want you to guess."

"Then tell me."

"I can't."

"But why not? We're friends, aren't we?"

"Friends?" Kristina grabbed her hands and squeezed them. "Hadley, of course we are."

"Well, I don't understand, then."

"Shouldn't some things just stay private?"

"So, it's a secret?"

"It's not a secret. It's just private."

"Okay," said Hadley. "It's just, when you said before that it was a long story, it felt like maybe you wanted to tell."

"Not really," said Kristina. "But if I did, you'd be the first person . . ."

"It's okay," said Hadley, "you don't have to say all that."

"You would be! Hadley, I promise you would. There's no one else here I'd rather tell. You're my best friend."

Hadley felt a ripple of pleasure. Kristina had tossed it so lightly, yet it didn't make it any less true. "Well, you're mine, too," she said back.

Kristina leaned in and kissed her on the cheek. Her breath smelled of the sweet apple liquor the barman had poured them to send them on their way. Her lips were cool as glass.

L'Institut Vaudois was a constant, the point

to which they all returned, no matter how full their days and nights. One afternoon they met up after their classes had finished, and Hadley suggested walking back into town. It would take them an hour and a half, perhaps more, but it was a brisk and beautiful day. Only the turning of the leaves on the trees, the canary-yellow patterns that stuck to the bottom of their shoes, gave away the true season. They came back into the outskirts of Lausanne through streets they had never walked before. They fell into slow step with an elderly lady and her lapdog, Hadley bending to ruffle the poodle's ears as Kristina chattered away in fluid French. As their ways parted, they wished each other *bonne journée* and walked on.

"Your French is so good. Is Jacques . . ."

"He's Swiss," Kristina interrupted.

Hadley blinked. "Swiss?" she said carefully, quietly, as though too much emphasis would send Kristina running.

"Did I tell you that I spent the summer on the Riviera? By Saint-Tropez?"

"Yes, you did."

"That's where I met him."

"But that's so romantic."

"Not really. I think you'd disapprove of the whole thing."

"How could I disapprove?"

Kristina hesitated, and her lips moved, as though there were lots of things she could say but she chose just one.

"Hadley, he's married. And that's why I can't talk about it. Because it's not right. None of it's right."

Hadley stared at her friend. She wanted to ask *Why him? Why someone married?* but Kristina's cheeks had turned so pale, and her eyes were suddenly so distant that Hadley knew she meant it when she said she didn't want to talk. She slipped her arm through Kristina's, and they walked on toward the town. Soon the hum of the approaching city, the rattling bicycle wheels, the wheezing buses, the clattering heels, filled the spaces in between.

Three weeks into term the English department at L'Institut Vaudois organized the promised drinks for students and faculty. They were held at a hotel on the shoreline, a place that from the outside promised some prestige and romance but inside had a faded institutionalized quality. The hotel's small bar was hired for the occasion, and about forty people crowded in among the wicker chairs and smeared glass tables. A thin-faced barman kept up with Joel's bombastic flow of drink orders, while Caroline moved with an airy sort of elegance, floating from student to student, exchanging a word here, a greeting there, never getting caught for too long. Joel, in contrast, was quickly buried by a clan of groupies, wilder boys who liked his style, and girls with heavy bangs and polo-neck sweaters, their chests crisscrossed with satchel straps. The bar's thinly piped music was drowned out by loudly voiced opinions on everything from the better places in which they could be drinking to the merits of Byron over Shelley. The counter grew sticky with spilled drinks. Joel took off his jacket and threw it over a chair and Hadley saw the dark patches under the arms of his gray T-shirt and the unexpected blueness of his leather belt. A girl wearing feathery earrings flittered her hands as she talked to him, twirling the ends of her hair with the tips of her fingers.

Hadley found herself trapped in a conversation about Shakespeare with a droning boy whose chin was stitched with the beginnings of a beard. He stood too close and insisted on tapping her arm with one finger every time he made a point. Earlier she'd spoken with a girl from Basel who'd introduced herself as Irene. She seemed sweet and unassuming, her eyes a cozy brown. She said she wanted to study abroad in England the next year, and when she spoke English it was perfect, and with a halfway American accent. Hadley tried to see the university that she had left behind through the eyes of a stranger. She pictured the tall blocks of student accommodation, separated by featureless hillocks and lines of spindly trees. The miles and miles of paint-scratched railing that anchored fallen bicycles, flapping notices advertising club nights and fundraising efforts, and, once, a dazed Fresher wearing only his underpants, handcuffed by his new friends, the steam of a night's booze rising from his sleeping form. What else? She pictured the library café with its gritty Eccles cakes and burning metal tea pots, and the old town that was a short bus ride from the concrete campus, where ancient buildings clung to the peripheries of a '60s high street. The pub that everyone went to, purported to be one of the most ancient in England, where beef-and-ale pies were served to the tune of whizzing, whirring, fruit machines, and was also the setting for one of the worst dates of her life.

"Don't you like England at all?" the girl had asked Hadley, her face crackling with amusement.

"No, it's not that," began Hadley.

"It's okay," she interrupted, "you don't

have to answer. I know what it's like when we talk about the place we come from. I could tell you about the snobby students in Lausanne. The impenetrable cliques. The foreign professors who come here only to play, not work. The classrooms that are crammed full of too many students. The exams that last for eight hours, more designed for torture than for testing. The drug addicts who sit every day on the church steps of Bel-Air, everybody pretending they aren't there. The way anyone who isn't Swiss doesn't quite cut it, you know, isn't quite the first-rate citizen. But, Hadley — that's your name, isn't it? — I know you won't see these things. I know that's not the place you want."

"Is that what you really think?" said Hadley.

"I love Lausanne," said the girl. "I'm just saying. Just offering a different view."

"Kind of a bleak one."

The girl shrugged. "Just playing devil's advocate. I can't stop you from thinking something's perfect."

"But I don't."

"I'll tell you who is perfect, though. We're in the same class, aren't we? American Lit?"

"I haven't made up my mind yet," said Hadley, cutting her short. "On any of it."

"Oh, sure you haven't," she said, offering a smile that was somewhere between a twinkle and a sneer.

The Shakespeare fan interrupted them then, and the girl from Basel moved away. Hadley looked for her later in the evening and saw her laughing in a group, talking Swiss-German double fast, holding her thin-stemmed glass between slimmer fingers. Hadley drank another glass of wine as she watched her, imagining her in the Union bar back home. Would she revel in lunchtimes of cheesy baked potatoes and weak coffee? Evenings of cheap pints and neon bottles? Would she join huddled groups; the theater club students tossing their hair and laughing in screeches; the hockey girls, stout-legged and hard-faced; the science boys, in misshapen T-shirts and with faces scotched with acne? Would she declare it all charming and be embraced, in turn, for her own exoticness? The thought that Hadley could find out the answer to these questions, for next year she'd be back home, too, her spell in Lausanne over, startled her into a mild form of action. As the evening wound to a close and the barman made ready to pull the shutters, she sought out Joel Wilson.

"Do you think it's naive to believe in the

good of a place?" Hadley said, the words falling a little loosely from her lips.

"The good of a place?" he said. "That's an interesting question, Hadley." His voice was gravelly from talking, and his eyes shone with the temporary light of whiskey and soda. "Have you been here all night?" he asked.

"I have."

"I'm sorry, I didn't see you."

This didn't feel true. He had seen her just as she had seen him, but she didn't say that. "You were always surrounded," she said instead.

"You've caught me as I'm just about to leave."

"You're leaving your own party early?"

"It's not my party," he said. "It's your party. It's for you students to get to know one another. And I'm not sure it's early anymore."

"Oh, well," said Hadley. "We'd better stop talking. We're breaking all the rules."

"But I haven't answered your question yet."

"So, what do you think?"

"Hadley," he said, tapping her arm just at the elbow, "I'd go so far as to say that ignoring what other people think is the trick of life itself." Instead of it irking her, as had the touch of the boy earlier, she found herself noting it, already knowing she'd want to remember it later.

"I'm not sure that's what I asked," she said.

He laughed, and she saw the tiny scar that ran above his lip, a slight puckering of the skin.

"Do you remember speaking to me on the street, before term started?" she said in a rush.

"Hmm?"

He leaned closer to hear her in the din.

"It was my first night here. I was walking home on my own. You said you were worried."

"That doesn't sound like me."

"It was you. I didn't expect your voice, it stayed with me."

"What was unexpected about it? That it came at all, or that when it did, I was American?"

"I don't know. It was my first night, so I guess everything was unexpected. It was all new, exciting."

"Exciting?"

"Afterward I decided you were probably from the university."

"You thought about it afterward?"

"Definitely a tutor. You had that air about you."

"I'm willing to bet that's not what you thought."

"Well, you don't look like a banker."

"I'll take that as a compliment."

It seemed as though he was about to say something else and then changed his mind. He glanced at his watch.

"I've got to run, unfortunately," he said. "I'm sorry we didn't have more time."

"It's okay."

"See you in class?"

"Of course," said Hadley.

As soon as he left, the party was over. She rode the bus home to Les Ormes, through the first splashes of a nighttime downpour. Rain streaked the window, and she thought again of the brief pressure of his fingers on her arm. It was so small a thing, and yet she hung on to it, without quite knowing why.

CHAPTER 6

Hadley and Kristina had arrived in Lausanne as equal outsiders. For all Kristina's Riviera living and her rapid French tongue, it was as strange a city to her as it was to Hadley. Together, they made it their own. They drank *renversée,* the Swiss *café au lait,* in a coffeehouse that was tucked at the edge of Place de la Palud. They walked in the full bright autumn sun at Ouchy, watching the swans tangling their necks in the shallows. As they passed the voluptuous exterior of the Hôtel Le Nouveau Monde, Hadley often found herself thinking of the old man she'd met, Hugo Bézier. There was something about him that stuck, although she couldn't quite say what. Perhaps, surrounded as she was by expats and internationals, it was simply his authenticity, his Lausanne stripes.

As the semester intensified, Hadley was consumed by reading. Meanwhile, Kristina had fallen to studying with fervor, spending hours poring over giant art books in the library, her hair tumbling like a curtain. L'Institut Vaudois was a perfectly orchestrated tangle of crisscrossing walkways, upper and lower levels, and glass partitions, so sometimes Hadley would see Kristina without her noticing. She'd spot her apple-green satchel or her blond head on the stairs, three flights beneath her, or the flick of her hips as she strutted in the opposite direction behind a glass wall or through a revolving door. Kristina always looked as if she was heading somewhere with purpose. It was in these moments that Hadley thought of Jacques. She imagined an affair with a married man to be conducted in stolen moments, snatches of passion here and there. Kristina could see him every day in this manner, and Hadley would never be any the wiser.

The commencement of the semester had sent them all in different directions. Bruno met a Spanish girl called Loretta, who lived two floors below at Les Ormes. When Hadley saw him, it was often through the puff of her dark and frizzy hair, as he stooped to kiss her neck or nibble her ear. Hadley grew to associate Jenny with her mobile phone, for it was perpetually pressed to her ear.

Hadley heard snatches of her conversation sometimes as she passed. *And what did he say to her?* And, *Did your mum go in the end?* And, *How's Dave doing?* She also noticed that Chase never seemed far away from Jenny. Sometimes she'd see them wandering about together, Chase wheeling his bicycle, Jenny strolling beside, a burble of laughter in their wake. Meanwhile, they would all still collide in the kitchen. As they boiled their pasta and crumbled their baguettes, they swapped talk of incomprehensible lectures, errors in French and new places they'd seen or heard about. Now that Bruno had Loretta, he seemed less eager to make plans to bind them all together. No more trips to the mountains were suggested; instead he talked of a shopping weekend to Milan but didn't offer up the extra spaces in his car. He told them he wanted to buy Loretta the most expensive bag he could find, to which Chase made a huffy noise, and Jenny tipped her head to one side and smiled with her eyes.

"How's your love life, Hadley?" Chase asked her once.

"I'm loving life," she answered, "thanks for asking."

And she'd glanced across at Kristina, who always seemed to be deeply distracted at such moments, rubbing at a spot of nail varnish on the sleeve of her sweater or hunting through her bag for a book. Kristina blinked back at Hadley, her face blank, her secret still hidden.

One evening, a little over a month into term, Hadley was working, cocoonlike, at her desk in her room. She had pulled the blinds and turned her lamp on and was bent low over her books. She had an essay to turn in the next week, her first, for Joel Wilson's course. She had called it "An End to Love" and had been looking forward to writing it, but now that the time had come she was struggling. She couldn't find the words she wanted. Everything that sounded good in her head looked so plain, once it was set down. A knocking at her door made her jump.

"Come in," she called.

"Hey," said Kristina.

She appeared to slide into Hadley's room, opening the door barely wide enough to enter. She wore a pink dressing gown, and her hair was bundled up on top of her head. She took a seat on the edge of Hadley's bed and twisted her hands in her lap.

"Do you fancy going out? We could go back to the Hôtel Le Nouveau Monde. A nice quiet drink."

"I can't," said Hadley. "I'd love to, but I've got to write this essay."

"You're always working these days."

"So are you. Or . . . aren't you?"

"Mostly."

She stood up and wandered over to Hadley's wardrobe. The door was open, and she pulled out an emerald-green frock, a slip of a thing, that Hadley had found in the bargain bin of a vintage shop.

"Can I try this on?"

"Help yourself," she said. "But you might take someone's eye out in it."

Kristina stepped out of her dressing gown, and it fell to the floor in a pink heap. Underneath she wore matching underwear. Red lace. Her back was perfectly smooth, and her legs ran on and on. Hadley turned back to her essay.

"I can't even get it over my boobs," she heard Kristina say with an exasperated giggle. Hadley looked around and saw that she had it stuck on her head, and her arms were waving in the air. Hadley got up and helped her. She carefully pulled the dress back up and at the same time heard a splitting. The stitching had torn at the seam.

"Oh, God, I'm so sorry."

Hadley slipped it back on to the hanger. "Don't worry, I can sew it."

"I should never have burst in here, and now I'm wrecking your clothes, too."

"Honestly, it's nothing. It's really old, it was always going to rip at some point."

"You're always so nice to me, Hadley."

Kristina sank down onto the bed. She picked up her dressing gown from the floor, but instead of putting it on she held it bundled in her lap. Hadley noticed that the lace of her bra was made of hundreds of tiny stitched love hearts. Underneath, her breasts swelled, barely contained.

"Are you okay?" Hadley asked.

Kristina looked up at her, and her eyes were rimmed red, her usually flawless skin was blotchy.

"I want to do the right thing," she said, "but it's just really, really difficult."

"Kristina, what are you talking about?"

"Jacques. God, I don't know what I'm doing. For the first time, I don't know what I'm doing."

Hadley glanced down at her essay. Work on it would stop now.

"Shall I make us some tea?" she said.

Kristina shook her head. "I don't want to be anybody's 'other woman.' I should just end it. Accept the hurt and move on. But I can't. I can't do it."

"What are you hoping? That he'll leave her?"

"He'll never leave her. Not fully. Not completely. Deep down, he still loves her, Hadley."

She shivered and wrapped her gown around her middle.

"Why don't you put it on?" said Hadley.

Kristina rubbed her arms, then slowly pulled it up over her shoulders.

"I just can't think straight right now."

Hadley reached into her desk drawer and drew out a bar of Swiss chocolate. She unwrapped the foil and broke it into squares then held it out. Kristina took a piece, her eyes pooling.

"It's something left over from my summer on the Riviera. I told you that much, didn't I? It's a dreadful coincidence, really. I didn't know that we'd both be here."

"In Lausanne?"

"No, no, not Lausanne. He's in Geneva."

"Tell me from the beginning," Hadley said.

"What, really? You want to know it all?"

So, finally, she heard the story of how Jacques and Kristina met, and once again Hadley thought how Kristina belonged to another world. For all her distress, Kristina chose her words carefully, with pretty embellishments and decorative flourishes. Hadley listened, a half smile at her lips.

Kristina said she'd been working as an au pair for a wealthy Danish family who had been passing the summer in Saint-Tropez. Her charges had been three little blond boys with mushroom haircuts and neat manners. As the mother rode palomino horses at a country club in the hills and the father paced the floor of a back office, talking conspiratorially with colleagues who hadn't been forced to spend the summer down south, Kristina had played with the boys in the villa's long and sloping garden. Or, rather, the boys had played and Kristina had cast glances at them from beneath the brim of her hat as she'd lain purring on a lounger.

The villa had been on a hillside that was clustered with similar-looking houses, all with smooth sculpted arches, colonnades twisted with bougainvillea and palm-ringed pools. The villa next door had been rented by a couple who, according to Kristina, had been spending the last days of their marriage there. As Kristina had leafed through magazines and painted her toes in sparkly hues, she'd heard the fierce pops of their arguments. And once, as the three boys had chased the wafting trail of a Frisbee, there had been the sound of shattering. A vase against a wall, or a fist into a pane. Kristina had watched from beneath her lashes. She'd seen Jacques, for it was Jacques, running onto the lawn like a man escaping a burning house. She'd seen him turn and stand with his hands clasped to his head, as everything before him had appeared to fall to ashes. And then he'd seen her watching, and instead of faltering under her cool, unwavering eye, his face had inexplicably turned to something like relief. That had been right at the start of the summer. The woman had left, leaving the man, Jacques, alone. Their first kiss was among the squat pineapple-shaped palms that had separated their gardens, a little over a week later.

As time went on, Kristina had started stealing away from the boys to snatch moments with him. She would slip next door and call up into the cavernous vestibule, waiting for his head to appear on the staircase three spirals up. Within no time at all they had become everyday lovers, he lavishing her with sprays of exotic flowers, she painting the rungs of his chest with sunscreen. And by the end of the summer, they were as much a couple as any other that walked the harborside promenade at twilight, or leaned toward one another across candlelit supper tables high up in the old town.

"A Riviera romance," said Hadley, and Kristina laughed reluctantly, showing all of her bright white teeth.

"And that's where it should have stayed," she said. "Probably. God, I don't know. You see, he was always married, even when he said he didn't want to be. Even when he said his wife didn't want to be. Even when I saw him take his wedding ring and hurl it to the bottom of the sea."

"He did that for you?"

"He was drunk and showing off. He probably went diving for it the next day. Anyway, now he's back in Geneva, and so is she. He says they're separated, living on opposite sides of the city, but it doesn't matter. Not if he still loves her."

"Do you love him, Kristina?"

"Love him? As if I could know a thing like that," she said, a peal of shrill laughter chasing her words. "Oh, Hadley, I wanted so much for you to like me. To not think I was a screwup. Now look what I've done."

Hadley moved over to sit beside her. She slipped an arm around her shoulders.

"You're hardly a screwup. At least you've got some drama in your life. Keeps things interesting, right?"

She smiled, weakly. "Well, it's not boring. Never boring."

"So, do you go to Geneva to see him? Is that why I haven't seen so much of you lately?"

"Or we meet halfway. There are some pretty lakeside towns. Old castles, things like that. We wander around them and scream at each other. Always the same argument. I tell him that I don't want to see him unless I know it's really over with his wife, and he's too honest, Hadley, he's painfully honest. It hurts."

Hadley couldn't picture a Swiss man screaming. In her mind they were all composed, rangy and elegant. *Jacques.*

"He can't be all that honest," said Hadley, "not if he's with you."

Kristina stared at her blankly. When she blinked, tears fell from her lashes.

"Has he ever been here?" Hadley asked, quickly changing tack.

"To Les Ormes? No, of course not. It'd shatter all illusions. I think he's under the impression that I'm quite sophisticated."

"I'd have liked to have met him," Hadley said.

"Hadley, you'd only disapprove," she said. "I know you wouldn't mean to, but you would. You're too good."

"Am I?" said Hadley. "Not deliberately."

"Please, let's change the subject. I've gone on and on. What are you writing? Or more like, what am I stopping you from writing?"

"An essay. For my American Literature class. It's on Hemingway."

"Your favorite."

"How did you know?"

"*A Farewell to Arms.* You told me."

"Oh, right. Favorite author. Yes, definitely."

"What's your tutor like?"

Hadley hesitated. "He loves himself a bit," she said.

She didn't talk about the way Joel Wilson's eyes always went to hers first when he made a joke in class. The way he'd tapped her elbow again as he'd talked to her after a lecture once, just as he had at the party by the lake. How she'd passed him in a crowded corridor one time and he'd doffed an imaginary cap in her direction and she had made to catch it like a blown kiss, only realizing her mistake when she was three, four, five steps in the opposite direction. The way her cheeks had burned red, and the hope, the desperate hope, that he might have thought that she was only waving. A strange, snappy sort of a wave, but only that, nothing more. She didn't say any of these things because, compared to Kristina's real romance, they felt like nothing. Hadley picked up her pen and began to chew the end. Kristina bent and kissed her, a slight press of lips against her cheek.

"Thank you, Hadley, for listening. And I'm sorry I didn't tell you all this before. I guess I'm not that proud of it, that's all." She groaned, "Oh, why can't I have a normal boyfriend?"

"You could leave him, you know. You don't need him. He doesn't deserve you, not like this."

"Oh, but I do. And he does." She looked down at her hands. "Hadley, I lied to you. I do love him. I really, really love him."

Hadley took her friend's hand and squeezed it.

"Maybe I'll see him tomorrow." Kristina went on, "Maybe I'll tell him how I really feel. And if he doesn't feel the same, if he's not *free* to feel the same . . ."

"What will you do?"

"I'll end it."

She went then, closing her door softly and going back into her room. Through the wall Hadley heard Kristina's door shut, and then a creak as she settled onto her bed. She sat for a moment, in the halo of lamplight, listening. But no more noises came from

109

next door. No trilling telephone, no whispered secrets. She read back over the words that she had written before Kristina had come to see her. They were flat and lifeless. She crossed them out with fierce black lines.

CHAPTER 7

On Saturday afternoon Hadley walked down the hill into town. It was a pert October day, a pale sun, the slightest bluster of cloud and breathtakingly cold. She shivered in the mackintosh that she had bought as soon as her grant money cleared. With its nipped-in waist and stiff collar, it gave her the continental air that she wanted. Unusually, for a weekend, Hadley was on her own. Just as she had said, Kristina had gone to Geneva to see Jacques. Her story had touched Hadley, for it was far-fetched enough to be perfectly true. She'd seen how when Kristina had spoken about Jacques, the hazel flecks in her eyes had shone amber and her lips had pursed as if to kiss. Hadley had never seen anyone look so hopelessly in love. She decided that she'd buy Kristina some chocolates to brighten her spirits, to tell her that, through it all, life was still sweet. After all, she had no real advice to offer, no brokenhearted tale to share in return.

The streets were full of Saturday shoppers, and there was a pervading air of grace about them; all sharp cheekbones, smartly tipped hats and silk scarves tied with a flourish. Even their purchases seemed elegant, a *tarte aux pommes* in a slim white box, a pair of pointy-end baguettes, peeping from a basket. The lapdogs were out in force, too, bumping at their owners' ankles or tucked into the crooks of arms. Hadley weaved between them, her quick pace taking her nearly all the way to the waterfront.

Chocolaterie Amandine had the air of an old-fashioned dispensing chemist, with a glass-topped counter and wooden shelves crowded with packets and jars. The smell inside was less sweet than she might have imagined; it hung heavily in the air, the kind of aroma you felt you ought to be able to see and feel. A bell had announced her arrival, but the lady behind the counter was busy with an elderly gentleman. He appeared to be selecting chocolates one by one, ruminating on their taste and compatibility. *Merveilleux!* she heard him exclaim as the last chocolate finally took its place in the gift box. He turned around with some satisfaction at that point, and Hadley saw his face. As he noticed her, a ripple of pleasure crossed it.

"Hadley," he said. "You're still here."

"I am," she said. "I'm in Lausanne for the whole year."

"Perhaps you told me that when we spoke. I'm afraid I'm forgetful."

"You remembered my name."

"So I did. And I'm not really forgetful. I like to play at being elderly sometimes. It gives one terrific liberties."

"Well, Hugo Bézier, I remembered yours, too."

"I'm immensely flattered. Now, where is your ebullient friend today?"

"Off being ebullient in Geneva." As she said it, her lightness felt like a betrayal.

"I don't care so very much for *Genève*. You were right to stay behind."

"Who are the chocolates for?" she asked.

"What? Oh, these?" He regarded the box in his hand with a mildly quizzical expression. "They could be for you."

"Is that what you mean when you talk about taking liberties?"

"Guilty as charged."

"I'm actually buying chocolates for Kristina. Said friend. What do you recommend?"

"The selection of chocolates is a fine art."

"I noticed. You were taking your time about it. A true old master."

His smile stirred. "Please, take these." He pushed the box gently into her hand. "I rarely eat them. I just enjoy choosing them."

"I can't do that."

"Please. I'd be delighted."

"Do you mean them for Kristina?"

"They're for you."

"But would you mind, if I gave them to her?"

"I think perhaps I would."

"No one's ever given me chocolates like that before. Randomly, I mean. A stranger."

"A random stranger? I'm not sure I appreciate that description."

"Thank you, Hugo. Really."

"C'est un plaisir," he said, bowing a little.

"Okay," said Hadley. "But I still need to pick some out for Kristina, though. Maybe you could help me choose?"

"I'd be delighted."

In the end they selected pralines that were shaped like rose blooms. Nine of them, placed in a perfectly square box and tied with a red ribbon. Once outside the shop, Hugo bent and kissed her three times. The left cheek, the right cheek, the left again.

"The Swiss way," he said.

"Are you going for one of your cognacs

now?" she asked.

"Certainly." He looked at her, his eyes as dark as treacle. He doffed his hat as he turned. "I'd ask you to accompany me," he said, "but I fear that would be a liberty on my part."

She watched him walk slowly off in the direction of the Hôtel Le Nouveau Monde. Before he was gone from sight, she took the lid from the box he'd given her and popped a chocolate in her mouth. It was curved like a seashell and dissolved on her tongue, as sweetly as a kiss.

Hadley didn't see Kristina until later that evening. She heard the jangle of her keys and the scrape of her door just as she was lying on her bed reading. She gave Kristina a few minutes then grabbed the chocolates, and went and tapped on her door.

"Kristina!" she called.

There was no answer, and she tapped again.

She heard muffled steps, and then Kristina appeared in her nightclothes. Thick woolen socks, leggings and a long sort of T-shirt. It bore a picture of a Pierrot, the mournful-looking clown of French folklore, perched on a moon. Stars pricked the sky behind him.

"Hello," Hadley said, "are you going to bed already?"

Kristina leaned against the door frame and shut her eyes for a moment. Her lids were dusky pink. "Geneva," she said. "I said I'd go and I did."

"And?"

Kristina shook her head. "The usual."

"What do you mean?"

"I don't control a thing in my life, you know, Hadley. Everything just happens to me."

"And Jacques . . ."

"He said he loves what we have."

"But, that's good, isn't it? Sort of?"

"It's not the same as loving me, is it?"

"Did you say that to him?"

She scratched the side of her arm absently. "I tried to," she said. "But, Hadley, he's very difficult to resist, in a lot of ways. I mean, I've been with him all day, and I'm exhausted, completely exhausted."

Hadley's face must have moved, maybe her eyes widened, or the corners of her lips twitched into something like a smile, because Kristina flapped her hands and laughed, suddenly not seeming very tired at all.

"No, I don't mean that! I don't mean that! But, yes, of course, that, *too*. But emotion-

116

ally, he's so exhausting. He puts it all on me. He says it's up to me if we carry on or not."

"But isn't that good? To be in charge of your own destiny?"

"I'm not, though, am I? Love doesn't work like that. Anyway, I want to be wanted. Isn't that what everyone wants? Isn't that what you want?"

"I wanted to cheer you up," said Hadley. "I got these for you."

She held out the box of chocolates. Kristina smiled sadly and shook her head.

"Oh, Hadley, you're such a sweetheart. But I can't take them. I don't deserve them. I always knew what I was getting into. It's all my own fault. You know what? I'll never tell him this, but I will tell you. The first time I saw Jacques, I thought he was the most handsome man in all the world." She paused. "And he made me feel like the most beautiful woman."

"Why wouldn't you tell him that?"

"I don't know. Because I'm me. I doubt I ever say what I really mean. I talk rubbish, half the time."

"That's not true. Kristina, please take the chocolates. I chose them for you especially."

"And you're so sweet, but you keep them," said Kristina, her voice thick with a yawn.

117

"It's my mess, isn't it? I'll just have to figure it out. Look, I need to sleep now, I'm so whacked. See you tomorrow, though? At lunchtime, maybe?"

Hadley went back to her room and plonked down on her bed again. She removed the bow from the box and the little circular sticker that sealed the ribbon. She took a chocolate and held it between her finger and thumb. It was shaped like a rose, with dark shining petals. Kristina seemed to move in a slightly different realm to the rest of them; a romantic dash from one foreign city to another to face the truth of an illicit love affair, that kind of thing didn't happen in Hadley's world. As to Kristina's own judgment of herself, whether the words she spoke were straight as arrows or a parade of shiny white lies, Hadley didn't overthink it. She wrapped the chocolates up again and set them carefully on her desk, to give to her another day.

Kristina and Jacques continued to see one another, and Hadley watched their romance from the sidelines. Sometimes Kristina's cheeks were sore from crying. Other times it was as though she was angry. Her face had a stiff set to it, her jaw tightly clamped. *You know what he said? That he "thinks he's falling in love" with me. What does that even mean? You either are or you aren't. It's just the idea of me, so no matter what I do, I can't change how he feels because you can't do a thing about someone else's ideas. You know?* And Hadley didn't, not really. Once, Kristina said she blamed Lausanne. She said she'd had no idea that Jacques would be just along the lake in Geneva; their fates were entwined, their fortunes running too close together. *Maybe I should just go,* Kristina said, *I could transfer to Paris or Lyon, or back to Copenhagen, I wouldn't even care. Anywhere but here.* But Hadley saw her come back from days in Montreux, her eyes shining sea-blue and in her hands a clutch of shopping bags bearing the names of designer boutiques. She talked of dinners in the vineyard villages where they sipped champagne from crystal glasses and afterward a helter-skelter drive down the narrow, winding roads. And one day she wore a new necklace, a piece of jet on a twisted golden chain. She sat in the kitchen at Les Ormes, unconsciously turning it between her fingers, touching the cool edges of the stone to her lips.

"I'd hate it if you left," said Hadley, watching her.

"You're the only reason I'd stay," said

Kristina, her face serious, and Hadley knew then that it was true. Only the finest thread held Kristina in Lausanne.

She tried not to be jealous of the time that Kristina spent away. Perhaps she would have minded less if Jacques weren't so much of a figment; to her he was just an idea of a person, not quite real at all, for Kristina only ever spoke about him in tantalizing snatches, shrouded with mystery. When Hadley found herself alone, which seemed to be more and more often, her thoughts frequently turned to Joel Wilson. Her own figment. And just as Kristina did with Jacques, she kept him for herself. Not that she would have known what to say to Kristina, but somehow Joel was proving himself important. She knew Kristina would have liked his lectures. The drama he bottled and served them. The importance and the frivolity as he talked about the ache of old sorrows, then the dangerous beauty of a grass-green glass of absinthe, all in the same breath. It would have been fun, winging their way into class together, talking it all over afterward, with cigarettes and martinis, as the rest of the day fell away behind them. But their studies took them in different directions, and some part of Hadley reveled in this. For all the pleasure she took in sharing, there was something to be said for a secret.

Hadley let the American Literature course shape her early weeks and color her days. She read everything Joel recommended, seduced by his telling of the Lost Generation, their stories of postwar abandon and excess. The broken men and brittle women, days eased by love affairs and the swill of liquor at the bottom of a glass that never emptied. She read of cafés with steamed windows and smoke-clouded corners, and the writers who wrote in them, ensconced in full view, courting attention and flaunting their notebooks. She read of jaunts to the races, wild horses with rippling necks and flying manes, and the reckless, hopeful gambles of men. She read of whole towns, gripped with frenzy, the narrow-hipped bullfighters who pranced at the very edges of death, the startling emotions roused in all those who could stand to watch. She read about the fast kisses and desperate clinches, the mistresses and the masters of nothing, the women who could melt a man just by looking at him, the men who could drive a woman to madness just by turning away. She read about the ill behavior of expatriates, people suspended in time, taking the best of a place and giving it their

121

worst. She read of Paris and Antibes, no more than a train ride away from Lausanne; so easily she could imagine tucking into a carriage and flashing along the lake, through the mountains then into the flatlands, and all the russet and emerald of a French autumn. She had never been to Paris, much less the South of France, but who needed them, anyway? Lausanne seemed like a blend of the two, with its expansive boulevards and frosted buildings, exotic sprays of palm and silver stretches of water. Hadley thought of those last rain-sodden pages of *A Farewell to Arms,* the torrents of sorrow, and wondered why more stories weren't set in the shine of Lausanne.

In class, when Joel talked of all the great literary traditions of expatriates, she pictured her and Kristina tripping about the city together, pleasure-seekers, in every sense. Sometimes she replaced the image of Kristina with that of Joel. She saw his arm draped around her shoulders, a dauntless smile at his lips. She imagined them sharing Lausanne's secrets with each other, and in this way her imagination ran on and on until, eventually, it ran out.

CHAPTER 8

"It's beautiful, right? If you like that sort of thing?"

Joel was standing at the window of his office with his hands in his pockets. His view took in the sweep of university lawn; the lake appeared like a distant silver thread, the mountains were lost in mist. Hadley was sitting in the low and sagging guest chair, watching him.

"Who wouldn't?" she answered, scrabbling for an elegant posture in a chair that seemed intent on defying it.

She was there for a tutorial, but so far their conversation had darted around and was yet to settle on the topic of her essay. She kept glancing at the clock, conscious of the limits of her time slot, but Joel seemed oblivious to any such constraint.

"It's easy to feel like an outsider here, is what I mean," he said. "Too much of the picturesque and nothing seems real."

She didn't think of Joel Wilson as a temporary resident. You wouldn't catch him wrestling with maps on blustery street corners, or passing the wrong coins over a *boulangerie* counter. She imagined him in a lakeside apartment, the walls lined with bookshelves and a jazz record turning on an old-style player. It would be the kind of place that a woman could only hope to leave traces in — a silky pair of pants caught just under the foot of the bed, a single earring beneath the bathroom mirror. No children, no dog.

"Could you imagine living your whole life in a place like this?" he said.

"Very easily," she replied. "I thought I'd feel like an outsider here, and I don't."

"Really? You don't?"

"Well, do you?"

"Absolutely. But I've never really minded that."

"I only wish I didn't have to count the days. There's a date stamped on my residence permit. It says when I have to leave. Do you have that? I hate it. Every day I'm reminded that I'm only here temporarily. That it won't last."

"Maybe it's good to be reminded of that from time to time. Carpe diem, *non*?"

"I guess so. That's a nice way of looking

at it, anyway."

He moved away from the window and took the chair opposite her. Hadley's eyes strayed beyond him, her attention caught by a poster on his wall. It was in the same style as the postcard she'd bought in the alpine village, that flat-painted vintage look, proclaiming all the joys of leisure, the golden age of travel. It offered up a world that was both superficial and of substance, one made of primary colors and sunshine and the Swiss Riviera. Striped parasols marked the lakeshore, blue mountains rose up from behind fuzzy-headed palm trees, and turreted hotels were beatific and imposing.

"I like your poster," she said.

"Oh, that? It was here when I came. They put it up to welcome me."

"That was nice of them."

"Wasn't it?"

"I've a postcard in the same kind of style."

"Of course you have," he said. "It's the perfect world. Tempered with distance, of course, we know that nowhere is as blissful as all that. So obviously our admiration is a little tongue in cheek."

"I use it as a bookmark. I don't need a poster, because all I have to do is look out my window, and the view's just as beautiful as anything that a doe-eyed artist might paint."

"Is that right?" he said. There was amusement brewing, showing in crinkles on either side of his eyes and at the edges of his mouth. It gave him a roguish but amiable look. "I'm going to have some trouble with you, I see. You're one of those romantics, aren't you?"

She laughed. "At my age, it'd be sad if I wasn't."

"Why did you want to come here? To Lausanne?" he asked her. And she knew already that she'd give him a real answer.

"I don't know," she said.

She hadn't meant it dumbly, and she could tell by the way he looked at her that he didn't take it that way.

"Because someone thought I couldn't. Maybe a little bit because of that. And they were probably right to because, God, I'd never thought of doing anything like this before."

"That's a good reason. But I doubt it's the only one."

"Oh, no?"

"You wanted to try on a different life," he said. "You liked the one you had, but you couldn't help wondering if there was more out there."

"How do you know that? I mean, why do you *say* that?"

"And is there? More out there?"

"I think there might be," said Hadley, trying not to smile.

His eyes fixed on hers, and they were like two blue marbles, the pupils sharp as a cat's. She blinked.

"You didn't like your college back home, did you? Sorry, your *university*?"

"Oh, I did," she said. "I liked it well enough."

"But you thought it'd be the start of the rest of your life, and it wasn't."

"Do you do this to every student, this mental examination? And anyway, shouldn't we be talking about my essay?"

"No. And yes."

Hadley looked away first. "Okay. You're right. It wasn't what I thought it'd be. I stayed at home, you see. I went to my local university. I thought it'd feel different and it didn't."

"And yet it brought you here."

"It brought me here."

"Now I feel a terrible sense of responsibility," said Joel.

"You're doing okay, so far," she said. "I mean, I love your course. It's all I can think about. All I want to read is Hemingway."

127

"A common complaint."

"I didn't expect to come to Switzerland and fall in love with an American."

He raised an eyebrow.

"Writer," she added quickly. "An American writer."

He made her a coffee after that. He handed it to her in a chipped brown mug that she curled her hands around, self-conscious suddenly, as she brought her lips to its rim. He studied the opening pages of her essay.

"An End to Love in the Novels of Ernest Hemingway," he read. "You could write twenty essays on that. But make sure you talk about beginnings, too. The beginnings were always fabulous."

Her tutorial ran over, twice the length of her scheduled slot, and she left knowing exactly what she wanted to write about. A Swiss boy with smooth dark hair and rimless glasses was sitting on the plastic chair outside Joel's office. He was next in line and looked up expectantly as Hadley came out, a crease of irritation showing in his brow.

"Sorry." She smiled. "He said you can go right in."

She held the door open, and he stalked through, his satchel spilling books. She heard Joel say, "Marcus, take a seat," in a voice that conveyed no particular enthusiasm, one that was, perhaps, imbued with the lightest dash of disappointment.

"We don't have long," she heard him say, "so, let's get to it."

Two days after her tutorial, Hadley saw Joel Wilson again in the English Language Bookshop just off Place de la Riponne. The store was a recent discovery of hers. It had no particular air of romance, no creaking floorboards or towering stacks of antiquarian books, but it possessed a *je ne sais quoi,* a certain something that meant she couldn't quite keep away. Perhaps it was the extensive Hemingway and Fitzgerald collection; the whole back wall housed shelf upon shelf of American literature, and Hadley always lingered longest in this section. She ran her fingers down the spines lovingly, as though she could glean the secrets that lay within by touch alone. She was holding a copy of *A Moveable Feast* when he came in. She had planned to meet Kristina there, but she had arrived early; and as the bell on the door clanged, she looked up, her face set to a smile. Joel Wilson stepped inside and smiled back. The wind outside had thrown his hair across his face, and he patted it down.

"Well, look at that for a welcoming smile," he said.

"Oh, hello," she said, "I actually thought you were someone else. I'm meeting my friend here."

"Ah, so that explains the expectant look. You should be more careful where you train that thing. Took my breath away, Hadley Dunn. What's that you've got there?"

Hadley held up *A Moveable Feast.*

"Don't tell me you haven't read it?"

"Of course I have," she said quickly, without adding that she had only read it that summer, and until then she hadn't known how full of "Hadley" the book was. She remembered the exact moment when she read the line where Hemingway said that he wished he had never loved anyone but her. Her mouth had dropped clean open and she'd felt a tugging in her chest. Just because everybody said it was flawed didn't mean it wasn't true. Faced with Joel Wilson, all she could say was, "I'm buying it for my friend."

"You are?" She noticed the creases at his eyes as he smiled. They deepened as he laughed.

"What is it?" she asked, smiling with him.

"Oh, nothing. Just, I used to give that book to any girl I ever dated. If she liked it, then I knew we were on the right road. If she didn't, well, game over. It was a juvenile sort of a test, but the results were pretty foolproof."

Hadley turned the book in her hand. "So, you didn't want to be with anyone who wasn't exactly like you?" she said.

"I was eighteen, and stupid with it."

She pictured a young Joel Wilson, smooth-faced, slighter of build, perhaps, but with the same deep dark eyes, the same flickering blue. And the same slow drawn smile. That Joel hadn't gone anywhere at all.

"Well," she said, "I'm nineteen and I'm giving it to someone because I like it. And if she doesn't, then that's fine, too."

"It's a romance, you do know that, right? A poetic imagining."

"I thought it was sort of a memoir."

"A pretty picture of one, that's for sure. Or not-so-pretty, if you ever got on the wrong side of him."

"I love all the lounging about in cafés. The way he talks about the mountains. And Shakespeare and Company, which just sounds too perfect to be true."

"Well, that probably all happened. And we could get on a train and go to Shakespeare and Company right now."

"It still exists?"

"It definitely does. What else do you like?"

"The way he writes about writing. What it takes, and what it gives back."

"What about the way he writes about love?"

"I don't know," said Hadley. "That's harder. Will we be studying it, as part of the course?"

"What, *A Moveable Feast*? Or love?"

"According to you, you can't have one without the other."

He laughed. *"Touché,"* he said. "While we're on the subject, I enjoyed your essay, Hadley."

"Did you?"

"It was very good."

"Thank you," she said, then, "It really helped to talk it through with you. I enjoyed writing it after that."

"I could tell. Now I've read the whole thing, my only problem's with your title. 'An End to Love.' I was expecting something suitably world-weary, but you didn't write that kind of essay."

"I didn't want to write that kind of essay."

"You find hope, apparently, in the most unusual places. I like that," he said. "Keep it up."

The owner of the shop tapped Joel on the shoulder then, and Hadley carried on

132

browsing. She felt herself glowing, inside and out. She glanced back, watching as Joel fell to speaking in garrulous French. She realized that when he spoke the language, he pouted, his lips appearing softer and more pronounced. She laughed suddenly, and turned quickly back, hurrying to a different part of the shop.

"Oh, what, you don't like my French?" he called after her.

All she could picture was the way his lips pursed, how he cocked his head to one side with a whole new set of gestures. She pretended to leaf through a different book, as irrepressible laughter came in waves.

"So, you think I'm ridiculous?" he said. His voice was close to her ear, and she turned around slowly, regaining composure. In his hands were two carrier bags bursting with books that he must have ordered. Hadley looked into his face and inexplicably wanted to laugh again.

"I'm sorry," she said, "it's not you, it's me. It must be the altitude. It's making me hysterical."

"Women." He shook his head, his face creasing with amusement. "I'll never understand them."

She watched him as he left, thinking about the way he'd said *women* and not *girls*. She noticed the way the shop owner was looking at her, and she smiled and turned away. She felt a little drunk. When the door clanged again, she half thought it was Joel coming back in, but this time it was Kristina.

"Oh, you're here already," she said. "I thought I was early."

"You are. I was just really early."

"What is it? You're grinning like a maniac."

"Oh, I'm just pleased. I found what I was looking for. I wanted to get you this." Hadley handed her the copy of *A Moveable Feast.*

Kristina's cheeks colored. She glanced away. "Oh, Hadley, I've already got it."

"You have? I thought you said you'd never read any Hemingway?"

"Well, no," said Kristina, shifting on her feet, "I haven't before, but you're always going on about him, so I thought maybe it was about time that I did."

Hadley thought of Joel Wilson and his once-upon-a-time girl test. She loved knowing that about him. People so rarely offered the small details of their lives.

"Well, did you like it?" she said.

"I haven't really started it yet," Kristina said. "I keep reading the first few lines, then something always happens to distract me. I just can't get into it."

Hadley bit down a smile. She imagined Joel saying "fail," and maybe writing a note in a pad, a cross next to a name.

"Not everyone likes Hemingway," she said, taking Kristina's arm. "I'm glad I checked before I got it. Come on, let's get out of here. I'll buy us some *vin chaud* instead."

A little over a week later, she saw Joel Wilson at the city baths. Hadley had taken to swimming in the evenings, and she liked the atmosphere of the pool. People chatted in the shallows, and loitered at the sides in couples and small groups. It was Lausanne's watery indoor meeting point. Often Kristina joined her, but sometimes she changed her mind and went to see Jacques instead. That night the two of them ran into each other just as Hadley was leaving her room.

"I thought you were in Geneva," cried Hadley.

"I was, but I came back early."

Hadley waited for more, but Kristina clapped her hands together dismissively.

"I haven't swum for ages," she said. "I could do with a chance to clear my head. You don't mind hanging on, do you?"

Hadley perched on one of the seats in the hallway. Five, then ten minutes passed. She wandered outside and leaned on the wall. Below her the city glittered. She thought ahead to the feeling of emerging from the pool into the night air, hair still damp at the nape of her neck, her cheeks slapped by the cold. Swimming in winter was something she never did at home.

Kristina strolled through the door, and Hadley turned at the sound of her approach. She was wearing a sports top, and her hair was slicked back into a high ponytail. Her neat rucksack gave her a buoyant look.

"Sorry, sorry," she said, "I'm here now."

Hadley felt as if she hadn't seen much of her in the past few days. She said so, and Kristina sighed dramatically.

"Oh, Hadley, tell me about it. I'm being pulled in just about every possible direction at the moment."

Hadley bit down a smile. "But you sort of like it, don't you? In a weird way?"

"Is that what you think?"

"I don't know. Maybe. A bit."

"Hadley, I'm not a drama queen."

"Well . . ."

"Am I? Am I a drama queen? Oh, God, that's just horrific if I am. I hate those people. Hadley, please, tell me I'm not."

She grabbed her hand and pulled on it,

squeezing all of Hadley's fingers. Hadley laughed and shook her off.

"Not in a bad way," she said.

"Are you fed up of hearing about Jacques?"

"I don't really hear about him so much anymore, you're with him so often these days."

"Am I?"

"It seems like ever since you told me about him, you've started seeing him more than before."

"Ah, but that's where you're wrong. It just feels like that to you because you know where I go now. That's the difference. All those times you thought I was so studious, slipping off to the library in search of some strange art history book . . ."

"I guess I just miss you a little bit, that's all."

"Oh, Hadley, but I haven't gone anywhere. Not really." She hesitated. "Actually that's not true. I have gone somewhere. I'm in a very big black hole. But there's a light right at the bottom of it. And as long as there's that light, I don't want to climb out."

"I don't even know what that means," said Hadley.

Kristina laughed hysterically. "God, and you think I do?"

They walked side by side, not talking for the moment. It was so cold that Hadley felt her lips tightening. Beneath their feet the pavement glistened with nighttime frost.

"How old is Jacques?" she asked suddenly.

"Older than us."

"What's that like?"

"It's like . . . nothing. It's not even a factor."

Hadley nodded. "I can see that," she said, her voice more wistful than she'd intended, "the right person's the right person. It doesn't matter how old they are, does it?"

Kristina looked at her indulgently. "Hadley, listen, there's a cute guy called Max in my Art History class. Maybe you'd like him."

"You don't have to match-make me, Kristina."

"No, but, wouldn't you like there to be someone?"

Hadley pushed her hands deeper into the pockets of her coat. She shivered.

"Or is there someone already? Someone you're not telling me about?"

"No," said Hadley, "not even close."

"You're blushing," said Kristina.

"That's not blushing. That's my cheeks freezing off. Yours are the same."

Kristina shook her head. "Whoever it is,

you should just go for it. Don't ask too many questions, just dive right in. I know I complain about what I have with Jacques, but when I'm with him, if I just close my mind to everything else, he makes me so happy, Hadley."

"Eyes wide shut," Hadley said.

Kristina yelped with laughter. "Exactly that. What do people say, just hold on tight and enjoy the ride? Sometimes there's nothing wrong with that, you know."

The pool was as busy as it always was. There was the crowded sound of splashing and calling and an indefinable hum that pervaded everything. Hadley wore goggles and a cap that hid her hair and felt boyish in her black bikini. She slipped into the water and began her fast lengths of crawl, slick as an eel. Kristina took a long time to emerge from the changing room, but when she did she dazzled in a fuchsia-pink one-piece that made Hadley feel as if she was wearing a P.E. uniform. From the deep end, Kristina paused, checked her space, then executed a perfect dive, emerging from beneath the water almost halfway across the pool. Hadley gaped, noticing the polo-shirted lifeguard was doing the same.

She didn't see Joel coming. She was

dawdling at the shallow end, catching her breath, when he tapped her on the arm. She turned around, thinking it was Kristina.

"You again," he said.

Joel looked different in the water. His hair was boot-polish black and shining wet, and his skin was deep brown. He had a sliver-thin scar across his right shoulder.

"Hello," she said.

He was so close to her, and she was grateful that they weren't standing on the slippery poolside tiles, their near-nudity entirely visible. She folded her arms across her front.

"So you're a swimmer, huh?" he said.

"Not really. More of a splasher."

"No, I saw you do a couple of lengths back there. You're a swimmer."

"I never get the breathing right, though," said Hadley. She exhaled slowly. "See, I'm breathless." She was conscious of her chest rising and falling as she said it.

"So, this is where the bright young things hang out, is it? The municipal baths, the favored haunt of the Lausanne literary set."

"Are you including yourself in that?"

"Youngish things, anyway. And my trunks are bright."

"It's the stench of chlorine, and the floating sticking plasters, we come for the ambiance, really."

He laughed, and his hand rubbed at his chin, scratching for the nonexistent beard again.

"By springtime we'll be swimming in the lake," he said, "a helluva lot more scenic than this place."

"I can't think of anything more beautiful than that," she said, "surrounded by mountains, the sky above. Totally undisturbed."

"Oh," said Joel, "I can take a hint."

He turned to go, but Hadley caught his arm. For the briefest moment her fingers brushed the hardness of his shoulder.

"No," she said, laughing out her embarrassment at the sudden touch, "I didn't mean that. Only that I love the way we're all here together. Listen to how *noisy* it is, and yet we're completely separate and in our own worlds."

She glanced away and noticed Kristina on the other side of the pool. She was preparing to dive again. She stood, oblivious of the eyes on her, then arced gracefully, with barely a splash as she entered the water.

"So, you came here on your own?" he said.

"Oh, my friend's somewhere here," said Hadley, waving her hand.

"Another Brit?"

"Danish."

"Have you made many Swiss friends yet?"

"I'd like to, but not really, not yet. You?"

"The staff at the Institute seem to keep themselves to themselves. Although Caroline Dubois hosted a dinner party the other night."

"How was it?" said Hadley.

"Very chic."

Hadley nodded, wondering if anyone else had been there, or if the sleek skirt and the ice smile would have been for Joel alone.

"You know what, though?" he went on. "Considering her husband's a wine lover, we drank from the world's smallest glasses."

Hadley felt a disproportionate rush of relief. "Was it very formal?" she asked, grinning.

"*Très* formal. I worry about returning the favor. My apartment has more of a box of wine and a take-out vibe."

"I don't think a box of wine would even fit in my room."

"Small?"

"But perfectly formed."

"Want to know something else about my apartment? I can't use the washing machine after ten o'clock at night."

"Wouldn't you have better things to do then, anyway?"

"Not the point, Hadley. Freedom starts with being able to wash your socks whenever you want. Don't the Swiss know that?"

"Is that right? You'd better get going then. You'll miss your chance."

"Nope, that's my Friday night. Right now I'm leaving here and going straight to the nearest bar. To warm up with my old friend Jim Beam, maybe."

Hadley laughed again, and it came out like a gulp. Beneath the water she shifted her weight from one foot to another.

"I only just got here," she said, "I've only done ten lengths."

"Then you must do more. *Au revoir, Hadley,*" he said.

"What bar?" she said, before she could stop herself.

"What bar? Not Mulligan's, that's for sure."

She might have considered it a snub, were it not for the way he looked at her just before he turned to go. It wasn't a too-hungry stare, but it was an acknowledgment, nonetheless, of her existence. In one glance he took in her wet body and pale shoulders and slim waist beneath the water. Then instead of taking the few steps to the ladder, he placed his hands on the tiles and hauled himself up and out in one deft motion. Hadley watched him walk smartly toward the changing rooms, the water slick-ing down his bare back. As he rounded the lifeguard's chair, she saw him slip on a tile, and for a moment she thought he'd fall. But he held his balance and kept going. It was an endearing hiccup in an otherwise smooth exit. She smiled and dipped down under the water. She felt entirely weightless and as though she didn't need to breathe at all.

CHAPTER 9

Hadley's birthday was in late November, and for the first time in her life she woke up on that day to find herself in a white world. She drew open the blinds and looked out over the snow-covered rooftops. The sky was smudged blue and gray, and the lake lay beyond, steely and unchanged. Her balcony had its own private drifts, with crystals forming at the window's edge. She pushed open the door and felt the sting of the cold air.

"Happy birthday, me," she whispered.

A card had arrived for her from home, and inside was a piece of Sam's finest artwork. He'd drawn her with a snowman again, but this time they stood in a patch of flowers, and the sun beat down overhead. His coloring had stayed inside the lines, and he'd written the first message inside — *Happy birthday to you, Hadley, love Sam, by Sam xxx.* Her mum and dad had written beneath and tucked inside was a fifty franc note. They'd written, *celebrate with your new Swiss friends*!

Her new Swiss friends. She thought of Jacques and imagined Kristina bringing him to her party later. Standing slightly awkwardly with his hair ruffled and a smear of lipstick on the side of his cheek. It would never happen. No matter how close she and Kristina were, it seemed that she and Jacques were never destined to meet. That evening Chase, Jenny, Bruno, Loretta, Kristina and Hadley had decided to go for dinner in the old town, a rare departure from their slapdash cooking in the kitchens of Les Ormes. Hadley would have been content for her birthday to pass unmarked, but Kristina saw the date of birth in her residence permit and was determined not to let that happen. She had rallied the others and booked a restaurant. It would be the first evening that they had consciously spent together in several weeks.

Hadley set the card on her desk in pride of place. She hadn't felt even slightly homesick since she'd left, but there was something about the day that made her wish, just for a passing moment, that she was back in the cheerful noise of her home. Her mum would be singing along to the radio, her dad

146

pretending to complain about a household chore, her brother kicking a blow-up football along the hallway, rippling the rug. She could slip into that world so easily; at home she was Hadley who always had seconds of mashed potato, Hadley who cried at films even when they weren't supposed to be sad, Hadley who could take the stairs three at a time, on the way up *and* the way down. It was strange that the very things she found irksome sometimes about being at home, the swaddling, the easy folklore, the suspension of the real world and everything in it, were, now that she wasn't there, turning out to be the most seductive. For the first time since she'd arrived in Lausanne she inexplicably felt as if she shouldn't be there, that she was in the wrong place. She shrugged the thought away; birthdays always made her sentimental. Her phone rang, and she answered it in a rush.

"Happy birthday, Hadley!" three voices cried in unison.

She closed her eyes and listened to her family sing. She smiled and smiled, and tried very hard not to cry. Ten minutes later, buoyed by their merry conversation and heartfelt wishes, she went into the kitchen to brew coffee and settled into looking out over the snow scene. It was a different angle from the view from her room; here the lake was a broader cut, and a band of burly elms stretched below Les Ormes. The snow was the perfect birthday gift, she told herself, and she would cherish it. If snow ever fell at home it never lasted for long before it grew slushy and gray. Council trucks sprayed grit grumpily, and people walked with teetering, uncertain steps. That day she vowed to dance in the street and throw her face up to the sky as the flakes settled on her lashes.

"Happy birthday!"

Kristina swung into the kitchen and deposited a paper bag on the table. Inside were two crisp and flaking almond croissants, their favorite *boulangerie* treat.

"These are for you. Happy Birthday, my sweet."

Kristina kissed her on both cheeks.

"I just made coffee. Want some?"

"Hadley, I have to run. I've got an early tutorial."

"Have you?"

"Yes. Oh, you're thinking of Jacques. Every time I say I'm going somewhere now, you think I'm actually going to see Jacques."

"Well, aren't you?"

"No, not today."

There was a snappish tone to Kristina's voice. She tore the corner from one of the croissants and nibbled at it.

"I'm actually going to buy you a present. That's what I'm going to do."

"But you already did." Hadley held up the paper bag. "I don't need anything else."

"Now you're just being silly."

"I actually mean it. Look, how about we dump the Institute today? Just run around the city in the snow. We could go back to the Hôtel Le Nouveau Monde. Or take a paddle boat out — I wonder if they let you do that in winter? Imagine the view from the water."

"Hadley, I can't. Anyway, it's Friday."

"So?"

"You've got your American Literature class."

"I can skip it for once."

"I know you think I don't notice, but I do, you know."

"Notice what?"

"You always make an extra effort on a Friday."

Hadley looked down at herself. Last night she'd painted her nails a cherry red. She had on her favorite winter dress, a checkered, woolen one that skimmed her thighs and made her look taller than she really was.

"It's my birthday," she said. "If you can't look nice . . ."

"Okay, sure, that's right." Kristina bent down and kissed her again, and the sweep of her hair brushed Hadley's cheek. "It's your birthday every Friday."

Kristina blitzed out of the door, throwing a *see you tonight* behind her. Hadley flicked a croissant crumb from the black of her tights. She poured herself another coffee, wondering if it was obvious to everyone, or just to someone who knew her like Kristina.

As she walked to the bus stop, her breath coming in white puffs, the snow squeaked beneath her feet. A cautious sun drew sparkles on the pavement, and she wished she had her camera with her. It was the kind of day you wanted to capture, that you'd need to see again in order to quite believe.

Joel Wilson's lecture had something of a hurried quality about it that morning. He seemed distracted, clicking his pen between his fingers, his usually fluent stream of talk broken with protracted *okays* and other fillers. It was as if he would rather have been somewhere else. On the bus on the way in, Hadley had overheard talk of the ski resorts opening early. Her mind ran on, and she saw those steep crystal-bright slopes, low-dipped skiers cutting new lines and the roar of a mountain bar afterward. She could

150

picture Joel there. She imagined him skiing bravely and with a hint of danger, finishing the day with burned red cheeks and his hair sticking to the back of his neck. She hoped that Kristina had meant it when she'd said that she would teach her that winter.

Despite racing through the class, as it drew to a close Joel fell to dawdling. He fiddled with some papers in his briefcase and appeared to search for a passage in a book. He looked up as she passed his desk.

"Hey, Hadley," he said. "How do you like all this snow?"

"I love it," she said. "I heard that if it keeps falling, they're going to open the ski resorts early."

"They are? No kidding. I'll expect a lower turnout for the next class, then."

It was the first joke he'd made in the past hour, and she took heart. "I don't think the Swiss are a nation of rule breakers. Remember your washing machine?"

"Well, sure, but you think nobody skips class here?"

"You tell me." She smiled.

"No students skip *my* classes," he said, "that's true. Now why do you think that is?"

"Their hearts couldn't bear the breaking," said Hadley, trying to sound cavalier. He looked at her, his face puzzled, and she opened her mouth to utter some qualification, to remind him that she was only quoting him, using some of the first words he'd addressed them with at the start of the semester.

"Your first class . . ." she began.

"So somebody was listening, after all. That's a relief."

They smiled at one another, Hadley grateful for the cover, and Joel with a glimmer of amusement that wasn't unpleasant, that pleased her, in fact, when she thought about it later. She said something about being late for her next class, and he walked with her to the door. In the corridor they said goodbye and went their separate ways.

She saw him again by chance at lunchtime. She was in the cafeteria eyeing the sandwich counter, when she felt a tap on her shoulder.

"Apparently I have to wish you a happy birthday," he said.

She smiled. "How did you know?"

"Student records. We have a file on each and every one of you, you know. Past misdemeanors, first pets, the lot. It's all in there. But I see you're on your own for lunch, what's that about?"

"Why were you looking at my file?"

152

"It's the best way to learn your names."

"But you know my name."

"And to check out your academic records. There are some knowledge gaps among the students, and I like to know who's taken what course. Yours was one of many, Hadley, and I just happened to notice your birthday. Now, lunch? Solo? I repeat, what's that about?"

Before she could reply, he said, "Want to grab it with me?" and without waiting for an answer, he put her baguette on his tray and took one for himself. "I get twenty percent off the prices here," he said, flashing his lecturer card like an FBI badge. "Go get us a table."

As she sat down she glanced around. She had seen other students with their tutors there before, taking coffee, leafing through essay pages at a corner table, and, if you didn't know otherwise, you might have thought Joel was a student himself. He had a youthful sort of posture, one leg cranked up over the other, the hems of his jeans straggling with loose threads. He wore a similar T-shirt to the one in the department photograph. White, and rippling slightly where it ran over his stomach.

"So, plans for later?" he asked.

"Just a dinner. At this place Le Pin."

"I've heard good things. That's all very civilized."

"It'll start off that way, at least. I expect we'll go on somewhere else, and it'll degenerate from there." She thought of Kristina, and eyes wide shut. She said, "You should come for a drink. If you're not doing anything else."

"I can't, I'm sorry."

"Of course," said Hadley quickly. "The last thing you want to do is hang out with students."

"Actually it's very tempting, but I have plans already. I'd have been there like a shot, otherwise." Perhaps he noticed her embarrassment, for he changed the subject deftly. "So, all this snow talk, you're a skier, then?"

"Well, no, I've never been. But I'd really like to. My friend Kristina's going to teach me."

And she talked on. She told him about the bungalow she grew up in, where she still lived with her parents and brother, when all of her friends had gone off to make new homes of their own. The flatlands that surrounded it. The absence of anything that could really be called a view. She talked about how she wanted to go up high into the mountains, higher than anyone probably ever needed to go, just to see how the world looked from up there.

"And ski back down," he said.

"Trying not to break all my bones in the meantime."

"You'd be good at it," he said. "I can see you liking the speed."

"What makes you say that?"

"And the danger."

"Not too much danger."

She sat back then and took a bite of her baguette. She chewed slowly and he was quiet. She decided she had said too much. Her mum and dad. Sam. The daily bus to university. There was no reason he'd be interested in all of that.

"I grew up in California," he said suddenly. He stirred a sugar into his coffee and clacked the spoon against the cup, once, twice, three times. "Soon as we were old enough my little brother and I used to ride up into the mountains in a clapped-out truck, me at the wheel, him playing with the radio looking for anything loud and with guitars. We'd spend the day on the slopes with junkyard skis, figuring things out for ourselves. We'd come home battered black-and-blue, all kinds of sprains and pulls and twists, muscles screaming for mercy, snow-blinded, because we never had the proper gear, and the sun always shone so hard it gave us these searing headaches, but . . . happy. Very, very happy."

"What's your brother's name?" she asked, not wanting him to end the story.

"Winston. Sounds like something you'd call a cat, doesn't it? No nine lives for him, though."

She looked for the right thing to say and only found, "Oh?"

"He passed away. Car wreck. Turns out that truck of mine wasn't the safest."

She looked down at her hands, her red nails feeling suddenly garish. She squeezed them together.

"I'm sorry. I can't imagine what that's like."

"You never lost anybody?"

"No."

"What, not even grandparents?"

"No."

"You're lucky."

He looked at her, and she felt her naïveté shining thinly, as though he could see all the way through her and out the other side. Hadley had no experience of loss, and in that moment, against all judgment, she wished that she did. Anything, a once-broken heart, an old but unutterable grief, just so that she could tell him about it and show that she understood.

"I don't know why I told you about Winston just now," he said, and she was relieved that his tone was contemplative instead of dismissive. "I usually don't. I keep him for myself. See this?" He pointed to the tiny scar, just above his lip. "Same car wreck. Had this since I was seventeen and it's never faded. I don't want it to, either."

Hadley met his eye and did her best to hold it.

"Well, this is fine birthday conversation," he said. "Great date, I am." She laughed easily but she noted the phrase; she'd remember it later, play it back. He skipped on, "What are you, twenty-one? Twenty-two?"

"Just twenty."

"Twenty." He shook his head. "I can barely remember it."

"Was it really that long ago?"

"I was mostly drunk, I think. And anyway, it was a long time ago. Truth is, you're just half of me, Hadley Dunn."

"Forty?"

"Thereabouts."

A shout of hysterical laughter burst out, and they both turned. A group of students across the cafeteria was fooling around. One was doubled over, laughing noisily, and her

157

friend was smacking her back as though she was choking. Hadley spotted Kristina in the group's peripheries, talking to a tall red-headed boy. She looked quickly away before she saw her back.

"Sorry, Hadley," Joel said, "I've got to go. Fridays are departmental meeting days, and you can imagine how long they go on for. Happy birthday, okay? And thanks for the company."

It felt like a sudden departure, and he left his sandwich half-eaten on his tray. Hadley drank the rest of her coffee slowly. *You're just half of me.* There were plenty of other ways in which he could have said it, but he chose that one. She held on to it, the precise phrasing, turning each word like a jewel in a necklace. The next time she looked up, Kristina had gone, too.

CHAPTER 10

Lausanne was small enough to feel as though you could always bump into someone, and already faces were becoming familiar — the boy with the giant headphones who went in and out of the Ouchy fountains on Rollerblades; the librarian from campus, a stringy-looking woman with a cloud of white curls and a rackety bicycle; Hugo Bézier, who appeared catlike, watching and waiting and smiling as he saw her. Hadley was beginning to treasure such people. They made her feel that she understood the city's rhythms and was part of them herself. And there was Joel Wilson, of course. Their paths crisscrossed at the pool, the bookstore and once on the creaking steps of the Escaliers du Marché, the market steps, where he offered her a finger-burning chestnut from a brown paper bag, and she took it, feeling that it was another thing shared. As long as there was the possibility of chance meetings, trips into town had an added charge about them.

She was getting ready for the evening when the phone in her room rang. Hadley expected it to be her mum and dad again, with another chirrupy rendition of "Happy Birthday."

"Hadley? I'm a terrible friend. I'm running late, really late. I had to go to Geneva in the end. Will you go on without me? I'll join you as soon as I can. I'm really sorry."

"Kristina, slow down. I thought you said you weren't going to Geneva."

"I know, I know."

"Well, why don't I call the restaurant and delay the table? We'll go for a drink somewhere first. It's fine."

"No, Hadley, that's really sweet of you, but I'm going to be really late. Please, carry on without me. I don't want to ruin things."

"Where are you now? Are you on your way?"

The train ride from Geneva took about forty-five minutes. It was the evening commuter time, and the carriages would be packed with stiff suits and their fast-ticking watches, and a clattering refreshment trolley that knocked the tips of shined shoes as it passed. She imagined Kristina applying lipstick to her reflection in the window, after

Jacques had kissed it all away. She could be in Lausanne within the hour.

"No, I'm still here. It's complicated. . . . And to make it all worse I've lost my phone, somewhere between there and Geneva, God knows how. I was flustered and must have left it somewhere. I'm on a pay phone. Look, I've got to go, the money's running out. Honestly sweetie, I'll get there as soon as I can."

She clicked off the line then. Hadley was left sitting with the receiver in her lap and the flattening feeling of disappointment.

"Happy birthday!" Jenny cried as Hadley opened her door.

Bruno pulled the cord in a party popper and spirals of colored strings fell about her feet. Chase shoved a bottle of beer into her hand.

"Come on," he said, "let's get going. Jenny, knock for Kristina."

"She's running late," Hadley said. "She'll see us there."

Jenny linked her arm through Hadley's in an unexpected gesture of intimacy. She was laughing loosely, her cheeks were flushed, and Hadley had the feeling that she was late to her own party. Jenny half dragged her along, Bruno and Chase close behind.

"No Loretta?" Hadley said, turning.

"She's meeting us at the restaurant. She's bringing her friend Luca. That's okay, isn't it?"

"Fine," Hadley said, absently. Her mind turned to Tonridge. If she were at home there would be a messily iced cake ablaze with candles. The television would be chattering with film after film. Sam would be throwing chocolate fingers at her from across the table. Despite the link of Jenny's arm and the close footsteps of Chase and Bruno, Hadley felt a biting sense of dislocation. She realized how adrift she felt without Kristina.

The restaurant, Le Pin, was tucked away on a street that lay between the station and the lake. With its arched windows, rows of wooden tables and scrubbed tiled floor, it felt like a Parisian café; a place more day than night. Crumpled newspapers thumbed by nicotine-stained hands hung on racks. A feathery-looking old man was sitting by the door drinking rosé wine, a racing newspaper spread out on the table before him. But the nighttime touches were there if you looked for them. Candle wax dribbled down the necks of wine bottles. At the rear, checkered cloths draped some of the tables. Baskets of thinly sliced baguette were stacked by the cash register, ready to be set down with the laminate menus.

"This place?" said Chase. "Really?"

"I love it," Hadley said. "It's actually perfect."

They took their seats at the back, and a waiter with oil-slicked hair greeted them indifferently. Everyone ordered wine, and lots of it. Loretta joined them, elegant in a black velvet dress, and the newcomer, Luca, who was tall and slightly stooping, with an ocean of curls. He kissed Hadley on both cheeks and wished her a happy birthday. The wine was red and thin. Bruno wrinkled his nose and ordered vodka instead. They looked over the menus, saw cheese fondue and horse steaks, wild boar with forest berries, dishes of sauerkraut and spindly pairs of sausages. Jenny said she wouldn't eat horse if you paid her, goading Chase into an argument that seemed to tickle them both more than antagonize. Loretta and Bruno had their heads together, plotting the sharing of a fondue, giggling over the games you had to play if you dropped your bread in the pot. Beside Hadley, Luca sat with his hand wrapped around the stem of his wineglass, smiling.

"What are you studying?" he asked, in a

163

bouncy sort of English.

"Literature," she said. "American, English and French. You?"

"French, of course. French language. With some Spanish, too. That's how I know Loretta."

He smiled again, and this time showed all of his teeth. He leaned toward her.

"And is it a happy birthday, so far?"

Hadley briskly flapped the menu. "Very happy," she said.

By the time the food came they were drunk and getting drunker. Hadley had chosen the daily special, a meat fondue, with thin strips of beef sizzling on the surface of a hot rock. She ate forkfuls of skinny chips, and Luca helped himself to one from time to time, grinning at her as though they were sharing a joke. He kept refilling her wineglass, splashing the cloth so the white squares in among the red turned pink. Chase and Jenny had matching beefsteaks, and Bruno and Loretta wrestled each other's fondue sticks and played with the flame beneath the pan. They were increasingly noisy. Just as Hadley was wondering if she was the only who had noticed that Kristina still wasn't there, she heard the trill of her phone in her bag. She jumped up, her chair screeching on the tiles.

She took the call, squeezed into a corridor by the toilet.

"Hadley, please don't kill me. . . ."

"Where are you?"

"Do you like the restaurant?" Kristina asked. "I thought it'd be like one of the ones you're always reading about in your books. Full of old writer types."

"Are you with Jacques?" she said, tasting the plaintive note in her own voice and hating it.

"Not for much longer," she said, "and actually, physically, no. I'm at a stupid pay phone again. What a day."

"What do you mean, 'not for much longer'? For God's sake, Kristina. You're always saying things like that, and you end up doing nothing."

"I'm sorry."

"You're not sorry. If you were, you'd just decide what you really wanted and leave it at that."

"Don't be like that, Hadley. You don't understand."

"You're right, I don't understand. Not tonight."

"I'm sorry I'm missing your birthday."

"It's not about that. Well, actually it is, a bit. You're the one that made me have this dinner, and made everyone come, and you're not even here."

"I didn't make anyone come. They all wanted to celebrate with you, Hadley."

"And there's some guy called Luca who I don't even know, and he keeps trying to touch my knee under the table."

"Hadley, I wanted to give you a special night, but Jacques . . ."

"Don't use Jacques as an excuse, okay? It sounds to me like he's never been anything but honest with you. You're the one who's making it into a drama. And you're the one who's there with him instead of here with me."

"Hadley, you sound jealous. Don't be jealous. And you really don't need to be, not anymore, because . . ."

"Why do you think I'm jealous? Wait, not because I don't have a boyfriend? That's what you think, isn't it? Was it you that invited this guy Luca? Nothing to do with Loretta at all? God, I'm so stupid, I didn't even put it together before."

"Hadley, I don't know anyone called Luca, and I wouldn't do that to you, anyway. Listen, I'm sorry you feel like I've ruined your birthday."

"You know what I think?"

"What?"

"You should just stay there with Jacques.

Your great mystery man. Just stay there, Kristina. You're excused from tonight. I'll send your apologies to the others. Forget it."

"I seem to be a letdown to everybody at the moment, Hadley. I just can't give people what they want." She gave a high-pitched laugh. "Jacques told me I'm infectious. He makes it sound like a disease."

"Well, seems like Jacques and I have something in common, after all."

Kristina was quiet on the line. When she spoke, it was in a small voice, devoid of all gusto.

"I'm on my way, anyway. I'm going to rush, and I'll get there as quickly as I can."

"I told you not to bother, so don't pretend to hurry because of me. In the end you'll do what you want, anyway."

Hadley ended the call and stood for a minute in the hallway. She'd never really argued with anyone before, and the fact that she had been quite good at it, and held her own in the face of Kristina's cajoling, depressed her. Instead of feeling righteous and boisterous, she was as deflated as an old party balloon.

As she returned to the table she saw that at her place there was a slice of cake crowned with flickering candles, and everyone erupted into uneven song. There was a hug from Jenny, followed by a virulent reproach of the still-absent Kristina. *It's really okay,* Hadley said into her wine, as Jenny pawed at her arm in comfort. And there was Luca, placing his hand on her thigh again, so lightly that it seemed to hover. She shook him off half heartedly. They ordered rounds of liqueurs, clear and spicy alpine schnapps, and all slipped a little lower in their seats. They talked over one another in unconnected lines of conversation, only Hadley seemed to fall quieter and quieter as time went on.

"I want to go dancing," she said eventually, to whomever was listening. "I want to go somewhere I've never been before. Anyone want to come?"

Chase talked about a cavern club near the station, where the Portuguese community danced and drank, and the music blasted the rails above. Hadley threw down the last of her schnapps and stood up unsteadily. They scattered their crumpled notes on the table and rolled out onto the street.

Outside, the weather had turned, and the gently spiraling flakes of early evening had become a rapid, blinding blizzard. Chase and Jenny danced along the pavement, their heads bent against the smack of cold, and were followed by a closely entwined Bruno and Loretta. Luca turned and waited for her, one arm crooked, gesturing for her to link with him.

"Come on," he said, "it's your birthday. You don't look happy enough to me."

Hadley shivered and pulled her hat down lower. She let him take her arm, and their feet skidded on the iced pavement. She fell against him.

"I've got you," he said, "it's okay, I've got you."

She looked up at him. She felt disorientated. Too much alcohol, too much food, the smarting cold air. She continued to hold his arm.

"I was horrible to my friend on the phone," she said, her words slurring. "I didn't mean to be. Why isn't she here yet, Luca?"

"Shh," he said, "I'm going to kiss you now."

His lips came toward her; she didn't move away. It was a long kiss and a deep kiss, and even though she didn't really want it, she let it take her. She heard a cheer go up somewhere behind them, and eventually Luca broke away as a swiftly hurled snowball smattered across his shoes. They both looked up to see Chase laughing, wiping his

169

hands on his jeans. Luca scooped a pile of snow into a ball. He threw it back, missing Chase and knocking Jenny's bobble hat askew, eliciting a squeal. Then they were all at it, grabbing and hurling and laughing, snow scattering down their coats and at their feet. Hadley stepped back and stuffed her hands into her pockets. She watched them, tired suddenly, with no real inclination to join in. Luca turned to her, his grin wide, and she smiled faintly back. She felt the soft whack of a snowball on her arm and looked to see Loretta, pink-cheeked and merry, waving at her from across the street. She waved in reply. Around her they played on, the blizzard whirling, like children caught in a snow globe.

Lausanne was a genteel city, by day as well as night. Certainly in those winter months, parties mostly stayed indoors, and rarely did the streets throng with reckless people. There were few of the drunken disputes and loitering that seemed commonplace in the streets of British cities past a certain time. If there was trouble at all, it was probably dealt with calmly and quietly, with none of the emergency of wailing sirens. But that night, as finally they walked on, their clothes damp from scattered snowballs, their voices loud and bright, the air was cut with a piercing chorus. They couldn't tell the difference between the Swiss ambulance, police or fire brigades, but there were at least two different sirens crisscrossing each other and just streets away.

"Can it be," said Chase, whirling around, "that for once something exciting is happening in sensible Switzerland?"

Hadley felt Luca's arm around her waist, pulling her close.

"I can think of something exciting," he said, his lips brushing her ear.

"Luca," she said, beginning to pull away, "I really don't think . . ."

And then he was kissing her again. Behind them the sirens pitched and fell, and she shut her eyes. Not kissing him back this time, not exactly, but just letting him. Her mouth just open wide enough. Her hands falling loosely by her sides.

Hadley woke up with a dull and throbbing headache. She pulled her sheets around her face and lay shrouded. The light in her room was bright but somehow heavy. It was probably still snowing outside. The events of last night came back in flashes. Luca's kiss from nowhere. The snowball fight. The tiny, crowded basement bar where they all seemed to lose one another. Chase lining up a row of bottle-green shots of absinthe and everyone taking one. The feeling of Luca's arm around her waist, as her throat burned and stars danced in front of her eyes. They had caught a taxi home, and only Luca, who didn't live at Les Ormes, had stayed behind, standing on the pavement in his long coat, one arm raised in farewell. *You could have let him come back with us,* Jenny had said with a giggle, and Hadley had pretended incomprehension. *He lives on the other side of town,* she'd said.

There was a knock at her door, and she groaned.

"Hang on!" she called. "Wait a minute."

She stumbled out of bed and pulled on her dressing gown. It would be Kristina, gushing apology. And she knew that she would instantly accept it, an apology of her own not far behind. Even though Kristina had no way of knowing where they'd ended up last night, Hadley had still found herself looking for her as they'd danced in the crush of the basement bar. She had kept one eye always on the entrance, turning whenever she saw a sleek blond head or heard a sudden burst of laughter. Simply, Lausanne wasn't Lausanne without Kristina. She opened the door, a ready smile at her lips.

A police officer stared back. And when he started to speak, even though his French was slow and measured, she couldn't understand what he was saying. She heard the name Rue des Mirages, but it meant nothing to her. Then he said Kristina's name. Hadley spoke in English, *I'm sorry,* she said, *I don't understand.* He turned his hat in his hands. His next words came very kindly, very softly, so gently, in fact, that she still thought she was mistaken, right up until the moment when she fainted in a fierce blaze of white light.

CHAPTER 11

The officer, with his slanting shoulders and
startling uniform, stood over her. She was
sitting on the edge of her bed, sipping a
glass of water gingerly. He told her that
Kristina had died straightaway and that it
was nobody's fault. It was the blizzard of
snowflakes, a slippery street, a sudden fall
and the unyielding corner of the curb meeting her head. *A tragic accident,* he said,
framing it with oft-used words that only
served to place it with all the other tragic
accidents that occurred all around the globe
each and every day. He had tried to smile
for her then, a half smile, lifting just one
corner of his sandy mustache. *She probably
wouldn't have felt anything,* he said, in well-
intentioned English, but it was as though he
was saying that, because of that, Hadley
shouldn't, either. At least not more than you
normally did, when one of those tragic accidents occurred. She couldn't meet his eye,

and yet when the moment came for him to leave, she didn't want him to. He had given her something she had never had before, this terrible piece of news passed so gently to her, its weight no less terrific. He couldn't just turn and go now, could he? Back out into the other world? She stared at the door as he closed it behind him, and it stared back at her.

The day that followed was made of strange details, blurred and imprecise. Jenny wore a hazy pink cardigan and made cup after cup of tea, pressing them into Hadley's hands as though a gentle form of medication. Chase smoked cigarettes out of the kitchen window, shivering in the blasts of cold air, a nervous red rash she hadn't seen before creeping up his neck. Bruno and Loretta sat beside one another, their fingers woven, their dark heads bent. The police officer had spoken briefly to each of them, careful questions that were met with shaken heads and incomprehension, and when he left Chase chewed at the edge of his thumb and said to them all, *is this real?* Outside, the snow continued to fall steadily, but there was nothing picturesque about it anymore. Clouds hung heavy and smearing. The streetlights clicked on early. At some point Bruno ordered pizzas, and the unopened

175

boxes littered the table. Hadley took one of Chase's cigarettes and smoked it on the balcony in the dark. She leaned all the way over, until her head filled with stars. Her teeth chattered, and the sound was so loud, so involuntary, she didn't realize at first that it was coming from her. She began to cry, new tears sticking to where the old ones had fallen. She felt a hand on her arm, and let Jenny draw her back inside.

"She was on her way to meet us, Jenny," Hadley said. The tips of her fingers were turning blue, and she yanked the sleeves of her sweater down. "She was probably only in those backstreets because she was trying to take a shortcut to the restaurant."

Hadley wanted to add that Kristina was only rushing, not looking and hurrying, her feet moving too fast over the white-iced pavement, because of her harsh words. She had made her feel so guilty and said such horrible things, things that weren't even true. But she choked back the words.

"People fall over all the time, don't they?" she said instead. "I don't get it. How could she slip, and bang her head, and have it *kill* her? How can we be so fragile, that the slightest fall means the end? People take all kinds of risks and they're fine, totally fine. Kristina was walking down a street. Or running, whatever, but that's all. She didn't jump off a building. She wasn't in a war."

"Sometimes things just happen," said Jenny, "and we can't explain them. You know, I heard about a boy when I was at school, the friend of a friend's friend, or something like that, anyway, he fell down dead on the rugby pitch, just from nowhere his heart gave out. Imagine . . ."

"What, he just died?" said Bruno, looking up.

"Collapsed. I think it was a really important game, and he was the star player, and . . ."

Hadley stopped listening and pulled at a loose thread in her sleeve. It ran a couple of stitches, and she pulled it some more. The pavements could be treacherous when icy, she knew that. She had skidded herself, flung out a hand to catch at a railing, and once fell down on her backside as they were rushing for the bus. She'd laughed with the shock of it, and Kristina had held out her hand and pulled her back to her feet. How could it be possible that a person's head, one so solid, so strong, so full of ideas and dreams and hopes and fears and cravings for rum-dashed hot chocolate and lime-lit cocktails and sweet-centered almond croissants and a Genevan man called Jacques, just stop at the slightest knock? Or perhaps it was heavy. A crashing to the ground. A hard smack to the softest part of the head. But were we so badly put together that life could be swiped away so very easily? As snow fell and people laughed in restaurants and said things that they didn't mean on the telephone?

"Hadley?"

She looked up. The four of them appeared to swim before her. Somewhere, deep in Les Ormes, a door banged, and there was a shout of laughter and running footsteps.

"We were just saying," said Jenny, biting down on her lip as she spoke, "Kristina's boyfriend, the one she thought we didn't know about . . . how will he know what happened? How will anyone tell him?"

Kristina's parents arrived at Les Ormes on Sunday morning. There were voices in the corridor and the clacking of a key against a lock. Hadley pushed open her door and peered out. They were standing with the porter, an elderly man who was bent double in his blue overalls, stooping with apology. And there was a woman she recognized from campus, with tightly curled brown hair and an officious air. She had always imagined Kristina's mother and father to be a

178

storybook pair, impeccable and quietly dazzling. Instead, she saw a dumpy man and woman, with old coats and cheap shoes. They held on to one another, their heads dipped. She began to close the door, but the woman from the university saw her.

"Excusez-moi, bonjour, vous êtes . . . ?"

"Hadley Dunn."

Hadley hadn't slept the night before, and her hair was matted, her eyes sore. She stood blinking in her pajamas.

"Une amie de Kristina?"

"Oui," she said. She glanced at Kristina's parents and saw that they'd turned to her. They still clung to one another, but their heads were raised now. Hadley tried to meet their eyes and failed.

"Kristina's parents are here to collect her things," the woman said, in a matter-of-fact voice.

"Of course," Hadley said, glancing at them again.

Kristina's mother came toward her then, and Hadley resisted the urge to step back.

"Were you good friends, you and Kristina?" she said, in careful English.

"Yes," Hadley said. "We were."

She had a thickset sort of face, but Hadley recognized the shades of Kristina. Her gray hair was threaded with gold. Her cheeks were dappled with freckles. The pale washed blue of her eyes brimmed with tears. She kissed Hadley on both cheeks, and her lips were cold and scratchy.

"Thank you," she said, and Hadley felt weak with pity. She had no words to make any of it better. In the end all she had was this.

"Mrs. Hartmann, I'm really going to miss Kristina. More than I've ever missed anyone. She was so . . ."

She wanted to say "full of life" because it was true, she had been bursting with it. Kristina had so much life that it spilled over into yours, too. She hesitated, and then said it, anyway. Kristina's mother clasped a hand to her heart, her five fingers pressing like a starfish, her mouth agape. Hadley regretted it instantly. But everything else was no good, either. How did a short-lived friendship, however important, compare to a whole life? The changing of nappies and kissing of her sleep-warm head? Helping with homework at the kitchen table and mopping the tears of first heartbreak? She knew her own grief was incomparable, but anything beyond it was impossible to imagine.

"Was she happy here?" Kristina's mum whispered.

Hadley nodded.

"And you were a good friend to her, weren't you? I can see that."

Hadley had ended the call so abruptly, and she had no idea how long Kristina had carried on speaking, after the click. Whether she had rung again, only to find Hadley's phone deliberately turned off, as they'd whirled back out into the night with no intention of telling her where they were going. Hadley was seized by the sudden desire to tell Kristina's mother everything, to fall into her arms and have her stroke her hair as her own mother would have. To hear her say, *oh, Kristina drove us all wild with her ways, never you mind, Hadley, she knew you loved her, of course she did.* But she couldn't do it. Hadley walked two steps toward her and opened her arms. Kristina's mother stepped into them as obediently as a child. Despite the press of Kristina's mother's body, the thick weight of her bosom pushing against her and her hot, gasping breath, there was an intolerable absence in the embrace; the inescapable feeling that they should never have met, never have needed to hold one another, and that they were each hanging on to the wrong person. The right person had wisped clean away.

Kristina's father took his wife gently by the elbow. He nodded at Hadley in brief acknowledgment, but his eyes looked through and beyond her. They went into Kristina's room and quietly closed the door. The porter idled in the corridor. *"Triste,"* he said, looking down at his feet, "very sad," and Hadley answered, *"oui"* in soft reply. She closed her bedroom door by degrees. She leaned her head against the wall. She thought of Kristina's parents folding their daughter's clothes, her silky shirts and mini-dresses. Taking her bursting makeup bag and the rows of dribbling bottles from beside her bathroom mirror. Her books, not neatly stacked like Hadley's but scattered carelessly, with cracked spines and bent pages.

They didn't take long to clear her room, about as long as it took Hadley to shrug off her dressing gown and put on some clothes, tug a brush through her hair and wash her hands and face. Kristina's parents were hollowed by grief, all scooped out. They would be back in Copenhagen by nightfall, Lausanne only a nightmarish memory, and there was nothing she could do to change any of it. There was nothing she could do at all.

Jenny's question about Kristina's boyfriend came to mind, then. *Jacques.* Worse than knowing had to be not knowing. To still be walking around, dogged by trivial worries, frowning at the snow clouds, tutting at a crowded bus or bemoaning the length of the queue for the train. Perhaps their connection ran deeper. Maybe Jacques was somewhere feeling a sharp yet indescribable sense of *wrong,* like a sudden blast of headache or sickness. One that made him pause in the street to look over his shoulder, feel in his pocket for his wallet or telephone his mother just to check that she still answered. She doubted that he would ever think of fearing for Kristina.

As Hadley splashed water in her bathroom, she heard the door open and the murmur of voices, the squeak of a rubber shoe on the linoleum floor. She hurried to her door and stepped out. They were standing in a cluster, the four of them again, Kristina's brown suitcases bunched at their feet.

"Mrs. Hartmann?" she said.

She turned to her, and for just a second Hadley saw something like hope cross her face. She stumbled over her words. She asked if they knew Jacques.

"Did she ever mention him to you?" she said.

Kristina's father picked up a case in each hand and began to turn away. Her mother took a woolen hat from her bag and placed it on her head, tugging it down over her ears.

"There were always a lot of boys," she said. "My daughter —" she paused "— my daughter was very much loved."

"Yes," said Hadley, her voice a whisper, as quiet as the falling snow, "yes, she was."

CHAPTER 12

Another day like yesterday would have been unbearable; the claustrophobia of the kitchen at Les Ormes, the five of them sitting around, Kristina's absence all the more noticeable because the rest of them were together. They might have felt surprise and shock with equal fervency, but their grief was separate and wildly different. Jenny had said yesterday, "I never felt like I really knew her," and Hadley had wanted to say, *that's because you didn't.* Chase and Bruno had murmured assent, and meanwhile she'd thought of Kristina playing with the three little boys in the French garden, the particular way she ate an almond croissant, swiping all of the filling with the tip of her finger and licking it quickly, and her "I'm talking about Jacques" smile, which was rueful and joyous all at once.

There was a knocking at Hadley's door, and she opened it to find Jenny.

"We're thinking of going for a drive along the lake," Jenny said, in a peppy voice. "Do you want to come?"

"No, thanks."

"Oh, go on, you're not doing anything else, are you?"

"I think I just want to be on my own today."

"But that's no good," Jenny said.

"No," said Hadley, "you're right. Nothing's good."

"Oh, Hadley, I didn't mean it like that."

"I know you didn't."

"Then why won't you come? We need to cheer each other up."

Hadley shook her head, and a wave of tears threatened to take her. It was the wrong girl standing at her door.

"Sorry, Jenny," she said, "and thanks. Really. But I'm just not in the mood."

Hadley forced the smallest smile for Jenny's sake as she closed the door on her. She didn't need *cheering up*. Children who felt poorly needed cheering up. Soft-willed girls who'd been snubbed by a boy needed cheering up. She thought of the four of them in Bruno's car, batting questions around just to fill the silence. They would stare blankly at the sights of lake and mountain and palm, then drink too much in a gaudy-looking bar in Vevey, eat anemic *croque monsieurs* and then wind home later proclaiming that the trip had been just the thing. All cheered up. She had lied when she'd said she wanted to be alone. She just didn't want to be with them, not without Kristina.

Hadley picked up her phone and started to dial her parents' number. She stopped. What would she say? That she had never felt sadder, or farther from home? She couldn't do it. Perhaps it made no sense, but as long as they didn't know she felt as though some part of her world could carry on. She stared instead at her desk. The pages of her essay for Joel Wilson's class were scattered across it. She considered sitting down to work, trying to lose herself in Hemingway. But she knew that for all the sparse, crisp words, all the things he didn't say would rise up out of the page and engulf her, and instead of being moved, or inspired, all she would feel was the pointlessness of it all. In her pile of books she spotted one with a candy-pink spine. She drew it out, and turned it in her hand. Kristina had lent it to her a couple of weeks ago. It was a schmaltzy romance that was set on the French Riviera, and Kristina had found it amusing. *It might as well be my fling with Jacques,* she'd said, *kissing under the palm trees, cocktails at dawn, it's all there. Here, I'll lend it to you.* Hadley had taken it and thanked Kristina, then added it to her pile and forgotten all about it, doubting it was to her taste. She hadn't known to treasure it then. The cover bore traces of beach life; it was sun-faded, with sand crystals buried in the spine. Hadley imagined Kristina lying on her front, her shades sliding down her nose. Jacques would be rubbing sunscreen over her shoulders, dropping a kiss between applications. Hadley held the book to her nose and could almost believe she caught the scent of Ambre Solaire. The silly cover, with its abandoned bikini and sparkling martini glass, blurred before her. She flicked through the pages and saw that a postcard had been slipped between them. It was one of those flat-painted vintage pictures, the ubiquitous kind that Joel had on the wall in his office. It showed undulations of distant purple mountains, stacked villas, explosions of palm and orange trees. *Cote d'Azur* was written in elegant capitals. She flipped it over and read the message. *There's nothing real about this place. Only you are real. Only being with you is real.* It was written in a messy, uneven scrawl, as though its author had consumed one too many drinks in the midday sun, or was writing on a bobbing yacht, eyes on the horizon. Hadley knew Kristina's writing, and it wasn't hers. It could only be Jacques. Hadley stared at the postcard, willing it to reveal some other detail, some clue to his identity, but there was nothing, just a standard scene of beauty and a chaotic, lovelorn scribble. Hadley read it aloud, tasting each word. She thought then of her own unsent card from the mountain village; another flattened and perfect picture of blue skies, white snow and a bronzed and happy girl leaning on her skis, her face to the sun. *A privilege and a trespass.* It could have been the same author. A couple of lines, jotted down because they refused to stay in your own head. She returned the card to its place in the book and felt again the pull between her and Jacques. A sweep of pity threatened to knock her from her feet. She staggered and flopped back onto her bed to stare at the ceiling. She felt as though it might fall, and she knew then that she had to get out.

It took her nearly an hour to reach the lakeside, and yet later she would be able to remember nothing of the walk. She didn't know it, but she marched across a road in full traffic, a cyclist swerving, a driver slamming his horn. She barged into a teenage boy as he wove on his skateboard and his face contorted with irritation, until he saw that she was only a pale-faced girl with tear-whipped cheeks. He watched her walk on. She only snapped back to life when her foot caught the open guitar case of a busker, sending his meager scattering of coins rolling across the pavement. She bent to her knees to apologize, knocking heads with him as she stooped to retrieve his money. He laid a hand on her shoulder, and she saw the note of pity in his face. She got to her feet and went on, and as she walked, she found herself consumed with one idea. Leaving Lausanne. Not because she wanted to go, but because she didn't know if she could stay. Without Kristina, nothing felt the same anymore. The city's spell was broken.

Hadley didn't particularly choose Hôtel Le Nouveau Monde that day. Rather, she would come to think that it chose her. She had come as far as Ouchy, drawn, as she always was, by the water and the mountains and the flat, wide sky, and there it was, the Hôtel Le Nouveau Monde. The place where Kristina had slipped her arm through Hadley's and said, *That's beautiful.* And then, *All we have to do is smile. And look like we belong,* they'd waltzed into luxury, covering their giggles with the flats of their hands. She wiped her eyes and walked up to the revolving door. The doorman stood to attention in his red coat and gold buttons. *Bonjour, mademoiselle,* she heard him say, and his words spirited her into the vast, shining lobby.

In the café, a waiter motioned Hadley to a corner table. She took off her coat and sat back in her chair. Through the plate-glass windows the sky was iron-gray, and the surface of the lake chopped angrily; inside, the atmosphere was one of cosseted warmth. She ordered a coffee, and when her drink came she avoided looking at the waiter, feeling the quick heat rising behind her eyes.

Hadley had always believed in the sanctity of a café, a place of cocoon and comfort. Back home in Tonridge there was a place called Le Boulevard. It had a poorly painted mural of the Eiffel tower on the back wall and French accordion music played through the stereo. Hadley used to go there after her university classes, and always imagined that it was the sort of place for beginnings and endings — the dipped heads and sorry mumbles of a fracturing couple, the locked and loaded looks of a new love affair. An appropriate stage set for the peaks and troughs of feeling. The Hôtel Le Nouveau Monde, however, seemed only made for beginnings. Everybody looked in the prime of their life, riding their luck with elegance and grace. Hadley watched them, her eyes as flat as windows. What had they done to deserve to carry on living? And did they know, as she now knew, that it could all be snapped out at any moment? She sat stiff-backed and stirred her coffee around and around. She glanced up and met the eyes of an elderly man across the room. It was Hugo Bézier again.

He lifted his hand, performing a funny sort of wave, halfway between one the queen might throw and a two-fingered salute. Hadley nodded back. She didn't have any words for other people, not today. He kept his eyes on her, and she shifted in her seat, looking away. When she looked back again, he was still staring at her. She saw him set down his newspaper and get to his feet. He looked taller than she remembered, and he held himself very straight. His shirt was powder-pink, and an indigo tie was held in place by a neat gold clip.

"You again . . ." he said.

"Yes . . ."

"I hardly would have recognized you, Hadley, *ma chérie.*"

He pronounced each word as though he was feeling its edges, rolling them across his tongue. His bright eyes startled her, as they had twice before. *Ma chérie,* he'd said, softly as a whisper, and it meant *my dear,* or *my darling.*

"When I saw you in the *chocolaterie,* you were so light, you appeared to blow in off the street, and I could sense your every pleasure. But today, you're different. There's a heaviness, light and heavy all at once. How is that possible?"

She picked up her cup but found her hand was shaking. She reset it, spilling coffee in the saucer.

"I don't know if that's true," she said.

"I've spent my whole life making people up. Rarely do they surprise me with their stories, anymore. Would you like another drink? Something stronger, perhaps? You know my habits a little now, I think."

She shook her head.

"It's good for the spirit."

"I don't think so," she said, "no, thank you." Her voice cracked.

He smiled, and it was so plain and true that without him saying a word, Hadley felt as though he understood. The small touch of kindness tipped her, and she began to cry. He reached into his pocket and took out a cotton handkerchief. It was starchy white, with a blue-lined edge. He passed it to her, and she dabbed her eyes with it. She sniffed. She blew her nose.

"Please," he said, "I'm sorry." He dipped a slight bow and retreated.

Hadley hid her face in his handkerchief. It smelled of washing powder and the homely press of a hot iron. She blew her nose again and looked up. Hugo was back at his table across the room, reading his newspaper again, as though nothing had happened. She took a note from her purse and left it beside her unfinished coffee. She had to pass his table in order to leave.

"Please," he said, lowering his paper just as she skirted past him, "I beg you, don't go on account of me."

"It's not you," she said.

"I made you uncomfortable. Really, it's the last thing I wanted to do. I have a blundering sort of way about me, that's all."

"It's not that," Hadley said.

"Would you sit, then?" He gestured to the chair opposite him. She shook her head again.

"I need to be somewhere else," she said.

"Your friends are expecting you?"

"No."

"Then, you have other plans. Places to be?"

She hesitated. When her voice came, it was small and tight. "I'll wash your handkerchief," she said. "If you give me your address then I'll post it back to you."

Hugo narrowed his eyes. She didn't fool him, and she could see that.

"You can just bring it here. I'm at the hotel most days. I'd say you could keep it, but I might not see you again that way. Although I must say, we do have a habit of running into one another."

Hadley sat down on the very edge of the chair. She smoothed her hands over her jeans.

"I don't feel much like company," she said.

"That's not like you," he said, "is it?"

The waiter appeared then with two voluminous glasses of brandy. He set one before Hadley and dipped a bow to Hugo.

"I must say, I do like it here," he said. "They seem to know exactly how to make you feel a little better, at precisely the right time."

He picked up his glass and tipped it in her direction, then drank. Hadley hesitated, then did the same. The brandy burned her throat in a sweet blaze, and she shut her eyes. When she opened them again, she saw

195

that Hugo was watching her from across the rim of his glass. In that particular light, his eyes seemed to be some of the kindest she'd ever seen.

She hadn't wanted to talk to anyone, but there was something about Hugo Bézier that drew her out. Perhaps it was no more than his age, an implicit reassurance that whatever she was feeling, he must surely have felt it himself. As they sat across from one another, she felt calm descend. The clamor and claustrophobia of Les Ormes felt a long way away. She told him the only thing that mattered.

"My friend just died."

His eyes widened, just the smallest amount. His fingers tapped the cloth.

"A close friend?"

"Yes."

Hadley waited, but he didn't say anything. Too much time passed. She started to get up, scooping her bag from the floor.

"Where are you going?" he said.

"I thought I could stay," Hadley said, "but I don't think I can. I'm sorry."

"No, *c'est moi,* I apologize. I'm not very good at talking to people in out-of-the-ordinary situations. Perhaps I never was, but I'm certainly out of practice now."

"It's really okay," she said. "You didn't know her. You hardly know me."

"Hadley, please sit down again. Tell me about your friend."

He was sitting a little back from the table, with his hands dropped loosely in his lap. His tie was nipped very tightly at the neck. Hadley saw an awkwardness then, a sudden shyness. She sat back down. She folded her arms across her chest and dipped her head.

"It was an accident," she said in the end, mostly addressing the cloth. "The stupidest kind, the worst kind, the most ridiculous kind. She fell over on the ice and hit her head. That's all. None of us even knew, until the next day. Yesterday. I only knew yesterday."

"I'm sorry," he said, and the unexpected strength of feeling underlying his words took hold of her and held her for a moment.

"How can someone be here one minute and gone the next?" she said. "I keep expecting her to knock at my door, or to come bursting into the room. People aren't supposed to just stop like that. It's not like she was ill, or old. . . ." Her voice cracked. "Sorry, I don't mean just because you're old . . ."

Hugo shook his head and made a dismissive gesture with his hand. Hadley pressed

197

her fingers to her temples. The headache that she'd had for the past two days seemed to lift slightly. She rubbed her eyes.

"It was my birthday," she said. "We were supposed to all be going out, but she was late. She's never late. When she called she was just so . . . I don't know. She made me really cross, and I told her that. I never do that, I never find the exact set of words, the words you know will really hurt someone. But this time I actually spoke my mind, and now I regret it more than anything. The last thing I said to her was really awful. And I can't do a thing to change that. It's so stupid, because even though I meant it, even though it was true, there were so many brilliant things I could have said instead, and all of them were true, as well. You'd think that nothing could be worse than her being gone. But this is worse. And I know that's selfish, but I can't do anything about it. You don't know what to say, do you? It's okay. There's nothing you could say that would make me feel better. You don't have to try."

He smiled quietly, and it was like a small break in the clouds.

"You haven't said any of that out loud before, have you?" he said.

"How do you know that?"

"Because you don't know what to think.

No one ever does."

"I do. I know exactly what to think. It's all a huge waste of time. It doesn't matter what we do, or how we do it, because it can all end just like *that.*" She snapped her fingers and fumbled it. "You think Kristina knew what was coming? Even as she slipped, even as she saw the ground rise to meet her? Maybe she just thought, *oh, I'm going to get my coat wet,* or, *shit, this is going to hurt a little bit,* but never, never would she have thought, *everything's about to stop. Forever.*"

"There's grace in that, somehow."

"Grace? There's no grace. It's chaotic and hopeless, that's what it is."

"It's not entirely hopeless," Hugo said. "All we can ask from this life is that there is someone who misses us when we're gone. You miss her, Hadley. She was beloved."

They sat opposite one another, neither one speaking for a few minutes. Hugo's hands stayed folded in his lap, and Hadley squeezed the stem of the cognac glass with her fingers. Her eyes pooled as she turned her head to the window. The lake looked full and fit to burst. For the first time since she had found out, Hadley was perfectly still. Her breath came evenly.

"I'm not the only one to miss her," said Hadley. "She had a boyfriend. Jacques. I don't know how to find him. I don't know if he even knows what happened to her."

"You never met him?"

"It was complicated. He was . . . married. Separated, apparently, but still married. And Kristina felt strange about it, guilty, I think. She kept him as a mystery. I can't stop thinking about him. How could he know? There's no one who could tell him."

"Only you, perhaps."

"I know. I keep thinking that maybe I should try and find him. Is that stupid?"

"No, it's not stupid."

"But I don't know anything about him. Only that he's called Jacques."

"That's something."

"He lives in Geneva," she said.

"There you are."

"I think he had a fancy job. Or maybe that's just how I imagined it."

"There are always ways to find people, Hadley."

"I wouldn't have a clue where to begin," she said, "and anyway, I don't think I'm going to stay. I don't think I *can* stay."

"You can't be thinking of leaving?"

Hadley shrugged. "Maybe. I think so. We did everything together, Hugo. Nothing here feels right anymore."

"And you think it'll be so much better if

you go home to England?"

"Not better, but . . . Lausanne's not the same. Nothing's the same."

Hugo's eyes widened, as if Hadley had said something truly startling.

"It'd be a terrible shame to throw it all away. To waste two lives," he said.

"It wouldn't be a waste," said Hadley, without conviction. "It'd be my old life back again, that's all. I'd just carry on."

"But you'd still be without her. And you'd be without all this, too." Hugo swept his arm. "You'd be bereft, in every sense."

"It used to be so perfect here, Hugo. It still is, on the outside. Maybe that's half the trouble."

"Ah. Of course you think that. It's far too beautiful a place for sadness, yes?"

"I was so happy here, now I don't know if I can be. That's all."

"I suppose you think Lausanne is a city full of golden people? A blessed place, *n'est-ce pas?* But, Hadley, you think no one cries among the fountains? You think that no one wakes up and stares out at that endless lake, those heaven-reaching mountains, and doesn't still feel that their life amounts to nothing? You think just because people are neat as clockwork and as smart as the shine on their shoes that they don't feel the same pain that you do?"

"I'm not that naive," said Hadley, "whatever you may think."

"And I'm not so very experienced," said Hugo, "whatever I may say. You're feeling, Hadley, that's all. You're feeling. And you're living. You're too young to know it, but not everyone does that. It's possible, in fact, to pass almost an entire life without doing too much of either. One day, you'll be glad. You don't want to get to my age only to look back and realize that you were too late for life. But I'm not worried about you, not like that. You're not really the running-away type, are you? No, not you. You're more stay and fight."

"Stay and fight? Fight what? There's nothing."

"There's everything." Hadley met Hugo's eyes, and they were shining with black intensity. He tapped his hand over his heart. Just twice, one-two.

Hadley glanced away. She thought of Kristina telling her *il faut profiter.* She looked back at Hugo. He spoke again.

"What about this Jacques? What of him? I think it's a noble idea to try and seek him out."

"I feel like it's something I could do," said Hadley quietly. "If I stayed, that is."

"Yes, you could."

"Maybe then I'd see if I still wanted to leave. After I'd found him."

Hugo nodded. "A plan, then. A fine plan." He took her hand very lightly between his own. His palms were warm and paper-dry. "You know where I am, if you need help, all you have to do is ask. The bar, the chocolate shop, the café . . ." He smiled and her cheeks tightened. "All of the finest places," he said.

"Thank you, Hugo. And for the drink."

"You're going now?"

She slipped her hand free and stood up. She noticed he stayed just as he was, his hands half-cupped, as though he'd let a small bird fly from them.

"Yes," she said.

"But you'll come back?"

"I'll leave the handkerchief at the front desk."

"Only if I'm not here."

"Yes."

"But then I often am. My sincere condolences," he said. "I don't know if that came across strongly enough before, and I'm sorry for that. I'm not very good at some things. I've been told that before, but I don't think I cared about the truth too much then. It seems to matter more, as one gets older. Isn't that strange? You'd think it would be the reverse."

"I want Jacques to know the truth," said Hadley, with resolution. "I do."

"And what's that?"

"That Kristina died. And she loved him. What else is there?"

The smallest, saddest smile tipped the corner of his lip.

"I would say that's enough," he said, "wouldn't you?"

Hadley fastened all the buttons on her coat, one by one, slowly, and then pulled on her gloves. Hugo was watching her, as if waiting for her to say one more thing. So she did.

"I keep replaying the last conversation we had, and she was upset, I mean, more than usually upset. I didn't really let her get a word in edgeways, I was too cross, but . . . maybe something wasn't right."

"A fight between lovers?"

"And she was late. She was never late for anything."

"Sometimes things just go wrong, Hadley, that's what people will tell you. Friends let each other down. Dreadful accidents happen. It's the way of the world, and there's no other explanation for it."

"I know that," she said.

"Do you? I'm not so sure if I buy it myself. It might be the common consensus, but then I've never been much of a believer in common. There is *always* an explanation, Hadley, a pattern of events, cause and effect. Something can seem un-piece-able, but we can always put it together in the end, if that's what we want to do. And maybe it'll only tell us what we already know — a random sequence, the worst stroke of luck — but that in itself is an explanation, *n'est-ce pas?* We figure a beginning, and an end, and then we can understand. For all of its senselessness, the world makes sense, and we can live with it."

Hugo's voice had lost its usual slow cadence; its formal parlor beats were replaced with a rapid, fervent tone. His hands cut the air as he spoke. He appeared, in that moment, very much younger.

"I'm sorry," he said, aware of her stare, "I like to make a puzzle out of a thing. Once upon a time it was my job. Now it's just bad manners."

"No," said Hadley, "you're right. She was my friend. My dear, dear friend. So it's up to me to ask the questions that other people won't, isn't it? And it's up to me to find Jacques."

She lifted her hand in farewell, and from

his sitting position, he stooped a half sort of bow.

"Oh, and what did you mean when you said 'your job'?"

"I was a writer, once."

"And you're not anymore?"

Hugo shook his head, and the weight of years appeared to return. His forehead creased into a frown. "No," he said, "not anymore."

CHAPTER 13

Walking home from Ouchy it was eerily quiet. It was a time of day that she had never paid particular attention to before; just before twilight, when lamps were clicking on in the cocoons of people's homes, and the outside world seemed as if it were closing down. Hadley felt a dull ache settle in her chest. It was an uneasy, flattening feeling, and she realized it was loneliness. She had never been lonely in Lausanne before.

The walk was long and uphill and slippery in places, but she couldn't take the bus, not with the dreary yellow of the interior light, the windows throwing back her sad reflection, people getting on and getting off, with purpose and direction and homes to go to. She walked through the chill and emptying streets with her head down and her hands thrust deep into her pockets. Not so long ago she would have found the same walk romantic, her and Kristina's laughter echoing off the shuttered buildings, the silver pools of streetlight, an American stranger stepping from the darkness. Now, loneliness persisted, and Lausanne wore a Sunday-evening gloom that felt as if it'd never end.

When Hadley returned to Les Ormes, it was humming with other people's conviviality. Tinny music and overlapping chatter rang from the kitchens, and there was the boom of an action movie coming from the television room. The corridors held the wafts of dinners, a vaguely spicy hum, and two girls that Hadley didn't recognize sat curled in the battered armchairs in the lobby, their noses pushed close as they whispered together. They screeched with laughter as she passed, and a nip of anger caught her.

Had there been no announcement? No official message, ringing down the halls? She had imagined a wreath at Kristina's door, or perhaps a photo of her pinned to the notice board in the hall — one of those pictures you saw flashed on television screens or in the pages of newspapers — people smiling their last smiles. Or maybe a poem, copied painstakingly in scratchy, trying-to-be-neat handwriting, by one of the Romantics, Christina Rossetti, perhaps.

People would pause as they hurried to the laundry room or the kitchen, dropping an odd sock as they read about Kristina's passing, later shedding a tear as they stared at the bank of washing machines, watching their load turn and turn. There would be a collective mourning, told in no more than a shared and sorry smile, as everyone's lives shifted a little, to take on the sad fact of Kristina.

But two days had passed, and none of this had happened. At Les Ormes, everything was as usual. Perhaps it should have been her job to do those things, to print the photograph, choose the flowers, copy the poem. It should have been Hadley who rallied people in the grief that they didn't know was theirs to feel. But she hadn't. She didn't want to think of marker pens and sticky tape and hunting for the words to talk about her friend in the past tense. Finding Jacques, understanding how Kristina's last hours had been spent, that was a different kind of commemoration. Hugo was right, you couldn't just let things lie. You had to question, and you had to try and understand. A sudden slip might be the cruelest luck, but there was a *before,* and now there was an *after;* and maybe she was it.

"You should have come with us, Hadley,

it was good to get away," said Jenny.

Chase had poured them all glasses of supermarket wine, the kind that was found on the bottom shelf in plastic bottles. It was vinegar-sharp, and her eyes stung as she drank it.

"We found this really pretty spot along the lake and drank hot cider, sitting outside. We just forgot everything, for the whole day. It really helped," she said.

"Bruno and Loretta were daring each other to go in the water, which was ridiculous as it was practically frozen at the edges. In the end Loretta took off her shoe and dipped her toe in, scaring a swan in basically the same moment, so the drinks were on Bruno. For a change."

Chase laughed and pushed his hair back from his face. It had grown long in the few weeks that they had been in Lausanne. It was almost the same length as Jenny's, and the same color, a watery sort of blond.

Bruno grabbed the plastic bottle from the table and read the label disdainfully.

"I clearly should have brought some home with us, this stuff is undrinkable," he announced with relish.

"We could go to Café Clio?" said Loretta. "I feel like dancing, doesn't anyone else? It's what we all need." She curled her fingers around Bruno's hand, prying them away from the bottle, setting one on either hip. She made as if to perform a feeble sort of lap dance, then peeled away, giggling into her sleeve. Jenny joined in good-naturedly.

Hadley was drinking her wine from a chipped blue mug, and she pushed it away from her. It spun across the table with unexpected force and fell on its side with a crack. Everyone looked at her.

"I just don't understand what you're all trying to forget," she said. "That she ever existed? That we had the inconvenience of being made to feel sad?"

"Hadley, you know it's not like that," Jenny said, "but what else can we do?"

"I don't think anyone's trying very hard to do anything," Hadley said.

"Listen, Hadley, we didn't really know her," Chase said. "It was different with you guys, but for us that's how it was. It's no less sad, no less tragic, but we can't all drag it out, pretending that we were such great friends when we all know that we weren't. I think that would actually be self-indulgent."

"Self-indulgent?" Hadley said, in a voice that was spiked and hard and didn't feel very much like hers.

"Hadley," pleaded Jenny, "Chase doesn't mean it like that, you know he doesn't."

Chase stood up, and she felt his hand on her arm. He dragged her into a quick embrace.

"I'm sorry," he said, stiffly, "Jenny's right. It's just that none of us really know how to be right now."

He sat down again, and she saw Jenny squeeze his knee, her face shining with sympathy. Beneath the table she saw their fingers twine.

"Come dancing, Hadley," said Loretta, her singsong voice taking on a cajoling note, "because it's about feeling better, right now, really it is. And Kristina would agree. I know she would. She always liked a good time, didn't she?"

Their attempts at levity were unbearable. Hadley thought of Chase and Jenny's hands finding one another beneath the table, and how long it had been since she'd heard Jenny mention her boyfriend at home. Just as with Bruno and Loretta, their togetherness seemed to promote a lighter mood, as if they wanted everyone to be as happy as they were, despite all obstacles. There was something so wrong in these obvious displays of pleasure, even if they were as passing as a wartime waltz. Hadley stood up to go. She started to say something, then stopped. She began again.

"I want to try and find Kristina's boyfriend," she said.

"The boyfriend she didn't want any of us to know about?" said Jenny.

"It wasn't like that," said Hadley in quick defense. "She had her reasons."

"What do you mean 'try and find'?" said Chase. "Don't you know how to reach him?"

"I don't even know his full name."

"Does he even exist?" said Bruno. "Girls make things up all the time."

Loretta gave a small cry of protest, and the two quarreled the point between kisses.

"It was in the local newspaper," said Chase. "I saw it. No picture, but an article, just a snippet really. Maybe he saw it. Maybe he already knows."

"I'm surprised there was no picture," said Jenny. "I really am. Normally when someone's so pretty, they put a huge great picture of them, as though that makes it even more of a tragedy."

Hadley stared at her. She felt her cheeks reddening with anger. Chase took her arm, and she saw Jenny's face splinter with surprise.

"Do you even know where to start looking?" he said, gently.

"Not yet," said Hadley, "but I'll figure it

213

out. I want to know what happened that night, Chase. When we were laughing and drinking and carrying on without her, I need to know what happened."

He looked at her as though he was about to say something, his lip curling in what seemed like disagreement, but he thought better of it. He shrugged.

"I guess it feels good to try and do something, right?"

She nodded. "Someone else said that. Stay and fight."

She felt the stares of the others, so she left them then, not caring that as she banged the door she heard their voices rise up behind her. A little later she heard them all leave. Soon they would be tripping through the still-snowy streets, merry and careless. In her room, Hadley changed into her pajamas early, and sat cross-legged on her bed, her pillows pulled askew. It was easy for the others to keep their distance; Chase was right, they weren't connected to Kristina in the way that she was. It hadn't been their party she had been late for, their frustrated words spurring her to hurry with abandon, without a care for blinding blizzards or icy patches. Nor had they seen the unperfected version of Kristina; in her Pierrot nightshirt with the ends of her hair splintering loose, how her cheeks grew pink-spotted when she got angry or upset or guilty as she talked about Jacques. They were already moving on, she could see it, and she knew that, for them, Kristina would soon be no more than a gasp-drawing anecdote they would recount when they were home for the Christmas break, a cautionary tale that even in a place as perfect as Lausanne there was tragedy.

She stood up and went over to the window. The gloom of her unlit room fell behind her, and the city sparkled as it always had, relentlessly optimistic, ceaselessly beautiful and pricked with thousands of tiny lights. Perhaps it was full of aching hearts; maybe it was, as Hugo had said, just like anywhere else, after all. She thought of Hugo sitting in a room somewhere, hunched over his typewriter, staring into a blank page. The writer who didn't write. What would have happened if she hadn't talked to him today? Would she be packing clothes into her suitcase, unsticking the postcards from her wall? She was grateful to him, this person she hardly knew. She laid the flat of her hand on the cold windowpane. Somewhere, too, beyond the rooftops and farther down the lake, was Jacques. Perhaps, without even realizing it, he was waiting for her to find him. Maybe she would just stay long enough to do that. She moved her hand from the glass and touched her cheek with her fingers; they were ice-tipped, and she shivered all the way to her toes. She yanked the blinds down on the city and turned back to the darkness.

CHAPTER 14

Student services had offered a counselor, and she took them up on it. In a blast of Swiss efficiency Hadley's appointment was that first Monday morning. She was shown into a room that seemed to promote caution and comfort in equal measure — lavender-scented, cushioned seats, a notice board patched with bold posters for contraceptive methods and diseases she had never heard of. The counselor offered tea and spoke in gently accented English as Hadley listened with her hands resting on her knees. When she said Hadley's name, she dropped the H, and it came out like *Ad-lee,* French and lilting, and she felt as if it wasn't her sitting there at all then, that it was some other girl, in a too-warm room, thinking about death as though it was a real thing that could happen to anyone. When it was Hadley's turn to speak she noticed that she was being excessively polite, even remembering a little French, until the moment when she realized she was crying soundlessly, and she stopped talking altogether. Afterward, when she walked out into the corridor, wrapping her scarf around her neck two, three times, there was only one thing the counselor had said that she remembered: *talking to someone who knows the nature of grief is the best thing you can do.* She was probably referring to herself, and gentle as she was, as warm as her palms had been as she'd shaken hands in farewell, Hadley didn't make another appointment. Instead, she thought of Joel Wilson and the tiny, white puckered scar above his lip. A mark you wouldn't know the meaning of, unless he'd told you about it.

"Hadley, I'm sorry, now's not a good time."

Joel Wilson opened the door of his office just wide enough for her to see that behind him, things were in disarray. Uneven stacks of books littered the floor, his desk had disappeared under a mess of papers and a dim smell of cigarette smoke yellowed the air. He rubbed his face with the flats of his hands and squinted back at her. He looked, for the first time since she'd met him, like a much older man.

"I'm behind on an article for a publication back home. Don't even ask. You students think you're the only ones with pressing deadlines, well, let me tell you . . ."

She waited for him to finish, but the end of his sentence fell away in a sudden drop. He was so slick in class that it was a stretch to imagine him being late with his own assignments. She felt angry suddenly, that he should choose today of all days to lose his hallway swagger and replace it with the desperate demeanor of an inferior, absent-minded professor.

"I need to talk to you," she said.

"Hadley," he pleaded, his eyes taking on a hunted expression, "I hate to turn a student away, but I really am up against a wall. I mean —" he swept his arm "— look at this place, it's chaos. I can't find any of the things I need. I'm feeling useless, right now."

"Kristina died," she said.

He was standing with his back half-turned, his arm still engaged in a full sweep. He held still.

"It's a real mess in here," he said. "I'm sorry, what did you say?"

"My friend was killed at the weekend. She's dead."

His hand went to his head and pulled at his hair. The kind of thing someone does when they're clean out of ideas.

"That can't be, Hadley."

"I know you're busy, and that this is a really bad time, and I'm sorry for that, but . . ."

"Come in," he said, "don't just stand there, come in. I'm sorry. I'm so sorry."

He kicked the door shut with his heel and dragged her toward him in an embrace. She almost tripped on the crumpled rug beneath her feet, and her bag fell from her shoulder. It was a fierce, hard hug, and she clung on to him. Her breath was stifled, her face pushed into his shirt, and for a second she thought she'd stopped breathing. She broke away.

"Why didn't you shut me up when I went on about my work?" he said. "You should have told me to shut up."

"I thought everyone here knew. Someone made me an appointment with a counselor. I've just come from there."

"I didn't know," he said. "I've locked myself away in here. In Hell." He quickly corrected himself. "What am I saying? You're in Hell."

Hadley set her satchel on the floor, then picked it up again. She folded her arms across her chest. Her breath came raggedly.

"Sit down," he said. "Here, wait."

He shifted a pile of papers from the low

chair, and Hadley sank into it. When she looked up at him, her breath coming surer, the color in her cheeks dropping, he was pouring two glasses of liquor.

"Whiskey," he said, handing her a half-full glass. "It helps, when words stop working."

She sipped from the glass he gave her, cradling it to her chest, then sipping again. It tasted hard and angry, nothing like the sweet heat of Hugo's cognac. But it loosened the knot in her chest, and she breathed in and out.

"Are you going to tell me what happened?" he said.

So she did. Everything she knew. If she stopped for a minute, she was afraid she would burst, so she ran on and on, and he was carried with her, just as she'd known he would be. He looked as shocked, as angry, as upset as she was. She realized that was what she had wanted to see in someone else. Fury.

"I knew if I came to you, you'd want to help," she said. "I knew it."

"I'll help you in any way I can, Hadley, if you ever need someone to talk to, or . . ."

"I mean something else," she said.

She told him about finding Jacques. As she explained it to him, as he crouched on one knee on the mat before her, his whiskey glass tilting in his hand, she knew without any doubt that she had come to the right person, that looking for Jacques was the only thing to do. Joel dropped his head, and when he looked back up, his eyes were glazed over.

"You really want to try and find this guy?"

Hadley nodded.

"Why?"

"He deserves to know," Hadley said. "Things weren't exactly straightforward with him and Kristina, but as far as I could see, he was always honest with her. And I do think he loved her. It must be terrible to not know the truth about someone you love. To think they've just disappeared, or just stopped caring." Her voice had grown cracked and hoarse. She smoothed her hair with trembling fingers. "I can't think of anyone else who could tell him. She kept him at such a distance, always such a mystery."

"Are you angry with her?"

"Of course not, how could I be?"

"But before . . . were you angry with her then? Over how she was with Jacques?"

"No, I mean, I didn't know enough to be angry, really," said Hadley, "but it didn't stop me, did it? I was rotten when I spoke to her on the phone. I just felt like she was making a drama out of it, expecting him to be someone he wasn't. But that's easy to say, isn't it, when it's not happening to you."

"And now you regret it."

"Yes, I regret it. I regret it massively. I hate myself for it. But I can't let it go, and I want to know what happened that night. For all the good it'll do, I want to know."

"Are you sure it'll help you? I'm not certain it will, Hadley."

"Joel, it's the only thing I am sure of. I did think about leaving. I was beginning to think that that was the right thing to do, and then someone made me realize that it wasn't. I owe it to Kristina to stay."

He sat back in his chair, thinking over her words.

"Maybe it's not such a bad idea to go home, Hadley," he said, after a time, "at least for a little while. Just to get yourself together. Find some balance."

"I don't want balance. Not yet. I need to do this."

"You could always come back again later in the semester. It doesn't have to be the end."

"I wanted to ask you for your help."

"Oh, Hadley."

"Will you help me? Find Jacques? Figure it all out?"

He didn't answer.

"Joel, please?"

"Isn't it better just to let this go?" he said, carefully. "This terrible, sad thing. Keep your head above water. Remember all the ways in which she was . . . great. And somehow find a way to let the rest go."

"I can't," she said.

"Well, do you have a friend who can help you do this? A boyfriend?"

She shook her head. "I came to you because I thought you'd understand why it mattered. I know that's stupid. It's got nothing to do with you, but . . ."

Her voice broke off. She felt a tear run down her cheek, and she quickly wiped it away. Another tear came, and she wiped that one, too. Joel turned away abruptly and set down his empty glass heavily on the desk. There must have been a crack in it, a fault line, and it shattered at the impact. Splintered shards covered his papers. He swore and held up his finger to the light.

"Goddammit."

"Are you cut?"

"Shit, there's glass in there," he said, and a trickle of blood ran down his hand.

"Let me," said Hadley. "Here, it's only tiny." With a delicate touch, she bent close and picked out the scrap of glass. "I've got it. See?"

A drop of blood fell on the pale carpet. He held his hand to his chest, and it smeared his shirt. "I'm getting it everywhere," he said.

Hadley rushed to her bag and dug out Hugo's handkerchief. She folded it over and over, then bound Joel's hand. An elaborate dressing, for so small a wound.

"You don't have to do that," he began.

She stepped back. "You're fixed."

"That thing's the size of a tablecloth."

"It's not mine," she said. "I guess I'll need it back afterward."

"Hadley . . ."

"Yes?"

He sat down on the sofa as she hovered by the desk. His good hand fiddled with the bandage. A dark red stain had begun to bloom through Hugo's handkerchief.

"It matters to you, doesn't it? Trying to find this Jacques."

"It's beginning to feel like the only thing to do."

"The problem is," he said, "I don't know where we'd start. And I don't know if we'd ever get to the end."

"I know."

"But if you want to look, if you want some help doing that, if you really think it'll make

225

you feel better . . . okay, then."

Hadley went to him. Without thinking she sat down beside him and leaned into his side, weak with relief. She rested her head on his shoulder, and she felt him stiffen. She closed her aching eyes, expecting him to move away. But instead he shifted in his seat. He drew his arm up around her shoulder and pulled her closer toward him.

"When my little brother died," he said, "my grandmother told me that I'd feel better about it one day, I just had to get through the shitty part first. And I hated her for saying that because I didn't want it to be true. I wanted to hurt. I wanted to hurt like hell, because it was all I had left of him, and I didn't want to believe that someone you loved, someone who mattered more to you than anyone else, could die, and how, after a while, that'd seem like it was okay, for them to have gone and died. So I held on to all of that hurt and all of that anger, and I didn't want to ever let it go. But then one day, without even noticing, it happened. I woke up in the morning, and you know what the first thing that I thought of was, Hadley? Coffee. A big, steaming, black-as-night cup of it. And then in the next second I remembered that Winston was gone. I hadn't forgotten, but the hole he'd left had just shrunk back, ever so slightly, just the smallest amount. I'd woken up every morning for three months, and as soon as I opened my eyes I thought, *Oh, Jesus . . . Winston.* But not that morning. Not at first. So I got up, and I drank my coffee, and I thought about him and I missed him still. And then I went on to the next thing, which that morning happened to be toast. A square of it, with a scrape of butter and burned edges. And it tasted like toast, too. For the first time since Winston died, it actually tasted like toast. Hadley, it's small stuff, it's stupid stuff, but when it happens you're ready for it, and you want it, because you're worn-out, and you're tired of railing. You never let the grief go, but somehow it begins to let go of you. Just a little, just enough. Enough to let you live again. Eat toast, drink coffee, breathe in and out without wondering how you're even able to do it. So here's the thing, Hadley. *This* is the worst time. Right now, you're in Hell. And nothing anybody says, or does, is going to get you out of it. God knows it'll feel like mourning Kristina is all you'll ever do and all you'll ever be. But it will get better. One day, down the road, it will get better. And when that day comes, you'll be ready for it, Hadley. Okay? You don't believe me, but that's all right, I didn't used to believe it, either. But you know what? People say that there's only one certainty in life and that's death. Well, let me tell you that they're wrong. There's two. The other is that eventually we'll always find a way to live with it. And that's the best thing and the worst thing about it."

CHAPTER 15

Rue des Mirages ran a few streets below the station, and on the way back from campus Hadley braved it for the first time. With Joel's promise, she was emboldened, and it felt as if he was with her, even when he wasn't. It appeared like any other Lausanne backstreet, with olive-colored apartment buildings and a bank of graffiti-blanched garages, more down at heel than most perhaps, but not a dangerous place, not the kind of place where lives were snapped out with sudden ferocity. She looked up and down the street, and there was no one about; a sideways step off the main thoroughfare and you could find yourself entirely alone. She looked up at the shuttered windows and the rear ends of old blocks. She looked down at the ground. That night there would have been a pool of spreading blood, ruby-red against the snow. Now there was only gray, grit-streaked slush. Kristina had dashed along Rue des Mirages and fallen, and there wasn't the slightest trace to show that any of it had ever happened. Hadley had seen memorials before, sad spots marked by spindly bouquets and rain-smeared messages, tied to the railings of a bridge or at a busy intersection. To a passing stranger they gave pause for thought, but what were they to the bereaved? It wasn't like taking flowers to a graveyard, a laying to rest; perhaps it was that same instinct she felt now, to stop the earth's spinning for just a moment, refuse to let the next day and the next erase all that had passed before. A desperate act, really, trying to make something matter, when the world rushed on regardless.

At the end of the street was a flower shop, and she went in, selecting a bouquet of twelve snow-white roses. She walked back up Rue des Mirages, looking for a spot to lay them. She chose the foot of a lamppost, and she set them gently down. *I didn't mean the things I said,* she began to whisper, then stopped. The only sounds were the far-off rumbles of traffic, the crunch of her feet as she shifted in the snow and the rustle of wind as it caught the plastic wrapping of Kristina's lonely bouquet. She walked away, and her words stayed zipped inside.

■ ■ ■ ■

Back at Les Ormes, the cleaners were in
Kristina's room. Hadley heard the whine of
their vacuums as she approached, and the
clump of their plastic clogs as they moved
across the floor. She listened and waited,
loitering outside her own room, and when
they left and didn't lock the door afterward,
she saw her chance. She was about to slip
inside, and then she stopped, first glancing
up and down the corridor. She held her
hand up to the door and pressed her fist to
it. She'd knocked so many times before, a
quick rat-a-tat to say, *fancy a coffee? Shall
we catch the bus together? The sun's shining,
so let's go somewhere, anywhere, how about
the lake?* She knocked now, just once,
gently. *Kristina?* Nobody answered. *I'm coming in,* she said.

It was empty, just as she knew it would
be. The bed was stripped, and a new white
bag lined the dustbin. They'd forgotten to
take her pin-board down, and it still hung
brazenly, stuck all over with signs of life —
Kristina's study timetable, all neon streaks
of highlight and underlined notes; the flyer
from La Folie, the club they'd been to at
the start of term, where they'd danced until

their hair had grown sticky and the soles of their feet had ached; and a picture postcard showing deep blue sea and bluer sky. She unpinned the last and flipped it over, but there was no message this time. Hadley glanced around the room. What had she expected? A business card bearing the name Jacques, tucked into the mirror's frame? An inkily written telephone number, blotted on a paper napkin? But there was no trace, nothing to make her search the smallest bit easier. There was only the sorrowful feeling of a recently evacuated room, the inescapable air of sadness in the crookedly pulled blind and the folded blanket at the foot of the bed. On her way back out Hadley closed the door quietly behind her. She noticed Kristina's name was still there in the little panel just below the room number. *Kristina Hartmann.* It was strangely comforting, to see it still.

Joel kept his promise and was there for her just as he said he would be. In those first few days, he was the only person she wanted to be around, and she didn't stop to examine the feeling or wonder at their growing intimacy; she only knew that he, more than anyone, understood. Between classes they pulled the blind down low, leafing through fat blue-paged telephone directories and student records. Joel dragged his laptop onto his knees and looked online, conducting exhaustive internet searches with every combination of suitable words they could think of. *Jacques Kristina. Jacques Geneva Saint-Tropez. Jacques Danish girlfriend.* Nothing ever came up.

"Maybe some of the students here might know something. Maybe you could try that," said Joel.

"What, Kristina's classmates? I don't think she would have told them anything."

"Sometimes it's easier to talk when there's a distance."

"Not about something like this. I was the only one who knew."

"I don't know, Hadley, it's just a place to start."

Joel rubbed his face with both hands. Hadley wondered if he'd turned insomniac just as she had, for the same telltale dark scoops were beneath his eyes, the mark of endless sleepless nights.

"You're right, I suppose they might know when she left for Geneva. She might have said something to someone. It's a good idea."

"Hadley, is this helping?" he said. "I mean, am *I* helping?"

"Of course you are. You know you are."

"I know how much I want to."

"Joel, you're helping me in ways you probably don't even realize."

"I just wonder if this fruitless searching only makes everything worse."

"It's the only thing that makes it better," said Hadley.

As she left, she leaned forward and kissed him lightly on the cheek. It was only afterward when she was walking down the corridor that she realized what she'd done, and she thought of how his hand had gone to his face afterward, an action as unconscious as the kiss itself.

She knew she would find Kristina's course mates in the corner of the main campus café. It was where they had been when she'd had lunch with Joel on her birthday, when she'd affected not to see them with Kristina, wanting only to focus on him. She watched them now as they lolled in their chairs, rolling cigarettes, their table strewn with coffee cups. There was the girl who laughed all the time, her hair falling in flame-red ringlets, the boy who wore the crushed-velvet jacket and stomping black boots, and an older blond man, with glasses and freckled cheeks. She said *bonjour,* and they looked blankly back at her, but threw a round of greetings in reply. None of them was British. The blond man might have been a Dane. She said that she was a friend of Kristina's, and he spoke up first.

"Ah, okay," he said, in English, "you're Hadley, then? From her student residence. Of course. Hi, good to meet you."

He had a detached air, and when he shook Hadley's hand, it was a cool, crisp gesture. The other boy waved his hand and smiled, revealing not quite perfect teeth. The red-headed girl spoke up, and her voice was sonorous, English laced with French, all lingering vowels and floating cadence.

"C'est tragique," she said, *"vraiment,* we can't believe it. She talked about you all the time, you know. How are you? Are you okay?"

For a moment Hadley wondered what it would be like to slot in with these strange half friends of Kristina's; they seemed to welcome her, they knew her name. But as she stood there, she sensed they were already moving on to other things; they stayed sorrow-struck and outraged just about as long as anyone would expect them to. The French-speaking girl was fiddling with the beads of her necklace. The others had spotted someone else they knew. Hadley spoke briskly.

"Did Kristina ever mention someone called Jacques?"

The girl shook her head, and her curls rippled prettily. She turned to the others, "Karl, Josef, you guys ever hear Kristina talk about a Jacques?" They shrugged, their smiles turned contrite, and they flipped quickly back to their conversation.

"We were friends but, like, campus friends, you know? A coffee after a lecture, a chat in the library, that kind of thing. I'm sorry, okay? *Vraiment.*"

"What about on Friday? Did Kristina say what she was doing afterward? Did she say that she was going to Geneva? To *Genève?*"

The girl shook her head again. She took a skinny cigarette and tucked it in to the corner of her mouth, a careless, carefree gesture.

"Listen, nothing was different. We had Art History before lunch, we all came in here afterward. Then we went different ways for the afternoon. I can't even remember saying *au revoir* to Kristina, to be honest. And that was the last time I saw her, so that's pretty terrible, you know? I feel shit about that."

She pronounced shit like *sheet,* and her version of *sheet* didn't look all that bad. It

236

was laughter and friends and light-passing regret, and that was just how it was. Kristina's course mates could give her nothing more, so Hadley thanked them, a tight-lipped *merci,* and walked away.

Instead of getting the bus, she took the long way home, her face hidden inside her hood. She thought about how Joel had said "we" when they'd talked about finding Jacques, and she felt less alone.

The Saint-Tropez idea came to her in the night. Her mind was looping in all directions, connecting everything she knew and some things she imagined. Jacques striding along Geneva's Rues Basses. Kristina reading stories to someone else's children. Jacques standing in his shirtsleeves under a melting sun. Kristina's hair falling like a wave, turning for a kiss. She had told Hadley that Jacques had been staying in the neighboring villa, a real, tangible place. As she realized the link, she jumped out of bed, all set to make a telephone call, but the yellow dial of her alarm clock told her it was only 3:45 a.m. She climbed back into bed and watched the numbers reshape themselves, clicking ever closer to a reasonable hour. At 7:32 a.m., she telephoned the campus administrative offices. She rang again at 7:40 a.m., and this time someone picked up; the Swiss began their days early. Minutes later she was scribbling down the number of Kristina's parents in Copenhagen. It had been easy, assuming the role of the distraught friend, desperate to offer her condolences. The digits were given up, and Hadley was already clicking off the line as the administrator offered consoling words of her own.

"*Hej*," a voice said, and even though he had barely spoken before, Hadley recognized Kristina's father. *Hey*, it sounded like, a greeting of unsettling levity, until Hadley remembered in Danish it simply meant "hello."

"Oh, hello," she said, "Mr. Hartmann. I don't know if you speak English, but it's Hadley Dunn. Kristina's friend. We met very briefly. . . ."

"Kristina's friend?"

His voice was all hollowed out, so thin it sounded as if it might crack at any moment.

"I'm so sorry to disturb you at home," she said. "Are you —" she lost her thread, then picked it up again "— I mean, how are you? I hope you're well. As well as can be, anyway."

"Why are you phoning?"

"I'm sorry, I really don't want to bother you, I just wondered something. I wondered if you could help."

"I think probably not," he said, not unkindly, just defeated.

Hadley took a breath and explained, carefully, gently, how she wanted to get in touch with the family that Kristina had au paired for that summer. She wondered if anyone had done that already, and if they could possibly give her a postal address. She expected a volley of questions, but he asked none.

"Sorry, no," he said.

"No? You mean you don't have it?"

"No," he said, "I'm sorry."

"Or what about the house in France, in Saint-Tropez, maybe, did you ever write to Kristina there? Or did she write to you?"

"Kristina was very independent," he said. "Her summer was, how do you say in English . . . her summer was her business. Who is this? You say you are a friend of Kristina's?"

"Yes, from Lausanne. I'm Hadley. I'm just trying to . . ."

"Hadley, here, we are trying to carry on."

"Carry on? Yes, of course. I know. I'm sorry, the last thing I wanted to do was upset you, I just thought . . ."

"We do not have answers to your questions. We did not know everything about

239

our daughter's life. Perhaps we did not know enough. We were not with her when she died. These are things that we are living with now. Trying to adapt to."

"I know. . . ."

"So, thank you, for your friendship with our daughter, but we cannot help. There is nothing we can do. Nothing we can do about any of it."

His words fell away, and Hadley heard a muffled sob. She shut her eyes and took a deep breath, hating herself for her persistence.

"Can I just ask, has anyone called Jacques phoned? Has any man phoned at all?"

"I'm sorry. Goodbye."

The line clicked off and Hadley groaned. Somewhere in the very south of France two villas sat side by side, but the occupants were ghosted and long gone. The voice of Kristina's father stayed inside her head, his diffidence turning to sorrow turning to irritation, and the uncomfortable knowledge that she had come across badly, questioning and impervious. She climbed back under her blankets. She cried until she had nothing left.

As the idea of Saint-Tropez flared and faded, Hadley went to Joel and suggested

Geneva. She sought movement, the tracing of a line along a map.

"What, just to wander the streets?" Joel said. "Holler 'Jacques, Jacques'?"

It was Wednesday, and she was sitting on the windowsill in his office, with her back flat against the glass. Below, the heads of poplar trees shifted in the wind. Scattered students crossed the walkways, their scarves blowing out behind them, their heads bent down to the ground. They looked happy, ordinary. She rubbed her eyes and turned back.

"Kristina said some things about the places they used to go together."

"Hadley, honey, why didn't you say that before?"

"Because she was always so vague. There's really nothing to go on, but . . . I could at least try."

"What sort of places?"

"The waterside. The old town. There was a café, I think, near the cathedral. I know it's not much to go on, but I don't know what else to do."

Hadley saw Joel think about it. She'd noticed that he always took his time with an answer; he had the same unhurried way about him in class, and you always waited to hear his answer. His fingers tapped a

241

rhythm on his desk. He nodded slowly.

"Okay," he said. "Okay. Maybe it's not a bad idea to get out of Lausanne. Try something different."

"I'll get the train, just like Kristina did. I'll go now. I might as well."

"Hadley, wait. Let me drive you."

"You don't have to do that."

"I do," said Joel. "You're not going on your own." He picked up his car keys from the desk and shrugged on his jacket. "Two conditions, though."

"What's that?"

"That maybe after tonight we draw a line. Accept that maybe Jacques just can't be found."

"I don't want to give up yet."

"Give up? Hadley, I think it's the opposite. Accepting something is never giving up. I've one other condition, too."

"And what's that?"

"That you let me buy you dinner. I'll bet you haven't eaten properly in a while."

Hadley reached for his hand. She held it as if it were the first hand she'd ever come across. She inspected its farmhand thickness, the tawny-brown skin, the giant half moons of his nails. She dropped it quickly.

"Thank you," she said.

■ ■ ■ ■

Back in September she had flown in to Geneva, *Genève,* on the very first day she'd arrived. She'd seen little of the city as the train flashed through its peripheries, just the usual high-rises, splashes of inexpert graffiti and the inexplicably depressing hangars of light industry. Nonetheless she had shaped the idea of Geneva as a dull, older brother to the playful Lausanne, stuffy and stiff-natured, in an expensive but ill-fitting sweater and box-fresh brogues. Lausanne, on the other hand, was artsy, and definitely a girl. No less pedigreed, no less moneyed, but with a blousy edge. Against the backdrop of Geneva, she'd seen the lake as a mere water feature, a placid piece of architecturally inspired landscaping for the flag-waving hotels. Along the Lausanne shore, Lac Léman was so much more arresting; you looked out over the rakish outline of mountains, saw the wild slapping of water against the jetties, and profusions of indignant gulls, and you were convinced of its vitality, its sunlit ripples hiding darker depths.

Kristina's accounts of meeting Jacques in Geneva had done little to change Hadley's view. She'd only ever pictured them in snatches, leaning on a railing watching the fountain, their legs touching from hip to toe; eating from an international menu in a gold-lit restaurant, champagne fizzing in frosted flutes. The city itself had seemed like nothing more than a bland backdrop to their stop-start romance. Then Hadley went to Geneva with Joel Wilson.

The restaurant Joel chose was tucked off a lamp-lit boulevard. It was Chinese and had a festive entrance decked with paper lanterns and papier-mâché cats. A girl in a wine-colored waistcoat, with her hair tied in two tight bunches, led them to a table at the back. The paper cloth rumpled as Hadley drew her chair in. She flicked a stray pea, left from the previous diners, to the floor. One wall of the restaurant consisted entirely of mirrors, while the other was vividly painted with a giant waterside scene. Sway-bottomed junks trailing colored lights floated nose to nose, while behind, blue mountains gave way to a rose-pink sky.

"Have you been here before?" she asked Joel.

"Never."

"But you thought it looked good?"

"No, but I thought maybe it'd be fun."

She looked at the giant menu. There were

at least two hundred dishes listed in tight type.

"I'll take 17 and 41," she said.

"Pot luck?"

"Why not?"

"See, I knew it'd be fun. I'm going 21, 50 and, hell, let's chuck in 80. But only if you split it with me."

They ordered tall glasses of fizzy lager and sat back in their chairs. It was ten o'clock and they were the only diners. Hadley ate a prawn cracker and tried not to laugh. It was, she realized, the first time she'd felt like laughter in several days. She drank her beer and stayed calm. It had been a strange evening so far. They'd arrived in Geneva without a real plan. Joel had parked in a cavernous underground car park, and their feet had echoed on the concrete as they'd looked for the exit. They'd climbed a set of sour-smelling stairs, the crunch of broken glass beneath their feet. She'd felt Joel's hand fall lightly on her waist as he'd motioned her through a swing door and out into the street. It seemed colder in Geneva than in Lausanne; the air had snapped her cheeks and seemed to cut through the layers of coat and sweater. She'd shivered, and Joel had wrapped an arm around her.

"You'll soon warm up," he'd said, walking

in step with her for a moment. She'd leaned into him, and he'd squeezed her shoulder before breaking away. She'd taken a folded map from her pocket and smoothed it with her gloved hand.

"I think the old town's this way," she'd said.

Had there been a plan that night? Yes, as much of one as there ever could have been. In the car she'd searched her memory and written down all the places that Kristina had ever mentioned, a feeble list of oft-visited landmarks and imprecise locations. She'd read it back to Joel, and he'd heaved a sigh, turned the music in the car up louder.

"You know, this is crazy, Hadley," he'd shouted over John Coltrane's frantic rhythms. "How do you feel about that?"

"But what else is there?" she'd shouted back.

"Just so long as you know," he'd said, drumming his fingers on the steering wheel.

If you asked Hadley what she hoped to find that night she would have told you this: she simply wanted to be close to where Jacques lived and worked. She felt that if she passed him in the street she'd recognize him, and perhaps he'd recognize her, her hope, marking her out like a shining beacon.

She knew that didn't make a lot of sense, but what else was there? Together Joel and Hadley had trekked all over the city. They'd stood in a cobbled square and watched a bar fill with young and beautiful *Genevois* as outside chalkboards offered cups of mulled wine and *coupes de champagne*. They'd looked up at the yellow squares of windows set beneath steeply tiled roofs, seen the shapes of people moving behind them, and once a child's face peeping up at the night sky as though counting stars. They'd walked through a dark and silent park, where statues stood hunched and watching. Neither had talked, both lost in their own thoughts.

"Is that enough for tonight?" Joel had asked eventually, turning to her. They had been back on one of the main streets, with weaving tramlines and brightly lit shoe shops. He'd blown on his bare hands and rubbed them together. She'd thought of her gloves with their sheepskin lining, and how natural it would have been to cover his hands with hers and warm them. Instead, she'd stuffed them deeper into the pockets of her coat. She'd nodded.

"Will you tell everyone what a waste of time this was?" she'd said.

"Tell everyone? I haven't said a word

about this to anyone."

"Not to your colleagues? Your boss?"

"I didn't think you'd want me to."

"But they know about Kristina?"

"Everyone knows about Kristina." He'd paused, then said, "But, in the English department, we didn't know her. I heard that her Art History professor held a minute's silence in his class."

"A minute's silence," Hadley had said, "one minute, then everyone rushes on just as before."

"The world has to keep turning, Hadley, it's the only way."

"Yeah, that, I know."

"And it was well-intentioned," he'd said. "It was a way of remembering. Everyone remembers in different ways."

They'd walked on in silence.

"Are you hungry?" Joel had asked, suddenly.

They'd stopped at the next restaurant they'd come across. The Chinese. They ordered too much food and watched each other across the table, past the bowls of sticky rice and mustard-colored curry, and drapes of wilted greens. They ordered more fizzy lager. Hadley chewed carefully, her nose wrinkling.

"Not good?"

"Not good."

Everything was either too salty or too bland. The meat was ragged and shot through with seams of fat. The prawns were woody, with pink eggs clustered in their folds.

"I'm sorry," she said, pushing her plate away, "I guess I'm not hungry, after all."

"Only because I brought you to the worst place in town," Joel said. "Unwittingly, by the way. I felt like taking a chance. Bad move, huh?"

"I suppose it's not right to be enjoying ourselves, anyway," Hadley said. She dabbed at her mouth with a napkin, and the lipstick she had applied earlier smudged on the cloth. She turned it over quickly, before he saw. "It's not why we came, is it?"

"I certainly set out to have a terrible time," said Joel. A smile pushed at his lips, and he let it break. "C'mon, Hadley, cut yourself some slack."

She smiled back at him and felt a lifting in her chest.

"Why did you say that you think it's time we stopped looking for Jacques?" she said. "I feel like we've hardly begun."

"I just think," said Joel carefully, "that maybe we need to accept that if he wants to be found, he'll be found." Hadley stared at him blankly, so he went on. "I mean, he knew about you, right?"

"Not necessarily."

"I'm sure she would have talked about you, Hadley," he said. He paused, then went on. "Look, think about it. It's far easier for this guy Jacques to connect with Kristina's world than it is for us to try and connect with his. We don't know anything about him, and even if Kristina didn't tell him much about herself, he'd still know enough to ask the right questions in the right places if he wanted to. If he were worried about where she was, or that he hadn't heard anything from her for a few days, if he knows *nothing* about her accident, then he'd be able to find out fairly easily, wouldn't he? And if he *does* know, if he saw the piece in the newspaper or heard about it some other way, maybe he wants to be alone with his grief. Maybe he doesn't want to try and know her friends. Maybe he thinks he doesn't belong with them. Maybe we should respect that."

"That's a lot of maybes," she said, looking forlorn. "But I hadn't thought of it like that. Why didn't I think of it like that?"

Joel shrugged. "It's just logic," he said, gently. He folded his paper napkin over and over until it was a tight square. He dropped it to the bottom of his empty glass. "But then, the heart doesn't always follow logic, does it? That's why we came here tonight."

Hadley picked up her beer and swirled the last of it. "There was something strange about her voice when we spoke that last time," she ventured. "She wasn't happy, Joel. And it wasn't just guilt about being late for my stupid birthday. It was more than that. I think she and Jacques had argued. I think she was upset."

"Every couple in the world argues, Hadley. And if he was married, they'd have had more to argue about than most."

"I just want to know what happened that night."

"We do know. It's senseless and terrible, but we do know."

"So, what, we stop?" A single tear trickled down Hadley's cheek. "I guess we do."

Joel leaned forward, and with the tip of his finger he lightly caught it. He glanced sideways, noticing the waitress watching them in the mirrored wall. "Come on," he said, "time to call it a night, I think."

They sped fast along the autoroute, and she willed the signs for Lausanne to grow farther apart, to carry a larger number, at least to be in miles and not kilometres. It was dark in the car, and she sat upright, her hands folded in her lap. She glanced across at him from time to time, noting the forceful outline of his features, the curl of his lip and the jut of his chin. He appeared rough-hewn, his eyes two dark scoops. He stared straight ahead as he drove, and his fingers thrummed a beat on the wheel. She turned away from him.

"Hadley? Are you crying again? Please don't cry."

"It's just been a strange day."

"It's okay. They're all strange days," he said.

"I've had a good time," she said quietly. "I shouldn't have had a good time tonight, but I have."

In the dark car, lit only by the passing flashes of other vehicles, Joel found her hand. He lifted it to his lips and pressed her fingers to his mouth. He kissed them. Once. Then again. She felt his warm skin, rough with stubble.

"We can't help feeling guilty," he said, his voice muffled by her hand. "We can't help looking back over the things we did or didn't do, the things we did or didn't say."

He had slowed right down and a car sped past, blasting its horn. Joel gently dropped her hand. He shook his head and clenched the wheel, speeding back up. Hadley's hand stayed on his leg. She felt the heat of him beneath her palm. She moved her hand away.

"Maybe that's why I can't let this go. The last words I said to her were in anger, Joel. I think I told you before, but I'm not sure. I know I told Hugo, but . . ."

"Who's Hugo?"

"Just someone I've got to know a little bit. An old man. He's the one who said I should stay in Lausanne. Even you said I should go, but he said stay."

"I didn't really want you to go anywhere."

"But you thought it'd be good for me, didn't you?"

"Maybe I thought it'd be good for me."

She glanced across at him. "I don't understand," she said.

"Yes, you do."

The neon signs of a petrol station loomed suddenly, and he swung into the forecourt. He pulled over, away from the bright lights and the luminous pumps.

"Hadley," he whispered, as he leaned toward her, "I shouldn't do this."

"I want you to," she said. "I always did."

Their two faces were close together. In the half-dark, Hadley felt his lips meet hers. She wondered if this was how they would

253

stay, not quite kissing, a warm press, sharing breath. Then she felt his mouth open, and the hot flick of his tongue. She shut her eyes, and tasted the salt of her own tears. His kisses, when they came, were hard and insistent. It was as though he had been keeping them for a long time.

Chapter 16

Hadley woke to a gray morning, with the sky hanging like sheet metal and half hearted drops of rain spitting at her window. She had forgotten to pull the blinds again, and she lay flattened by the weighty covers. *Oh, Kristina,* she thought. Her hand went to her face, and she felt the delicate grazing on her chin. She knew that if she looked in the mirror there would be a reddened patch, a minor irritation that prickled as she touched it. It was the only lasting proof of the night before. No one had ever kissed her like that, and she had never kissed anyone back with that half-cut desperation, needing to be swallowed up so completely. All she wanted to do was to knock on Kristina's door. They would have stood facing one another in their pajamas, and she'd have pointed to her chin. *You'll never guess what happened.* Perhaps they would have giggled, and the kiss would have seemed funny, or exciting, or both. But without Kristina it was a different sort of kiss. If everything had been ordinary, beautifully perfectly ordinary, it would never even have happened.

They had driven the rest of the way back to Lausanne in near silence, not a pleasant, companionable quiet but an atmosphere thickened with words not spoken. After Joel had kissed her, he'd muttered, *I'm sorry, I don't know what I was thinking,* then hastily put the car in gear and roared back to the autoroute. She had turned her face to the window, pretending not to hear.

"Hadley?" he'd said.

"It's okay," she'd replied. "I'm sorry, too."

"Maybe we both need some distance, maybe that's it."

She had knotted her hands in her lap and watched the window, wishing he had said something different, or maybe even nothing at all.

Joel had pulled into the pavement just past the turning for Les Ormes, and sat with the engine running.

"Okay from here?"

"Okay from here," she'd said. She'd climbed out, turning back to say, "thanks for tonight."

"See you in the week," he had replied, tight as a clam.

She had slammed the door, and he'd driven away on up the hill. Hadley had held up her hand to wave. There had been no possible way of telling whether he'd seen it or not.

Hadley showered, and afterward she watched herself in the mirror, her chin tipped with defiance. Things would be different now, she knew that for certain. She wasn't due on campus until the afternoon, and an idea came to her as sharply as a pain in her side; she would go back to Rue des Mirages. She'd lay new flowers. Last night, for the first time since Kristina had died, she'd enjoyed herself, and no matter how fleeting a sensation it had been, it had felt wrong.

Rue des Mirages was gray and silent. Her bouquet of roses was still at the foot of the lamppost, and when she lifted it, the browned petals fell to the ground like tarnished snowflakes. Hadley laid a new bouquet in its place, exotic-looking sprays of color, island-flowers, marooned in a cold Swiss street.

"Kristina," Hadley began, "something happened last night."

"Elle ne peut pas vous entendre."

Hadley spun around. A woman was standing on the other side of the road, watching her. Her hair hung in two girlish, tangled plaits. Her jogging bottoms were ripped at the knee and sodden at the ankle.

"*Excusez-moi?*"

"*Anglaise?* I speak English. She can't hear you, the girl who died. *Elle n'est pas là. Elle est partie.*"

"I know she's not there."

Hadley stared at the woman. It was ten o'clock in the morning, and she had a can of beer in her hand. An unlit cigarette fluttered between her lips. Hadley turned away again. She bent and straightened the new bouquet, busying herself, ignoring the sound of the woman's shuffling footsteps coming closer.

"I told you, *elle n'est pas là.* She's not there. They took her."

She spoke English with a zigzagging French accent, but it was entirely comprehensible. Hadley stood up straight and faced her. She could have been anywhere between twenty and forty. Her cheeks were pale and sunken, and a scarred track of worry lines ran along her brow. Her eyes were gray and sharp, and staring directly at Hadley.

"Were you here when the police came?" said Hadley. "*Avez-vous vu la police?*"

"*Il neigeait.* It was snowing. It never stopped snowing."

"Did you see Kristina? Did you see my friend? *Mon amie, la fille qui a été tué?*"

"Your friend?"

"She was my friend."

"She was running in the snow."

"You mean you saw her before? Did you . . . Did she . . . You saw her fall?"

"*Je veux une cigarette.*"

"You've got a cigarette," said Hadley, nodding to her, "do you mean a light?"

"*Je veux une cigarette.*"

"You've already got one," said Hadley, and pointed to her lips. "Please, tell me, *dîtes-moi,* what did you see? *Qu'avez-vous vu?*"

The woman reached her hand to her mouth and pulled out the cigarette. She held it between two fingers, and started laughing hoarsely.

"I haven't got a light," said Hadley. "I'm sorry. Look, please go on. *Continuez, s'il vous plaît.* Tell me what you saw. She was my best friend. *Ma meilleure amie.* I just want to know that she didn't suffer. At least that."

The woman tucked the cigarette behind her ear, and a grin split her lips.

"You think it's funny?" said Hadley. "Forget it. I can't talk to you." She started to walk away.

"You're the only one who came," the woman called after her.

Hadley kept walking.

She spoke again, louder still. "Nobody brings flowers."

"Yeah, well, they're pretty pointless, aren't they?" said Hadley over her shoulder.

"*L'autre n'est jamais venu.*"

Hadley didn't turn.

"*J'ai dit,* the other person didn't come."

Hadley froze. She spun on her heel. "What other person? *Qui?*"

"With the car."

She thought of Jacques, driving from Geneva. Kneeling a moment in the street, placing the flat of his hand on the hard ground.

"What car?" she said. "Did you see a car? *Qu'avez-vous vu?*"

The woman flapped her hands in front of her face with sudden animation.

"*Personne n'a rien vu. Il neigeait.*"

"I know it was snowing, I know. But . . ."

"Nobody saw anything. I didn't see the car. The car didn't see the girl. The girl didn't see the car. Nobody saw anything."

Hadley's mouth dropped. "What? You mean the night it happened? Oh, God, how do I say that in French? There was a car? *Y a-t-il une voiture?"*

"It didn't stop. It disappeared. In the snow, everything disappears."

Hadley willed her breath to come evenly. She placed a hand gently on the woman's arm.

"S'il vous plaît. Il est vraiment important. Please, tell me what you saw. *Dîtes-moi."*

"Nobody saw anything."

"But you did, didn't you? You saw a car. *Une voiture.* It was snowing, *il neigeait,* but you still saw a car. *Qu'est-il arrivé?* What did it do? Did it . . ." She stopped. Collected herself, breathing deeply. "Please. Just think. *Cette voiture que vous avez vu . . . qu'est-il arrivé?"*

"La voiture ne s'arrête pas. Elle a disparu."

"Wait, hang on, did you say *'disparu'?* It disappeared?"

"Yes."

"It didn't stop?"

"Non."

"Why didn't it stop? Did they see her? See that she'd fallen?"

"She was running, and then the car came, and then she fell."

"They hit her?"

"Catastrophe. Bang. After . . . gone."

Hadley covered her mouth with both hands. She felt physical shock for the second time in a week. She staggered with it, and a cry escaped her lips. The woman started to turn away, but Hadley reached out and grabbed her shoulder.

"Please. Wait. Don't go."

The woman shrugged her off. *"Ne me touchez pas."*

"Sorry, I'm sorry, I won't touch you. *Une question . . . La Police? Avez-vous leur dit?"*

"Salauds."

"What does that mean?"

"No police. I don't talk to anyone."

"You talked to me," said Hadley. "You told me. You wanted me to know the truth, *la vérité.*"

"I just want to smoke a cigarette," said the woman.

"Then smoke it! Or don't smoke it! I don't give a shit, just stop *talking* about it. You can't say something like this and just carry on like it's nothing. Or like you don't understand what you saw, because I know that you do. I know you know exactly what you saw and that's why you started talking to me. Because you wanted to tell someone. Because you knew that what you saw was wrong."

The woman looked dazed, her face shutting down.

"Please, just please. *S'il vous plaît.* You're

262

the only one who knows anything. The police think it was an accident, just a careless fall on a slippery street. They don't know about the car. They don't know it was a hit-and-run. Nobody knows that Kristina was killed except you. And now me. We can go to them together. *Nous pouvons aller ensemble, okay?*"

"*Non.*"

"*Oui.* I'm going to the police. I'm going now. Please come, please. And then they'll be able to trace the car, and . . . What's your name? I'm sorry, I'm rude, I'm so rude. What's your name? *Comment vous appelez-vous?*"

"Lisette."

"*Lisette, je m'appelle Hadley. Je suis désolée, vraiment.* But you don't understand, *vous ne comprenez pas,* what you've just told me, what you saw, it changes everything."

"I didn't see anything."

"You did, you saw the car. *La voiture.*"

"I don't know anything."

"But you know what color it was? Maybe you saw a number plate? Even just part of a number plate?"

"*Ad-lee?* I don't remember anything. I never remember anything. Not now. Not anymore."

"But you remembered my name! And it's a weird name, people hardly ever get it right. And you remember how to speak English. Did you learn it in school? See, it stuck. Maybe if you think back . . ."

Lisette tapped the side of her head, and her plaits twitched. "Sorry. I'm sorry. How do I say in English? There's nothing left."

With that, she ambled away. Hadley watched her all the way down Rue des Mirages until she was out of sight, and all that she was left with was a half-told story about a car that hit a girl and didn't stop.

Hadley pushed through the revolving doors of the central police station. She sat on a creaky plastic chair and tried to avoid looking at the small child who was crying into the neck of his string-thin mother. The same police officer who had spoken to her before, the one with sandy hair and apologetic eyes, took her into a room and sat her down. He listened to what she had to say, his hands folded on the table before him.

"Thank you, *mademoiselle,*" he said when she'd finished, "and we're already aware of the development. If you had been on Rue des Mirages a day earlier, you would have seen our officers."

"Thank you? *Thank you?* Is that all you

can say?" Tears popped at her eyes, and she blinked them away. "I don't understand how you could have thought it was an accident. How long have you known that it wasn't?"

"The results of the autopsy were not immediate."

"But how come it wasn't obvious? I mean, just from looking at her?"

He explained that close inspection had revealed the dark stain of a bruise on Kristina's thigh. No broken bones, but evidence of a blow that wasn't from the hard surface of the road, or the edge of the pavement, or any other part of the city.

"Kristina was not killed by the impact of the car," he said, "that much we do know. She died because her head struck the pavement. She was very unlucky. The same accident, on another day . . ."

"But of course, the car killed her. If there hadn't been a car, she wouldn't have fallen. How can you say that?"

"A hit-and-run case such as this is extremely difficult, *mademoiselle*. We have very little evidence. And it wasn't a powerful impact."

"But there must be evidence. The woman I told you about, Lisette, if she saw it, then maybe someone else did, too."

265

"Lisette Colombe is, sadly, of very little use. A clean and sober witness, who actually heard and saw something other than a bang and a blur . . . now, that would be helpful, *n'est-ce pas?* The fact is, the snow was falling so quickly that any tracks or footprints were completely obscured. It's possible the driver got out, but we cannot be sure of that. We're pursuing all lines of inquiry, but I'm afraid, *mademoiselle,* you should prepare for the possibility that we might never know exactly what happened to your friend."

"Unless you catch the driver."

"Yes."

"You are trying to catch them?"

"We've appealed for witnesses. We've gone door to door. But it was a bad night, the weather was severe. There was no one outside who didn't have to be."

"Lisette was outside."

"*Oui,* she was. Lausanne has its problems like everywhere else."

"But it was the middle of the city, there must be someone else who saw."

"It was a backstreet, *mademoiselle.*"

"So, what, that's it?"

"We'll find Lisette and question her again; unfortunately, we know her well. But it's just as you said, she told you everything she knew, Hadley. She even spoke English to you. She wanted to help you, but she couldn't. When she said that nobody saw anything, I do believe that, for once, she was telling the truth."

"But you'll keep investigating? You'll keep trying?"

"We'll do our jobs, *mademoiselle,* which means doing all that we can to solve this case. More than that, you know I cannot promise."

Hadley blinked quickly. She started to get up, then sat back down. "Is it okay if I go now?" she said.

"Of course, this isn't a formal interview. You've told us everything you know. Thank you for coming in."

Hadley pulled on her hat and knotted her scarf. She shook hands with the officer, because it felt like the right thing to do. She walked to the door, then turned suddenly.

"Do the drivers ever come forward?" she said. "I mean, days, weeks later? Do they ever wake up one day and realize that they can't live with themselves, after all? That they didn't get away with it, because their conscience, their humanity, their *something,* wouldn't let them? And do they come to you then, and tell you the truth?"

The officer hesitated. "That can happen,"

he said. His voice was flat and without a trace of anything like hope.

The words *hit-and-run* echoed down the halls of Les Ormes. Chase and Jenny were in the kitchen when Hadley returned from the police station, and she saw how their eyes flickered with undisguised excitement as she told them. When she spoke of the unoptimistic police and absence of witnesses, they squeezed her arm and patted her hand and said that what she really had to do was try and move on. Alone again in her room, outrage threatened to choke her, sobs blistering the back of her throat. She paced back and forth, her head in her hands. On impulse, she grabbed her coat and slammed out of her room.

She walked across campus with a heightened sense of self-consciousness, as though everyone she passed knew her business; her lips still smarted from Joel's kisses, his stunted goodbye rang in her ears. It was a spiky, cold day, and the sky held the threat of another snowfall. Students moved in dribs and drabs, their mouths hidden by scarves, their hands stuffed into pockets. Conversations were muffled and hurried. Glances were snapped sideways. Inside the main building Hadley loosened her scarf and took her hat off, teasing her hands through her hair. She slipped into the toilets and checked herself in the mirror. The wintry wind had drawn tears from her eyes, and her mascara was smudged. She tidied her appearance, combing the ends of her hair and marking her lips with a dash of ruby-red. It helped, to paint a face.

Joel's office was up two flights of stairs, at the very end of the English department corridor. Hadley reached his door and knocked. There was no answer, so she knocked again, more insistently.

"Professor Wilson isn't here today."

Hadley turned to find Caroline Dubois standing behind her. She had taken off her glasses and held them loosely in one hand. Hadley noticed that the inside of their arms was violet-colored. She twirled them between her fingers, majorette-like.

"Oh," Hadley said. "I needed to see him."

"He's unwell," Caroline said. "His classes were canceled for the day."

"I didn't know."

"How could you?" Caroline narrowed her pale green eyes. "It's Hadley, isn't it?"

Hadley hadn't properly met her before, not even at the welcome drinks, but the department was small. She presumed she was aware of all the exchange students, for

269

there was only a scattering of them.

"I'm so sorry about your friend," she said. "Professor Wilson mentioned in the last staff meeting that you might need some extra support. It can be difficult, I know, when you're a long way from home. It's easy for things to run out of control. If you ever want to have a cup of tea and a chat, my door is always open."

Her English was perfect, with only the slightest trace of an accent. It was, in fact, a gentle, milky voice, imbued with kindness.

"I love English tea," Professor Dubois went on. "I have a sister in London who sends me over boxes of it. If you miss the taste of home, you know where to come."

A few days ago, Hadley might have taken her up on it. She could have imagined herself drinking loose-leafed tea, letting Caroline's soft voice steep around her. But would she have understood about Jacques? And now, this crime, would she have been moved to do anything about it? Somehow Hadley thought not. Her feelings were too irrational and directionless for someone like Caroline Dubois.

"He has a stomach bug, if that's not too much detail."

"Who?"

"Professor Wilson."

"Oh," Hadley said. "Oh, right."

Professor Dubois looked puzzled for a moment. She opened her mouth as if to say something else and then closed it again. She set her glasses back on her nose and laid her hand very gently on Hadley's arm. It was so light a touch, she barely felt it.

"Remember the tea, Hadley," she said, "anytime."

Hadley retraced her steps down the corridor. She felt Caroline watching her, but when she turned, she'd disappeared back inside her office, and this time the door was shut fast. Hadley took out her jotter from her bag and tore off a page so that she could scribble a note. She thought of last night's bad Chinese food, and how Joel had carried on eating when she had stopped. Illness was plausible. But what if he was just embarrassed and going to great lengths to avoid her? After they had kissed, he had barely been able to look at her, and the sense that they had done something wrong had stayed with them all the way back to Lausanne. If he only knew what had happened to Kristina, that another dark line had been drawn, he surely wouldn't care about anything else. She decided on simplicity, in case someone else found and read it. *Sorry you're ill, Joel. When you're back — which is now, I guess, as you're reading this — can we talk? It's urgent. Not about what you think. Thank you. Hadley.* She marked it with a kiss, then changed her mind, scribbling it out. She tore another page of her jotter and wrote the whole thing again, in cold, hard capitals this time. She took it to his pigeonhole and tucked it right at the back of the space, between a sheaf of essays and internal mail. Then she did the only other thing she could think of. She went to the Hôtel Le Nouveau Monde.

Chapter 17

"I'd quite given up," Hugo Bézier said, as soon as he saw her.

He gestured to the empty chair across from him, and she hesitated.

"You don't mind?"

"The very opposite," he said.

She slipped into the seat.

"I thought perhaps you had found your man Jacques and run away with him," he said, smiling at her over the top of his coffee cup. "I'm delighted to see that you're here, of course. That you stayed, as I knew you would. And fought, I think, too, for you look tired. How are you, *ma chérie*?"

She pressed her fingers to her eyes and took a breath.

"Hadley, what's wrong?"

"There's been a development," she said, using the police officer's words.

"What kind of a development?"

She stopped before she spoke. She held

the words for a moment longer, and they felt as unreal as ever, as though she was reading aloud a passage from a book in class, or a line from a newspaper. She told him about laying flowers on Rue des Mirages, the appearance of Lisette and their broken exchange and finally her trip to the police station, where the terrible fact was already known, but there was so little promise of progress.

"Everything's changed," said Hadley, "and yet nothing has. How can that be? After the police I wanted to tell someone who would know what to do, someone who'd really care, so I went to see my . . ."

Hugo laid a hand on her arm to still her. "I'm glad you came to me," he said.

"No, I mean . . ." She started to correct him, then stopped. "Yes," she said.

"A hit-and-run, and a self-acknowledged unreliable witness. Good God."

"Lisette was there, but she wasn't there, Hugo. She didn't really see anything, and even if she did, she can't remember. It's useless. I can't believe the police didn't realize there was a car from the beginning. And I can't understand what coward . . ." Her words tailed off.

Hugo pursed his lips, taking in a little air. "Very few of us know how we would react in an extreme situation," he said, evenly.

"You wouldn't stop? If you hit someone? You'd just drive off, as though it never happened?"

"I very much doubt it would be as though it never happened. For anyone. But, me? I can't say. I like to think I'd stop, but how can I say?"

"That's a terrible thing to admit to," Hadley said.

"Better, surely, than not admitting to it?" he countered. "If I know them at all, the police won't be able to find the driver who hit your friend. Forgive me, again, for what you probably see as quite brutal honesty."

"Is this your idea of helping, Hugo?"

He seemed to reset himself. "My apologies," he said. "Now, tell me, things have, of course, changed, and changed significantly, but since we last met, have you made any progress? With finding Jacques? With any of it?"

"I'm stuck. So is Joel. He . . ." She stumbled as she said his name, then righted herself. "He thinks we should stop looking. He said that if Jacques wanted to be found, then he could be. I actually hadn't thought of it like that. I thought it was all one way."

"Joel?"

"My professor. He's been helping me."

"And here I was thinking that I was the only man of distinguished years in your life."

"He's not that old, Hugo," she said.

Hugo straightened his tie at the neck. He coughed stiffly.

"Did you think about an advertisement in the local newspaper, perhaps, appealing for a Jacques to come forward?"

She shook her head, for that felt too dramatic, like an authority's call for information. She imagined her Les Ormes telephone number printed in smudged newsprint and a picture of Kristina, that *last smile* again.

"It would seem like a trick," she said, "as though there was a suspicion that he was involved. So, you think I should carry on, then? That I shouldn't give up on Jacques?"

"Never give up, Hadley. And the police, you feel you've exhausted all avenues with them?"

"For now. And even though they won't admit it I'm afraid they're feeling the same way."

"You mustn't be deterred. I can see your professor's point, of course I can, but that's no reason for you to stop looking for Jacques. He can still come to you, at any moment, that doesn't change. Listen, what would you say if I were to get you a list?"

"What kind of a list?"

"I have a friend in the force still. An old boy, but one of the good ones. I can ask him to generate a list. Young men falling within a certain age, in Geneva, with the first name of Jacques."

She set down her cup with a crack.

"You could get that for me?"

"Yes, I'm sure I could."

"Hugo, could you really do that? Are you . . . Were you . . . a policeman? I thought you said you were a writer."

He laughed, and it was a well-practiced sort of laugh, as though she had told a joke he'd heard a good many times before but never ceased to find amusing.

"Once upon a time, I wrote detective fiction. A good deal of it, too. I always rather enjoyed the research element. I cultivated some great friendships, in the name of authenticity."

"And you know people there still?"

"One or two. Most have gone out to pasture, to the golf fields of the Algarve or the San Diego coast. People say the Swiss don't like to leave Switzerland, but I'd say the opposite for old detectives. Perhaps they've seen too much beneath the perfect surface. Beyond the neutrality." He gave a low chuckle. "Or some have simply died, too, of course. An occupational hazard, for us old-timers."

She knew, without having read a word of his work, that he would have been a good writer. For this much was obvious — he chose what to tell and when to tell it, and by quiet tricks, politely proffered handkerchiefs and offers of assistance, he kept you coming back for more.

"Could you do it?" she said.

"I will certainly try."

He pressed her for any other information that she might have on Jacques, however vague. She saw him write down *under 45, decent job, city dweller, childless* in spidery writing. He told her to come again in a few days.

"Hugo, thank you. Really, that's amazing. I had no idea you could be so . . . helpful."

"I'm rather surprising myself. I'm flexing muscles I haven't used in a long time. Now, we have to begin with the rest."

"What rest?"

"This crime, Hadley. For it is a crime, not an accident, not a careless fall, and solving it, or 'working out what happened that night,' as you said to me in the very beginning, is more important now than ever, *n'est-ce pas?* Listen, no one will ever care about this as much as you do. Every single

278

thing that you can think of, you have to try and do. You and only you."

His voice wavered as he spoke. Hadley saw his dark eyes glisten, and his passion choked her. She glanced away, trying to collect herself.

"I can't think," said Hadley. "I don't know, I mean, what else is there?"

"Go back to Rue des Mirages."

"And do what? Even if I found her again, I don't think Lisette can tell me anything else."

"And you did well, questioning her like that, getting as much truth as she was able to give. Other people might have walked away from someone like her, Hadley, so see, you're already fighting, just like I knew you would. Now listen, she might not have been the only one to see the accident. The police will have gone door to door, but you should do it for yourself. Someone else may remember something. Someone, Hadley, always knows something."

"Can I do that? Can I just go and knock on doors like that?"

"You can do anything you want to. Anything you can think of, you must do."

She thought of asking if he would go with her, this old man who seemed so pin-sharp, who knew exactly how to turn impotence to action, but he hadn't proffered his company, he spoke only of "you" not "we." Hadley thought of Joel and felt a pang of regret. How long would he think the kiss mattered for? Would he be away tomorrow and the next day? Would he find her note, and if he did, would he know how to reach her? She imagined him snarling with regret, pacing in his apartment, a place she had never seen and probably never would. She knew then that she missed him, even if she hadn't known him well enough or long enough. She missed him.

"Hugo," she said, "do you think you'd be willing to come with me? To Rue des Mirages? I'm afraid to do it on my own. I know you probably think that's silly. And my French isn't good enough, either. I wouldn't know what to say or how to say it."

Hugo looked pleased. "I thought you'd never ask," he said.

They walked uphill from the waterfront as tiny snowflakes, light and infrequent, danced in front of them. Hadley watched Hugo as he wiped a solitary bead of sweat from his brow with the tip of his handkerchief, his breath quickening.

"We could have taken a cab, if you'd have preferred," she said.

"No, no, I'm enjoying the walk. I don't commonly come this way, that's all."

"Whereabouts do you live?"

He waved his hand behind them. "Oh, back there somewhere. Nothing extraordinary about it. Now, by my estimation, I believe we are just two streets away. Onward."

Hadley slowed her step to match his, and they came to Rue des Mirages a little after seven o'clock. It looked as ordinary as ever, a street of buildings with weary expressions and closed shutters. There was no startling yellow police tape, no chalked outline. It was as deserted as ever, and there was no sign of Lisette.

"So, this is where it happened," said Hugo, removing his hat and smoothing his hair. "I don't believe I've ever been on Rue des Mirages before. Or perhaps I have, a long time ago, maybe. I tend to move in similar patterns, these days. The same places, the same faces."

"I'm sorry to break your routine."

"You're apologizing? I thought my gratitude was obvious."

Hadley gave a small smile and shrugged. "Okay, so how do we do this? Start at one end and just . . . knock?"

"Nothing else to it," Hugo said.

Together they went from one end of the street to the other. They buzzed every buzzer and knocked every knocker and rapped at every door. Their questions were met with suspicion, concern, contrition and apology, but the answer was always the same. *We only heard the ambulance siren. That was the first we knew.*

They came to the very last door. 148 Rue des Mirages, a top floor apartment of a block that, once inside, had the tight, caustic smell of bleach and cold concrete. A young woman in a silk dress answered, her hair piled on top of her head in an elaborate series of curls and twists. Her eyes bulged with sympathy as she listened, and her head bobbed with agreement. She spoke delicate French with Hugo, and Hadley tried to understand. They talked for some time, and she grew hopeful; but when Hugo shook her hand and gently led Hadley away, she knew she'd been no more helpful than anyone else.

"She said that people use these backstreets as a cut through, a way to avoid the main routes. Rue des Mirages has quieter traffic than most, but it is near the station and there are always trains rattling past. Residents are used to the noise. They turn up their television sets and their music, they

282

don't go running to their windows when they hear something."

"What else did she say?"

"That was it, *plus ou moins*, more or less."

"But you were talking for ages."

"She wanted to know why we were there together, whether we were related. I think she was intrigued. I didn't give very much away."

"There's not much to say, is there?"

"That depends on your point of view."

They reached the bottom of the staircase and stepped out onto the street. A blast of ice-sharp air hit them and Hadley blew on her hands to stay warm. They started walking.

"So, what now?" she said. "Lisette was right, 'nobody saw anything.' She kept saying that, over and over. She meant Kristina, she meant the driver and she meant every other nonexistent witness. The police were right, too. *Salauds.*"

"Hadley!" said Hugo with a shout of laughter. "Your French is astonishing."

"I don't even know what it means. Lisette said it."

Beside her Hugo stumbled suddenly, and Hadley caught his elbow. She took a little of his weight and was surprised at his lightness. He looked so solid.

"Are you all right?" she said.

"Yes, yes, fine," he said, hurriedly. "Just skidded a little, that's all."

"It was exhausting," she said, "going to all those doors. And the walk here was uphill."

A lock of his perfectly groomed hair had come unstuck, and it fell over his forehead, giving him an uncharacteristically bedraggled air. Hadley resisted the urge to pat it back into place.

"I think there must be a little ice underfoot," he said. "Watch your step, too."

"I will," she said, gently.

"You look tired yourself," he said, glancing sideways at her.

"I haven't been sleeping very well. And then this morning . . . it's the shock. None of it feels real."

"You need to look after yourself," said Hugo, stopping. "Do you have friends where you live? Do they care for you?"

"Kristina was my friend," said Hadley. Then, "It's different with the others. We just don't connect in the same way. But they do try. I don't think I make it very easy for them. In fact, I know I don't."

"A boyfriend, then?"

"No boyfriend," she said, shaking her head.

"No?"

Hugo looked at Hadley, and her hand unconsciously went to her chin. She felt the mark of Joel's rough kiss, his stubbled cheek.

"Thank you for today, Hugo, I really appreciate it. You don't have to care this much and yet you do. Why do you?"

"Anyone would."

"They wouldn't, not like this."

"Tomorrow, I'll see about your list. We'll soon know about every Jacques in Geneva. If you haven't got classes, you should go to the police again. Ask them what they're doing next. If you possibly can, make a nuisance of yourself." He stopped, took a breath, then went on, "Then take a photograph of Kristina to the train station. Just in case anyone who works there saw her. It might not give you anything, but why not? Try anyway. You must always try. And, Hadley, it's shut now, but there's that flower shop at the end of this street. Go in and ask if they have a security camera. You never know, they might have picked up something. Now, I think that's about all. You know where I am if you need me. I'd come to all these places with you, only . . ." His voice tapered off.

"I've already dragged you about enough," said Hadley.

"But you'll tell me of your progress?"

"I will. Do I need to say anything to the police? Let them know that we're doing this?"

"Only if you find something."

"Okay. Hugo, I'd never have thought of all those things on my own. I'll do them, every one, no matter how long it takes. I couldn't care less about classes at the moment. Anyway, my professor's off sick."

"Fortunate timing, then."

Her hand went to her chin abstractedly again, and she saw him notice, his eyes widening just the smallest amount. She dropped her hand. She didn't know what else to say, so she wished him good-night and watched him walk slowly away. She hoped he'd take a taxi home, for it was cold out, and for all his bright words, he looked ghost-pale. He turned and they waved at one another. Then Hadley walked the length of Rue des Mirages on her own, her feet crunching on the ice-bitten pavements, listening for cars.

CHAPTER 18

Over the days that followed, Hadley kept away from everyone at Les Ormes. She waved briskly as she passed Chase in the hallway, she didn't answer the door to Jenny's soft *tap-tap* and she slipped out of the kitchen before Bruno could appear with his bottles of wine and eagerness for conversation. They'd all made it clear that they thought her efforts were well intentioned but pointless, and that judgment was too disheartening and infuriating to hear again and again. Once she overheard Bruno and Chase as they sauntered past her room. *How long is she going to be like this? It's tragic but you have to move on,* Chase said. Bruno murmured a reply she couldn't catch, but she was sure it was agreement.

She had been a wanderer before, but the thought of the car charged her grief and made her restless. She began to avoid the kitchen at Les Ormes altogether, skipping breakfast in favor of hastily grabbed cafeteria coffees. She took supper in bland and anonymous department store cafés, glasses of expensive Coca-Cola, triangles of quiche and bitter curls of red lettuce, eaten from a sticky tray. Wherever she went, Hadley watched the seemingly respectable Lausanne people, their smart and formal kisses, their ceremonial *café-croissants* and their impeccable tight-lipped smiles as they bid you *bonne journée,* "have a good day," without any of the American fizzle and pop. Was it one such person, fiddling with their car stereo, turning to answer a child's question, their attention diverted for just one moment from the business of the road, who'd killed Kristina? Such a person who peered from behind their door when faced with the old man and the young girl, and said, *non, monsieur, mademoiselle, je suis desolé, j'ai rien vu; I'm sorry, I saw nothing.*

Meanwhile she saw Kristina everywhere, flitting across the city, just a flash of apple-green satchel and honey hair to mark her; her perfect profile through the window of a bus as it passed in the opposite direction, the delicate V-shape her face made as she turned; fifty yards ahead on the hill up to Les Ormes, her languid, unhurried steps as Hadley bustled breathlessly to catch up.

These apparitions deserted her as soon as she made it to her room. She'd lean against the scratchy wall that once separated them or go on to the balcony and peer around at the dark glass of her windows, and she'd see and feel and hear nothing. It seemed that whenever she tried to conjure Kristina, she was unforthcoming, but when she wasn't looking, Kristina was all that she could see.

She heard nothing from Joel, and his absence haunted her, too, in smaller but no less disturbing ways. Despite the tarnishing effects of uncertainty, the idea of him still burned gem-bright. In the bustle of Place Saint-François Hadley once turned at the sound of an American voice, only to see a bearded, big-bellied man, dressed in mountaineering regalia, swinging his walking poles. He grinned at her and cracked a *bonjour.* And another time, at the entrance to the metro, she glimpsed someone from behind, dark leather, brown-black hair, faded jeans, but it wasn't Joel, even though she followed him three, four, five steps to be sure. If it wasn't for Hugo Bézier, his belief and insistence, sometimes she felt sure that Lausanne would turn to a city of ghosts and take her with it.

Hugo's suggestions gave her focus, and

she took them all on, even though they didn't feel anything like real life. She printed a picture of Kristina and carried it folded in her pocket to show blue-capped railway workers, hoping for a sign of recognition. She traced Kristina's footsteps, out of the back of the station, down the steps, across the alley, around the corner into Rue des Mirages. She walked slowly and deliberately, looking left and right, down at the ground and then up at the sky. She looped back and did it again, faster this time, running like someone who was late for a party. The last snows hadn't settled, and the streets were wet and black. She didn't slip, there was no fall, no car came roaring from behind her, and traces of Kristina were nowhere to be found.

Once she saw Lisette again, hurrying from the station's back exit, but the woman looked right through her as she said her name, not the slightest flutter of recognition crossing her face. *Lisette!* she called again, and a passerby glanced at her sharply, nostrils flaring with disapproval.

Hadley went to the flower shop and inhaled its tough, bright scents all over again. She spoke poor French and tried to mime a security camera, waving her arms as she did so, the sleeve of her jacket streaked with the dark stain of lilies, and was met only with blank looks. She returned to the police station where she asked for information and got nothing. *There is nothing new to report*, she was told, and she shook her head and said all the French words she had written down precisely for the purpose. Leads. Inquiry. Perpetrator. Cold, hard-edged words that she'd found in the dictionary, one finger marking the page as she scribbled them in her notebook. She went back a second time, later on the same day, and a third on the day after that. The sandy-haired policeman became too busy to see her. He said this as his radio crackled at his hip and a fellow officer stood watching, chewing on the rim of a plastic coffee cup.

Nearly five days had passed since she had first gone to the police, and most of them she'd spent in the city. Joel's uncomfortable silence and Caroline Dubois's inquiring eyes had kept her away from the campus. She'd attended a French language class, just for appearance's sake, and checked out three books from the library if anyone cared to look; the kind of track-covering that Hugo approved of. Otherwise she went back, again and again, to the Hôtel Le Nouveau Monde; the café and Hugo sometimes felt like her only consistencies. Every time,

291

Hadley thought of her first night with Kristina in that very spot, soaking in late-summer rain, their cocktail laughter and talk of unimaginable snow. How Kristina had taken her arm, and she'd liked that version of herself, the easy, breezy girl who tripped along by the lakeside in a strange and beautiful city. That was the thing about Kristina, her friendship somehow came with a new you, as well. Hadley had said that to her once, or something like that, and Kristina had laughed sweetly and said "it's nothing to do with me, it's Lausanne," and perhaps that was partly true, for the two had always been perfectly entwined.

Hugo was always waiting for her, in his usual spot, and when all her efforts got her nowhere, he reassured her that it had still been worth it, that trying her best was all that she could do. He listened as she told him about the unforthcoming police, the perplexed but kind lady at the station's ticket office who simply saw Kristina's picture and smiled, saying "belle," the woman in the flower shop who had laughed when she'd asked about *un caméra de sécurité* and said, "who wants to steal flowers?" When she floundered, he tried very hard to right her.

"It's all useless, Hugo, useless," she said

to him. "I'm scrabbling around, trying to change things, and why? Kristina's still gone."

"You don't see the point of it?"

"I just don't know what to do next. Perhaps there isn't a next. Perhaps this is it."

"It's better to have run out of ideas than to have had none at all," he said.

"But they've all been your ideas. Every one."

"Well, you're still here, aren't you? You didn't run away. That counts for an awful lot."

"I would have, if you hadn't stopped me."

"You underestimate yourself. You're a force, Hadley."

"A force? What kind of force? I don't feel like one."

"Life," he said, "you're brim full of it. And that gives you a responsibility, a responsibility to do as much as you can with it. Why don't the young know that? Somebody said as much to me once, and I laughed at them, I pointed to all the books I'd written, my latest fine review. Oh, yes, I thought that all counted for something very grand indeed."

"I don't see how that has anything to do with . . ."

"I'm rambling, I know I am. Forgive me, *ma chérie.* But take the knocks and carry on, because that's what life is. Real life, that is. Now, I have failures of my own to report. Not failures, exactly, but lack of progress . . ."

Caught in her story, he burned brightly. His eyes darted, his mind whirred. He was so easy to talk to that sometimes she even thought of telling him about Joel. Then she remembered the way that he had stared at the mark on her chin, accusingly, almost. When he'd been a student, professors wouldn't have gone about in leather jackets and torn jeans, kissing girls in dark cars. He would probably have said that he was right to stay away, that he was doing her a favor, in the end. Or perhaps she was doing him a disservice, maybe once his life had been full of dash, and Hugo a rakish type, with a sweep of fair hair, dark eyes and a darker mind. She wondered if there had ever been a Madame Bézier, a straw-thin Swiss woman, with a slick of insouciant lipstick and a doll-faced dog tucked under her arm. Perhaps someone who had brought him his *petits* bowl-glasses of cognac as he wrote, stealing the cigar from between his lips before bending for a kiss. For all his consummate good manners and ready geniality, under the veneer a part of him remained that she knew she'd never know. Sometimes

294

she caught him looking at her, and just like the time that he had talked about his puzzles, his planning and plotting, the years fell away; she saw it in his blue-black eyes and all the things he didn't say and some of the things that he did.

"What is it, Hadley?" he said, on the fifth day, as they sat across from one another at their usual table. "There's something you're not telling me."

Hadley didn't think she'd said or done anything to give him such an idea.

"There's nothing. Nothing more, anyway. Have you got anywhere with the list?"

"In the next day or so, I hope. But that wasn't what you were thinking about. What's new?"

"Nothing's new."

"No?"

Hugo was watching her, and his stare was comfortably penetrating. She found she didn't mind his attention.

"Nothing that's relevant, anyway. Nothing that's important, especially not compared to everything else."

"Ah," he said, "then I was right." He ran his fingers over his chin, pointedly, it seemed to Hadley, and in the exact spot where her own had been marked. It had faded to nothing, but that didn't matter to Hugo.

"Right about what?" she said.

"There's a boy, I suppose."

"It's not that simple," she said.

"It ought to be," he said, "for a girl like you. You should have the world at your feet."

Hadley looked down. "I don't even want that," she said. "I just thought someone would be around this week, and they're not. It's my fault, I guess. I made a mistake. Actually, we both made it, but . . . I let it happen. I even wanted it to happen."

"I like a brainteaser," said Hugo, "a plot to unravel, but you, *ma chérie,* are talking in riddles."

"I shouldn't be talking like this at all. Not with Kristina gone. I shouldn't be thinking about anything except her."

"I suppose she knew all about this boy of yours?"

"No, she didn't. I wish she did, but . . . there wasn't much to tell . . . before. In a weird way, it's because of her that anything's happened with him at all. It was starting to feel like a good thing, and then it all went wrong."

Hugo smiled quickly, clicking his tongue. "I see," he said, and as Hadley looked at him, she felt sure suddenly that, without her saying a thing, he did see. She tried to think back to whether she had ever mentioned Joel. *My professor,* said deliberately casually, her cheeks tingeing pink. Nothing escaped Hugo.

"I miss Kristina so much," she said. "Thinking about anything else, feeling anything else, just seems wrong."

Hugo took a cigar from his jacket pocket and ran his fingers the length of it, a touch at once casual and reverential.

"Missing something," he said, "I wonder, is that better than never having had it in the first place? We all know what the poets say, of course."

Hadley met his stare. She held it.

"You're a writer, what do you think?"

"*Was* a writer."

"Was, is . . ."

"Do you know, I couldn't possibly say. The more I think about it, I'm convinced that I saved most of my living for the page."

His voice was a little rackety then, devoid of its usual aplomb, and she wondered for the first time if Hugo was, for all his fine clothes and quick wits, a lonely sort of man.

CHAPTER 19

As she walked back to Les Ormes, a cold rain started to fall, intermittently at first, and then with real intent. She had neglected to bring an umbrella, and her hair grew slick and seal-like. Her beret was folded and forgotten in the depths of her bag. She sneezed, and sneezed again. The back of her throat was starting to burn, and it felt like the beginnings of a cold. When Hadley had finished *A Farewell to Arms,* on a drizzling day back in the English summer, the image of Frederic Henry walking through the rain-soaked streets of Lausanne had stayed with her. For all its desolation, it had a pictur-esque quality, and a sense of *rightness* that had appealed to her. But reality was an aw-ful lot colder, the sad days of real life encouraging no such appreciation. She didn't give Frederic Henry a moment's thought as she cut up some steps and onto a side street. She had inadvertently wandered onto Rue des Mirages again. She began to run, her feet slapping in the puddles. She ran all the way back to Les Ormes.

As she opened her door her phone was ringing. She dashed to it and grabbed the receiver, her mind flashing immediately to Joel.

"Yes, hello?"

"Hadley! We've been so worried. Your dad told me not to fret, but I couldn't help it."

He didn't have her number. Of course it wouldn't be him.

"Hadley, dear, are you all right?"

How do you drop in the news of a death? With Joel and Hugo, she had blurted it right out, as if her words were magnetized, irrepressibly drawn by their respective force fields. Her parents were worriers. For all their puff-cheeked rallying, she knew they'd rather she wasn't so far away. She had kept her postcards home warm and jolly, conjuring a world of Twenties-style pleasure-seekers, tempered with honest graft in the university library. If they thought she'd flown their nest, then she'd wanted them at least to think that her trajectory was smooth.

"I'm so sorry, Mum," she said. "I kept meaning to phone, and then something always happened."

"You're busy, of course you're busy, that's wonderful and how it should be, you don't want to bother with us. But a quick call now and again . . ."

"I know . . ."

"And your birthday, we never did hear from you after your evening out. Did you all have a lovely time? It sounds so glamorous, Hadley, a birthday in Switzerland."

She felt her throat tightening and worried that when she spoke it'd be with a croak. She willed her mum to keep talking.

"We've been reading about all the snow you've had. All across Europe, it said. I expect you've been out playing in it. Or are you too old for all that? Here, have a word with your dad. He's snorting in my ear like an old dog, bless him. He's been desperate to hear from you. Sammy's at school, he'll be cross I rang without him, but I couldn't wait a minute longer."

There was a small ruckus on the line as her mum passed over the phone. Hadley heard her dad settling himself on the stool in the hallway. Hadley knew then that she wouldn't be telling them anything about Kristina, not this time. Instead, they talked of a goose for Christmas in place of the usual turkey, and she said that maybe, just maybe, she'd be persuaded to go with her mum to midnight mass, for once.

"Tickle Sam from me," she said, "right under his arms where he hates it. And give him a kiss. Tell him . . . tell him I miss him."

Hadley hung up then, leaving them excited and counting down the remaining three weeks before the break. She didn't want to tell them lies, but nor did she think she could manage the truth. Their sympathy, sent down the line and from miles away, would batter her heart. And when they asked her if she wanted to come home, as they inevitably would, she worried she'd fall apart, burst at the seams, and forget everything except the words *yes, please yes.*

Perhaps it was due to the soaking she had received, or her ceaseless tramping about the city, but Hadley developed a cold that sent her to bed for the rest of the week. She had all the usual afflictions, a rasping throat and an unstoppably runny nose, but she was also haunted by headaches and a listless feeling that she couldn't shift. Jenny brought a stack of English magazines to Hadley's door, much-thumbed, dog-eared copies that carried with them wafts of the doctor's surgery. She never stayed long, for Hadley, with her flushed cheeks and rumpled pajamas, looked too contagious for company. Jenny would back away, depositing her offering and smiling her dimpled smile as she made for the door.

She fell in and out of sleep, and unsettling dreams pushed up from the inside. Kristina and Joel had appeared together in her dreams before, when Joel had been no more than a silver-tongued stranger and Kristina simply held the sparkling promise of a new friend. In her illness, Hadley dreamed about them both again, and for all the intimacies of their shared reality, in her dreams they were indistinct and barely recognizable. Kristina was wispily beautiful but pale and fading, and Hadley couldn't focus on her; it was as though every time she looked in her direction, she had the sensation that she was falling into a faint. There was no solace in this glimpse of her, no otherworldly re-assurance, just an emptying sense of disloca-tion. Joel was there, but he offered no comfort, no company; instead, he turned his back and refused to meet her eye. In the dream it wasn't clear if they'd ever kissed. She didn't think they had, but the longing she felt as she pulled at his back, willing him to face her, was unpredictable, a base-less, rabid want. Jacques was there, too, but just in spirit, a ghost-voice that taunted from the sidelines. Only Hugo was clear and sharp-edged. Whenever Hadley turned, he was at her shoulder, stepping back as neatly as a dancer, smiling kindly but always maintaining his distance. They moved in quick patterns, the five of them, like in an amateur magician's game of cups where the coin never reveals itself and the truth remains unknown.

The residue of her dream lingered into the following morning. She awoke exhausted, feeling as if she hadn't slept at all, and cold with the knowledge that Kristina was gone and never coming back. For all her moonstruck glimpses, she had never felt more out of reach. Hadley tried to concentrate on real, so-solid things, to wash away the uncertainties of the night. Hugo would likely have the list by now, and he would be wondering where she was. And she had missed another of Joel's lectures. She wondered if he would have turned up as usual, sauntering to the front of the class and spreading his arms in that way he had, a grin of welcome on his face. Perhaps he would have noted her absence and read too much into it, faltering in his delivery or losing his place in his notes, doubling his smile for cover. She hadn't meant to stay away as long as she had, but he didn't know that. Perhaps, in a very different way, he was disappearing, too, slipping away from her, a little more day by day.

Just as the interminable afternoon was finally rolling toward evening, there was a tap at her door. She heard a man's voice call out *Hadley*? Because she had been thinking about him, and really, when she thought about it later, that was all it was, she felt sure, beyond any clouding doubt, that it would be Joel. Her heart leaped in her chest. She looked down at her faded pajamas, raked her hand through her limp hair. She didn't dare face a mirror for she knew a washed-out version of herself would be staring back, eyes bleary, a feverish speckle to her cheeks.

"I'm in bed," she called out. "I look awful. You can come in, but only if you shut your eyes."

She heard the door open, and the squeak of a shoe. She tried to arrange herself more comfortably on her pillows. She threw a wad of balled-up tissues under the bed. He stepped around the corner and into her room.

He had his eyes closed, just as she'd asked. His long lashes were dark against his olive skin, and his curly hair was pulled back into a half ponytail. He was holding a bunch of yellow tulips, his lips parted in a foolish sort of smile. There had been no sly remarks from Chase, no airy droppings of his name by Loretta. *Luca*. Their kisses in the snow-filled street, their hot tangle in the cavern bar, his fingers teasing the edges of her dress; she realized she hadn't given him a moment's thought; it had all been wiped out by everything that had happened since.

"I wanted to come sooner, but Loretta said it wasn't a good idea," he said. "And then I came, anyway, and knocked, but you were never here. Then I saw Bruno in the city, and he said you were ill, so I knew I had to come."

He kept his eyes closed as he spoke. Hadley stared at him and realized he looked awkward by day. She remembered how he'd seemed so slick and self-assured before, and how she had let him kiss her, despite herself. She didn't even know what she'd thought of him that night, if she'd liked him even a little bit. It was horrible, not to be the person that someone else wanted.

"Luca, you can open your eyes," she said. "It's okay."

He opened them and smiled at her. "Hello, Hadley," he said. "Things have been difficult up here for you all, haven't they? I should have come before. I'm sorry. I suppose I didn't know if you wanted to see me. You look beautiful, by the way. *Bella*."

"You're a good liar," she said. "I mean, about looking okay, not the rest of it. But thanks. Thanks for, well, both things."

"Is it all right that I'm here?"

"Of course," said Hadley, "I mean, I don't recommend you stay long. I'm probably still contagious, you'll catch something, for sure. If you go down the hall, I'm sure Bruno's about. He's always ready for company."

"I don't want to see Bruno."

"Oh, okay." Hadley shifted on her pillows and folded her arms across her chest. "But perhaps we should go into the kitchen. I could make us some tea. Maybe Jenny's around, she always has a good stash of biscuits."

"I'm not interested in Jenny and her biscuits."

"You would if you knew what she had. She gets them sent from England, pink wafers and marshmallow things and all sorts." She realized she was gabbling and slowed down. "Actually I think it'd do me good to stretch my legs. I haven't left this room in days. Shall we go and see if anyone's about?"

"I came to see you, Hadley. You and only you. Ever since your birthday I've been thinking about you."

"Oh."

"Hadley, I . . ."

She interrupted him. "It was a weird night, Luca. Nothing ran properly. Kristina should have been there and she wasn't. I had too much to drink, and I really wasn't myself. I'm still not. Nothing felt right then, and nothing feels right now. I'm sorry. I know that's not what you want to hear."

"You're upset about the accident, Loretta and Bruno told me. Of course, everyone is. And I know you probably can't separate the two events in your head, you know, the night that we were having, Hadley, and then what happened to Kristina. That's okay, I understand that. But I really like you, *bella*. I'd like to make you happy."

Hadley shook her head and pulled the sheet closer to her chin. She wanted him to leave and take his bouquet with him. Her head soared to an ache.

"You're really kind, Luca, you are, but I feel like I gave you the wrong idea. Before, definitely before, and now, too. To be honest, when you knocked on the door, I only said come in because I thought you were someone else," she said. "I'm sorry."

"You didn't mind who I was on your birthday," he said. "You liked me then." ·

"We were all drunk, Luca, you know we were."

"Not that drunk. And I don't think you

can kiss someone and then just forget about it."

"Well, I've had a lot on my mind since then," she said. She felt tired suddenly. She'd given him a chance to exit gracefully and he hadn't taken it. "And anyway," she said, quietly but distinctly, "there's someone else."

"Who?"

"Nothing's really happened with them but I want it to. That's all that matters. I want it with someone else, Luca. I'm sorry."

He laid the bouquet down on Hadley's bedside table, beside her empty bottles of water and discarded magazines and box of spilling tissues.

"I don't care about anyone else," he said. "A kiss is always the start of something."

"Not always. Sometimes it's the end."

He glared down at her, his cheeks reddening. "I don't give up that easily," he said.

He banged the door behind him on his way out. Hadley rolled over onto her side and faced the wall. She ran her finger over the whitewashed concrete. They couldn't both be right, Luca and her, but they had to be, otherwise it wouldn't work. None of it would work. In the end it was Luca's words that she held on to, as she drifted into an early night's sleep. *A kiss is always the start of something.* A convenient fragment that threaded its way through her dreams. Breaking and coming together again, like the flimsiest of promises.

CHAPTER 20

Anyone who dreams of a picture-book winter should spend December in Switzerland. In Lausanne's old town, felt-hatted merchants in leather aprons sold brown paper bags of hot chestnuts and cups of spiced wine. Sturdy, apple-cheeked men and women set up their tables in the Place de la Palud, laying out discs of hard cheese and bouquets of lavender. At nightfall, the frost-licked shopping streets were swept with quiet, perhaps just a blast of music as the door of a cavern bar was pulled open by the wind, or the click of an elderly man's tongue as he politely waited for his dog to do his nighttime business. Christmas was approaching, and Lausanne glittered, serenely, quietly.

By the weekend, Hadley was feeling better. She went out onto her balcony for the first time in days and stood in the biting morning air, her dressing gown wrapped around her, her slippered feet sticky on the iced floor. She looked out over the December city. It was a day for leaving two crisp trails of footsteps, for drinking rum-dipped hot chocolate in the corner of a café, for laughing by the water and your breath coming in white puffs. Whatever Joel said, it was impossible to imagine a new day without thinking about how it ought to have been Kristina's, too.

She had woken with resolution. After the weekend she would go and find him. She would say what she had done and where she had been, and how she had tried her best even though it hadn't been good enough. She would slot back into his class, fall back into his world of Hemingway, a place of promise and hope and heartbreak. If he wanted to forget whatever else had passed between them, then that would be fine, because he was part of her Lausanne life and she didn't want to lose him, as well. That would be Monday, and every day thereafter, but first there was Hugo Bézier and his Jacques list. She had made resolutions about that, too. It would be her last effort. Everything else had yielded nothing, and her amateur detective work, her creased photographs and tapping at the doors of strangers, all that was over now, whatever

Hugo said, and whatever passions he tried to stir in her. Perhaps there would be twenty names on the list, or a hundred, but there couldn't be too many more, surely. Jacques could be within her reach. She would do this useful, vital thing, for Kristina and for him, and then carry on. Not quite as she was before, but moving forward, step by step.

Hadley smiled involuntarily as she glimpsed Hugo at his usual table, and he looked up and caught it. There was reassurance in the stability of his patterns. He rose from his seat to kiss her on both cheeks, and there was something courtly in the gesture. She saw the corner of his lip twitch with a smile as he drew back from her and sat down again.

"I'm sorry I've only come now," she said. "I was ill."

"You do have that look of one who is recently well again," Hugo said, his head tipped to one side. "You look newly washed."

She smiled. "I feel much better. So, Hugo, did you manage to get the list?"

"They're terrible things, these winter colds. At my age, they can be the death of you. Literally. I wonder if I'm not placing myself in extraordinary peril by taking coffee with you."

"I don't have to stay," she said. "If you give me the list I can take my vile body away and you'll be quite safe again."

"You're quoting Evelyn Waugh," he said, gleefully.

"Well?"

"Well." He removed the cloth napkin from his lap and folded it carefully back into a square. "I'm afraid it's not quite what we were hoping for."

"How could it not be?"

The waiter came and poured coffee from a silver pot. Hugo waited until he had finished. Hadley closed her hands around her cup and waited, too. Eventually he spoke.

"Jacques, it turns out, is a common name in this part of the world, but then perhaps I should have warned you of that possibility. I was naive, too, and there's no excuse for that."

"I thought it would be," she said. "But you don't understand, Hugo, to have anything at all is great. I've been groping in the dark. I'd stopped trying."

"Even with your benevolent professor's help?" he said, and there was extra emphasis on the word *professor,* she was sure of it.

Hadley ignored him. "Well, here it is, then," he said.

He passed her a wad of paper, every page packed with minute type. Her eyes ran over it, attempting to make sense of the continuous flow of information.

"It's how it comes from the computer," said Hugo. "Mind-boggling, isn't it?"

She turned the pages and saw *Jacques Jacques Jacques* again and again. *Jacques Legrand. Jacques Arnaud. Jacques Petit.*

"There are hundreds of them," she said, "thousands, even."

"If you only had a surname . . ."

"If I had a surname I wouldn't need the list at all."

"That's quite right."

"All I'd have needed was the phone book, or the internet, or . . . it would have been easy. So easy."

She hung her head despondently, all of her morning buoyancy disappearing.

"In grief . . ." Hugo began, and then pulled back. "We never know how we'll react. You wanted very badly to do something. To be helpful. You've done everything that you possibly could."

Hadley looked up at him, and her cheeks were flushed red.

"And none of it was enough," she said,

"was it?"

"Shall we step outside?" said Hugo. "A little air will help."

They sat on one of benches by the water, as in front of them a circle of ducks pecked at the lake's edge. Hugo seemed slighter tucked inside his woolen coat; at his neck his tartan scarf was folded just so. He wore his fedora, and the tips of his shoes shone with new polish. Sitting beside him she suddenly wanted to lean and rest her head on his shoulder, as she had done with Joel that one time in his office. It was a different feeling, but in some ways it was the same, that need for touch, for something solid amid the uncertainty. She wouldn't have minded if Hugo's gnarled hand came down and for a moment patted her knee, a small gesture of comfort. In her hands she held the wad of paper printed all over with *Jacques Jacques Jacques.*

"I should just toss it in the lake," she said, waving the pages, "watch it sink. Joel said we should stop looking, and I should have listened. We spent hours, you know, looking in phone books and on the internet, even just pounding the streets of Geneva. Stupid, pointless hours."

"Joel? Oh, your professor again. Well, the very fact that he was willing to go along with

315

it all should be a comfort," Hugo said. "It can't have been time entirely wasted."

Hadley glanced across at him, and there was that wry smile creasing his lips. She pretended not to have seen it.

"But you helped, too," she said. "We never needed the list, did we? You must have known it would be a mile long. Was that just 'going along with it,' as well?"

"I think not. And the fact remains, you don't know if Jacques knows, and you feel bad about that."

"Yes, I do. We're connected, we are, even if he doesn't know it. Kristina mattered to both of us, and that should count for something."

"Well, I feel bad about you feeling bad."

"Hugo, why do you even care so much?"

"Why does your professor care?"

"I'm not sure he does anymore. But he understands what it's like to lose someone."

"Ah. That."

"Don't you?"

Hugo furrowed his brow. His face was lined but only barely. He had the appearance of polished wood, and an expression that was just as impervious.

"I've written loss, over and over. It's a feature of every one of my books, I suppose.

But do I understand it? No. I can't claim that."

They both sat quietly, their separate minds turning as they looked out over the water and across to France. After a while Hadley spoke, and her voice sounded thin and fragmented.

"Hugo, listen, you've already helped me more than you'll ever know. And we've tried everything, we really have. I don't see what else we could have done. The police say the case is still open, so there's still a chance they'll turn something up, isn't there? I just think that, maybe, I should leave things now. It's time."

"With Jacques? Or your professor?"

"Why do you keep talking about my professor?"

"Because I distrust his motives, of course. I'm suspicious, Hadley. I expect he's terribly handsome? It's an age-old story. Has he tried to get you into bed yet?"

Despite his words, his tone remained one of airy detachment. She moved away from him on the bench.

"Is your life so dull, Hugo, that you have to make up stories all the time? Oh, I'm forgetting, that's your job. Or was, anyway. You've been enjoying all this, haven't you? The twists and turns of an unsolvable case.

I suppose you go home and write it up afterward."

"I haven't written in many years, Hadley. I gave it up long ago."

"Yet you can't seem to stop yourself. You go on about Joel's ulterior motives, but what about yours?"

"I have none."

"Anyway, I'm done now. I'm done with looking for Jacques, and I'm done with trying to make sense of something that is, in the end, senseless. The police know it, Joel knows it, yes, that's right, my *professor,* and now I do, too. *C'est fini.*" Hadley swept her hand, taking in the hotel, the lake, the far-off mountains and the tips of Hugo's shined shoes. "How's that for drama? Is that brightening your day?"

She watched him stand up, and his arms were loose by his sides. The punch had gone from him.

"Whenever I say goodbye to you, I wonder if I'll ever see you again," he said. "Don't look at me like that. I'm not that old, and I'm not that morbid, but the grace of your company has always felt like borrowed time. I could be wrong, of course, I often have been, but today feels rather like the end of our road."

"Are you breaking up with me, Hugo?"

she said, and she meant it as a joke but it came out tight-lipped.

"Our mutual desire for truth is perhaps waning," he said.

"I do want the truth," she shot back. "But you know what, I want a different kind of truth. I want to feel something different. Something that isn't sad, or bad, or hopeless."

"I wish you luck with that, too, Hadley."

He doffed his hat and walked away before she could reply. His gait was slightly stiff. She thought she heard him whistling, but she might have been imagining it.

The Café Grand was different from the composure of the Hôtel Le Nouveau Monde. The room was packed and conversation roared. Fur coats were slung over the backs of chairs with their hems trailing, and cutlery clattered against china. There was the fizz and pop of pouring wine and sparkly drinks as waiters performed a high-speed dance between the tables, silver trays held high above their heads. Bruno and Loretta were tucked in a corner table by the window, leaning toward one another with their noses touching. Hadley made her way toward them.

On her way out of Les Ormes that morning, she had run into them, and Bruno had asked her to join them for a drink. They had been planning to spend the day shopping, and he'd clasped his palms together pleadingly and said, *Please, dear God, give us a break from the shops, Hadley.* She had been noncommittal, but after her exchange with Hugo, a meeting that had left her deflated for reasons that had nothing to do with the failed list, the thought of their company was appealing. She wouldn't tell Bruno and Loretta what she had been doing recently, and she knew that in their desire for easy pleasure, they wouldn't ask. Instead, she would smile and drink glasses of whatever wine Bruno had chosen, and it would feel good to lose her edges, let the afternoon blur into the evening in a way that she hadn't done in ages. Loretta would be wearing something pretty, so she'd remark on it. And perhaps Luca's name would only come up fleetingly; she'd make sure she adjusted her features to appear contrite as she said, *he's just not right for me.*

As she approached their table, she summoned a "hello," and they both turned their heads and beamed at her.

"Hadley! You came! Let me get you a seat."

Bruno darted up and went in search of a

third chair.

"Hadley, sit down," said Loretta, "take Bruno's chair. How are you? You don't look so well. Is it your cold still? Poor thing."

It was hot in the room, and she set about removing her hat and scarf and gloves, saying that she was fine, *great*, in fact. Bruno came back with a chair held high over his head, making a show of not hitting people with it, muttering *scusi, scusi*. They huddled at a table that was really meant for two. Bruno poured the last of the Prosecco into Hadley's glass, then looked around for a waiter to order another bottle. Loretta managed it with just the tip of her chin and a quick nod.

It was then that Hadley saw Joel Wilson. He was sitting at the far side of the room, just by the door. She had walked past him just moments ago, without even noticing. His leather jacket hung from his chair, and he was sitting forward, his elbows on the table, reading a newspaper. He was on his own, and despite his distance and posture of repose, she felt his blast of energy from across the room. Hadley stared at him. She hadn't seen Joel in over a week, and yet she felt an absurd sense of surprise that he looked just the same. It was almost as if she could saunter up and throw a breezy "hi," just as she used to do. But something inside her tugged, and she felt her cheeks explode with color; she had been deceiving herself if she thought she could go back to how things were before. Desire didn't let you off that easily. She watched him as he folded his paper, tucked it under his arm and slung his jacket over his shoulder. She saw his face then; his forehead was lined and his mouth set hard. He had what looked like a smear of gray newsprint on his cheek. She watched him go toward the door and throw it open, disappearing into the Lausanne afternoon.

"Hadley? Did you hear any of that?" said Bruno, snappily.

Loretta was watching her, her wide eyes agog with questions.

"See someone you recognize?" she said.

"Yes," said Hadley, "yes, I did. Sorry, give me a minute, I just need to catch them. I'll be right back."

She was out of her chair and hurrying across the room without another thought. She burst onto the street, her eyes searching left and right, and almost fell into him. Joel was standing just outside, a cigarette between his lips, a struck match in his hand.

"Hadley," he said, his voice lifted with surprise.

She realized that she didn't know what to

say. Between his fingers the match carried on burning. He dropped it to the floor and stamped on it. He took the cigarette from his lips. He shook his head.

"Were you in there the whole time?" he said.

"No, I just arrived. I only saw you as you were leaving. Why were you leaving?"

"Because I finished my coffee."

"Not because of me?"

"Hadley, I didn't even see you. In fact, I haven't seen you in nine days. No, ten. Where have you been? I was worried."

"You were?"

"Of course I was. I wondered if you'd got the same bug as me, but then Caroline said she saw you and you looked fine."

"I was ill," said Hadley, "but a cold, nothing to do with any bad Chinese food."

"Serves me right for taking you there, doesn't it? But no one has a cold for ten days straight. Where were you?"

"I had some things to do," Hadley said. They stepped aside as a group left the café, girls and boys with bright cheeks and dark coats, laughing and linking arms. Hadley watched them go, then spoke again. "I did try and find you, Joel. Everything got turned upside down. I heard about Kristina and the car and I had to see you, I wanted to see you so badly, but you weren't there."

"What about Kristina and a car?"

"You don't know? I thought you knew. I thought everybody knew. It was in the paper. I left you a note, in your pigeonhole."

"I didn't see it, I hardly ever look in there. You must know that I'd never ignore a note from you. Hadley, tell me, I don't know."

Some part of her wilted with relief. He set a hand on each of her shoulders, steadying her as she talked. She told him everything — Hugo, Lisette, her search, the door-knocking all along the street, and for all of it Kristina still gone. She felt the press of every single one of his fingers.

"Hadley," he said, "Hadley, Hadley. I don't know what to say."

"I didn't think it could get any worse, and then it did."

"I never would have wanted to leave you alone with that. Why didn't you come and find me again? Why didn't you try? You weren't in class, I didn't know what to think."

"I thought you didn't want to see me," she said, "not after Geneva."

"I thought it was *you* who didn't want to see me," he said. "Damn it, Hadley, what a mess. I handled it so badly. I'm sorry. For all of it. What about the police? I expect they say there's nothing they can do?"

"I thought they'd given up without really trying, but then I tried and didn't get anywhere, either. Joel, how can someone do that? Just drive on? And then just carry on with life, as if nothing happened?"

"If we think about it we'll go crazy," he said, and she heard the "we" and felt its comfort and knew how much she'd missed it. He took his hands from her shoulders and folded his arms across his chest. He looked bigger then, like an American foot-baller barreling forward as frill-skirted girls leaped in the stands. "In fact, I don't know how you haven't gone crazy," he said.

"I found an unexpected friend."

"You did? Look, Hadley, I hate to do this, but I'm late for someone. Maybe we could talk about all this later? Will you call me?"

"There's nothing more to be said, not about this. I want to talk about other things. Happy things."

"So, call me. Call me for that, too."

"I don't have your number."

"I never gave it to you?" He gave her a rueful smile. "That was careless of me."

He took out a pen from his pocket and went to tear a corner off his newspaper. Hadley held out her hand, palm upward.

"Write it on me," she said.

She smiled as she spoke, for it didn't sound much like her at all. It was a bolder, brighter Hadley. It was, she thought later, more like Kristina than her. Joel took her hand, and he wrote slowly, the pen tickling her palm. When he'd finished, she folded her fingers over it.

"I will call, you know," she said.

"I hope you do."

She tapped her cheek with her finger. "You've a mark here. Newsprint."

He found the spot and wiped it away. He studied the tips of his fingers, and then looked back at her. He smiled, absently.

"Gone?"

"Gone. Joel . . ."

"Yeah?"

"It's felt strange, not seeing you. I mean, everything's felt strange lately, but . . . that's been part of it. I don't know if that's right or wrong."

Joel didn't look to see if anyone was watching. He didn't glance down the street, to the left and to the right, or through the windows of the Café Grand. He simply leaned forward and kissed her. If anyone had seen, perhaps it would have appeared as simply a quick peck, their lips meeting but only just. Hadley, however, felt the heat, and the firm press, and then the strength of his fingers as they curled around her shoulders. She knew then that the kiss in the car wasn't the end of something. It was, perhaps just as Luca had said, only the beginning.

Back inside the café Hadley worked hard to keep her features still. She'd slipped between the tables, her feet barely touching the ground.

"Where did you go?" cried Loretta.

"Sorry," she said, laughing in a gulp, "sorry. I had to see someone. Now, Bruno, what were you saying? You sounded like you had a fantastic piece of gossip." She shuffled in close to them and gave them all of her attention. Their indignant faces softened.

"Only that I think angelic Jenny and our American friend Chase are up to no good. Nothing interesting or anything," said Bruno, pouting.

"What about Jenny's boyfriend?" asked Hadley.

Loretta shook her head. "Over, I think, and you've never seen anyone look less sad."

The waiter came and recharged their glasses. Hadley watched the bubbles explode in her flute, and let Bruno and Loretta run on, happy that the conversation had turned away from her. They spent the rest of the afternoon drinking Prosecco, Bruno and

Loretta reveling in speculation over other people's love lives. Hadley sat with one hand resting on her knee, her fingers curled around Joel's carefully inked telephone number. She drifted on a tide of amber fizz and did a passable impression of someone who cared about the same things as them. She smiled in almost all of the right places.

CHAPTER 21

She rang him in the early evening, just as the kitchen at Les Ormes was humming with activity. Chase and Jenny were absorbed in the making of macaroni and cheese, and Hadley spied their romance for herself then; their close-bobbing heads, their secret smiles. Without anyone really noticing, she slipped away to call Joel Wilson. The numbers on her palm were precise and deliberate. She traced their shape with her finger and dialed his number. It rang and rang, and just when she thought she'd have to leave a stumbling message, he answered.

"Joel Wilson."

He spoke quickly and abruptly. It almost threw her off.

"Oh, hi. You said to call. It's Hadley."

"Hadley! Hadley, Hadley. Yes, I did."

"So . . . I'm calling."

"Yes, you are. Thank you. Look, I'm just going to come right out and say it. I haven't been very professional, and I apologize for that."

"I never asked for *professional*."

"It's implicit. A student-teacher relationship has to be professional. There's a code, something I probably signed, along the way. Everybody else, in this place, is the very model of *professional*."

"And they gave Kristina one minute in class, and then they moved on. Didn't you tell me that? I think I prefer unprofessional, don't you?"

There was silence on the line.

"Joel?"

"The problem is, Hadley," he said, in a quieter voice that made him sound as though he was speaking from a long way away, the heights of the ice-white peaks or the bottom of the searing-cold lake, "I'm not normally like this. It's a strange version of me, this me in Switzerland. I seem to have come here and turned in to somebody else." He hesitated, then said, "I don't normally tell anybody anything, and I seem to be telling you everything."

"But you can," she said.

"No, I can't. It's not very smart, none of it's very smart."

"Well, I've got something I have to tell you, so please, listen. Hugo made me realize it. The Jacques hunt, me roping you into it all, dragging you to Geneva. Even yesterday, making all the right noises when I said I'd done all that door-knocking, all that retracing of footsteps. I'm sure you thought it was all pointless. I'm sure you were just being kind, pretending that any of it was a good idea. But then I realized something else. Maybe there's another reason why you wanted to help me with all this."

"What do you mean? What kind of reason?"

"Well . . . maybe you like me. Maybe you like spending time with me. Maybe that was why we went to Geneva. Maybe it's complicated, but, also, maybe it's really simple."

He didn't say anything.

"Joel?"

He still didn't say anything, so she went on. "It's okay, you don't have to answer. I don't really know what I feel about anything at the moment, but you, and the way you are with me, I like it. I know that much. And I think you like it, too."

"Is that what you think, Hadley?"

"Well, don't you?"

He laughed then, a great eruption. Something swelled inside of her, and she clamped her teeth to ride it out.

"Why are you laughing?"

"It's laugh or cry," he said.

"What?"

"Am I that obvious?" His voice was still thickened with mirth. "I thought I was being a little cooler than that. No, I guess two kisses gives it away." She started to laugh, too, then, a lighter, uneasy sound beneath his far deeper one. "Oh, God, Hadley, if you knew what was good for you, you'd walk away now. Really you would."

"Maybe I don't want what's good for me."

"You don't know what you're saying."

"I do. For once, I really do."

"This is your chance. I'm serious, you should take it. Hang up on me now. Find yourself a Swiss boy, with neat hair and good shoes and the right manners. It's not too late for that."

"I think it probably is," she said.

"You're too nice a girl for this."

"I'm not. Or, I don't want to be. Nice doesn't count for anything. Joel, these past few weeks, everything's come crashing down. But you're still here."

He seemed to disappear and then come back. He spoke slowly.

"So, you're telling me you want to do this?"

"I want to do this."

"Whatever 'this' turns out to be . . ."

"Yes."

"No one can ever know," he said, and he sounded as if he was talking to himself as much as to her.

"No," she said. "But we will, won't we?"

"Yes," he said, "and that's all that ever matters."

There was no setting up of their next meeting; he'd just said, *Good night, Hadley, try and sleep well,* as if they both had a big day ahead of them. The next morning on campus she inexplicably found herself avoiding the English department. She took a table in the library's Natural History section, by the books on rock formations and alpine flora. She had over a week of catching up to do, and she hid behind a stack of books and papers, ploughing through all that she'd missed. When she returned to Les Ormes in the evening, her cheeks drawn pink by her fast climb up the hill, there was a note waiting in her mailbox. It bore no stamp; perhaps he had slipped in with a hat pulled low over his eyes, or handed it to a passing student with a muffled remark about news from home or a graded paper. Either way, it lay in her mailbox, a page torn from a jotter and slipped into an envelope, with the quick-dashed handwriting that she recognized from the margins of her essays.

New Year's. It needs to be marked and I'd like you to mark it with me. Skiing, then?

Her first thought was that he'd sent it to her by mistake. That it was intended for a friend back home or a colleague from the department, deposited in her mailbox in error. And then she knew. They had said that they were doing this, whatever *this* was. Maybe *this* meant a trip into the mountains. Perhaps he'd remembered what she'd told him on her birthday. That Kristina had been planning to teach her. And what had been her words, as she'd sat across from him in the cafeteria, her legs crossed self-consciously, as somewhere behind them a girl had exploded with sudden laughter? *Speed,* she'd said. *Danger.* She only remembered afterward, when she was trying to fall asleep and failing, that it was Joel who'd talked like this, that they hadn't been her words at all. But she'd nodded, agreeing, because he was right. It was exactly what she wanted.

CHAPTER 22

There was less than two weeks left of term, and Christmas was everywhere. At Les Ormes, doors banged late into the night, and small-hours revelers giggled in the corridors. One morning a raggedy tree appeared in the foyer, as if by flat magic, its silver-gray plastic arms bent by gaudy baubles. Kitchens were strung with fairy lights and looping paper chains. Hadley had gone in one night and discovered Jenny and Loretta busy at the table cutting out paper stars. Chase was balancing on a chair, his T-shirt riding up as he stretched to fasten tangled lengths of tinsel to odd hooks and cupboard corners. Bruno was stirring a pan of mulled wine and cramming cinnamon biscuits in his mouth. He ladled out a sloppy serving and passed it to her, and she joined their uncharacteristically familial scene, realizing it was the first evening that they'd all spent together in weeks. She also realized that she remembered how to fold and snip paper to make a string of cutout figures, rows of girls and boys holding hands. She concentrated on the task, sipping the sweet, warm wine and listening to the aimless talk of the others. Chase nudged her with his elbow.

"Going home for Christmas, Hadley?"

Chase had seemed to lose his barbed edges lately, and Hadley preferred this softer version of him.

"My mum and dad can't wait," she said. "What about you? Back to the States?"

He nodded. "I wouldn't mind staying here, seeing a bit more of Europe, just hanging out, but there's no way my mom would let that happen. It's home to New Jersey, and my kid brothers and sisters. And I still don't have plans for New Year's, there's something wrong about that. I think my friends have forgotten I even exist."

"No kisses for you at midnight, then," said Jenny, licking the edges of a blue-tipped paper chain. "That's a shame. What about you, Hadley? Are you meeting up with university friends?"

There were a few ways to answer, and none was quite the truth, but she wanted to run close to it. She wanted to feel the words and hear how they sounded.

"I'll be back here, actually," she said. "I'm going skiing for a few days."

"Oh, wonderful! Who with?" piped Loretta. "Luca's parents have an apartment in Cortina."

"It's not with Luca," she said, quickly. "Just some Swiss friends."

"Have you got Swiss friends, Hadley?" said Jenny. "I haven't so much as talked to anyone who actually comes from Lausanne. There's a guy from Zurich in my class but he's kind of weird."

"A couple," she said, cautiously, "not many."

"A guy?" said Loretta, twinkling at Hadley.

"Maybe," she said. "Anyway, it's not definite yet, it's just an idea."

"Hadley!" Jenny gasped. "You're such a dark horse! Don't hold out on us . . . who is he?"

"He's no one yet," she said. "It's only the beginning. Honestly, there's nothing to say. If there is, I'll tell you. I promise."

"That's a promise that won't be kept," said Chase.

"Oh, and why?" Hadley said.

"Girls love secrets," he said, shrugging. "You and Kristina were always whispering together."

"We weren't whispering. We were talking to each other. That's what people do."

"That secret boyfriend of hers," piped up Jenny, "I just think it's really strange he never came here, after everything that happened."

"It's really not that strange when you think about it," said Hadley quickly. "He was nothing to do with us."

"Not even you?" said Jenny.

"Not even me. Chase, Jenny, come on, do you really want to talk about this now? You don't know anything about it. Neither do I, barely, and that's the sorry truth."

"I actually didn't mean to make it about Kristina," said Chase. "Just girls and their secrets, that's all."

"It's okay. It's fine." Hadley picked up one of the paper stars and turned its edges. "She'd have loved this, you know. Not the talking about her bit, but all the Christmassy things. She'd have loved it."

She could picture Kristina at the table with them, sipping from her cup of wine, cutting love hearts to hang on the kitchen cupboards. Or could she? More likely she would have blasted in, her cheeks kissed pink, just as they were all thinking of going to bed. And Hadley knew she'd have stayed up with her, stifling a yawn, wanting to hear another Jacques story. There would have been squares of silver-wrapped chocolate and whispers, their laughter muffled as someone passed in the corridor. Kristina was the only person in the world that she wanted to tell about Joel.

"Hadley," said Jenny, leaning across and squeezing her hand, "I think it's great if you've got a boyfriend. You deserve someone to make you happy. It's been a really crappy term."

Hadley smiled. She fished an orange slice from the bottom of her cup and nibbled it.

"It's just skiing," she said.

She'd had boyfriends before but never anyone like him. There had been Ed, who had a prickle of white-blond hair and liked Chaucer and French hip-hop, and Paul, who played center forward for Tonridge reserves, and could never shake the endearing habit of calling her dad "Sir." But they were boys she'd seen without ever really using her imagination, just ways to pass the small-town summers that stretched out never-ending, someone to be with just as everyone was pairing off, sitting side by side on park benches and sharing headphones. She'd never been in love, not really, not in her first year of university, and not at home, either.

Joel was nineteen years older than Hadley, thirty-nine to her twenty, and she was sure he'd had his fair share of romance. He smiled too easily, he watched you too avidly, he had altogether too much dash, not to have seduced a line of women before her, but she never felt as if any of them, or any of that, mattered. What had losing Kristina proved? That the future could never be known. That on the most ordinary of days, when fast-falling snowflakes filled the air, when candles on a cake flickered beneath the breathy song of "Happy Birthday," when Lausanne people folded their clothes and removed their shoes and made for their goose down beds, someone's world, at least one person's, could fall apart. In the face of such fact, the past counted for little. All that remained was the present.

Joel and Hadley couldn't stroll arm in arm through the streets of Lausanne like other couples, kissing beneath the chestnut trees or by the Ouchy fountains. They couldn't sit at corner tables in cafés and hold hands past the sugar bowl. Sometimes she tried to picture them doing such things, and she never could. She wondered if that mattered, the inability to imagine an ordinary future.

Often, she couldn't believe he was there with her at all; he seemed too reckless for a place like Lausanne. His hair kicked up at too rough an angle, his cheeks weren't shaven enough, he didn't shine his shoes and he wore odd socks. Instead, she could see him yanking giant fish from a salted ocean, cramming into the crowds at a bull-ring, throwing back drinks in a sawdust-strewn bar. With such pictures she made him into her version of Hemingway, and she became his bob-headed consort; lithe and devoted, lips stinging with kisses.

The day after the skiing message, Hadley stayed behind after class. She hung at the back of the room as Joel threw his papers and books into his case. She scratched her arm idly and glanced away. When the last student left, the door closing behind them, she approached the lectern and slipped her hand tentatively into his. Joel's breath was hot and whispery in her ear. They clattered up the stairs to his office and kissed there, pushing up against his creaking bookshelves, sinking into his well-worn sofa, perching on the corner of his desk, as his hands raked through her hair. The door was locked, the blinds were drawn, Coltrane, as ever, drowned out the ringing phone or the pass-ing tap of a visitor. He slipped off her top, a

341

plaid shirt with usually testy buttons, zipping through it without blinking, peeling it from her shoulders and letting it drop to the floor. He kissed her breasts, teasing down the lace of her bra, his lips brushing her nipples. Hadley gasped and ran her hands over the curve of his back, pushing him closer into her. But then he stopped. He tidied her bra. He stooped to pick up her shirt and gently slipped it back over her shoulders. He kissed her on the tip of her nose.

"You're undoing me, Hadley Dunn," he said.

"I'm already undone," she said, reaching for him again.

He took her hand and held it firmly. "Soon we'll be in the mountains. A long way from this place. There won't be any stopping then."

"That's not until next year, days and days and days away. Might as well be months."

"You need more time to decide that I'm not too bad for you," he said.

"You're not," she said, "you're good. You're great."

He buttoned up her shirt, one by one, as though he were putting her back together after taking her apart.

"It would be nice if I was," he said.

"You sound like Jake Barnes."

"You can't talk about *The Sun Also Rises*," he said, "and expect it to end there." He began to unbutton her shirt again and then stopped. "Actually, I'm tougher than that," he said, "but nice try, Hadley."

She sighed and reached for her coat. "There won't be much skiing, will there?"

He shook his head from side to side. Smiled.

They didn't only meet behind closed doors. For all its manicured presentation, L'Institut Vaudois had some wilder parts. Between the Language block and the Arts building there was a patch of brushlike grasses and scrawny pine trees, and they kissed there once, with dazzling brazenness. One moment they were walking along, Joel with a folder tucked under his arm, Hadley with a stack of library books, then they stepped off the path. Within a couple of paces they were unseen, the perfect place for a rendezvous, a tête-à-tête. She wondered why it was that French words were often used at these moments. Perhaps it was because they carried with them a hint of mystique, not found in phrases like "we need to talk" or "can we meet?" She knew the word for "affair" in French was *une aventure*. An adventure. There was some-

343

thing impossibly perfect about that; it was spry and thrilling, and held the recognition that it might not last, that it probably wouldn't, but it would be no less shiny because of it. She knew this was how Kristina had felt about Jacques. Just steps away from the campus path Joel kissed her, and later she remembered how they'd heard approaching footsteps, and he'd held his hand gently to her mouth to still her; she'd pressed her tongue flat against his palm and tasted salt, wanting more. She knew he was holding back because he felt guilty, and she understood it, them both pretending that a line had been crossed but not entirely kicked away. She also knew that it couldn't last much longer, the waiting. She thought of this as she picked pine needles from her hair. There was mud on the soles of her shoes, and she smiled.

One afternoon, when Hadley came home to Les Ormes, she opened her mailbox to find a package. Her first thought was of the man she had just left. A gift perhaps, a Hemingway first edition or a copy of Joel's own collection of critical essays printed by an American college publisher, with a note written in his sloping hand, the kind that years later a teenage grandchild might find and run their fingers over with a romantic fizzle in their eyes. *Who was Joel?* They would ask, their lips a tiny crescent smile. She was running away with herself, and she knew it. Joel's place in her history was still uncertain. The handwriting, however, wasn't his. It was calligraphic and gigantic, sprawling unapologetically across the brown-wrapped parcel. Hadley opened it standing in the hallway and found a book inside; a yellowing paperback, with a corny cover — a gloved hand, a gun, a rose. A postcard was slipped inside its pages, and the picture was of the Hôtel Le Nouveau Monde. On the back, in the same extravagant hand, a message was written, tamed and miniaturized to fit the space.

"Hugo!" she gasped, with happiness and relief.

For all her distraction, she hadn't forgotten Hugo, not the sharpness of her last words to him, nor the resignation in his. She'd tried going back to the Hôtel Le Nouveau Monde, but he was never there. She'd stopped at the chocolate shop, but he wasn't there, either. She'd found herself walking along Rue des Mirages, not looking for clues, not with eyes darting left and right, just slowly, sadly. A few days later, she had tried again at the hotel, and the waiter she recognized from before had asked her if she was looking for Monsieur Bézier. She'd nodded. *He isn't always well, mademoiselle,* she was told, *he does not always come.* Hadley trailed back outside. *He always came before,* she'd wanted to say, and then she'd wondered what was wrong. She'd worried, irrationally, that she wouldn't see him again. For some reason she had avoided saying anything to Joel about him. She could still hear the tang in Hugo's voice as he'd said *your professor.* They were better kept as separate worlds.

She read the card now, with relief.

Forgive me for my foolish insinuations. They were the ramblings of a childish old man. On the subject of which . . . I offer you this . . . one of my better books, I think. Ignore the cover, it has aged about as well as its author. The words inside are not as bad as they might have been. It's in French, so you might require a dictionary. Unless, of course, your interest in American Literature has been replaced by a keener study of the French language (again — I'm sorry) in which case you will find it pitifully easy to read. Happy Christmas, Hadley Dunn. My very best wishes, Hugo Bézier. Post-script: I am, in fact,

Henri Jérôme. Un nom de plume, as you can see from the cover. Perhaps we could meet again in the New Year. The days seem awfully tired without you.

Hadley flicked through the novel and saw the tightly packed type, blotchy and aged. She wished she knew enough French to be able to read it. Perhaps she would take it home with her at Christmas, armed with a dictionary. She flicked to the back and saw the author photograph, a thirtysomething man but unmistakably Hugo. The slant of his jaw was the same, as were the roguishly hooded eyes; had the picture been in full color, they would have beamed treacle-brown. He wore a black roll-neck, a perfect sweep of blond hair falling across his forehead. His lip was curled with insouciance. *Henri Jérôme.* Hadley wondered why he'd chosen that name, for it seemed unremarkable to her. Perhaps she would ask him, if they met again. In the New Year, when she would perfect an insouciant smile of her own and say, *actually, Hugo, you were right. Joel was only interested in one thing. I'm not half as nice as you thought I was.* And they'd laugh, and he'd shake his head indulgently and they'd order a couple of stiff drinks.

Hadley carried the book back to her room.

She knew why he'd sent it, and she understood. It wasn't just an olive branch. She felt sure that he'd wanted her to see the picture of him as a young man, and the praise-filled quotes from the newspaper giants, *Le Monde* and *Le Figaro;* he wanted to say, *this is who I was, and who I am still.* For the strangest moment she imagined him and Joel facing one another, eye to eye, shoulder to shoulder, fists clenching. A younger Hugo, bristling just as Joel did now. *Henri Jérôme.* She placed the book carefully on her shelf. Beside it was Kristina's Riviera novel, its lovelorn postcard from the unfound Jacques still caught between its pages. Her bookcase was filling with treasure, unremarkable to a stranger's eyes, but infinitely precious to her.

CHAPTER 23

The night before she was due to fly home, Joel and Hadley met for drinks. He drove her to a small lakeside town, on the road to Vevey. It was no more than a scattering of villas, with a line of sailing boats moored in the reeds. A single café bar, with a once-cheerful awning, ripped now at the edges, fluttering in the night wind. They sat beneath the dense warmth of an outside heater and overlooked the dark water. She huddled into her coat, and Joel folded his arm around her.

"Are you warm enough?" he said.

"Getting there," she replied.

They drank whiskeys, and Joel smoked cigarettes one after the other. The moorings of the nearby boats chinked.

"It's amazing this place is even open," she said. "Who comes here?"

"People like us," Joel said. Then he kissed

the top of her head. "There's no one like us."

"This is the first time we've really been out together," she said.

"But you understand why," he answered, turning. In the gloomy light his face appeared gray. "I'd love to take you to all the best places, but I can't. We'd run into someone we know."

"We could just go to your house," she said.

"But that's not going out," he said.

"Well, no, but it's doing something. That isn't after class, or in your office, or in the back of the library."

"The back of the library?"

"You put your hand on my bottom in the poetry aisle," she said.

"Well, I'm sorry," he said.

"Do you think it would matter that much if people did see us?"

"Yes."

"Then why don't we just go to your house?"

"But I'm giving you all this." He swept his arm, taking in the bladelike reeds, the jet water, the gray-white plastic chairs of the terrace. "Isn't it something?"

"It just feels a bit like we're hiding."

He drained his glass. "I don't want you to feel like that, Hadley. You know I don't. I've hesitated taking you back, because . . ."

"Nosy landlady?"

"No." He laughed.

"Nosy neighbors?"

"Nosy? Nonexistent, more like. I live in a block where everyone tiptoes around. I've ghosts for neighbors, I'm sure of it."

"Then, what?"

"Then, nothing. You're right. What *are* we doing here?"

"Maybe you thought it'd be romantic," she said.

"Romantic? Yeah. Maybe I did."

He kissed her, then. One of his long, deep kisses, the kind he gave her only sometimes. She surrendered herself, wholly, and he was always the one to pull away. But his bitten-down lip and pale eyes told her that he didn't really want to.

"Let's go, then," he said.

All of the times she'd pictured Joel's apartment it was always full of *him* — loaded bookshelves, rows of records, every inch of wall covered with pictures, splashy paintings and darkly photographic prints. She had somehow forgotten that he was as much of a visitor in Lausanne as she was, and his lodgings probably just as sparse.

His apartment was in a building a few streets back from Place Chauderon, up a narrow, steep residential street and hemmed in on either side by old apartment blocks, five stories high. Joel slowed down, searching for a space to park. The streetlights were few, but she could see that the building was buttermilk-yellow, each window set with shutters. Some had wrought-iron balconies, crammed with up-ended bicycles and plant pots with straggly winter growth. One window was plastered over with sun-faded newsprint. Approaching the door, there was a bank of buzzers, at least twenty.

"How many people live in your building?" Hadley asked.

Joel fumbled his key in the lock. "I told you, I never see anyone." He shoved the door with his shoulder, and they went into the lobby.

The floor was tiled and the air smelled musty. She wiped her feet on a stiff-bristled mat and looked at the rows of mailboxes. The light overhead blinked.

"Come on," said Joel, "let's get upstairs. It isn't exactly the lobby at the Ritz."

But it might as well have been. She hung on to the rail for steadiness, her excitement making her jittery. She almost fell into his back as he stopped abruptly and rattled a key in a door, at the turn of the landing.

"And we all wondered why this place was

available at short notice," he said, throwing open the door. "I'd say make yourself at home, but that's probably ambitious."

He flicked on the lights, and she looked around. It was a relatively large studio, possessed of a scratched parquet floor and high ceilings. A black leather sofa was pushed into the corner. A coffee table was scattered with old copies of the *New Yorker,* a full to the brim ashtray and a plate with a fork, remnants of tomato sauce congealing on its surface. There was a low bookcase, every shelf crammed, and a lamp with a tasseled shade like an old lady's skirt.

"Hadley, it's a hole. It really is. What can I say?"

"It's not a hole," she said. She went over to the sofa and sat down on it. "Where's your bed?"

"You're on it."

"You sleep on the sofa?"

"I kept meaning to get a bed and then never got round to it. It's actually pretty comfy."

"I can see that," she said, leaning back.

"What time's your flight tomorrow?"

"Late afternoon."

"Packed?"

"Mostly. Oh, hey, I nearly forgot." Hadley went to her bag, pretending to be casual, and pulled out a gift. It was wrapped in blue paper and tied with white ribbon. "This is for you."

"You got me a present?"

"Of course." She watched him as he turned it in his hands, shy suddenly, biting her lip with anticipation. "It's just a small thing," she said.

He removed the paper carefully, his fingers smoothing it as he went. "Very smartly wrapped," he said. "You shouldn't have done this."

Inside was a book. It was a collection of photographs of their corner of Switzerland, all taken in the 1920s and '30s. She had found it at the Ouchy market, in a box packed with smoke-stained paperbacks and French comic books. At first she'd wanted it for herself, and then she'd thought of Joel. She watched him now as he turned the pages; the three hills of Lausanne, a sway-backed steamer making its way to Montreux, snow scenes with chiseled villages and slabs of rock, all in black-and-white and painted color. There were pictures of pleasure-seekers, lithe men and women in sun hats and knitted jumpers, merry and bright.

"And look who it is," she said, pointing, leaning closer to him.

Ernest and Hadley Hemingway were standing in the snow. They wore clumpy boots and tweedy garb, billowing trousers and roll-top socks. They were turned toward one another, trading sweet but level stares, to all eyes a well-matched pair. *Chamby, 1922,* the footnote said.

"They look happy, don't they?" said Hadley.

Joel smiled, as if greeting old friends. "Perhaps deceptively so. See that date? If it's the end of that year, she'd just lost all of his work."

"Was that then?"

"That was then. Imagine it, getting to Lausanne, that's right, our city, and knowing that you'd lost a suitcase containing everything your man had ever written, somewhere on the train from Paris. There's hell behind that picture."

Hadley traced her finger over their faces. "I don't know," she said. "They look happy to me. I wish they'd stayed together."

"History's full of people making monumentally bad decisions," Joel said. "You'd think we'd learn, but unfortunately, fear doesn't seem to fade with evolution. And fear's nearly always the reason."

"Did Hemingway say that?"

"No." He took her hand and kissed it.

"Hadley, it's a beautiful gift, it really is. I'll always keep it. You know, your present is the ski trip. I mean, you can't unwrap it, but . . . it'll arouse less suspicion on Christmas morning. Well. Maybe. Depends what you tell people."

"I don't want to think about other people. Tell me what we're going to do in the mountains."

He set the book aside and sank down beside her on the sofa, his legs sprawled out in front of him. He had kicked off his shoes, and he stretched like a cat, the toes of his odd socks pointing. He turned to her, his smile a crinkled line.

"We're staying in a cabin that's not near any of the others. There's a fire that chokes out the whole place and will make everything you've got smell of wood smoke and make you want to eat it. There's a track we can ski down to get to the village, and the only prints you'll see will belong to deer or marmots or fox."

"You've been there before?"

"In my imagination, plenty of times."

"Tell me about the bed."

"It's a big bed. It's a small cabin, but the bed's big enough to fill the whole thing."

"I thought the fire filled the whole thing?"

"No, the smoke from the fire. The fire

itself is small and picturesque. It'll keep itself to itself and won't bother us unless we want it to."

"It sounds very romantic."

"Doesn't it? And I'll teach you to ski, of course."

"What if I'm hopeless?"

"You won't be."

"But what if I am? What if I fall and get lost in the woods?"

"I won't let you out of my sight," he said. "You'll be sick of me by the end. You'll wish we'd never met."

"Impossible."

"Can I kiss you?"

"You never asked before."

"I'm trying to remember to be a gentleman."

"Please, don't," she said.

She leaned in, and they kissed, Joel pulling her onto his lap as though she weighed nothing at all. Hadley's lips burned. She shut her eyes tightly, but once, just once, she opened them and saw his eyes were wide and staring, his pupils misted.

She closed her eyes again.

For the first time, she let him all the way in.

Hadley woke up the following morning on

357

Joel's sofa. She stared at the ceiling and sank as she always did when she remembered Kristina. She stretched, her back stiff from the crooked angle she'd slept at. At first she couldn't see Joel at all, and then she spotted his silhouette by the window. He was smoking and looking down at the street below. She thought about the night before. How afterward, he'd clasped her to him, held her so hard and so long that it felt as if everything he needed, everything he wanted, everything he was afraid of, was in that embrace. *I didn't know him until now,* she thought.

"Good morning," she murmured.

"You're awake," he said. "Hello."

He stayed by the window, the expression on his face unreadable with the bright light behind him.

"How are you doing? Are you okay?" he said.

"Okay? I'm better than okay."

"That's good. That's great."

"Aren't you?"

"Me? Course. Hungover, that's all."

"We didn't drink much."

"Makes no difference. I'm bad in the mornings."

He moved away from the window, and his face was clear now. His eyes were rimmed red and his countenance pale, haunted by ghosts of the night. Perhaps he hadn't slept at all. She had no memory of him beside her in the small hours. She'd had the sensation of being washed up on a shore, her energy quite spent, and as Joel had relaxed his hold on her, she had drifted toward sleep. Faced with his bluntness, she felt too naked suddenly, and pulled the blanket around her top, covering her breasts. Her clothes were strewn on the floor, and she made a sort of toga and bent to reach them.

"I'd have thought that this morning you'd be feeling a little better than usual," she said, shaking out her jeans. She let the blankets drop and put them on. She stood facing Joel, her chest still bare. "Or is this just an everyday occurrence?"

"Hadley, I didn't mean it like that," he said. "I'm sorry. I'm being an asshole. You were — are — much too good for me."

He walked toward her, bending to pick up her T-shirt from where it lay rumpled on the floor.

"Here," he said, putting it on over her head. He fed her arms through the holes, his hands encircling her wrists. He pulled it down over her waist.

"You forgot my bra," she said. Her nipples pointed through her T-shirt, and Joel stared down at them.

"So I did," he said. His arm hung by his side, and she saw his fingers flutter. He put his hands into his pockets. "If you want to take a shower, go ahead. I'll get you a towel."

"Joel?"

"Yes?"

"Nothing," she said. "I'll take a shower."

A quick exit was probably best. She decided this as she stood beneath the cooling blitz of the water, soapsuds stinging tears from her eyes. When she came out, she attempted to be brisk and bright. A cup of coffee awaited her on the side, and she took it without looking at Joel. She sipped, holding the cup with both hands.

"Hadley," he said.

"What?"

"Whatever you may think, I don't make a habit of this."

"It's okay, I don't think anything."

"Well, I just want you to know that. I haven't actually been here, in this exact situation before."

"How could you have? This was our first time. Maybe that's not a big deal for you, but it is for me."

"I'm your tutor, Hadley. I do think about

that now and again, you know. Don't you?"

"Of course I do. How can you even ask me that? And I know you're risking far more than me . . ."

"Don't say that, I couldn't care less about that."

"But I do think about it, Joel. Yes, you're my tutor, yes, you're twice my age. . . ."

"Hadley," he began to say, but she rolled on.

"But those things, they just don't matter anymore. How can they? Nothing matters like it used to."

He stared at her. He rubbed his face vigorously.

"I just don't know what to do with you sometimes, Hadley."

"You knew last night."

She glanced around for her coat and bag, and glimpsed them thrown over a chair. They were exactly where she'd tossed them as she'd stood in the middle of his flat with her hands on hips and said, *I like it, this place of yours, it's got a good feel to it,* and he'd stepped toward her, his face cracked with laughter lines. She gathered them up.

"Please, don't go," he said. "Stay."

"I think I've probably stayed too long already."

"And now you regret it?"

"What's to regret? What's left?"

She threw her arms wide, with her palms turned out.

"Everything just happens," she said, "and when it's done, it's done. No traces."

He stepped toward her.

"No traces?" he said.

She shook her head.

"What, nothing? I know you don't believe that," he said.

He took his finger and brushed her cheek very lightly with it. He wiped away a tear, a single drop.

"Don't cry, Hadley. There's no reason to cry."

"Whenever I'm with you and I'm happy, later I feel bad about it. But that's okay, I know that's just how it is. I don't want it to be any other way, not yet. And I know Kristina would want me to be happy, even if I failed her, even if I couldn't help her at all. I just hope she knows I tried my best for her, too. . . ."

"You couldn't have done more."

"But this is the first time that it feels like you're not happy, either."

"Hadley, I am."

"I don't believe you. Look how you were when I woke up."

"You're too precious to screw around

with, Hadley."

"Everybody's too damn precious."

"I want it to be serious with you. I want it to matter."

"Serious isn't the same as sad."

"I'm not sad, Hadley. Far from it."

"Joel, I just wish we were normal."

"Us? We could never be normal."

"But what if we'd met some other way? Wouldn't that have been better?"

Joel took her hand and pulled her into him. His eyes were a darker blue than usual, sea-colored. His lips were apart.

"You were a woman in a bar. And then you were on the street, in a coat that was too big for you, your cheeks all smacked red by the cold air, looking at me as though you were half afraid that I'd pounce, and half afraid that I might not."

"Oh, come on." She laughed. "I didn't look like that."

"I wouldn't change anything, Hadley," he said, "because if I did, it wouldn't be us, would it? When I saw you in that awful bar I figured you were maybe a student, but I didn't care. I followed you outside because I wanted to talk to you. And then you wound up in my class. *Hadley Dunn.* Watching me that whole hour as though I was telling you a secret. And then you came to me.

When you were at your lowest, you sought me out. What choice did I have but to help? How could I resist that, any of that? And how can I resist you now?"

"There's no answer to that," she said, "is there?"

She laid both hands on his chest. Beneath her palm she felt the banging of his heart.

"None I want to hear," he said.

"Then let's stop talking."

"Hadley, I . . ."

She stepped in and stole the next words from his lips. Wrapped in a kiss, they sank slowly to the floor, and all things spoken slipped away.

Chapter 24

Her flight wasn't until later that afternoon. She walked through the streets of Lausanne, catching glimpses of herself in plate-glass windows. The keen air on her cheeks made her feel spry and invigorated. It was new, this feeling. Was it how Kristina had felt, zipping home to Les Ormes after seeing Jacques, on the good days, the best days? *Alive,* thought Hadley, *I feel alive,* and instead of crumpling at the thought, it made her smile.

She was headed for the lakeside. She wanted to try and see if Hugo was there, one last time before Christmas. In her bag was a new handkerchief for him. The old one was washed and dried and only a little creased, but it bore the dark stains of Joel's blood. As much as he had scrubbed, he hadn't been able to get them out, he'd said. She had bought Hugo a new handkerchief to replace it, a Christmas present, she supposed. It was made of cream cotton with a blue trim, and it came in a box with a ribbon.

At the Hôtel Le Nouveau Monde she saw that, at last, Hugo was back in his usual spot, stirring his spoon in his coffee, contemplating the lake view that must have been as familiar to him as a bedside picture. His eyes were glassy when he turned to Hadley. He looked thinner in the cheeks.

"You!" he said, a beam lighting his face. "I thought you were long gone, back to your fair isle. You're not here for Christmas, surely?"

Hadley explained she was leaving that day, and she wanted only to say Merry Christmas, and to thank him for the book. She didn't mention the two weeks that had passed or her attempts to find him in his usual spot.

"Ah, the book," he said, "the book."

"Am I to call you Henri Jérôme, then?"

"Henri Jérôme," he said, "I haven't felt much like Henri Jérôme for a long time."

"I liked your picture," said Hadley, sliding into the seat opposite him. "You looked like a cool guy."

"Cool? I don't think so. I was a lot of things, but I don't think cool was ever one of them."

"Okay, you were handsome. Very handsome."

"Ah, now that I cannot quarrel with. Coffee?"

"Please. I'm sorry I got so angry with you last time," said Hadley, watching as he poured her a cup from a silver pot. "It wasn't very gracious of me. But I felt so helpless, suddenly it was the end of the road, just like you said, and I didn't know what to do with that. You did your best for Kristina, and you were so kind to me. That earns you the right to tease a little, I'm sure."

"Just as I wrote, they were the foolish insinuations of a jealous old man. And I don't like to be defeated, that's why I was irritable, really. In real life, people get away with the bad things, the accidents that turn out to be crimes. Perhaps that's why I always preferred fiction."

Hadley took a silver teaspoon between her fingers and inspected it. She twirled it twice, then set it back down.

"Real life isn't so bad," she said.

"But I am sorry that I wasn't more help to you. Not that that errant professor of yours was very useful, either."

"Oh, but he has helped," she said, "just in a different kind of way, I suppose."

"Yes, I can see that," Hugo said, bringing his coffee cup to his lips. "I knew, in fact, the moment you walked in today."

Hadley looked up quickly. "What's that?"

"*Mais oui,* you have a definite spring in your step. I'd like to think it was due to your elation in seeing me again, in finding that, in coming here and seeing me drinking my coffee and cognac at always the same time, there is at least some constancy in the world. But, I fear, that is self-flattery of the most futile kind."

She laughed and looked away. This time she wouldn't grow angry; this time he was perfectly and absolutely right.

"You're mischievous, today, that's what it is," he said. "I thought that the very first time I ever saw you, you know. On account of the hair. Or lack of it, rather."

She ran her hand through it, mussing the ends. "It needs cutting again. It's getting too long. Oh, here —" she reached into her bag "— I've a Christmas present for you. Well, not really, but it's your handkerchief. After all these weeks, sorry for the delay. Actually, it's a new one. I thought that would be nicer than giving back your old one."

"A very fine specimen," said Hugo, turning the box in his hands. "Thank you." He looked at her again. "You do seem impossibly brightened. But then they say that the young bounce back more easily than the old."

She dropped a sugar lump into her cup and stirred it, watching the crystals ebb away. She licked the spoon.

"I've bounced nowhere, Hugo," she said. "I don't know what I am."

Her eyes wandered across the café and out toward the lake. Despite the flatness of the day the waters were churning. Crested waves bashed the fleet of paddle boats, just visible by the jetty's edge, and a blitz of twenty or more seagulls spun in looping circles.

He took her hand then, and held it firmly.

"Be careful," he said.

"Why do you say that?"

"I felt moved to, suddenly. Is my intuition wrong?"

"I don't know. It's intoxicating, really." She gave a high-pitched laugh. "I'm surprised you haven't ordered cognac, so you can keep up."

He released her hand. *"Be careful,"* he said again. This time he wasn't looking at her at all, but somewhere into the middle distance. When he spoke again, his voice had changed.

"While you've been busy elsewhere, I've been thinking," he said. "I've been trying to figure it out for myself."

"Thinking about what?"

"Jacques."

"Jacques might as well be a phantom, Hugo. We both know that."

"What if that's precisely what he is?" he said. "What if he is, in fact, not Jacques at all? It's just an idea I had, but it came to me as I wrote that card to you, as I dusted off old 'Henri Jérôme.' Kristina needs a nickname for her secret boyfriend, so why not Jacques? It has a pretty enough ring to it, *n'est-ce pas?* And if that is the case, then Jacques, my dear, could be anyone. It's a thin sort of disguise, but an effective one. Perhaps you should look at the people in Kristina's life. The people you both knew, even. Could any of them be Jacques?"

"She met him on the Riviera, Hugo. He's nothing to do with Lausanne."

"And it was a good story, wasn't it? Their meeting? A perfect fiction."

"Hugo," Hadley started then stopped. She began again. "Some people have those kind of lives. Dazzling, perfect, picturesque lives. Maybe you did once. Maybe I will one day. Do you really doubt everything? Suspect everyone?"

"Not everything," he said. "Not everyone."

"I've stopped looking," she said, "you know that. I'm trying to do what everyone wants me to. I'm trying to move on. Can we drop it now? Please?"

They drank the rest of their coffee quietly, swapping fragments of small talk back and forth. They both admired the slow dance of the waiters and turned to watch as a magnificent patisserie trolley laden with fruit-decked tarts rolled past and was greeted with delicate exclamation.

"Would you like something?" offered Hugo. "The cakes here are quite delicious."

"No, thank you," said Hadley, then added, kindly, "maybe another time, though."

In the end she began to put on her coat. "I should get going," she said. "I haven't started packing yet." She pulled her hat from her bag and set it on her head then. She smoothed the tips of her hair with her fingers. Hugo watched her with his head cocked to one side, and the corner of his mouth trembled.

"What would it take to get Henri Jérôme writing again?" she said, suddenly.

"Now that's a question I can't answer."

"I think you miss it."

"Perhaps," he said, "but that chapter is long finished."

"You've still got it, though, haven't you?" said Hadley. "The writer's sense. You know a story when you see one."

"What's all this?" said Hugo. "Compliments. Encouragement. Ridiculous flattery. If I observe again that you're in a particularly good mood, will you refrain from biting my head off?"

"You deduced correctly, Hugo."

"Hmm?"

"You were right about me and the professor," she said.

"What was I right about?" he said, slowly.

"Thinking that there might be something there," said Hadley.

"L'amour?" said Hugo.

"You're the one who saw it coming. God knows how, but you did."

He laughed soundlessly and scratched lightly at the side of his mouth with just the tip of his finger.

"Ah, but is it love, Hadley?" he asked.

"I don't know about love, but . . . maybe. Maybe it will be. In a strange way, it already is."

Hugo snorted. "It's an old story, you know," he said, "a professor dabbling with his students. I thought you were a little more original than that, Hadley Dunn."

"Didn't Henri Jérôme ever write about love?"

"He wrote about death."

"Never love?"

"Sex. Not love."

Hugo looked at her, but she found she didn't have anything else to say. She shrugged. For some reason, the words that came to mind were, *I'm sorry*. She didn't say them. She stood up to leave and they gave each other three kisses, cheek to cheek in the Swiss way, Hugo turning his face to her with a slightly injured air.

"Well, Merry Christmas, Hugo. I'll see you in the New Year, I hope."

"Only if you've time, you sound like you're going to be busy," he said, just as she was walking away. "So, in the end you found yourself a Jacques, after all," he added, "without even looking. A secret boyfriend all of your own."

"I'd have loved to have told Kristina about it," said Hadley, ignoring his tone. "It's the last thing she would have expected of me, I'm sure."

"You could have whispered about your indiscretions together, and become quite unbearable around your other friends."

"The others wouldn't understand, Hugo. They'd just think it was fantastic gossip and go on about it all the time."

"So it really is a secret affair? Oh, my."

"You promise you won't tell anyone?" she said.

Hugo sat erect. He looked a little princely, sitting there so straight-backed. He waved his hand dismissively.

"My dear, who on earth would I have to tell?" he said. "Except, perhaps, if I am to take your bait, the page. The blank and staring page."

Hadley laughed. "Write what you want, Hugo. It doesn't bother me. In fact, I think you should. You might enjoy it."

Their farewell stretched. Hadley waved and turned, but Hugo's voice stopped her.

"What a Christmas present you've given him," he said. "This professor of yours."

There was something in his look that made her wrap her coat more tightly around herself. She walked back toward him, feeling the eyes of the waiter on her.

"He's been good to me," she said, in a low voice. "Okay? When Kristina died he was the only one who really understood how I was feeling. That was how it started. Not with anything else, but with kindness."

"It won't be how it ends," Hugo muttered.

"And now he's turned my world upside down," she said. "In the best possible way."

"You sound as if you're trying to convince yourself, my dear."

"It's fine," she said. "I get it. You don't like love stories."

"I don't believe in them," said Hugo, flatly.

"And I don't believe that," said Hadley.

"This professor of yours, what's his name?"

"You know his name. It's Joel."

"Joel," he repeated, with added emphasis. "What do you think he believes?"

"He believes in life. And living it. Not hiding away, watching from the sidelines."

He held her eye, unblinkingly. Hadley looked for the thread of humor that would twitch his mouth into a smile, but there was none. She looked away first. "Merry Christmas, Hugo," she said over her shoulder.

CHAPTER 25

The bungalow was ablaze with colored fairy lights. It wasn't like her mum and dad to go so over the top, but this year was different, they said, this year it felt like a real holiday. On the front door a plastic Santa with a swollen belly hung crookedly. Hadley nudged her dad and raised an eyebrow.

"I know, it's a bit naff," he said, "but your mum couldn't stop herself."

Inside, the familiar rooms shone with loops of tinsel and strings of Christmas cards. A plump tree stood in the same red-painted bucket they always used, and every decoration glittered with family nostalgia.

"You're home!" cried her mum, in a blaze of jubilance, and hugged Hadley to her. Sam flung himself at her legs and hung on to her knees, attempting to inch himself up like a monkey.

"She needs fattening up," said her dad. "Look at her, thin as a rake. So much for

Switzerland being full of cheese and chocolate."

"It's so great to have you back," said her
mum, squeezing her. "You've got no idea."

"It's good to be home," Hadley said.

Her mum eyed her. "Hadley, are you all
right?"

"I'm fine," she said. "Tired from the
journey, that's all." Her smile faltered.

"Something's wrong, what is it, love?" Her
mum placed a hand on each of her cheeks
and cupped her face gently. "We've missed
you so much," she said.

The ache behind her eyes had started as
they'd driven the last stretch into Tonridge,
past the rows of pudgy tan-brick bungalows
and manicured shrubs; it had been quietly
heartbreaking, the familiarity of her old
world. She had turned her face to the
window and managed to keep her tears at
bay, but they got the better of her now. As
her mum and dad folded her into their
arms, she told them all about her friend
called Kristina. For a while they stood in a
tiny scrum, in the middle of the sitting
room. Sam clung to her ankles and began a
song about a red-nosed reindeer.

Hadley was at home for a little over a week,
but it felt longer. She took Sam to the park

and pushed him back and forth on an ice-cracked swing, his yellow Wellingtons pointing at the sky. She talked with her mum and dad until late in the evening; they played cards, the old games she used to love, and drank Irish Cream from mismatched glasses. She felt herself being drawn back toward her old world, a place where she could almost imagine that she had never been to Lausanne; but this feeling never lasted longer than a moment or two, and most of the time she was glad.

One day she showed her mum and dad her Swiss photographs, and Kristina was there, smiling back at her, just as she knew she would be. Kristina posing by the fountain in the old square, one leg cocked jauntily, an arm thrown out in a wave. She could almost hear her laughing, *hurry up and take it, Hadley,* and squinting at the accidental flash. Kristina leaning against the wall at the entrance to Les Ormes, the city falling away behind her, a gust of wind catching her sweep of hair. The hat she wore was wine-red and fur-trimmed, and Hadley could remember the day in bright detail. They'd sneaked into a café for hot chocolate laced with rum and cream and sat giggling, licking the long spoons. A sharp-eyed waiter had watched Kristina from his spot in the corner. She'd done that — stopped people in their tracks without even realizing.

The next day Hadley caught her mum looking at Kristina again, holding the photographs in her lap. And she saw her dad as he came in from the garden, stamping the mud from his boots, saying to himself, *her poor parents.* Hadley let her home do its work; she drank its tea and sank into its sofas, her parents' words and Sam's simplicity a comfort.

The only time that Hadley was really on her own was when she was in the bathroom and when she went to bed at night. These were the moments when Joel found his way in. In the bathtub she sank under, closing her eyes and feeling the rush of water in her ears. She held her breath until she gasped. Pulling herself back up, she rubbed soap between her hands, smoothing the foam over her winter-pale arms and chest. On her last night in Lausanne, Joel's hands had been everywhere. His fingers had traced shapes as though writing on a misted mirror, delicate messages that had run across her back and down her front and along the inside of her thigh, and yet miraculously her body bore no prints. She closed her eyes and found herself drifting, smoothing the soap in circles, the water growing tepid around her. *You're so brand-new,* he'd said in a voice that had seemed shot through with marvel. *Don't let me ruin you, Hadley Dunn.* She'd raked her fingers through his hair and told him to stop talking.

Her first night in Tonridge, she went to sleep feeling the weight of him, inside and out. She pushed the bedsheets away from her face so that she could breath. She wanted to be in Lausanne with Joel, not here without him, and yet inexplicably she was grateful for the things she knew, the rattle of her dad's cough down the hall, the scratching of their old cat Brady at her bedroom door, the hulking outline of her old wardrobe. Some small shred of her hung on to these things as she hurtled toward the unknown.

On Boxing Day she told her mum and dad about her plans to leave. They were in that aimless post-breakfast holiday time, when the whole day stretched ahead, but no one was quite sure how to spend it. Her dad took a seat at the piano and brushed the keys back and forth with the tips of his fingers. Her mum folded and refolded the crinkled sheets of wrapping paper, keeping an eye on Sam as he potato-painted at the dining room table. Hadley curled in an armchair with a book, a jotter balanced on her knee and her pen poised for note taking. She had two assignments to turn in after the holiday, and she was yet to make a start on either.

"So," she said suddenly, setting her pen down, "we haven't really talked about when I'm going back."

Her dad tinkled at the high end of the piano, a cheerful ripple of music. He didn't turn around.

"Oh, don't talk about leaving, Hadley, not when you've only just got here."

"I've been here for ages," she said, "and I've still got three full days left."

"Three days?"

Her mum held a square of creased gift wrap to her chest. Her hands looked redder than usual, as if she'd done a batch of hand washing and forgotten to wear her rubber gloves.

"Yes," she said, "I have to be back in Switzerland for New Year's. I thought I'd mentioned it. . . ."

"For New Year's?"

Her dad shifted on the piano stool, and it creaked ominously.

"Oh, no," she said, "did you think I was staying longer? I'm sorry. You don't mind, do you? It's my only chance, maybe ever, to spend New Year's in Switzerland. I was asked to go skiing."

"Skiing?" they both said, simultaneously charmed and taken aback. Sam turned around, adding to the chorus. *"Skiing, skiing, skiing,"* he sang, as he carried on painting.

She put her books down and went over to them. She took the folded gift wrap from her mum and pulled at her dad's sleeve. Sam carried on at the table, smearing pink and yellow paint.

"We thought you'd be here for longer. We've got a joint of beef in the freezer. We'll never eat it all without you," said her mum.

"Your mother was going to make a beef Wellington," said her dad. "We've been reading up on how to do it."

"I didn't know you were planning that," she said. "I'm sorry. Do you mind, though? Do you mind if I go? I've got the money to cover it."

"It's not the money, Hadley. Of course you want to be with your friends," said her mum. "It's important to have fun, what with . . . everything."

They held her hands, and she felt traitorous. She thought then about telling them about Joel. But what part? Maybe the way he read passages aloud in class, his voice deep and unbending, and peppered with unself-conscious pauses. Or perhaps how he'd smile reluctantly, as though you'd drawn it out of him, and somehow in doing so you'd gained something more than just his slow, broad grin. Or even how he'd taken her to Geneva, to look in vain for a person who possibly didn't even want to be found, and had folded his arm around her shoulders as they'd crossed a snow-dusted road. But not this — how on the sofa in his apartment on a Lausanne side street he had made love to her, and that was exactly how it'd felt, more than sex, and she'd forgotten about Kristina for one huge and seemingly unending moment, and instead of raging, she was glad.

But instead her mum said, "These friends of yours, they'll look after you, won't they? They do know you've never skied before?"

She nodded, and *yes* was all she said.

On Hadley's last night, her mum came to her room just as she'd gone to bed.

"Can I come in?" she said, appearing shy, standing at the threshold.

"Of course," said Hadley, and patted her covers. Her mum sat down, crossing her feet in their well-worn moccasins.

"I know you're excited about the skiing,

but, what with everything else . . . you know, you don't have to go back. Not if you don't want to."

Hadley rolled over so that she was resting on her elbows.

"But I do want to go back," she said.

"I'm glad you do, very glad, but . . . I just want to say that no one would blame you if you felt differently, if you wanted to carry on the year back here. After that poor Kristina . . ."

"Mum, really, it's okay. I want to be there."

Her mum took her hand. "You're far braver than I ever would have been," she said.

"It's not really brave," said Hadley. "I wouldn't call it that. Mum, I did think about leaving, but then I changed my mind, someone helped me change my mind, and I'm so glad about that. It's strange, but in Lausanne I've never been sadder, but I've also never been happier. I don't even know how that's possible, but it is."

Her mum smiled a slow, sad smile. "Hadley, can I ask you something?" she said, smoothing the quilt with the flat of her hand. "Is there a boy?"

Hadley laid her head back on her pillow. On her ceiling there were scattered bunches of glow-in-the-dark stars. They had been there for years, and they'd lost their luminosity long ago. A boy called Simon had given them to her, no doubt hoping that he would be the one to organize them into constellations, to one day lie back and see them glow for himself, but he hadn't, and nor had anyone else.

"How did you know?" she said, still looking at the stars.

"I'm your mum, Hadley."

She finally looked at her.

"Okay," she said, "but he's not really a boy. I guess he's more of a man."

"A man? How old is he?"

"I don't know," she lied, "a little bit older. Not much, really."

"Where did you meet him?"

"At the Institute."

"Is he in your class?"

"Yes. The American Literature one. He's American."

"What's he doing in Switzerland?"

"The same as me, just a visitor. He's only there for a year."

"Was he friends with Kristina, too?"

"No, he wasn't."

"Perhaps that's a good thing," said her mum. "Is he very handsome, Hadley? One of those wonderful square-jawed Americans?"

"I don't think he has a particularly square jaw," she said, "not really."

"What do you love about him?"

"Love?" Hadley started smiling, she couldn't help herself, "I didn't say it was love, Mum."

Her mum leaned forward and kissed her on the cheek. Then she stood up, her hands smoothing her skirt.

"But it is, though, isn't it?" she said. "I can tell."

CHAPTER 26

Hadley had never been met at an airport before, and she almost wasn't. Joel's disguise was too good. He was standing several steps behind the eager row of greeters, the types who leaned on the railing with their home-made welcome signs, cellophane-wrapped bouquets and expectant smiles. He was wearing a hat she hadn't seen before, a trapper cap with a furry lining that tickled the lobes of his ears. His smile was self-conscious, and his eyes watchful; one too-long glance in his direction and he looked as though he would turn and run, skidding down the escalators and back into the swell of anonymity. He caught her elbow and drew her into a fast kiss. His lips were tight and unyielding. His cheeks were just-shaven and unusually smooth. To Hadley, he didn't feel a lot like Joel.

"You came to the airport," she said, wheeling back to look at him.

"Let's get out of here," he said.

He relaxed when they were inside his car. He reached across and put his hand on her knee, his fingers rubbing back and forth on the denim of her jeans.

"I had a whole story worked out, you know, in case I saw anyone I knew. I even began to believe it myself. I was starting to look forward to seeing my old friend Jim, flown in from Madrid. That was the flight in after yours. I checked the board."

"Good cover," she said.

"Jim and I were thinking it'd be a smart move to drive straight on up into the mountains tonight. That way we'd get to wake up to a whole new day. A fresh start. What do you say?"

"I love that idea," she said, thinking they'd drive fast through the night, the car thick with jazz. Joel would keep his hand on her knee, spinning around the hairpin turns, as craggy pines in winter coats stood looking on. The roads would be slick with ice and maybe they'd slide a little, Joel grinning as they spun deeper into the mountains. Hadley settled into her seat and loosened her scarf. Her lips were stinging with the kisses he'd given her as soon as they were out of sight of the crowds.

"Oh, I do just need to call in at Les

388

Ormes, though," she said, "I want to pick up some more clothes."

"We can buy you what you need," said Joel.

"No, that's crazy. I just need to stop by quickly. I'll be in and out in five minutes."

"Okay. If you have to. I just don't want us getting pulled back into Lausanne. It's supposed to be a getaway. I want it to feel all new."

"Of course it'll feel new," she said, turning her smile to him. "How could it not?"

She already knew how to quash his reluctance. She would pull him into her funny little oblong room and push him down onto the bed, as beyond the unshuttered windows the Lausanne night glittered. Then they'd carry on up into the mountains, and it would be just like Joel said, *all new.*

"I think you'll be glad we stopped," she said, "when we get there."

They joined the autoroute and drove quickly toward Lausanne, bumper to bumper with flashy Swiss cars. Joel stared straight ahead, and his face was striped with light. Hadley glowed with the heat of her intention, glancing sideways now and again, as if daring him to guess the reason for her smile.

■ ■ ■ ■

Les Ormes was deserted, just as she knew it would be, but she'd still had to practically drag Joel inside. He wanted to stay in the car, and it was only her lips brushing his ear and the heat of her breath that persuaded him to follow her. His trapper hat went back on, and he shoved his hands into his pockets and bent his head.

"If anyone recognizes me, Hadley . . ." he said, his sentence hanging unfinished.

They slipped inside like fugitives, clicking the corridor light into reluctant action. It blinked and fizzed, and they squeaked down the hall, past the bank of mailboxes and the scrawny Christmas tree, the deserted leather sofas. No music came from the kitchens, there was no slamming of doors or chatter. Everyone had left for the holidays.

"This is me," she said, stopping by her room. Her hand fumbled as she pulled her key from her bag. She turned to Joel, but his attention was caught.

" 'Kristina Hartmann,' " he said, reading the name on the neighboring door. "You lived next door to her?"

"You knew that," she said. She reached for his hand. "Come on, this is my room."

390

"You never said you lived in the next room," he said.

"That was the whole point. That's how we were friends."

"Why is her name still on the door?"

"I guess they haven't got around to changing it."

"What, so every day you walk past and you never think to take it down?"

She had noticed, and it had surprised her that the fastidious porter or the sleek-haired woman from the university hadn't removed it. They must have forgotten, that was all. As to Hadley, she didn't want to take it down. It was the last trace of Kristina, and until someone else was in there, it was still her room.

"Hadley, it's not right that you have to look at it every day," he said.

He flicked the slip of paper out with his finger and held it in his hand, his thumb obscuring her surname. *Kristina.*

"I think I quite like it," she said. "Actually. In a weird way. Can you put it back?"

"No," he said, "it's macabre."

"But it's still her room."

"I'm not putting it back," he said, stuffing it into his pocket.

"Then give it to me, at least," she said.

"What, you want this paper? With her

name on it? Why?"

"Just . . . I don't know. I don't want you to throw it away."

"Hadley, I thought you wanted to be happy."

"What's that got to do with anything?"

"You don't need to be reminded of her at every turn. This —" he patted his pocket "— it's a nothing."

"If it's such a nothing, then why do you care?"

He draped his arm around her and pulled her into his shoulder but instead she wriggled free.

"Joel," she said. "Please. Until someone else is in there, it's still her room."

He kissed her on the top of the head, his caress quietly insistent.

"Your hair smells like honey," he said.

"Joel . . . can I have the paper?"

"Hadley," he said. "You know what's part of accepting that someone's gone? Letting go of the little things. This —" he patted his pocket again "— is a little thing. You have to let it go."

He took her key from her hand and opened the door. He nudged it with his shoulder and led the way inside.

"It's practically a new year," he said, "it's a fresh start. There's so much to look forward to, isn't there?"

"Okay," she said, "okay, then."

In the room she turned on the bright overhead light. The whispered promises were forgotten, and they both ignored the bed. She walked over to her wardrobe, saying over her shoulder, "I just need to grab a few things."

If he was disappointed, he didn't show it. He turned to the window. "This view," he said, "it makes you feel like you want to just run and jump right on into it, doesn't it? Like it'd swallow you up."

He opened the balcony door, and she felt the blast of cold air. She heard the crunch of his feet as he stepped outside. She hastily pulled a few clothes into a bag. Glancing out at him again she could just see his outline in the dark, a lone figure, facing out over the city. She pushed a last sweater into the bag and snapped it shut.

"I'm done, then," she called.

He came back into the room, his cheeks red with the cold. He rubbed at his eyes.

"It's windy out there," he said. "We should get going before it starts to snow."

The drive up into the mountains would have been perfect. The black night air was crisp and clear. The snow was banked at the sides of the road, and it shone bright white under the glare of the headlights. Hadley watched the outside temperature drop on the car's dial, as she huddled deeper into her seat, pulling her scarf tighter. They didn't play music or talk; the only sound was the rushing of the tires on the smooth road. Joel stared straight ahead, concentrating on the tight bends and the steep climb. She wondered what she would have done if back in her room he'd taken her in his arms and kissed her. If he had gently lowered her onto the bed, whispering that he was sorry, and that he only wanted her to be happy. Would she have loosened, tipped back her head and let him have her, as she had imagined having him? But instead he'd stayed on the chilly balcony, chagrined, their whispery, complicit mood stolen by a ripple of disagreement over a name on a door. She wasn't grown up enough to feel her way deftly back into equanimity. They climbed higher into the mountains, and she kept quiet, gazing from the window at the white world. She felt as raw as a stripped fruit, and just as easily bruised.

In the end it was simple beauty that smoothed the wrinkles. Joel drove over tight-packed snow, the tires crunching, and they climbed out of the car beneath a canopy of still pines. The freezing air bit Hadley's cheeks and stole her breath. In the distance the lights of the village twinkled, but their patch of the mountain was dark and silent.

"It's this way, I think," said Joel, and he took her hand, curling his fingers into hers.

The outline of a small cabin was just visible, tucked off into the trees. A lamp hung under its eaves, and they made for its light, wading through knee-deep drifts. The air was so still and hard and cold that it seemed to blast right through her, taking any lingering uncertainty with it. At the porch they stomped their feet, kicking clods of snow from their shoes. Joel took a key from his pocket and turned it twice in the lock. She followed him inside as he clicked on a lamp.

It was a simple chalet, a home built for two, with a floor of slate and walls of honey-colored pine. Wooden rafters reached to the roof, and sheepskin rugs lay underfoot. A fire was already prepared in the grate, and Joel put a match to it. The flames jumped hungrily and filled the room with a flickering light. A basket had been left for them, with two bottles of wine and bars of Swiss chocolate, a block of hard mountain cheese and a box of salted crackers. There was a note from the owner, a loopy handwritten card that said *bienvenue et bon ski.* She asked Joel again how he'd found the place, and he shrugged. "I got lucky," he said, and he bent to kiss her.

"It's like a stage set," she said, dodging his lips with a smile. "It's far too pretty."

"What, I brought you all the way here, and you won't kiss me?"

"I feel like a heroine, a fairy-tale one. I need to keep you at bay for a little longer," she said, and slipped from his grip.

"We'll picnic in front of the fire tonight. How's that for a fairy tale?"

"It sounds okay," said Hadley, "not too bad."

"We'll eat upside down, chocolate first, then the cheese. Glass of wine?"

"Let's just take a bottle each."

"Hadley, listen to me. I was a bore on the journey up," he said.

"You weren't a bore," she said. "You were silent as the grave."

"Sorry I annoyed you at Les Ormes, then," he said.

"I don't want to talk about it," she said.

"Okay, well, I'm sorry I haven't done this yet, then."

He began to undo the buttons of her blouse. She reached down and flicked the end of his belt from its clasp.

"You're forgiven," she said, and he pulled her into a deep, dark kiss. They disappeared somewhere else entirely, a place where there was no more talking, only bitten lips and whispers and easy grace. Just once, Hadley's thoughts flitted, and she was struck with the idea that here, in the heights of the mountains, perhaps the only things that mattered were extraordinary.

CHAPTER 27

When Hadley woke she felt every point of her body touching his, the ridge of his anklebone, the curve of his back, her nose pressed to the lobe of his ear. They hadn't made it to the bed the night before; instead they had fallen asleep twined on the sofa, blankets caught around their waists. Despite the warmth of Joel, she felt chilly; the fire in the grate had long ago fallen to ash. She carefully untangled herself, pushing her lips together for silence. She found his sweater on the floor and pulled it on, then padded barefoot to the kitchen where she found coffee and fresh milk. She set a pot on the stove and went over to the window, drawing the curtain aside. Outside it was a white, white world, and the sun was already climbing in the pale blue sky. Traces of wispy cloud clung to the tops of trees. She could see as far as she ever had, across hurtling mountainside, undulating snowfields, gray-white peaks and cloaks of forest.

She felt his hands on her shoulders, and she turned to him. Joel's hair stood on end, and when he spoke his voice was still groggy with sleep.

"When you woke up this morning, and found yourself here, what did you think?" he said.

"What do you want to know?" She smiled. "Yes, I'm grateful to you for whisking me away. No, I don't regret it for an instant. And, yes, I'd really like it if you wrote my American Lit essay for me later, as I was kind of distracted over the holidays. I kept thinking about this man, you see."

He hung his head and gave a gruff laugh.

"No. I mean," he said, squeezing her shoulders, "was it like I said it would be? Did you open your eyes and think of something else? Like I said, that time in my office?"

"Oh, that."

Hadley turned her head to the window. Outside, the sun threw blue shadows on the snow. Winter-coated pines stood in gossiping clusters. She watched the drip of an icicle hanging from the roof, its sharp point translucent. Everything had an unreal quality. From where she sat, so long as she carried on looking out of the window, there was nothing to place them in the world they knew. She turned back to Joel.

"I meant," he said, "did you think about Kristina?"

"I know what you meant," she said quietly.

"And?"

"And . . . I know that it will get better. It already has, Joel, so much better. I'm just not . . . there yet. But don't worry. Never worry."

He reached out and took her hand. She wore a single ring on her finger, a tiny star set in a silver band. He took it between his fingers and lightly turned it.

"Will you tell me?" he said. "The day when you wake up and think of something else? Toast. Coffee. Those stupid, necessary things I talked about. Will you promise to let me know when that happens?"

She closed her hand around his and told him *yes.*

Joel took Hadley onto the slopes, her feet pinched by hired boots, her calves at first protesting as she floundered around. She surprised herself by taking to skiing more readily than she'd thought. She liked how the slightest action, a bending of the knee, a leaning of her weight, could alter something, drive her faster or sharpen her turn. Joel watched her, leaning on his poles, his hair licked back by the breeze. In his ski suit he looked like something from an old picture postcard, nut-brown and racy.

"Kristina was going to teach me to ski, you know," she said as they stood catching their breath off to the side of a run. "I'll bet she was brilliant at it."

"I remember you saying that," he said.

"Skiing, I mean, I'll bet she was brilliant at skiing. She might have been a really bad teacher. I can't imagine her standing around waiting for me, like you do. She'd have wanted to ski off. Jumping over things, probably. She was more daring than me."

"You're plenty daring," he said.

"I don't know if I am."

"You're here with me, aren't you?" he said.

She went to lean into him and slipped, her skis moving in different directions. She ended up in a heap in the snow, collapsed in laughter, her poles crisscrossed. He joined in, reaching out his hand for her. The mountains caught their peals of laughter and returned them, over and over.

Back on her feet, her skis in position, Hadley whipped him a smile.

"Try and catch me," she shouted.

She pushed off, her knees bent, and the speed soon took her. The wind drew tears from her eyes, and her lips formed a boundless grin. She heard the hiss of Joel's skis behind her, but he never overtook. Her skis wobbled, her poles pointed, she let slip a cry, but she stayed upright, she kept moving, and the mountain kept coming. At the bottom, he pretended she'd beaten him.

"You don't need to fake it," she said, red-cheeked and jubilant. "I don't even care. That was amazing. It felt like flying."

"You've got it," said Joel. "You don't need my help anymore. You're expert."

Hadley brushed the snow from her skis.

"Shall we go up again?" she said.

In the cocoon of the lift, as it swung up over the mountain with the slopes rolling beneath, Hadley pushed her goggles up on top of her head.

"Joel, without you, I'd never have come here."

"You'd have made it out eventually," he said.

"No," she said, "you gave me this. You gave me all of this."

Their days in the Alps were full of the kind of startling natural beauty that Hadley knew would stay inscribed on her memory, moments that she was already beginning to miss before they were quite gone. The powder-soft light at sunset, the salmon tint to the snow as they walked back to the cabin. The spindly deciduous trees on the lower slopes, impostors in the thick evergreen forests, and the way that in the chill mornings each tiny shoot was painted with ice, like pointing fingers. And she knew she'd remember the taste of water from the tap in the cabin, as crisp-cut as diamonds. She'd drink great gulps of it in the middle of the night, while behind her Joel rolled toward sleep, his spent form lying still beneath the sheets.

Disruptive thoughts intruded only sometimes. Walking back through the village once they passed a group of young Swiss men, newly arrived for the weekend. Hadley watched as they stood around their gleaming cars, pulling on their ski boots, their hair already sun-slicked. Their number-plates were marked GE for Geneva. She strained to catch the sprinkle of their chatter, searching faces for one more pallid, more haunted than the rest. Jacques was everywhere and nowhere, which was as hopeless a thought as the driver being everywhere and nowhere. Untraceable people haunted her, and no good could possibly come of that. She was grateful then for the solid reality of Joel. She told him this, and he smiled. *I'm glad I'm good for some-*

thing, he said.

Joel seemed different in the mountains. In Lausanne he had been tightly coiled and somehow bristling, popping on his toes like a boxer. Here, his movements took on a more languorous air, and he never once looked over his shoulder or pulled his hat low over his eyes. Lausanne sprawled somewhere far below them, packed with all-seeing people, the likes of Caroline Dubois and the crowd at Les Ormes, its wet streets marked with lines that couldn't be crossed, and Hugo Bézier, with his sharp edges and insinuations. It was as though the pair of them had taken flight, and the world they'd left behind spun somewhere far beneath them.

Joel was different in other ways, too. One day on the slopes, Hadley grew tired and took a spot on a sunny terrace while he carried on skiing. She cupped a hot chocolate in her hands and looked down over the mountain as he went on without her. He was easy to spot, not by his red suit but by his crouched stance, his whipping speed, the flurries of snow that were thrown up in his wake. She saw him cut across the *piste* and jump the low rope onto the untamed side of the mountain. To her it looked like nothing but a steep field of rocks, all craggy slopes with scrawny, wind-beaten fir trees clinging to the ledges. Just the narrowest chutes of snow ran between. She watched him barrel into a drop; there was nothing but gray-black stone in front of him, not even a dusting of snow. Her hand went to her mouth, and her drink spilled in the saucer as she saw him suddenly take off and fly through the air. If he was falling, he was doing it gracefully, but wasn't that how everyone looked as they plummeted? A sudden serenity, an abandonment of struggle as the ground rushed ever closer. Joel held a tuck position, and at the last moment, just as he looked certain to crash-land on the rocks below, he flung out his arms and his poles pointed to the sky. He seemed to be tipping forward, and Hadley could only watch with a gasp. Then he was out of it and shooting on down the mountain, a flash of red between the rock and the snow. He'd found the smallest strip of powder and had taken it perfectly, and now he was skiing faster than ever before. He disappeared from sight. He might as well have dropped off the ends of the earth.

She waited for him, and he didn't come. She ordered another hot chocolate, and it went cold before she had finished it. As the afternoon sun disappeared behind the peaks, a fiercer cold swept the mountain-side. She took the sheepskin blanket that was thrown over the arm of her chair and wrapped it over her knees. She was the only one left on the restaurant terrace. She kept her eyes on the slopes, looking for the flash of his red ski suit, turning expectantly whenever she heard the clatter of boots behind her. In the end she paid her bill and rode one of the last lifts back down to the village. She looked for him everywhere as the small compartment swung on its rope. Her eyes combed the steeply wooded hill-sides, the piles of rocks, the ravines that scarred the snow's smooth face. As the last straggles of skiers headed for the village, she walked in the other direction, back toward their cabin. Her feet ached in their stiff boots, her skis were cumbersome to carry and she was cold from sitting still for so long. Fear pushed her faster, and by the time she kicked the snow from her feet at the door and fumbled with the key, her heart was pounding. She let herself in. The cabin was in the shade of a clutch of pines, and without the lamps it was dark.

"Joel?" she said, even though she knew he wasn't there.

The bathroom door opened, and she let

out a small cry. Her fear was replaced by anger.

"Where did you go? I thought something had happened. I was frightened."

He stood in the gloom. He had pulled his ski suit to his waist and his chest was bare, a towel wrapped around his shoulders. He still wore his boots, and as her eyes adjusted to the dark she noticed the trail of melting snow from the front door. She went to him, her hands raised.

"Joel, what were you thinking?"

"Careful," he said. He flicked the light switch on, and she gasped. The side of his face was streaked black and red with half-drying blood. His shoulder bloomed with a giant bruise.

"Joel, oh, my God."

"It's not as bad as it looks," he said.

"How did it happen? I watched you jump from those rocks but you landed. I saw you land."

"That was the easy part," he said. "It was just a misjudgment, that's all. I got too close to a damn tree."

"Why didn't you just stay on the *piste*? Why did you have to go off? Honestly, I was watching you, and it looked like you had a death wish. Here —" she touched his cheek gingerly and he winced "— let me help.

What can I do?"

"It's looks worse than it is," he said again. "It's my own fault, I got it wrong, that's all. I'm sorry you had to wait so long, Hadley. I tried, but I couldn't ski back to where you were. I just came down."

"I didn't know what'd happened, but I knew something must have. I just had that feeling."

"Hadley, I'm fine. Come on, kiss me. Just on the side of my mouth."

"Joel." She laid her hands gently on his shoulders and saw him flinch. "I'm hurting you."

"You're not," he said. "You're the best thing. I feel better already."

"What can I do?"

"Nothing. Some drinks, maybe. One apiece."

"Do you need a hospital?"

"Definitely not. It's nothing, really. I just got a little banged up, that's all. You can't avoid it in the mountains."

He walked into the bedroom with labored steps, then. He sat down on the edge of the bed and began to pull off his boots. Hadley poured two whiskeys and carried them through, her fingers leaving prints on the cold glass. She handed him one and watched him drink it quickly down. He exhaled slowly. He set the glass aside and grinned half heartedly.

"You know, there is a way that you can make me feel better, Hadley."

"Oh, come on," she said. Then, "What, really?"

"Really."

She stood before him and he laid his hands on her hips. He pulled her gently toward him.

"Just lie here with me," he said, "put your head on my chest, and I'll tuck my arm around you. That's all I want, nothing else."

That night they watched the fire until the small hours. First, Hadley had coaxed Joel from his ski suit. Then they'd bathed, and she'd run her hands over his bruised shoulder, dabbed carefully at his cheek, and he had closed his eyes, gritting his teeth as the water ran in his cuts. Afterward, his fingers traced a pattern over the curve of her back, and she imagined what he was drawing, two looping love hearts or a bird in flight. Every now and again, he would clasp her to him as he bent forward to toss another log on the fire. As they settled back, they breathed in the wood smoke. Hadley rolled over and kissed him; she tasted burning pine in his hair and skin. They saw the shadows their bodies made together on the rolling wooden walls of the cabin. Hadley slim as a child, Joel ox-strong and square-shouldered and not hurt at all.

Afterward, he went back to drawing shapes on her skin. "There's so much you don't know about me," he said.

Hadley sighed and shifted. The fire crackled as the flames guzzled the dust-dry logs.

"And there's so much you don't know about me," she said back.

"You?" he said, "You're bright white. You're the kind of girl a man looks at and sees the worst of himself looking back. No one's good enough for you, Hadley. Least of all me."

"Lies," she said, lazily, "all lies."

Joel bent and kissed her head. His lips stayed pressed into her hair. When he spoke, his words went all the way through her.

"What if I hurt you without meaning to?" he said.

"You wouldn't," she said. And it really did feel that simple.

"I'd never want to," said Joel.

"Then you won't."

Outside, the snow was falling quietly and heavily. Hadley closed her eyes and opened them again, and everything was just the same. Hissing logs. Shifting shadows. Snow banking at the window, the pane misted. Joel's hand was in hers, and it was warm and rough-edged, as real as anything else.

"Tell me a story, Joel," she said. "Tell me something about you that I don't know."

"What kind of a story?"

"A true one."

So he began to talk. He told her how he'd fallen in love with books when he had just turned ten, plundering his grandparents' bookshelves and finding a copy of *Grimm's Fairy Tales*. How he'd spent the summer holidays lying in the parched grass of their lawn, reading of frog princes, lost children and shoes that wouldn't fit. How afterward he had still tossed baseballs, ridden his bicycle along the boardwalk, chased his brother in and out of the orange groves, but all the time his head had been full of stories.

He told her how one day when he was twelve he'd hidden on the roof of a barn and smoked his way through half a pack of stolen cigarettes. He'd coughed and spat and his feet had skittered on the uneven tiles. He'd fallen and broken his arm, smashing the bone in three places, and he took hold of Hadley's fingers then, and made her feel the slight bump beneath the sleeve of his shirt. He said he could still remember the moment of falling, the

411

ground flying toward him at the strangest of angles, as though the world itself had tilted, and the waving heads of the angry nettles that, instead of cushioning his blow, had stung him through his clothes, from top to toe.

He told her how one day, in the sorry wake of Winston — his brother, who would always be fourteen and freckle-faced and laughing just before they'd spun off the road in a no-good truck — a hard-edged, seventeen-year-old Joel had discovered Ernest Hemingway. And his heart, bent out of shape as it had been, beating with life but not much else, had lifted once more.

Hadley watched him, and in the end he looked back at her.

"I wish I'd always known you," she said.

"I'd have been better, if you had," said Joel. He smiled for her, but his eyes stayed far away. "Now it's your turn. You tell me a story."

"I only have one," she said.

"Well, I want to hear it."

"You know most of it."

He settled himself in the armchair. Hadley stayed sitting on the floor and wrapped her arms around her knees. She watched the fire.

"It's a love story," she said.

"I don't think I do know it."

"I came here without expectation or design," said Hadley, turning to him, holding his eye. "I hardly knew anything about Lausanne. But I fell in love with it, right from the very beginning. Do you remember how we saw each other, on my first night?"

"Do I remember?" He shook his head. "Hadley, of course I remember."

"I was walking back to Les Ormes, through all the streets of the old town. At one point I turned round and looked back and saw the lights glittering on the other side of the lake. And I realized that I knew exactly how that scene looked by day, as well, with the mountains rising up behind, it was like a painting, like nothing real. And I couldn't believe any of it, Joel. I couldn't believe that I was there, on my own, in a foreign city. That this life was mine. Then, well, it only got better. I met Kristina. And we started doing everything together. I'd never had a friend like her before. She was Danish, but she seemed so exotic to me, it was like she didn't come from anywhere, she came from everywhere. Isn't that a silly idea? But being here, something changed. I guess I felt something I'd never felt before."

"What was that?" he said, quietly.

"Like anything was possible."

He was out of his seat, and Hadley thought he was coming to her, but instead he bent to the fire. He had the poker in his hand and jabbed at the logs, the flames shooting up into the darkness.

"Joel?"

He didn't turn. And when the fire roared and embers scattered over his bare feet, he barely flinched. Hadley stood up and wrapped her arms carefully around his shoulders.

"You couldn't have done more. I hope you know that. Because it matters, that kind of thing, the way people are when . . . disaster strikes. When you were telling me about Winston you said I'd be in my own private hell. But you've been right there with me. You've never made me feel alone in any of it. And you've given me something else, too. Something I didn't even know I was looking for. That was what I really wanted to tell you."

He faced her, and she saw that his eyes were burning. In that particular light, he almost looked as if he were crying. She reached out her finger to brush his good cheek, but he caught it and held it lightly in his.

"Your love story," he said, "I just wish it

414

ended differently."

"But it's not over yet," she said, "is it?"

CHAPTER 28

On New Year's Eve they dined in a chalet-style restaurant in the village, a place that was all dark corners and sloping wooden ceilings. Their table was crowded with a giant pot of fondue, and they ate as the locals did, never allowing the forks to touch their lips, deftly skimming the cubes of bread from the bubbling cheese. Hadley had only thought about a Lausanne New Year's once, earlier, as she'd pulled on her fur-topped boots and hunted for her gloves. How might it have been? She and Kristina crowding into the bathroom together, jostling for mirror space, marking their lipstick and flicking their hair. They would have been bound for somewhere dazzling. Or would Jacques have lured his girl away, instead? Quick kisses on the cheeks and a florid wave, and Hadley left wishing she had someone, too. Now she did, and he was right there with her. She drank champagne and let it fizz on her tongue.

"This is perfect, Joel," she said. "Just perfect."

"Let's never go back to Lausanne," he said. "Let's stay here always." His cut and bruised cheek gave him a roguish air. His smile was more lopsided than ever. Their evening had begun with mountain-frosted whiskeys. Joel had snapped ice spears from the roof of the porch. *Fire and ice,* he'd said, opening his palm and revealing the glittering shards. After their second glass, Hadley had stopped trying to match him.

"You know we're not so far from the places where the Hemingways used to stay," Joel said. "Chamby, Les Avants, I haven't been yet but I will, in the spring. Maybe if they'd stayed in the mountains they'd have been happy always."

"You really think that?"

"No."

"So you're just being romantic?"

"Willfully so."

"Well, I wish we could stay and be just like them, however misguided."

"We'd be nothing like them," he said.

He refilled their glasses, the champagne fizzing all the way to the rim. He drank his back, thirstily.

"Actually, I don't think I'd even want to stay," said Hadley, "not for too long, anyway. I'd miss the bustle, the people. You could live here, in a tiny snow-filled bubble, and forget that the rest of the world exists. Your life would never collide with anyone else's."

"Exactly its charm," said Joel.

He looked at her, and his gaze was hot behind the eyes. The candle between them was guttering, and the wax blobbed on the table. He pressed its edges, kneading it flat with the tips of his fingers.

"What would you want to be, if you weren't a professor?" she asked suddenly.

"There's a question. I honestly couldn't tell you."

"So you really like teaching?"

"I really do."

"You like teaching me, that's for sure."

"Well, you're a gifted student."

"So, have there been other gifted students?"

"Hadley . . ."

"It doesn't matter, I'm just curious."

"No. No one like you."

"What does that mean?"

"This is a career-threatening move, Hadley. I'd be stupid to make it too often."

"But you have before?"

Joel took hold of her hand. "No, Hadley. I

haven't. I'm in Lausanne for one year only, just like you. I'm not fleeing a scandal in the States. I haven't left behind a string of broken hearts. Okay?"

"I was only teasing you," said Hadley, her smile ringing with obvious pleasure.

"Well, tease away, Hadley Dunn. That's your prerogative."

"I'm just so glad you came to Lausanne, too. I can't imagine the alternative."

"You'd have found one."

"I don't go for just anyone, you know. I am, actually, very choosy."

"Then how the hell did you end up with me?"

"It's a puzzle, isn't it? I guess I dropped my guard."

Joel topped up their glasses, then kicked back in his chair, his brow crinkled.

"Last term I wasn't all that happy in Lausanne," he said.

"But, I thought you loved it. You said so in your first lecture, how all the literary greats came here, escaping too-crowded Paris, the stifling Riviera, you said they walked and skied and stayed in glamorous hotels. You made it sound like we were treading in all the best footsteps."

"I don't know, maybe it's just me, but I feel watched here. There's no imperfection."

"I thought California was like that, too."

He picked up his glass again, but he'd already emptied it. He turned it in his hand and stared, mesmerized.

"Yeah, but it's all artifice there," he said. "You can see the set design, hear the lines being spoken. Everyone goes along with it and that's the fun. Here, it's real. Everything's real."

"Hugo Bézier said it's not so very perfect. Scratch the surface and it's just the same as everywhere else. Just sharper suits. Better watches. Prettier views."

"This Hugo Bézier, what's the story there?" he said, looking at her, his glass set down. "Do I need to challenge him to a duel, or something?"

"Joel, he's over seventy."

"And what did you say he was, some kind of crime writer?"

"A *retired* crime writer."

"That kind of mind never stops turning, does it, though?"

"Oh, I think his has, a long time ago. It's funny, you know, I can't work out if he cares about everything, or nothing. If he's lonely, or perfectly content."

"Does it matter?"

"I don't know. I guess not. It's not like I could make a difference, anyway."

"You'd be surprised, Hadley, you'd be surprised."

"I'm grateful to him, I know that much. If it wasn't for all his 'stay and fight' talk, I'd probably be back home now. I wouldn't be here with you. Imagine that."

Joel rubbed his eyes. When he moved his hands away his pupils were bleary.

"We need to get something else to drink. Shall we change it up? Red wine?"

"I've still got a full glass," said Hadley.

"Well, you drink that and I'll get us some red."

He called out to a passing waiter and exchanged quick words.

"Your French is even better when you're drunk."

"I'm just getting started. You know, I thought about leaving, too, Hadley," he said.

"What? When? You never told me that."

"Around the time I got to know you."

"So what made you stay?"

"A less-than-compromising boss and a nice salary."

"Oh."

"No. Actually it was you."

"You're just saying that."

"I didn't feel like my life was here, and I didn't feel a lot like me."

"I guess a lot of people feel like that, when

they go to another country."

"You didn't."

"I made a great friend."

"Yes. You did. I wanted to go home, start the year over. And then, suddenly, you made me feel needed. As though I could actually do something good, after all."

"Kristina brought us together, didn't she? I like the idea of that. She thought I was straitlaced, you know. She wouldn't tell me anything about Jacques because she was sure I'd disapprove. But an affair with my tutor? Well, she'd have loved that."

"Hadley, we're not only here because of Kristina," he said.

"But don't you think it's true, in some ways?"

The wine came, and Joel poured two glasses. The wine ran down the stems, pooling on the pale cloth.

"You know, part of why I wanted to find Jacques . . ."

"Hadley . . ."

"No, listen, I'm not dwelling on it, I'm not. It's actually romantic. I wanted to tell him just this one thing."

"What one thing?"

"It was something Kristina said to me once. When she talked about Jacques, she left so much out, but she did say this one thing, and I loved it."

"Come on, Hadley, what was it?"

"That when she first met him she thought he was the most handsome man in the world."

"She said that?"

"And that he made her feel like the most beautiful woman. I just think that's the most romantic thing I've ever heard."

Joel took hold of her hand. He caught her ring as he always did and turned it on her finger, around and around.

"Don't you think that's beautiful, an amazing thing to say? I wanted Jacques to know that. I wanted him to have it to hold on to. I think people ought to know things like that."

"You're a romantic, aren't you, Hadley? I always knew you were. I like that about you, it's a nice way to be."

"I don't know what I am. A quitter, maybe. I stopped looking, I stopped bothering the police. Hugo didn't say it but I know he thought it. But then he'd run out of ideas, too."

"You moved forward. You started something new. Isn't that better?"

As he spoke, Hadley saw how, in the candlelight, his eyes blazed. She wanted to be back in the cabin suddenly. She didn't want New Year's to be anything else, or anyone else. Was that moving forward? Perhaps it was, perhaps it wasn't, but she knew that she wanted the countdown to be hot whispers, and closed walls, their two bodies moving in time, only that.

The waiter came then, bringing them shots of syrupy *eau de vie.*

"Bonne année!" he said, as he set them down.

Joel looked at his watch, then held it up to her. Midnight had come and gone, and they had missed it.

"Hadley, it's a new year."

"We didn't count down. Is that bad luck? That we missed it?"

He took her hand. "Let's get out of here," he said.

They spilled out into the sharp mountain night. Joel's steps were ragged. He'd finished the last of the wine and hers, too, swilling it down after their celebratory liquor shots. She laughed at him and slipped her arm through his. Around them, revelers kicked through the snow, shouting and calling. Fireworks exploded in the valley. Hadley felt someone pull at her arm, and she spun around, smiling, ready to cry *Bonne année,* Happy New Year, to anyone she met. But her expression changed instantly as she looked into a face she knew. For a moment she struggled to place him, the curling dark hair, the plump lips. Her mind went blank. Then she put it together. She dropped Joel's arm.

"Luca, what are you doing here?"

"Same thing as you," he said, looking past Hadley and on to Joel. "Or maybe not exactly."

"Loretta said you had a place in the Italian Alps. . . ."

"My *parents* have a place in the Italian Alps. I'm here with friends. So are you, by the look of it."

Hadley glanced at Joel. She began to shape a quick answer. *Oh, we just ran into one another, too,* but Luca stopped her.

"I saw you in the restaurant," he said. "My friends and I came in for a late drink. We were in there at midnight."

"I didn't see you."

"You were busy," he said. "With Professor Wilson." Luca turned to him. "A friend of mine, or should I say, another friend, for Hadley and I have been friendly, too, is in your class. She's always talking about you. She thinks you're the best. Evidently, she's not the only one."

"Yeah, and who are you?" said Joel.

425

"Luca, listen," said Hadley, "I know this looks bad, but . . ."

He turned to go, flapping his hand dismissively.

"Luca, wait."

"Hadley? Is he bothering you?" said Joel, the words falling messily.

"Happy New Year," Luca said, over his shoulder, "to both of you. Oh, hey, and stay out of fights," he added, nodding at Joel. "You don't want to damage your looks."

Hadley watched him swing off into the crowd. She turned to Joel. He had one hand held to his face and was feeling his bruise as if he'd forgotten it was there.

"What now?" she said.

He shrugged, with exaggerated casualness.

"Joel, what now?"

"I'm sobering up," he said. "I know that much."

"Oh, God, what are we going to do?"

"An old flame of yours? Seemed like a man walking wounded."

"Is that all you can say?" said Hadley. "Anyway, no. Not really. I . . . kissed him. The night Kristina died. Before we knew."

"You were with him that night, were you?"

"It was my birthday. He's a friend of a girl I know at Les Ormes. It was a bad idea."

"Only a kiss, Hadley," he said. "What's a

kiss? Nothing."

"Luca said that it's always the start of something, and at the time I wanted to believe him."

"Because you did like him?"

"No. It was just after Geneva. When we'd kissed in the car. That's why."

Joel looked down and kicked his feet in the snow.

"And now he's seen us," he said, "but that kid won't do anything. He's spineless."

"You don't know that," said Hadley. "Why . . . Hang on, are you jealous?"

"I couldn't give a rat's ass if you kissed half of Lausanne," said Joel.

"You're jealous," said Hadley. Then, "I like that."

As they walked, their footsteps crunching, the clamor of the resort fell behind them, and moonlight showed the way home. The mountainsides were empty, the night workers, the hulking machines that bashed the snow and groomed the slopes all ready for morning, must have stopped early. It was beautiful and eerie all at once. Underfoot there was ice and drifted snow, and their feet skittered in different directions. Hadley led the way home.

"What I think we should do," said Joel, "is get away from here altogether. I thought the mountains would be far enough, but I was wrong. What we need, Hadley, is an island, some place exotic. How'd that be?"

His words were a little slurred, but she liked the feel of his hot breath on her cheek and the weight of him pressing against her. She felt as though if she stepped away, he'd trip and fall.

"That'd be just fine," she said, "perfect."

"You and me and no one else, as far as the eye can see."

"Sounds pretty great."

"It'd be hot, of course, so there wouldn't be any need for clothes. No clothes, at all, not a stitch."

"Naturally not."

"Coconuts. Rum, lots of rum. Monkeys in the trees. We'd grow our hair long."

"You don't like my short hair?"

"What? I love it. Of course I love it. But I'll grow mine. Or maybe just a great old beard, just like Hem's. Would you still kiss me, with a beard like that?"

"On our island, I'd do anything."

"Castaways, we'd be. Tanned, drunk and happy."

Hadley laughed, and the mountains threw it back. They hung on to one another for steadiness. They held each other up.

■ ■ ■ ■

New Year's Day brought a snowstorm that hadn't been forecast. On waking they peeped at the outside world and saw nothing but whitewash, swaths of mist and falling snow.

"Shall we stay inside today?" said Joel. "I'm a little stiff. I thought I got away with that fall, but I guess not."

She looked at him. His eyes were rimmed red and his sun-gold tan had paled to nothing.

"Nothing to do with your hangover?" she said.

He smiled, and crinkles appeared at the edges of his lips and the corners of his eyes.

"And you feel fine, I suppose?" he said.

"No, I feel awful, too."

They disappeared under the covers and stayed there for most of the day, drowsing and happy. Once he woke her, and twice she woke him, their bodies remembering the shapes they'd made before. She cried out his name, and he whispered hers, across her collarbone and into the nape of her neck. The day passed, and they saw only one another.

In the early evening, as Joel slept on, Hadley took a bath. She lit a single candle, and it guttered beside her, an unfelt breeze twisting the flame. "So this is what a new year feels like?" she said out loud, a smile at her lips. In the dark water she lay quite still. Her body felt exhausted; scattered, yet more whole. She thought of how before, she used to prize Joel's slightest touch, the brief tap of his finger on her arm, a small squeeze of her shoulder. Every contact, no matter how light, how passing, had felt like a promise, or something just less perhaps, a whispered intention. Then had come the grazed patch on her chin, all that had been left of their kiss in the car, and she remembered how the physical mark had pleased her, its eventual fading feeling like a loss. Now, Joel knew her inside and out, no part remained untraced, no place untouched, and she wanted him more than ever. She smiled again, and in the bath she drifted.

Against her wishes, her mind turned to Luca and the night before, and she groaned at the intrusion. Deliberately, the day had been about closed curtains, the retreat to bed and never any talk of the night before. What would Luca think if he could see them now? Caroline Dubois? Even Hugo? She felt the combined weight of their disapproving looks and slipped beneath the water, closing her eyes, dismissing everybody. The only person she ever wanted to tell about Joel was Kristina. She imagined them back at Les Ormes, perched on the balcony wall, legs dangling, swapping stories of Riviera romance, Hadley's made of frost-licked palms and boats moored in ice-water and mountains silently watching. She'd say how once Joel had spelled out her name in kisses, from the tips of her fingers to the crook of her elbow. She'd tell about the creases in his smile, and how sometimes when she looked at him, she wanted to cry, for a very long time, and was that real happiness, that intolerable, heart-snapping knowledge that nothing could last forever? She imagined what Kristina would say back. That she'd felt the very same with Jacques? She heard her voice and the peal of her laughter and it was unbearably, beautifully close. Hadley leaned toward the candle and blew it out, plunging into black.

Hadley spent a restless night, and in its depths she woke. She'd been dreaming, but as soon as she opened her eyes, it was gone, only an uneasy taste remaining. She rolled onto her side and reached out for Joel. He lay with his back to her, and she moved up close to him. She wrapped her arms around him and pushed her cheek against his back.

She listened for the shallow, steady breathing of the sleeper, but his breath came unevenly.

"Joel," she whispered, "are you awake?"

She kissed the ridge of his bruised shoulder blade.

"I had a bad dream," she said quietly, her lips against his skin, but he didn't stir.

She slowed her breathing to match his, but it wouldn't work. She was too restless. She rolled back over to her side of the bed, and it felt like another country.

Morning finally came, and the low winter sun split the room in two. It was a welcome return after yesterday's whiteout. She squinted and rubbed her temples. Joel turned in his sleep and grunted as she kissed his shoulder again.

"Morning," she whispered, "I'm going to get us some breakfast. Croissants?"

He murmured assent.

"I feel like a walk," she said. "It's the cabin fever. Literally. I'll be right back."

They would be back in Lausanne by lunchtime, and the spell of their winter retreat would be broken. Luca might already have started telling people. Loretta would know and then Bruno and before long Chase and Jenny. And what if it didn't stop there? You could shut up a secret in Les

Ormes, but it would soon find its way along the corridors of the English department, down the lecture halls, into the staff room and out onto the campus. She had never been *that girl* before, the one whom people talked about.

Hadley looked in her purse and saw that she had only a few coins. She went back into the bedroom and bent close to Joel, whispering gently.

"Joel, have you got any cash? I haven't enough for breakfast."

He rolled over.

"Joel?" she insisted, as quietly as she could.

"My ski pants," he grunted, "there should be twenty bucks."

"Thanks. Go back to sleep."

She found his ski pants discarded, lying in a heap. She searched the pockets and could find only a scattering of coins. She tiptoed back into the bedroom, but Joel was asleep again, a rumble of a snore at his lips. She saw then that his jeans were hanging over a chair, and his wallet peeped from a pocket. She glanced again at his sleeping form, and, deciding that he wouldn't mind, she took his wallet. She ran her fingers over its old, brown leather. She loved everything that belonged to him, no matter how banal a possession — a striped sock strewn across the room, a ballpoint pen, its end chewed boyishly.

Inside, the wallet was lean and well kept, without any of the usual detritus of crumpled receipts and old bus tickets. She drew out a twenty-franc note and then hesitated. She had a sudden fancy that she would find a picture of herself in there, a Polaroid perhaps, snapped when she wasn't looking, her eyes cast down coquettishly, or a passport photo, taken in an automatic booth, the pair of them crowding in for the shot, their faces pushed together. It didn't matter that they had never posed like that, or that she couldn't recollect Joel ever having had a camera in his hand; against all reason she could imagine it.

She delved deeper, but there were only the essentials, folded notes, a clutch of cards, a driving license. And then she saw it. Tucked into the bottom, a small, white strip of paper. *Kristina Hartmann,* written in a black, typewritten font. The creases from when he'd screwed it up and stuffed it into his pocket had been smoothed out, not the work of an accident, but rather a deliberate and repetitive press of the thumb. He was supposed to have thrown it away, to stop it from reminding her of sad things, he'd said, but instead he'd kept it. It hadn't simply been forgotten, balled at the bottom of his pocket with his loose change, he had expressly moved it to his wallet. He'd smoothed it. Kept it.

CHAPTER 29

After the storm, the mountains were doing their best to show the world as newly washed. The snow was dimpled where it had started to melt, and the sun threw jagged blue shadows beneath the fir trees. The snow-cloaked streets were tranquil, for it was early and the ski lifts were yet to crank into motion. As Hadley walked to the village, her mind turned, wondering at how easily she could be snapped back and forth. Yesterday, she'd been ready for the New Year; it had held all of the promise of brightness.

At the *boulangerie* Hadley asked for a baguette and two croissants in English, forgetting the simplest of French words. She tucked her purchases under her arm and wandered slowly back to the cabin with her head down. She wanted to see Joel and hear him say normal things, have him kiss her first on the side of her cheek and then on the lips, and yet an uneasy feeling persisted. It was such a small, insignificant thing, a name on a piece of paper, and yet somehow it seemed like more than that. Just as lovers might slip trinkets and pictures into their wallets, Joel had smoothed and kept Kristina's name.

Back at the cabin, Joel was standing in his boxer shorts, waving at her from the door. His face was cracked with a grin, his hair sleep-tousled. It was such a simple image that she fell into a smile. He ran a few steps into the snow in his bare feet and swept her into a kiss.

"Are you mad? You'll freeze!"

"I watched you walking all the way up the hill. You looked like you were concentrating so hard, one foot in front of the other. Come on, give me that hand of yours."

Inside the cabin he took the bread from her. "I'm ravenous," he said, tearing the end off a baguette and chewing it loosely. The creases appeared at the edges of his eyes, giving him a knavish look. "And I missed you, of course. If you're gone for five minutes, I miss you."

"How will you cope when we're back in Lausanne, then?" she said. She perched on the edge of the table and swung her legs. It made her look breezy.

"Don't even talk about Lausanne," he said. "It's five worlds away."

"But maybe we do need to think about it. I'm in your class again next week. Should I sit at the back? Hide?"

On the countertop she could see his wallet, as innocuous as a pair of folded glasses or a paperback novel. She tried not to look at it.

"How good are you at hiding things?" he said.

She watched him. "Pretty good," she said.

"Well, I'm terrible." He took her chin between his finger and thumb and searched her eyes. "I don't want to cover anything up any more than you do," he said.

"But what if it's not even a case of covering it up?" she said. "What if Luca tells everyone? What if it gets out that way?"

"Then we deal with it."

"You're not worried," she said, "are you?"

"Because, you know what? Some kid seeing me kiss you really isn't the end of the world. If the faculty raps me over the knuckles, I can take it. If I get dismissed . . ."

"You wouldn't, would you? Not for a little thing like that?"

"A little thing?"

She laughed, and it was a relief. "You're right, maybe none of it matters." She decided to say nothing more.

They left the mountains by the same road they had come in on but it looked completely different in the full blaze of the winter sun. It was an unseasonably mild day for January, and the bonnet of the car pinged with drips from overhanging branches. Hadley wore a pair of face-swamping sunglasses. She felt glamorous, and loosened. She was glad she hadn't mentioned anything about the contents of his wallet; she'd had no point to make, she didn't know what she would even have wanted to say. They'd made love in the cabin for the last time; his skin had been cool from the outside air, but his touch had been feverish and full of want. Afterward they had lain tangled, their chests rising and falling in a rhythm that she'd had no desire to break.

On the drive home it seemed as though Joel did everything he could to delay their return. He pulled over in the crook of a bend, just so that they could watch a tumultuous river flash through banks of old gray snow, the valley falling away behind them. He stopped at a roadside shrine, a display of Catholic devotion with an ancient-looking cross made from blackened wood. Such shrines dotted the mountain roads, and Joel told her they were erected by God-fearing alpine folk in the dead of harshest winter, praying for a beam of white light.

"I didn't think you were religious," said Hadley.

"Why not?" said Joel. He ran his hand over the knotted wood. Patted it. "You're right. I'm not. But I'm glad that some people are."

They climbed back into the car, and she caught him glancing in the rear mirror.

"You know, Kristina was religious, I think," she said.

"What made you suddenly think of that?"

"She always wore this tiny gold cross around her neck. I just thought it was jewelry, but maybe not."

"So, perhaps she wasn't afraid of dying."

"I don't think that equates to being ready to stop living," said Hadley, quickly. She sank down in her seat. "I don't know, Jacques was married, wasn't he? She wasn't exactly pious."

"She only told you he was married."

"But why would she bother making that up? It didn't particularly make her look good."

"Maybe it made her look exciting."

"I didn't find it exciting. I found it sad.

You know, it's funny that you said that about her. Sometimes I do wonder if she always told the truth."

"What do you mean?"

"I don't know. It's just something I've been thinking about recently. I always believed every tiny thing she told me, without question."

"That's what friends do, Hadley."

"Maybe. I know she held things back about Jacques, I think she felt guilty about it, but when I was trying to piece it all together afterward, where she was that Friday night, who she was with, why she was late, it never really occurred to me that she might not have been telling me the whole truth. I don't know. I don't know what I'm really saying."

"That kind of thinking is a surefire way to go crazy."

"Yeah, that I know." Hadley turned her head to the window. "What about you? Do you always believe what everyone tells you?"

"Unless they give me a reason not to."

"That's the thing," said Hadley, "isn't it?"

They drove on, the car humming through the otherwise silence of a white-blanketed world.

By the time they hit the autoroute, joining

the lines of traffic bound for Lausanne and Geneva, the sun had dwindled. The cool, soft brightness of the mountains seemed, just as Joel had said, five worlds away. In the bottom of Hadley's stomach, unease twitched and turned. She could already feel the questioning eyes of her Les Ormes friends turning on her, and hear the mounting babble of Luca's gossip. And there was something else, too, a feeling that was vaguer, indistinct, but no less unsettling.

She focused on Lausanne. She wanted to feel about it as she did in the beginning. She'd had an appreciation for all of the details then, making the city seem as if it was truly hers. They'd been the equivalent of the things that a lover might notice — a half moon on a nail, a beauty spot, a lone hair on a man's shoulder. But she couldn't keep her mind where she wanted it. Her thoughts flitted back to this, *Kristina Hartmann.* A name. Sixteen letters. Her dear friend, reduced to the thinnest slip of paper. Smoothed and kept and guarded. Was it one of the reasons of which Joel spoke, sufficient motivation for doubting someone's word? But to doubt *what*? It was such a harmless thing, yet it persisted in her imagination.

For the first time in days, she thought of Hugo. She knew what he would say, and she could picture his face as he said it, his eyes darkening, then brightening, a barely perceptible inclination of the head. *If we don't ask the question, we'll never know the answer.* Had he said that once? Perhaps she had simply assigned the words to him because they felt like Hugo, and they felt like last year's Hadley, the one who'd torn about the city with a photograph folded in her hand. She glanced across at Joel as he drove. His hands were resting lazily at the bottom of the steering wheel. He turned to look at her and smiled.

"What are you thinking about?" he said.

"Just getting back to Lausanne. What this year's going to be like."

"You don't sound so very enthralled by it."

"Oh, I am. But I'm not sure I want this part to end."

"I'm with you on that."

"I like being driven around by you, you know."

"Well, let's just keep on driving, then. On into France, the length and breadth of it, we'll wind up on the Riviera, chasing the sun."

"The Riviera?"

"You got it. *La France.* You'd fit right in there, Hadley, with your leggy legs and your

443

boy-short hair and your sweet, sweet smile. With my arm around you, I'd fit right in, too."

"I didn't know you'd been to the Riviera."

"I'm an American Lit scholar, Hadley. Fitzgerald practically invented the place. Hemingway wrote *The Garden of Eden* . . ."

"Eden?"

"I suppose it is a kind of paradise, in a twisted sort of way."

She didn't know where her next words came from. When she thought about it later, she supposed they had been threatening all day, shining at the lake's tip, certain but slippery as a mirage.

"Joel," she said, "this is going to sound strange, I know. But when I looked for the money for breakfast, in your ski suit like you told me to, I couldn't find it, so I took it from your wallet instead."

"That's fine, honey, nothing strange about that."

"I found something in there. That was the strange bit. Sort of strange, anyway."

"You did? And what was that?"

"The piece of paper from Kristina's door."

"From Kristina's door?"

"You know, at Les Ormes. You said it was morbid to keep her name up there, and you took it down. You were going to throw it away."

He didn't flinch. "Okay, sure."

"Well, I found it in your wallet. You didn't throw it away."

"Okay. So what?"

"It was all smoothed out and tucked in there like it was, I don't know, like someone might keep a ferryboat ticket or a photograph. Like a souvenir."

"A ferryboat ticket? Hadley, what are you talking about?"

"I don't know, I just thought it was odd that you kept it. You made such a big deal about taking it down. You said you didn't want me to be sad anymore."

"I don't want you to be sad, anymore."

"And you said that I didn't need reminding of Kristina at every turn. So you took it down."

"Yes, I did."

"So, why did you keep it?"

"Hell, Hadley, I don't know. I just hadn't gotten around to throwing it away yet."

"But how did it get from your pocket to your wallet? That's a conscious thing. You must have taken it out and thought, 'I know, I'll keep this.' "

"*I know, I'll keep this?* Hadley, have you gone completely crazy?"

"Yes. I think I have. I'm sorry. Forget I spoke."

"Hadley, what the hell?"

"For a crazy moment I thought . . . I don't know. Why would you keep it? That's all."

"That's crazy."

"But . . ."

"If you want to know, I kept it for you. I felt stupid for insisting it came down. That's it. Okay?"

"Okay."

"Hadley, I didn't think that was you . . . going through my stuff, hatching theories. . . ."

"I'm not hatching theories, really, I'm not. I'm sorry. I'm an idiot. Can we just wind back the clock?"

"How far? How long have you been fretting about this sort of stuff? How far do we have to rewind? Hours? Days?"

"Minutes, only minutes. Hours, tops."

"I'm playing it safe. I'm taking it all the way back."

"Joel, honestly, it's only since today. When I took the money, and I saw the paper. I was just . . . thrown by it."

"We're starting over," he said, with resolution.

"So, where are we?" she said.

"Remember my very first class? When I

446

asked Hadley Dunn to stand, and up you got? All embarrassed but kind of pleased."

"Yes. I mean, *no*. Okay."

"Well, we're back there."

He was serious. His hands were no longer lazy on the wheel.

"So, all the things that have happened with us . . . that's all wiped?"

"Yeah."

"We haven't even kissed yet?"

"Nope."

"So, what, we're literally starting all over again?"

"Right at the very beginning."

She sank down in her seat and leaned her head against his shoulder.

"That's a little forward," he said, "considering we only just met."

They drove like that all the way back to Lausanne.

Despite what Joel had said, the silt of their argument lingered into their goodbye. It was there at all the edges, marring them. He stopped to drop her off at the bottom of the steep hill that ran up to Les Ormes. Outside it was twilight, and the city had fallen to cold again, all snow streaks and glistening pavements.

"What, you're going to make me walk?" she said.

"I can't risk parking outside. Everyone's returning from vacation. It's not worth it. Unless your friend Luca has already spread the word, in which case, well, I guess none of it matters."

"Well, why don't we presume the latter? At least then I get a ride to the door."

"It's safer this way."

"Right. Safer. Whatever. It's fine, I'll get the bus up."

Joel had pulled into the thin slice of car park by a small hotel. It looked all shut up, and the chalkboard with the day's restaurant specials was wiped clean.

"I thought perhaps you were taking me here," she said, her voice lighter, "one last night before reality hits."

"Too late, Hadley," he said, "I'm afraid it's upon us." His tone was morose, all earlier spark fizzled out. He leaned across and kissed her. Just once. Smartly.

"So . . . what next?" she said, her head tipped on one side, watching him.

"I'll see you soon. In class, I guess."

"Not before?"

"I've a ton of work I need to catch up on. Papers to grade. With you around, it's fair to say I've let things slide . . ."

"But, I mean . . . nothing's changed, has it? We're still . . ."

"Still what, Hadley?"

"Whatever we were before."

"Before what?"

"I don't know. Look, I had a great time. I really did."

"So did I."

"No one's ever done anything for me like that, Joel. It was magical. Thank you. Thank you so much."

"You're welcome," he said. He drummed his fingers on the wheel. "Thanks to you, too. That was . . . a grand New Year's, Hadley. Better than I ever imagined it would be." His voice was stretched, and it cracked at the end.

"I loved it, too," she said.

She leaned in for a better kiss and he obliged. Just.

As he drove away, she was left with the feeling that she'd handed him something and he hadn't quite taken it.

CHAPTER 30

Even from a distance Hadley could hear that the kitchen at Les Ormes was buzzing. As she opened the door and the faces of Jenny, Chase, Bruno and Loretta turned to meet her, she immediately knew that Luca had told them. It was in the strength of their gaze, as though they were looking for the one thing in her that they'd neglected to spot themselves. They turned on their smiles, and Hadley wilted in the doorway. Her hand stayed on the handle, her next step unsure.

"Here she is," said Jenny, "at last!"

"We thought you'd run away to the mountains and were never coming back," said Loretta.

"Make any resolutions?" asked Bruno. "We're just discussing ours, but they're all really boring. I bet yours are much more exciting."

Only Chase spoke plainly. "It's okay," he

said. "Luca just left. He told us you ran into each other, and he told us who you were with. He's just pissed because he can't have you, and he doesn't want anyone else to, either. Don't worry about it."

"Oh, Hadley, how could you? Your tutor? Isn't he all wrinkly?" said Jenny, sticking her tongue out with an exaggerated shiver.

"I'd say it was sexy," said Loretta, "if it wasn't for Luca. He really likes you, Hadley. He thinks you led him on."

"Well, Happy New Year, everyone," said Hadley, "it's just great to be back. And I didn't even come close to leading Luca on." She went to the sink and ran the tap. She filled a glass with water, then threw it away again. "And you all know that, by the way."

"We don't know anything," said Jenny. "You don't tell us anything."

"But you see why I couldn't," said Hadley, "don't you?"

"If Kristina had been here, would you have told her?"

Hadley stared at her. "No," she said. "No, I wouldn't. Because, if Kristina was here, I doubt I'd be with Joel at all."

"Joel," said Jenny, "is that his name? *Joel.* It even sounds old."

"Why do you say that, Hadley?" said Bruno.

"It doesn't matter," she said.

"Hadley, you're always so secretive," chipped Jenny.

"And you're so nosy," said Loretta, planting a kiss on Bruno's forehead.

As the others giggled together, Hadley let herself on to the balcony. She climbed onto the wall and sat with her legs dangling, wishing Lausanne would swallow her up. Or perhaps Joel was right: everything would be simpler if they stayed in the mountains. Chase followed her out.

"Don't worry about it," he said. "They just love to gossip. They don't mean anything by it. Did you have a nice Christmas?"

"Jenny's so offended," she said. "I don't see why. And I did, thanks. It was good to be home."

"She likes to think she knows what's going on round here, that's all."

"And you? Do you like to think you know what's going on?"

"I couldn't care about most things," said Chase. "Certainly, no offense, your love life. Though I'm glad you've got one, of course."

"Thanks, I guess," said Hadley.

Jenny rapped on the window. "Chase," she called, "it's freezing out there. Come back in."

He rolled his shoulders. "Summoned," he said.

"You don't have to go, you know," said Hadley. "What about your Christmas? How was America?"

He took a cigarette from his pocket and rolled it between his fingers. "America was exactly as I left it. I might stay and smoke this," he said.

"Chase!" called Jenny, through the glass. "How did you enjoy skiing? You had great weather for it. I saw the reports."

"It was beautiful," said Hadley.

"Bluebird and pow, that's what they call it, means blue skies, fresh powder. So, he's a skier, this guy of yours?"

"He is," she said, "and he taught me how to do it, too. I wasn't bad by the end."

"Very cool. Hey, there's a new girl, by the way," he said. "In Kristina's room. I noticed as I went past. Her name's on the door."

"There's a new name on the door?"

"Helena Freemantle. She was in the kitchen earlier when Luca was here. It wasn't going to stay empty forever, Hadley, but, are you okay?"

"Of course," she said. She tore at a loose nail and worked hard not to meet Chase's eye. *Helena Freemantle.* A new set of letters, a new slip of paper, slid neatly into the space where the old one had been.

She escaped the kitchen by saying that she had an essay to finish. Once in her room, Hadley breathed a sigh of relief, but almost straight away there was a knock at the door.

"Oh, what now?" she snapped, unintentionally saying it aloud. She opened the door with her face already set to contrition.

"Sorry to interrupt you, I just wanted to come and say hello."

Helena was as tall as a flag pole and had flame-red hair tied in a thick plait. Her face was blasted with freckles, not the polite scattering that Kristina had but an eye-popping amount. Her teeth were huge and perfect and she smiled easily.

"I'm your new neighbor," she said. "Helena Freemantle. Or just Hels, plenty of people call me Hels."

"Hi, Helena. And sorry, I didn't know it'd be you at the door. I'm just trying to lie low, that's all."

"Do you want a cup of tea? I've got a kettle in my room. Saves me having to go all the way to the kitchen every time."

"That's wise."

"Not that I'm antisocial but, you know, sometimes you just want a quiet cup of tea without having to go into everything all of the time. I was there when that guy Luca came around, getting them all whipped up."

"I don't really want to talk about all that."

"They weren't being cruel. They were just surprised. Nosy. Excitable. Whatever. Well, Luca wasn't exactly excitable, but you know what I mean."

"It's all right," she said. "And, you know, I was just about to finish up an essay, so, I haven't really time to stop for tea. But . . ."

"You were friends with her, weren't you? The poor girl who had my room before me?"

"Yes, I was."

"I'm sorry I'm not her," Helena said.

"Not your fault," said Hadley, and she couldn't help smiling back. "But thanks, anyway."

"Go on, one cup of tea," Helena said. "Please. Honestly, I was sitting in the kitchen listening to them all go on and on about you, and I just thought to myself, she sounds so much more interesting than you lot."

"I'm not," said Hadley, "not really. Just because I've slept with my professor doesn't make me interesting."

"Come on, Hadley, let's have a cup of tea together. I don't know who this professor is. I don't know anyone here yet. I'm safe territory. I'm . . . Switzerland."

Hadley laughed and acquiesced, letting her door click behind her as she followed Helena into her room. Inside, it didn't feel as if it had ever been Kristina's. Helena gabbled away easily, and Hadley sat back and listened. She was from the north of England, from a tiny town near the Scottish border. She'd had glandular fever and had missed the start of the year. She had been worried she couldn't come at all, so she took her eventual arrival in Lausanne to be a gift from the gods. As Helena put the kettle on to boil for a cup of tea, Hadley was surprised to find that she wanted to tell her about Joel — not the moment when he first kissed her, nor how he took her into the white world of the mountains — but the slip of paper from the door; how before *Helena Freemantle* there had been *Kristina Hartmann,* and he had kept her name. But it was too soon for that. Those kinds of confidences, if that was what they were, couldn't be so loosely scattered.

"Oh," Helena said, jumping up, "that reminds me. I found something you might want. It was under the bed. The cleaners must have missed it. I kicked my slipper under there, and when I scrabbled about to get it, I found this. Here."

She handed Hadley a book. It was Hemingway's *A Moveable Feast*. Traces of dust clung to its edges, but otherwise it was shiny and new, its spine uncracked.

"They said you were studying American Literature. When they were talking about your . . . Sorry, they were gossiping . . . Your professor . . . Anyway, you've probably read it. But I thought, you know, if it belonged to Kristina, maybe you'd want it."

With the tip of her finger, Hadley wiped the dust from the cover. It was the book that Kristina wouldn't let her buy her because she said she had it already, and she had loved that about her, the thought that she wanted to understand why Hadley liked Hemingway so much. It was also the book that Joel Wilson had taken from her hand in the English bookstore, grinning ruefully, as he'd said, "I used to give that book to all the girls I ever dated," and she'd loved that about him, too, the idea of a young Joel, wanting to be with a girl who liked the same things as him.

"I had a quick flick, and there's a cool bookmark in there," said Helena.

Hadley drew out the card. There was nothing written on it. She turned it over and saw a scene that she recognized. Rising mountains, spinning parasols, crystal lake waters, all painted in flat and colorful hues. It was just like the picture that graced the wall of Joel Wilson's office, a welcome gift from the department, he had told her then. *The Swiss Riviera*, immaculate and beautiful, a vintage traveler's dream.

"I know those pictures are sort of ubiquitous," said Helena. "There were loads of them at the airport. But it is lovely, isn't it? And to think we live here, in that perfect world. Oh, sorry, that's insensitive. I know it's not perfect, not really. But it seems it, doesn't it? To an outsider like me, anyway."

Hadley looked up at her. She kept her voice as level as she could. "Can I keep it?" she asked.

"Of course you can. I thought you'd want it. It was lucky that the cleaners missed it. I'm sure they'd have thrown it away otherwise."

Hadley slipped the card back inside the book. She clapped it shut.

"Thank you, Helena. Thank you so much."

After that she went back to her own room, refusing a second cup of tea, a shortbread biscuit. She professed that she was fine, not pale at all, no problem, none.

Hadley got ready for bed with mechanical

movements; back and forth with a tooth-brush, the flicking of a comb through her hair. Her phone rang, and she eyed it uncertainly before picking it up.

"Hadley, I'm sorry," said Joel's voice.

"What for?" she said, carefully.

"In the car. I went on and on. A dog with a bone."

"Don't worry about that," she said.

"Listen, here's a plan for next weekend. Have you ever been to Locarno? I hear it's . . ."

"Joel, wait. What did you mean, in the mountains, when you said that you were afraid of hurting me?"

"Did I say that?"

"You know you did."

Hadley could hear music in the background, the low rumble of jazz.

"Well?" she said.

"I was afraid that you think I'm perfect, when I'm not."

"Nobody's perfect," said Hadley, "and I'm not as stupid as all that."

"It's not stupid, it's lovely," he said. "Hadley . . ."

"Yes?"

Silence.

"*Yes?*" she urged.

"I do love you, you know."

It was a strange way of saying it for the first time. It came across as more of an afterthought, or an affirmation, a reminder of all previously uttered *I love yous,* when, actually, there had been none. Not as they'd rolled together, or kissed together, or whispered with hot breath. Not as they'd careered down slippery slopes, walked in the never-black alpine nights, fallen into sunken beds. Not one single *I love you,* and that had never mattered. Not before, anyway. Her hand went to her mouth. She shut her eyes.

"Hadley?" he said. "Are you still there?"

"I thought I'd know what to say," she said, "but I don't."

CHAPTER 31

She didn't sleep. In the bathroom she peered at herself in the mirror, and the doubt that burgeoned inside her seemed to cloud her face. Reflected in the glass she appeared pale, her eyes as flat as buttons. She showered, staying under the hot blast of the water until steam clouded her tiny bathroom, and afterward she sprayed perfume and painted her lips scarlet. She donned her thin mackintosh and trod quietly past her slumbering neighbors' doors, out into the stiff cold of the morning.

Lausanne seemed all elegance. The paving stones were frosted, and the first breaths of sunlight reflected the pastel shades of the shutters. Neatly dressed office workers walked snappily, woolen scarves knotted at their necks, leather-soled shoes tip-tapping. Hadley wove between them, cutting into the backstreets, until eventually she arrived at the Hôtel Le Nouveau Monde.

Inside, Hugo's usual table was empty. She sat down just beside it, her back as straight as a fence post, her hands knotted on the cloth. A waiter came from nowhere and bent down to her, solicitously. He'd served them the last time they were there, and she remembered his licorice-black hair, his sideways smile.

"*Mademoiselle,* if you're looking for Monsieur Bézier, he isn't here. But he telephoned with a message for you last week."

"Oh," Hadley said, "a message? What kind of a message?"

"Only to say that if you came to the café we were to tell you that he is staying at the Résidence Le Printemps, on the Rue des Roses."

"Why would he want me to know that?" she said.

"It is a convalescence home, *mademoiselle.*"

"Is he ill?"

"Monsieur Bézier is a very private man. He wanted only that we pass on the message, if you were to come, which you have. *Merci, mademoiselle.* Can I bring you something? *Un renversé,* perhaps?"

Hadley hesitated. "Um, I don't know . . . perhaps not. Perhaps . . . Well, I only came to see Hugo. Rue des Roses, did you say? Is that near here?"

"Just three streets away, *mademoiselle.* Turn right at the Maritime Restaurant, and then it's the second on the left."

She stood up, her chair screeching in the quiet of the dining room.

"*Mademoiselle,* one moment. I must give you the message. He wanted me to tell you this — *He's been thinking about the story, and the plot has taken an unexpected turn.*"

"The story? What story?"

"Monsieur Bézier is a writer of novels, I believe, *mademoiselle.*"

He bowed and retreated.

Printemps meant spring, and there was a fitting freshness to the convalescence home on Rue des Roses. The entrance was gated, a subtle gold plaque set in stone proclaiming its identity, and a short sweep of gravel drive led to the columned doorway. Its countenance was that of a discreet but luxurious hotel. Beneath every window lay carefully tended rose beds, blooming even in midwinter.

Hadley hesitated at the entrance. She took off her beret and ran her hands through her hair. A nurse in a pistachio-colored uniform came down the steps toward her, and despite her clumpy shoes, she was the picture of elegance. Hadley mustered her best French.

"Monsieur Bézier?"

The nurse smiled. "Please, come with me. He will be delighted to see you, Mademoiselle Dunn," she said.

Hugo was sitting in a chair by the window, wrapped in a tartan dressing gown. He had a silk scarf tied loosely at his neck, and his hair was perfectly combed, but his face was set in tones of gray, and there was a prickle of stubble at his jawline. Hadley felt a surge of affection for him. She hurried over, her footsteps breaking the quiet of the room.

"I knew there was a reason to hold on," he said, as she took his hand.

"What happened?" she said. "Are you all right?"

"I've never much cared for Christmas, so I thought I'd miss it this year. I had a perfectly timed heart attack on the twenty-third and spent the festive period in the hospital, presided over by a rather stern band of nurses. I checked myself in here for a little holiday. It's a pleasant sort of place."

"Oh, my God, a heart attack?" said Hadley. "But you're okay?"

"Right as rain," he said. "You know, I've always liked that expression of yours, so very stoical, somehow. But that's all very dull, so enough of me. What of you, Hadley, are you well? Is it a happy new year?"

"I'm fine. Hugo, I went to the Hôtel Le Nouveau Monde, and they gave me the message. But what if I hadn't gone? I wouldn't have known. You should have sent a note to me at Les Ormes."

"That was precisely the point," he said. His dressing gown was belted, and he curled the end of the cord around his fingertip. This small action, in one usually so composed, was unsettling. "I didn't want any kind of a pity visit," he went on. "I only wanted you to come if you were seeking me out, anyway. I was somewhat frosty with you the last time we met, and I've berated myself for it ever since."

"So, you left it to chance?"

"Not chance exactly," he said. "I wouldn't say that."

Hadley saw the tip of his finger turn quite white. He unwound the cord and dropped it in his lap. Hadley glanced away.

"So, what is this place?" she said eventually.

"It's a very expensive hotel for the infirm. They do excellent smoked salmon for breakfast, of which I'm served the tiniest strip, with an absolute absence of scrambled egg.

Now, considering what I pay to be here, I hold that to be a significant crime."

Hadley eyed Hugo's battered slippers and the cane propped at the side of his chair. He noticed her looking, and flapped his hands with unusual animation.

"I'm horribly underdressed," he said, a little theatrically. "If I had known you were coming this very minute, I would have prepared quite differently. What a sight I must look, what a frail old thing."

"But you're recovering all right? You're going to be okay?"

"I am," said Hugo. "I don't think I've ever been so pampered. And it was a minor attack, I'm told. As you can see I am quite unharmed. No damage that's obvious to your young eyes, anyway."

"Are you sure you wouldn't prefer that I left you to rest?"

"Rest!" he harrumphed. "I've had nothing but rest. The days run on, you know, punctuated by small, unsatisfying meals and passages of sleep. The odd exchange with another guest, or patient, or client, or whatever we're supposed to call ourselves. I was quite turning to dust. And then . . ."

"And then?"

"Lately, I've been bothered, Hadley."

"I'm sorry," she said, "is it . . . Are you in pain?"

"I haven't been bothered in such a long time," said Hugo. "Not since I wrote my last book, all of seventeen years ago. When I was writing, I spent my life in a state of perfect agitation, my mind pulling in every direction. That was my way. I didn't realize how much I missed it, until I felt it again."

"You're writing again?"

"Not yet."

"I wondered about your message, *'the plot has taken an unexpected turn.'* "

"Ah, yes, I hoped that would bring you here."

"What do you mean? And what are you bothered by?"

"An idea for a story."

"But, Hugo, that's great, it's something to focus on. That's brilliant."

"No, it's not. Not really. It's a cruel idea. I feel enormously guilty even imagining it. But I told myself that if you didn't object, if you allowed me this . . . liberty, then you might be giving an old man a most tremendous gift."

"I don't understand. What do you want me to do?"

He took her hand. He smiled, but only just.

"You like happy endings, don't you? Love conquers all. And in life I want you to have all the happiest endings possible. But in the story . . . Let me begin at the beginning, Hadley. I've been too much apart from the things that matter, for too long. Every single one of my days has been shaped by routine, down to the very smallest detail. When I was writing, my days were upside down and back to front. I would begin work at three o'clock in the morning, because an idea seized me and I couldn't sleep. Or I'd simply work all the way through the night and sleep the whole day. A story would take me by the throat and refuse to let me go. All my days were filled with life and death and sex. My nights, too. What else? Beauty. Evil. Generosity. Pettiness. I lived every emotion and wrote every possible character, all of my beginnings, all of my endings. Henri Jérôme published eighteen novels. People wanted to read what he had to write. And then, one day, I just stopped. No reason. No deep psychological blow. No lost love, searing disappointment or any of the things that people try and use to explain away the miserable romance of a writer who doesn't write. I simply felt, Hadley, that I had said all the things that I'd ever wanted to say."

"But that's amazing, Hugo. Not many people get to say that," she began, but he hadn't finished. He spoke on, his hands jumping with agitation.

"And now, without the writing, comes . . . nothing. Empty days, blank and staring as the unwritten page. Without words, I've filled them with watching others. I no longer make up lives. Instead, I sit on the sidelines and simply watch. Impotently, but quite contentedly, don't mistake me. Did you know I live only a two-minute stroll from the Hôtel Le Nouveau Monde? I've a cavernous apartment, with one of the finest lake views in Lausanne, and yet I choose the hotel for my coffee, for my cognac. There's a sense of order there, that all is right in the world. One day is very much like the other, you could almost believe that time has stopped turning. I've grown to like that, the feeling of everything slowing down, almost to a stop. And then, you walked in. You ignored all of those fools at the bar and allowed me to talk to you instead. After that evening, for the first time in, well, a very long time, I thought about writing again."

He shook his head, with a mild sense of wonder. Only the ripple at his jaw betrayed the depth of his emotion.

"You're my story, Hadley, or rather, my

469

story is yours. Everything I've been turning over, the things that have been keeping me awake, it's all yours. Kristina. Jacques. Your professor. And you. Especially you."

Hadley stared at him. She didn't know where he was going, but it felt like somewhere they had never been before. She folded her hands in her lap and dug with her nails, a sharp little track, marking her palm.

"When I was writing," he said, "I used to dream my plots. I would go to sleep thinking on a problem, and in the depths of the night all would be revealed to me. I'd keep a notebook by my bed so I could jot it down the moment that I woke. If I left it any longer, past waking, coffee, breakfast, it would all slip away again. So as soon as I opened my eyes, I'd scribble it all down. Some of my finest ideas came to me while sleeping."

Hugo sat back in his chair as an attendant in the same pistachio-colored uniform brought them a carafe of iced water and a pot of jasmine tea. She set it down with painstaking exactitude, and Hugo waited until the last cup was laid and the teapot perfectly positioned. Hadley kept her eyes on him.

"Go on," she said.

Hugo felt in the pocket of his dressing gown and took out a notebook. It was black and bent at the corner, as thick as a hotel bible. He held it with both hands.

"Of course, a lot of dreams are nonsense. Crazed ramblings. And God knows I've been on some fantastic drugs recently, but . . ."

He shifted in his seat, and his foot nudged the tip of his cane so that it fell to the floor with a clatter. Neither reached for it. He opened the notebook and folded the cover back on itself, cracking its spine.

"So you must forgive me," he said. "You must not think me . . . vindictive. I know in the past you've considered me something of a jealous old fool, and quite rightly, too. But, Hadley, I had the most wonderful idea for a story . . . so wonderful, in fact, that I'm afraid it's not fiction at all. I fear, irrationally but no less resolutely, that it's very much the truth."

He handed her the notebook. She clapped it shut, and the sound reverberated down the halls.

"I don't know if I want to read it," she said, "not after that build up. You're scaring me, Hugo."

"I'm not scaring you."

"You've barely told me anything about

your life, and suddenly I get everything, in one great rush. I'm touched, I am, but . . ."

"Just read it, Hadley. Please."

She looked down at the book. She opened it and flipped through the pages. Each was packed with a dense scrawl, the marks of a streaking ink pen, scribbles and crossing-outs.

"Your handwriting's impossible," she said. "And anyway, it's all in French." She went to hand it back to him, then stopped. There were two names she recognized.

"What's this?"

Hugo leaned forward and tapped the page. "It says, *Joel est Jacques.*"

"I know what it says, but what does it mean?" Her voice was ice-cold, sharp-edged.

"Joel is Jacques," he said.

"For God's sake, Hugo, my French isn't that bad."

"Well? Aren't you going to say anything?"

"What can I say? It's a fantasy. You said so yourself."

"I said that it began as one. But I believe it now. I believe it to be the truth. And from the expression on your face, Hadley, I think perhaps you do, too."

Hadley tossed the notebook back to him, and he caught it in his lap, his fingers curl-

472

ing around it protectively.

"Oh, you do? And what makes you so sure? Because how can you, shut up in here, dare to pretend to know something like that?"

Hugo watched her, sitting quite still as her questions whistled past.

"I mean, it's crazy, Hugo. It's lunacy. You've never even met 'my professor' as you always insist on calling him in that disdainful voice of yours. You don't even know what he's like. You haven't got the slightest idea."

"I haven't met him, you're quite right."

"And you didn't know Kristina, either. So, she's a liar, too, is she? Everything she told me, she made it all up? It's a ridiculous idea."

"You're right to be angry, Hadley."

"I'm not angry. It's too stupid to dignify with anger."

"And you're right to be upset."

"I'm not. I'm not upset."

"Hadley, please know this — the last thing that I would ever, ever want to do is hurt you."

She opened her mouth, a stony response at her lips, but she faltered. "That's one thing I do know," she said quietly.

"Then you must listen to me, Hadley. I'm certain that if you cast your mind back, if

473

you try to think along the same lines that I have, you'll see what I see. There will be reasons, two or three things that just don't quite fit. Things that at the time didn't seem that unusual, because there are always excuses, and there are always explanations. But now, in this light, on this day, think again, Hadley. Think again and tell me it's not a possibility."

It had begun yesterday, as something small and dull and niggling, and last night it had crept and crawled, an ever-mounting sense of unease starting to shape itself. Now, as she let herself listen to Hugo's words, it became whole. She knew then that realization wasn't something that lived in the mind, instead it was a physical sensation, a strangling hold, a flat-out blow.

"A possibility?" she said. "No, I don't think it is a possibility."

"Hadley . . ."

She was breathing heavily, her chest rising and falling rapidly. As soon as she became aware of it, she couldn't slow down, she couldn't begin to catch her breath. She closed her eyes to concentrate. She felt Hugo's steadying hand on her arm. Tears fell from her lashes.

"She teased me about him once," she said, her voice as tight as a knot.

474

"Who?"

"Kristina. She teased me about Joel. She told me she'd noticed that I always wore something nice when I had American Literature. I had on a dress, and I'd painted my nails. It was my birthday. I told her it was just for my birthday."

"Ah."

"I wanted her to meet him because I thought they'd get on, but I wanted to keep him to myself, too. You see, I thought that if he saw her, if he got to know her even just a little bit, he wouldn't . . ."

"Hadley?"

She was speaking into the cup of her hand, muffled, delicate words that Hugo strained to hear. He bent closer, his eyes never leaving her face.

"He was my tutor. But I never really saw him like that, because I met him before term started, and it didn't occur to me that he was anything to do with the Institute. I just thought he was someone like me, another person on their own in Lausanne, excited to be here, finding their way."

"A chance meeting," Hugo said, "two strangers."

Hadley stared at him and he stared back, with perfect symmetry. At last, they were matched.

"Joel," said Hadley, "Jacques."

"Mon Dieu."

The room around her ceased to exist. Gone were the flat-footed orderlies and the dim smell of expensive disinfectant and the china pots of tea served at all the wrong times. Everything went, and all that was left was Hugo and the pieces of his story.

Outside, beyond the rows of pom-pom-headed trees, sunset was falling over the water in a blaze of iridescence. Hadley sat slumped in a chair, an invalided pose, with her back to the window. Hugo watched her intently, the color high in his cheeks. She'd told him about the tiny, insignificant strip of paper that said *Kristina Hartmann,* and how pathetic she had felt as she'd challenged Joel over it in the car, her voice brittle and quavering. *He stuffed it in his pocket and said he'd throw it away because he didn't want me getting sad every time I saw it, but instead he kept it. He kept it into his wallet, Hugo, and I found it and I didn't know if it meant something or nothing.* She told him about the dust-scuffed copy of *A Moveable Feast* that Helena had discovered kicked beneath the bed in Kristina's room. *Joel gave it to her, didn't he? Because he told me that he used to do that, he used to give all of his girlfriends a copy of that book as a kind of test, to see if they liked it. I laughed when he told me that, because I loved that book. And when Kristina told me she bought it herself I believed her.* Hugo listened and nodded, his eyes wide, for there were no such florid idea scribbled in his notebook.

"He never gave me a reason not to believe him, Hugo," she said. "Just since yesterday I started feeling like something wasn't right, but I didn't know what. I never thought it was this. Never this."

"Didn't you? Hadley, try and think. Did you tell him about Kristina, or did he already know?"

"I told him. I went looking for him. I wanted his help."

"And what was his reaction?"

"He was . . . shocked. Like anybody would be. No, wait, there was something. He was stressed. Before I got there he was already stressed. He said it was over a deadline. He was tearing his hair out. Do you think he was already lying? Was that *grief*? It can't have been, Hugo, because he was so kind. He set himself completely aside. He listened, and straightaway he was kind. And supportive. He was so, so supportive. He was the only person I really wanted to talk to about Kristina because he understood.

Oh, God."

"He understood," said Hugo.

"He understood better than anyone."

The last of the sunlight had fizzled from the room. Hadley got up and walked over to the window. Down the lake toward Geneva, there was the smallest strip of burned orange. Then it went, quick as a switch, as overhead the sky thickened with a band of snow clouds. Everything ran to a blur, and she rubbed fiercely at her cheeks. She turned back to Hugo.

"It was all right there in front of me, and even then I couldn't see it. I don't understand how you worked it out, Hugo."

He told her that he had moved the pieces of the puzzle, this way and that, until they created a pattern that made a sort of sense. *Just an idea for a story,* he'd said, *at first,* and as he talked, Hadley's mind ran on, tracing miserable shapes. It all made dreadful sense. Kristina concocting the story of the broken marriage, a cover for the real fact of Joel's position at the Institute, the illicit romance with a tutor that she now knew all about herself. *Jacques.* A French dream of a name, a clean white lie. Perhaps they did meet on the Riviera; Joel had a deep and even tan, and in class he clicked through slides of palm-tree-lined promenades and bathing-suited socialites, talking of the Fitzgeralds, the Hemingways, speaking of the summers that changed everything with an aficionado's familiarity. Yet it still would have been a coincidence that he was bound for Lausanne. She would have changed all the details, who he was and what he looked like, and where he lived, to keep the veil of secrecy. Just as Hadley had gone skiing with Swiss friends. And just as the American she gave her mum was a student in her class. A fluttering line of little white lies. But Joel hiding who he really was? There was nothing little or white about that. A picture began to root itself. It was the thought of how perfect the two of them would have looked together. Kristina all long, blond hair and endless limbs, eyes as wide as windows, and Joel chucking an arm around her carelessly, dragging her into a kiss. They would be the same height, their lips would match perfectly. *The most handsome man in the world, and the most beautiful woman.* Hadley remembered the pained look in Joel's eyes as she'd told him what Kristina had said about her lover. She had mistaken it for sympathy.

"Hugo, it wasn't just one lie," said Hadley. "It was layer upon layer of deception. We walked all over Geneva, looking for someone who doesn't even exist. How he could lie and lie, again and again?"

"Perhaps he felt he didn't have a choice," Hugo said. "Consider it from his perspective, just for a moment, if you can bear to. If the girl he wasn't supposed to love was killed, a student, an illicit romance, he'd have had to mourn in private. And then you arrived at his door. What could he do? He couldn't show you his grief."

"You're defending him?"

"Far from it."

"I fell for him, Hugo."

"Yes, you told me that, *ma chérie.*"

"What, and you didn't believe it?"

"You were terribly unhappy, and he managed to change that. I witnessed as much with my own eyes. And you, without realizing, perhaps did the same for him. I wonder if that's the same thing as two people coming together under ordinary circumstances. I think perhaps not."

"Nothing's ever ordinary, is it? Not for the people involved."

"You and I met in a bar. Hasn't that got a terrific ring to it? I could fancy I was forty years younger."

"And was it ordinary?"

"It was the most extraordinary thing to happen to me in a very long time."

Hadley let her face drop into her hands. She felt Hugo's hand on her shoulder, a barely-there touch.

"It's not inconceivable that in the time that you spent together, and the comfort you drew from one another, you replaced Kristina in his affections."

"I don't want to replace anybody," said Hadley, "and especially not like that."

"But no one is a clean sheet."

"I was."

Hugo sat back in his chair and stared across the lawn toward the lake. His face trembled, as he struggled to find something to say to her.

"I wasn't looking for anything, Hugo. It was enough just being here, in this beautiful place. And then everything fell apart, and he was there."

"He was never the only one."

"No," she said, "but he was the one who really mattered."

"He never deserved you, Hadley."

"He told me he loved me," she replied, quietly.

"When?"

"Yesterday."

"And?" he replied.

"I didn't say it back."

Hugo sighed. A long, slow exhale. His

briefly brightened cheeks were pale again.

"He'd know, though, wouldn't he?" he said. "People always know."

"Do they? I'm not so sure. I'm not so sure about anything. The girl in your story, what does she do?"

"I didn't get that far."

"But what would you have her do? And him, what about him?"

Hugo slipped the notebook into the pocket of his dressing gown and clasped his hands in his lap.

"I'm sorry," he said. "I can't see the rest of the story anymore," he said. "It's gone."

Hadley stared at him, frustration swelling. She had the sudden desire to shake Hugo, grab hold of his arms and rattle him until he told her something different. She bit her lip and looked away from him.

"This fiction, this *truth* . . . it didn't just occur to you in a dream, did it? You suspected it before. Long before. I can see that now, with all your talk of phantoms and pen names. You hinted, but too softly. You should have just come right out and said it. What were you afraid of, Hugo? That I wouldn't want to hear? That you'd scare me away?"

"It was only an idea. A foolish fancy. One fueled by my somewhat prejudiced distrust of his motives. You would have laughed at me, Hadley. Or yelled."

"Yes, probably."

"And you would have been terribly hurt," he said.

"And now?" she said. "What am I now?"

"Perhaps you're someone who knows the truth."

His voice was as soft as the snowflakes that had started to fall outside the window. They both turned their heads to look.

"Jacques is Joel, and Joel is Jacques," said Hadley, in no more than a murmur.

She watched as each snowflake spiraled gently, melting just as soon as they touched the ground.

CHAPTER 32

Before she left the Résidence Le Printemps that day, Hugo tried to warn her.

"Let him speak, Hadley," he said. "We may still be wrong."

He had stroked her fingers as he spoke, brushing the length of them from knuckle to tip. Hadley moved her hand gently away, and Hugo nodded. A rueful smile.

"I'm going to wait," she said. "I want him to tell me first. I think he will. I know he will."

"Don't be so sure."

"You never liked him, did you? Even without this."

"No," said Hugo, "but I shouldn't think that's any kind of comfort now."

She walked down the dark sweep of the drive. At the gateway, she turned and looked back. Hugo was watching her from his window. He held up one hand in farewell. She nodded and briefly raised her hand in silent reply.

She sat through Joel's class the next morning. She took a seat right at the very back and watched him. He appeared brisk and bright, but Hadley was looking for the cracks of a grieving man and she saw them. They were there in the dark stains beneath his eyes, the creaking in his voice, the pressure of his fingers as he leaned on the desk, their tips turning quite white. Yet he still made the students in the front rows sway with easy laughter. People still wrote down the things he said and underlined them for emphasis, swept them pink with highlighters and threw their hands up in the air as he turned a question on them. At the end, eager students crowded his desk, and Hadley hung back. She heard banter about his ski accident. His cheek had bloomed into a yellowing bruise, blackened scabs beneath his eye, but he no longer looked daring to her, just broken. She saw him glance in her direction, peering past the earnest figures that circled him, just as he had all throughout the class. Hadley stared back at him evenly. In front of her, her jotter page was etched with black lines. Her pen was cracked along its stem. She left before the crowd at his desk had cleared.

In the cafeteria at lunchtime she saw him standing at the counter, slinging back an espresso, Italian-style. He was with Caroline Dubois, and they were deep in conversation. Caroline's loose chignon had uncurled, and a lock of auburn hair fell across her shoulder. She leaned close to Joel as she talked. Hadley looked down at her plate of *frites*. She selected a fry and dipped it in a pool of ketchup. She nibbled it, intently.

Later that afternoon, he caught her arm in the corridor as she passed.

"Hadley, what are you doing this evening? I want to see you."

"I'm not sure," she said.

"Hadley, please."

He gripped her arm and said only that he wanted to see her again. No, when Hadley replayed it later, he'd said that he *needed* to see her. And amid it all, it still felt like a good thing; his inconsumable desire for her.

That evening, she buzzed at the door of Joel's apartment block. There was no answer, and so she buzzed again.

"Hello, yes?"

"It's me."

"Hadley?"

"Who else?"

He let her in. The vestibule looked shabbier than she remembered. Empty bottles of wine were scattered like bowling pins. She kicked through a flood of free newspapers and pizza leaflets. She hadn't felt nervous until now. A wave of nausea hit her, and she hung on to the banister as she climbed the stairs with shaky steps.

He had left the door to his apartment ajar, and she pushed at it. Joel emerged from the kitchen, a dishcloth in his hand. He blinked at her, and his look was so heavy-hearted that she felt her insides wrench in pity.

"You wanted me to come over," she said, as levelly as she could.

Joel passed the cloth from one hand to the other, and Hadley shifted the weight on her feet with matched unease.

"No kiss?" she said, attempting brightness.

Joel threw the cloth at the countertop, and it missed, falling to the floor. He ignored it and took Hadley by the shoulders. He pulled her toward him. But he wasn't all there. His lips were tight and hard. Hadley turned away, her own masquerade a failure. She wished, fleetingly, that Hugo Bézier were there with her; far better for him to tell this far-fetched story. She sat down on the edge of the sofa, her body set tight. He hovered beside her, loose on his feet.

"You hung up on me the last time we

spoke," he said, not quite looking at her.

"I didn't plan to," she said.

"I told you I loved you, Hadley."

He met her eye then, and she held it. She tried to see all the way inside him, but all she got were pale mists, a wash of blue, shrinking pupils that told her nothing.

"I know you did," she said.

"That's it?" he said.

"I didn't know what to say."

"Right."

"I'm sorry."

"Hadley, listen. It's me who should be sorry. It was too soon for what I said. And too late for other things."

"Joel . . ." she began.

"You deserve better," he said. He crouched beside her and took hold of her hands. His palms were dry and warm and she held on tightly. "I said it at the beginning, and I always meant it. I've been doing a lot of thinking these last couple of days. Hadley, I need to end it."

It was a slap. The last thing she expected.

"So, you said *I love you* and, what, now you don't?"

"That's not it."

"And what about this weekend? Locarno? We're not going anymore? Just like that?"

"I wish we could."

"I don't believe you," said Hadley.

"I don't blame you," he said.

"What kind of answer is that?"

He turned away and went to the window. The same spot he had stood in on the first morning when she'd woken up at his house, when he was hunched and smoking and staring at the street, instead of lying beside her.

"Joel," she said again, as forcefully as she could muster.

She saw then that his shoulders were shaking. At first she thought that he was laughing, and she wondered briefly if it was all a bad joke, a misjudged piece of playacting, but then she heard a sob, a strangled sound that seemed to rip from him, possessed of a life of its own.

"Joel," she said, the same sob threatening her own words, "it's okay. I know."

She saw him freeze. Heard his intake of breath. She went over to him, and her steps across the room were slow and steady, one foot in front of the other. She curled her arms around his waist and leaned her head against his back. She moved with him as he shook. She hadn't planned to do any of this, but she did.

"How?" he said, turning to face her. "Not because of that damned slip of paper?" His voice was a hoarse whisper.

"Jacques . . ." she said.

"Kristina . . ."

As he said her name, his face was locked in a soundless scream. Silence roared around them, and the name, *Kristina,* twisted in the wind. Hadley tightened her hold on him, her fingers pressing into his arm.

"There's so much I need to say to you," he said, "but the one thing you need to believe is that I do love you."

She stared at him, her eyes watering. His hair was awry and falling into his eyes. He was a man split open with sorrow. How could there be any love left for her, in all of that? It was only then that she realized she hadn't really believed it before, not wholly, not completely. But now, every single lie he had ever told was all around them.

"I don't know who you are," she said, "do I?"

"Hadley, I barely know myself."

"I shouldn't be here," she said. "I have to go."

"Hadley, I need to explain . . ."

"I don't see how you can."

"You have to let me."

"You made a fool out of me. Maybe you had your reasons, and maybe you never meant to, but you did. So, I can't hear anything yet. I don't want to know. I will, but not yet. Not now."

She walked out of the apartment, pulling her coat around her, fumbling with the buttons. As soon as she was out of the door, she dashed down the spiraling stairs. When she got to the bottom she heard a sound and paused to listen. It could have been the wind moaning outside the building, the whine of a passing car, perhaps, even the growl of an old man's tethered dog. It could have been any and all of these things, or it could have been Joel Wilson weeping.

Two days passed, and he didn't try to contact her. Hadley skipped class, eschewed Les Ormes and kept away from Résidence Le Printemps. She lost herself in the city. She walked the length of Rue des Mirages, looking for something and nothing. In the end, the mountains pulled her to the lakeside. The Alps that day were mud-gray and massive, with burly rolls of cloud scudding the low slopes. It was a landscape that rooted her and gave perspective, and she stared into it, letting it take her. Just a few streets away Hugo would be sitting in his dressing gown, his bony ankles showing beneath the roll of his pajama bottoms. She knew he would wake up each day and wonder if she'd come again. Was he scribbling in his notebook, even now? *I wanted to write my own story.* That was what she would tell him later.

Suddenly she knew that what she really needed was to hear her parents' voices. She took out her phone and rang.

"Mum?" she said, cupping her hand to her mouth as the wind upped its roaring.

"Hadley, oh, Hadley, what a lovely surprise."

She shut her eyes. "What are you doing?" she asked.

"Oh, the usual," her mum said. "Sam's at his friend's house, your dad's just in from work. Where are you? It's noisy."

"I'm down by the lake," said Hadley. "It's the wind."

"You're not on your mobile phone, are you? It'll cost a bomb."

"I wanted to speak to you, that's all."

"Well, that's very nice. Love, we didn't hear from you after your ski trip. Was it everything you hoped?"

She passed the telephone to her other hand and blew on her freezing fingers.

"I've never been anywhere as beautiful," she said.

"And could you do it? Could you ski?"

492

"I could," said Hadley.

She thought of how once she'd spun out of control and Joel had caught her, his arms encircling her waist, her legs with their skis sliding between his own. They'd sunk into the snow, laughing and laughing as she'd pulled him down on top of her. His skin had tasted of sun-cream, and his lips had been roughened by the cold, hard air. Then she thought of him skiing through the rocks, the deafening speed, the crazy leap, not seeming to care if he lived or died. It made sense now, the erasing of all feeling except that which existed in the moment. The grim abandonment.

"Tell me some things," said Hadley, struggling to keep her voice even. "What's Dad up to?" she said. "Is he okay?"

"Oh, he's fine. You know your dad," her mum said. "Here, have a word with him. He'll be so pleased to hear from you."

Hadley shut her eyes again as she heard the telephone being passed between them.

"The cat wants letting out," she heard her dad say.

"Never mind the cat," said her mum. "Hadley! We looked for you on Ski Sunday, and we couldn't see you."

"Hi," she said weakly. The bars of their fire would be glowing red and they would

493

probably have drawn the curtains early. When Sam came home, he'd be pink-cheeked and full of chatter.

"And you're all right?" he said. "Everything's all right?"

"Always," said Hadley. One word was all that she could manage. She bit her lip and hoped he'd launch into a torrent. A detailed account of the latest piece of mischief from Sam, or the winners he'd had from his small bets on the horses.

"You enjoy yourself, Hadley, but don't forget your studies. Now, what's all this about an American boy?"

She heard a muffled admonishment in the background. She saw her dad shifting on his feet like a slow old boxer as her mum wrestled back the phone, her laughter chirruping.

"Never mind your dad, Hadley. You have the time of your life," she said. "Don't waste a minute of it."

She knew then that she had to go. She mustered an exuberant sort of goodbye, one that smacked of things-to-do and places-to-go and happiness, happiness above all else, but in the end it came out as a whisper. Her parents' voices rang out in their own farewell chorus. In their bid to wish her well, they had missed the fact that she wasn't, and that was exactly as she needed it to be. She imagined them settling back into whatever they were doing before, but with a new charge about them, a sense of brightness.

Hadley held the phone in her hand, turning it over and over. Joel was the only person who'd ever torn the earth from beneath her feet, in all of the good ways, and now in an unimaginably bad way. But the good ways were still there. They still counted. Wasn't it her choice, to decide how much it mattered that he had lied?

She thought of what she knew, and what she could imagine. Joel had caught the sun in the Riviera, she saw that now; the creases around his eyes were from squinting past spiky palm trees and glittering water. He wasn't a departing husband, but a new professor on foreign shores, a romantic, treading in the footsteps of his literary heroes. Maybe he'd noticed Kristina's hair first, the way it held the sun's light in every strand. Lausanne would have been a talking point over a harborside dinner, a realization that, miraculously, their fates were bound. Joel would have kicked back in his chair and folded his hands behind his head, a fine mess, a love affair with a soon-to-be student, but he'd tasted her honey skin, her frangipane lips, and it couldn't be the end just yet. They had decided on *Jacques* on their last night down south, Kristina's idea, proffered with laughter. Maybe she had imagined Joel in a shirt and tie in a lecture hall, chalking love hearts on the board, thinking she would catch his hands later and press them against all the places that he couldn't touch by day. *Jacques.* She would weave a story for the other students, *a failing marriage,* she would say, *a stop-start romance.* Perhaps she hadn't counted on the English girl who became so dear a friend, and grew so starry-eyed whenever she said *love.*

Hadley pushed her hands to her eyes. Quietly, into her gloved hand, with only the water as witness, she began to talk.

"So, I figured it out in the end, Kristina," she said, "with a little help. You could have told me, you know. Or would that have been no fun? Because you liked to tease me about my American Literature professor, didn't you? Would it have been so very bad to have just told me the truth? You could have trusted me, you know. I don't think Joel ever set out to make a fool out of me, but what about you? You weren't perfect, no one ever is, but I was so sure that you were better than that."

The wind whipped easy tears from her

eyes. Through the burly chestnut trees, she could glimpse the shape of the Hôtel Le Nouveau Monde. She walked toward it.

"And now? What now?" she said, beneath her breath. "You're gone. I hate it, every day I hate it, but it's true. And we're still here, Joel and I, Jacques and I, me and him. Kristina, what if what we have is real? Despite the lies, and despite everything that's gone before, what if it's true, too? Hugo thinks it's all wrong, but you, what do you think?"

Sometimes Ouchy teemed with people, but today it was quiet. She kicked through piles of iced leaves, and gravel crunched underfoot. She had felt the heat of Joel's hands as they'd closed around her, and the press of his body in the cabin in the mountains. The unquestionable truth contained in a kiss. Out of the dark came these things, and she knew that they were hers. She wound her way through the chestnut trees and thought of Joel's hole of grief, and how, for all her presence, he had been so alone in it. If she had only known, if he'd only trusted her with the truth, how different things would have been. Or maybe not? Perhaps everything would have been just the same.

As she walked, she began to warm up. He

had comforted her, when she needed it most. That was true. He had kissed her and held her. That was true. He had distracted her from all that was sad and bad and taken her into the white Alps and loved her there. That was true. Any trickery had always been accompanied by warming words and hope, the hope that one day things would be better than they were now. And that had been true.

She stopped when she got to the hotel. A momentary lull in the wind had left its flags drooping. The doorman stood rocking on his heels. He nodded to her. Perhaps he recognized her; more likely he was just being polite. She walked on past, her mind turning on Joel. She had always thought him bristling, contained of an energy she couldn't fathom. And it was true that there always seemed to be a part of him she couldn't reach, as they lay beside one another in the dark, as she watched him when he wasn't looking, how he turned the music all the way up in the car and gripped the steering wheel as though he'd rip it from the dashboard. Perhaps she had been warned, after all. He had looked into her eyes and told her to keep away, to run while she still could. *Find a nice Swiss boy with impeccable manners and neat shoes,* wasn't that what he'd said? And yet she had fallen all the same.

Jacques. She smiled a tight little line of a smile. She had always thought that she and Jacques shared an affinity, bonded by their affection for Kristina, unified in their separate grief. It was Kristina, her sweetest friend, who had brought them together. She decided there and then that it would not be Kristina who pulled them apart. There was no Jacques. There was only Joel.

CHAPTER 33

It was nightfall when Hadley rode the bus home to Les Ormes. Around her, Lausanne glittered and twinkled as it always had. Perfectly presented shop windows beamed brightly, and the fine hotels were illuminated like stage sets. Hadley closed her eyes. She wanted more than anything to sleep. In the morning she would see Joel. She would tell him that she was ready to listen, and that she was ready to try and understand.

Les Ormes was its usual ominous hulk. A jaundiced streetlamp lit the passageway to its foyer. A group of international students stood smoking on the steps, and in their black winter coats they appeared like a clutch of jackdaws. They chattered among themselves and laughed into their cigarettes. Hadley slipped past them. She was barely inside the hall when Helena appeared, and rushed up to greet her. She must have been waiting on the leather sofas, flipping through

500

the free newspapers and torn-edge magazines, and now her cheeks were candy-pink with excitement.

"Hadley, there you are! I've been looking for you all over."

"Hels, I'm so tired. I'm just going to crash . . ." she began.

"But there's someone here for you. I saw him as I walked in after class. He was sort of loitering in the corridor, looking quite shifty, actually. But he's so handsome, you'd never just go up to him and ask him what he was doing or who he was looking for. He so obviously wasn't a student. And then once I was in my room, I heard a knocking at your door. I just stuck my head out, to see who it was, in case it was Jenny or Chase or someone to say hello. But it was him."

"Helena, who?"

"Your professor's here."

"What, Joel? Is he?"

"I let him wait in my room. I'd have shown him to the kitchen, but the others would have torn him apart. He's very monosyllabic. All he said was that he was here to see you, but I knew straightaway who he had to be. God, he's handsome, Hadley."

He was standing with his back to them. He

501

was staring through the window, across the balcony and down toward Lausanne's tiny lights and the dark shape of the mountains beyond. Perhaps he was in a world of his own, for he made no move to turn at the sound of the door. Hadley had the chance to study his blond hair, his lofty height, his dark coat that fell to somewhere near his knees. She closed the door behind her. It was not Joel Wilson.

"Hello," she said.

By some miracle, the word came out in one piece. He turned around. He made as if to smile, then stopped himself. Instead, he nodded, as if the sight of her affirmed something essential — joining dots and solving puzzles, Hugo might have said. He held out his hand to her, and she walked toward him. She took it.

"You're Hadley," he said.

She found that she couldn't let go. She felt her fingers squeezing his, holding on for dear life. His eyes widened, and hers filled with tears.

"You're real," was all she said back.

It was almost six weeks since Kristina had died, and all that time Jacques had been in the Middle East on business, staying in a sky-high desert hotel. His wife had walked among the impeccable gardens and silver-burst fountains as he'd driven about in icebox cars, running meetings in his shirtsleeves. He had cut all ties with Kristina before he'd left, finally choosing to save his marriage over the ebb and flow of a summer romance that had lingered too far into autumn. He had fallen for Kristina, *complètement, totalement,* he said, in an accent that was everything that Hadley had imagined when she used to think of Jacques. His blond hair would have been smoothed back that morning, only it fell messily now, raked by tormented hands. His sunny brown skin had turned ghost-pale. He had learned of Kristina's death only by accident, he said, almost as soon as he returned to Switzerland. He'd seen a tiny printed snippet in an old newspaper, the last to be delivered to his Geneva apartment after he'd given the order to cancel. He had collapsed with the shock of it. For he'd loved her and wanted a life with her, once, before he'd decided what was right. *Was it possible,* he said, *to love two people at once?*

"I don't know," said Hadley. "I don't think so."

"We argued the night she died, because I was ending it, because I was going away. We went round and round in circles, and she kept saying that she was late for you, that she couldn't do this now, but I had to make her understand that it was over. I didn't want to leave on a lie. I owed her that, at least. In the end, she ran out in a fury with me. I thought it was the last time I'd see her for a long time. Not forever."

Hadley watched a single tear glisten on his cheek and wondered why it didn't drop and run. She thought of the Pierrot nightshirt Kristina had worn, the painted sadness. She saw him brush it away with the back of his hand.

"I found you through the university," he said. "I hope you don't mind. I've been so alone in my grief, and so late in my grief. I've only been back in Switzerland two days, and I had to find someone who knew her. She talked about you, Hadley. *My sweet English friend,* she'd say."

"I tried to find you, too," said Hadley.

"You tried?" said Jacques. "*Merci.* For trying."

They were in Helena's room. Kristina's room. Jacques was sitting on the edge of the bed. Helena was on the floor with her back leaning against the door, her arms wrapped around her knees. Hadley had wanted her there when she'd seen it wasn't Joel; she'd caught her sleeve and said, *stay, please stay.* Hadley stood by the window, just another

Lausanne night falling away behind her.

"I hate the thought that she died un-happy," said Jacques. "That she died with the words of our argument still in her ears. Were you with her? Was it after your party? Had she had a good time? Had she smiled? Please tell me she smiled."

Hadley hesitated. A white lie would be so easy, and so gentle.

"She never made it," she said. "She was late and I was upset, and we went to a different bar. You were the last person to see her."

"The last person?"

"Yes."

He sank his head into his hands. She knew that posture, she knew how it felt.

"We argued, too," she told him. "She phoned me on her way from Geneva. I was horrible, I told her not to bother coming. I can't change that, Jacques, but I also know that it can't be the thing that I remember. Because there was so much more."

He didn't say anything.

"Kristina told me something about you once," she said. "I thought it was the loveli-est thing. She said that you were the most handsome man in the world, and that you made her feel like she was the most beauti-ful woman."

"She said that?" He lifted his head, blinking fast. A sad smile crossed his face.

Hadley nodded. In her chest something shifted, and she breathed deeply.

She walked him out to the street. It was dark and quiet, and bone-cold.

"You're shivering," Jacques said. "You should go back inside."

"I'm fine," said Hadley, her teeth chattering. They made for the bus stop, their arms linked together.

"In fact, I won't take the bus. I'll walk to the station from here," he said. "Hadley, I'm glad to have met you. So very glad. If I hadn't, I might have tricked myself that Kristina never existed. I might have tried to pretend that we never mattered to one another. That's the coward's way to avoid pain. It always gets you in the end."

Hadley stared back at him. She unlinked her arm.

"What is it?" he said.

"I don't know," she replied.

"Are you angry with me, Hadley? That somehow I mistreated her? I wouldn't blame you if you were," he said.

"Kristina knew what she was doing with you," she said.

"Then, what's wrong?"

"It's nothing," she said, then, "Just, what you said before. About pretending she didn't exist. I'm confused, I guess."

"Confused about me?"

"Confused about someone who isn't you."

He looked sideways at her. "I don't understand," he said. His manner was brisker now that they were on the street, now that all had been said. "I'm sorry, but I really do have to go now. I've stayed too long already."

He kissed her on both cheeks, three times, in the Swiss style.

"I did love Kristina, Hadley," he said. "Once, I would have dropped everything for her. But then I made a decision, and I had to stick by it. That was all. If I hadn't ended it, things might have been different. I have to live with that guilt."

"Or they might have been just the same. It wasn't your fault, Jacques," she said. "It wasn't anybody's fault."

He looked momentarily grateful, but then his face clouded again. "Except it was, wasn't it?" he said.

She stayed on the street. The past hour had rinsed her. She leaned against the wall and watched Jacques walk away in fast strides, his legs moving like scissors. For all his sorrow, he was just as Kristina had said. He

507

had come and gone, and everything had changed again. She watched him as on the street he stepped aside to let someone pass. A man was dashing up the hill with uneven steps. He trod into a pool of streetlight, and her heart bolted in her chest. It was Joel. He was running, and he could only be running to see her. Joel passed Jacques, and they were within inches of one another, their feet pounding the same piece of pavement, their misted puffs of cold-night breath disappearing into the same patch of air. Two quite separate people, after all. She could have flattened herself against the wall, dropped into the shadows, and Joel would likely have blasted past, for his head was down. Instead, she stepped into the middle of the pavement. He pulled up, his breath gasping.

"Hadley? You're here," he said.

He reached for her, as though she were a figment that might slip away. His hand, usually so deft and warm, was slippery and chill to the touch. He seemed as though he had run all the way from downtown, his heart hammering in his chest. He was drenched in a cold sweat.

"Did you plan it?"

"Plan it?" he said, with disbelief. "You're not serious?"

"That was Jacques," said Hadley. "That man you just passed. *Jacques.* He's really real. He's everything Kristina said."

Joel wheeled around, and his open jacket flapped. His hands went to his head. Jacques was almost out of sight. Streetlight illuminated his last steps, and then he was gone.

"I thought she'd lied, I thought everybody had lied," she said. "All that looking for Jacques, and then he found me. How did you know he was here? I don't get it."

"Hadley, I don't know any Jacques. I never did."

They stared at one another, and oceans rolled between them.

"But you said it was you," she said. "I was so sure it was you, and you said that it was. You loved Kristina, you were Jacques. I thought that was it. Hugo thought that was it."

"I didn't even know her, Hadley. I didn't know her at all."

"But in your apartment, you knew that I'd worked it out. But I hadn't, had I? I got it wrong. So, why did you do that? Why did you pretend to be him?"

"I didn't pretend to be him, Hadley," he said.

"But then I don't understand. If he's

Jacques, if you're not Jacques, why were you so upset? Why are you upset now? Joel, I don't get it."

His arms hung at his sides, and he appeared shrunken inside his jacket. All of the stuffing was gone from him.

"Please, say something," she said. "Please, tell me something that makes sense."

Joel rubbed his face with both hands. "Can we go inside?" he said. "Can we talk someplace else?"

"No. Here," she said, "talk to me here."

He placed a hand on each of her shoulders. It was a delicate touch, as though she, or he, might break.

"Hadley," he said, "when you came to my apartment, the way you were talking, I was so sure you understood. And it was such a relief. Such a dreadful, sickening, awful relief." He gave a short, sharp bark of a laugh, a sound entirely lacking in mirth. "Then, afterward, when I thought about it, hell, I couldn't *stop* thinking about it, I realized you must have gotten it wrong. That whatever you were thinking, it had to be something else."

His lips moved loosely, and at his jawline his stubble had thickened into a beard. His eyes searched hers, and she stared back, looking for the Joel that she knew.

"You're frightening me," she said, stepping backward. His arms dropped, and he caught at her hand.

"Hadley, I'm frightening myself. I haven't slept in two days. You're the first person and the last person that I needed to talk to about this. I've been the worst kind of coward. The absolute worst. So, whatever's coming to me, I deserve it. I'll take it, I'll take it all."

"What are you telling me, Joel?" she said, her voice peculiarly level.

He didn't answer. He just looked at her as though she already knew.

"Say it," said Hadley, very slowly, each word spiked as though it would cut her tongue. "Because what I'm thinking is absolutely, completely, *impossible*. So, you need to say it. Or I'll get it wrong again. I'll think you're someone you're not. Again."

"Hadley . . ."

"Tell me. The truth."

"I love you."

"Not that. Never that."

"Hadley, I can't . . ."

"One true sentence. Isn't that what your Hemingway would say? The truest sentence you know, Joel. Say it."

"I'm going to the police."

"Why?"

"Because of the accident."

"Why?"

"She came from nowhere, Hadley. Like the blizzard, from nowhere. She just stepped into the road. I didn't even hit her hard. I wasn't driving fast. But she fell. And she must have hit her head on the pavement, because when I looked back, I could see she wasn't moving. And there was blood on the snow. And I didn't do that, I know I didn't, I didn't hit her that hard. She must have slipped on the ice. I barely brushed her, I know I didn't. Perhaps I was just driving by. The worst timing. The worst stroke of Fate. And before I knew what was happening, I was driving on. Why? You want to know why? I want to know why. I've asked myself that question a hundred times, and all I have is this — I didn't want my life to end because hers had. This girl I didn't know. This girl who just stepped from the darkness, this girl who slipped and fell. And I know exactly what that makes me." He paused for breath. Hadley was open-mouthed, her hands clasped. "I shouldn't even have been there. I was a fool to have been there. You want to know why I was? You'd told me you were going to some restaurant, Le Pin, some place near the station. And I was at home, in my apartment,

512

and I suddenly thought, to hell with it, to hell with everything, I'm going to go and see her. I'm going to go and wish Hadley Dunn happy birthday, buy her a drink and just see, just see what happened when I did those things. Because I liked you, Hadley, because I wanted to take a chance on it, run a risk, and see what happened. So I got in my car and I drove, because the weather was so bad, and the blizzard was so rough. I was looking for a spot to park, and then I saw you. You were with that kid from the mountains, the Italian, and you were kissing him. On the pavement, right there in front of me, in front of everyone, barely coming up for air. And I realized then what a fool I'd been to think that it could have gone any other way. So I carried on past, I drove around the block a couple of times, and maybe I was angry, maybe I was distracted, maybe I was thinking 'what does this kid have that made her choose him?' and maybe I wasn't looking where I was going on Rue des Mirages."

She'd listened in disbelief, her feet rooted to the ground, everything frozen, but as he reached for her hand, she leaped away from him.

"It was *you*?"

"It was me."

"It can't have been you. It wasn't you."

"Hadley . . ."

"You hit her, and then you ran? *You?*"

"Hadley, I was frightened. I didn't know what to do. I'd had two glasses of wine, barely two glasses, but it might have looked like more. They might have thought that had something to do with it, and it didn't. Suddenly I was driving away and I didn't stop."

"And you forgave yourself?" she said, her voice looping with incredulity.

"Never."

"But you lived with yourself," she insisted. "You did, you know you did."

"Barely, Hadley."

"You expect me to believe that?"

"If you hadn't come to me that day I would have gone to the police. You have to believe that."

"You're lying. Everything's a lie. You're a lie."

"I was going mad with the weight of it, and it got mixed up with everything else, old grief, old wrongs, Winston and that godforsaken truck. And then you came to the door, and changed everything. *Almost* everything. Hadley, you gave yourself to me. All your despair and need and want, you placed it in my hands with so much trust. And I suddenly thought that here was

514

someone I could help. What good would it have done, if I'd turned myself in, then? What use? I could be helpful to you. I could comfort you. I could right a wrong. It felt like the best thing I could do, to make you happy. That was all I tried to be, the person who could make you happy. Then I failed at that, too."

She stepped toward him and shoved him hard in the chest. They grappled for a moment. His feet were unsteady, the hill was steep and he stumbled, falling back onto the pavement. He went down heavily, and he stayed down as she screamed at him.

"You're making this somehow about me? And my need? Whatever I needed, it wasn't this."

"Hadley . . ."

"No! Kristina was . . . so much alive. And she . . . she fell in love when she wasn't supposed to, and everything she told me about Jacques was true, even though I'd begun to think it wasn't, even though I'd begun to doubt her every word. And now she's gone, Joel. She's *gone.* Her parents came. They drove up this exact street. They stood in Les Ormes and cried. Her mum kissed me on the cheek, and her lips were so cold. And I had nothing to say to her. Nothing that would make any difference. And all of it was because of you . . . It was you, all you."

She gasped and stopped, choked by sobs.

People didn't ordinarily yell in the streets of Lausanne. They didn't tussle and brawl on pavements. Respectability was everywhere, or the veneer of it at least. A police car, cruising the quiet midweek streets, where civilized Swiss were tucked up in bed, rolled down the road toward them. There were no quick-switching lights, no bleating sirens or spinning tires. There had been no panicked telephone call, no rat-a-tat voice coming over the radio. It was simply a quirk of timing, just as when Joel had turned into Rue des Mirages in a gathering snowstorm, his windscreen blurred and whipped. Just as he had turned his head in a waterside bar and seen a girl he knew he couldn't forget. It was the work of moments. The police car began to slow down, and to the officers inside, they must have appeared as the very picture of strife, the kind of image that hangs in a gallery in old Lausanne, a masterful rendering in fine strokes of oil. The man on the street floor, looking as if something had caught him and was pulling him to hell, the girl trying to step away from him, her hands thrown up to heaven.

Hadley saw the car first. She turned from Joel, and for a second she stood quite still.

516

Then she stepped into the middle of the road, her hand raised. One, two, three paces, and she was there. It was a quiet night, and there were no other cars. It came on toward her, and she let it. She braced herself, curled her toes inside her shoes, stood straight and kept her gaze level. There was no great drama, no screeching of brakes and screaming of tires. Instead, the Swiss police pulled over tidily, and Hadley was left in the middle of the road. The officers slid from their seats. Joel clambered to his feet.

The four of them stood on the hill outside Les Ormes looking at one another. For a second, she entertained the dark fantasy that they could carry on pretending, after all. Tell the officers that she hadn't meant to step into their path, that it was all a mistake. And they'd go to Locarno just as Joel had said they would, see the Italian blue lake and lick ice cream from each other's cones, pose for photographs, their laughter turning to kisses. But Joel had his wrists out, upturned, as though he had seen the films and was following the script. He addressed the officers in French, and she understood the words for *accident,* and *girl,* and *dead.* It was dark on the street, but she could see his face as clearly as if it were lit by a camera flash. His eyes were blue-black. His mouth a ragged hole. His cheek was battered still, and one of his cuts had opened. His lick of hair had fallen and plastered his forehead. She had never seen him looking as devastated as that. Except, perhaps, that day in his office, when she had come with news of Kristina, when she'd asked him for his help. Hadley moved to him and caught his hands. She wrapped her fingers around his wrists, and she squeezed with all that she had.

"It's time," was all he said.

Before she knew what she was doing, she tried to kiss him. She leaned forward, pushing her lips toward his, but he turned his head away. She caught the bristle of his cheek, the lobe of his ear, the salt-hot part of his neck behind his collar. Then she felt a hand on her shoulder that wasn't Joel's. It couldn't have been, for there was nothing transmitted in the touch. She let herself be blankly, coldly, steered away.

"We'll need to talk to you, too, *mademoiselle,* just a routine statement," one of the officers said, and his voice seemed to come from a long way away. Hadley nodded, dumbly. She confirmed her name and address. She reeled off the digits of her phone number, stumbling once, starting again. "Tomorrow will be fine," he said, and Hadley stared at him as if he'd slipped into a strange language, for the idea of a tomorrow was too abstract, too impossible to conceive of ever happening.

Just as Joel got into the blue-striped car, he reached into his pocket. He held a small, battered book in his hands.

"Please take this, Hadley," he said. "It's all true."

"I don't want it," she said. Then, "What is it?"

"The first time I saw you I wrote about it. The second time I saw you I wrote about it. And the third. I carried on writing. You, and only you. I want you to know what I saw in you from the beginning. What I kept on seeing in you. Even after what happened —" he stumbled, then collected himself "— I kept writing about you. I want you to believe that you existed for me before, and that you'll never stop existing for me after."

"I can't read it," she said.

"Hadley, I know how wrong this is, but whenever you looked at me, I thought that you could see all the way inside. Without either of us ever saying anything, it was like an absolution."

"You really thought that?"

"In the beginning. Not in the end."

He looked at her, and it felt like a last

look, as though he was seeking to remember her before she had quite gone.

"If you want one true sentence," he said, "it's in here."

Her fingers closed loosely around the book's cover and its jagged spiral binding. Gradually her hand tightened its hold. By the time the car drove away, the rear windows reflecting nothing but the night, she was gripping it as though she would never let it go. That was how Helena found her. Standing on the pavement, clutching Joel's words, staring down the hill toward a city that seemed, to all appearances, to carry on regardless.

CHAPTER 34

Spring came overnight to Lausanne, just as Hugo Bézier said it would. Early March was milder than usual and full of sunshine. By April, trees with puffed heads of pink-and-white blossoms lined the streets and parks. At Les Ormes the residents were embracing the turning of the seasons. Balcony doors were propped open, blankets were spread on top of the flat roofs and a string of sausages was barbecued over hot coals. Hemingway might have written about a false spring, but this one seemed to feel true.

Hugo had insisted that they continue with their old habits, so Hadley still drank coffee and cognac with him at the Hôtel Le Nouveau Monde, except he followed his doctor's orders and took water with sliced lemon instead. As he watched Hadley drink a cognac, some part of him seemed to revel in it, too. Perhaps he liked the flush it gave her cheeks, maybe he remembered the taste, how the sweet burn in the throat felt like a long-forgotten kiss. Sometimes they took tea at his vast apartment, the one that was just three streets back from the hotel, where from his balcony the fluttering flags and the voluptuous curve of the roof were just visible. A maid called Brigitte brought their tray out to the terrace; her silver hair parted with a girlish clip, and her every movement as light as a dancer's. Each morning now before breakfast, Hugo slowly walked the gardens of the Musée Olympique. The air was as crisp as it always was at that time of year, but he seemed to take more of it in these days. With every breath, he told Hadley, he could taste the bite of the snow-capped mountains, its crystal edge.

In the end he'd outstayed his welcome at the Résidence Le Printemps, the clack-clack of his typewriter driving the fellow guests, and particularly the pistachio-coated orderlies, quite mad. For Hugo was becoming Henri again. Word by word, line by line, page by page, he was writing. And Hadley was reading, which was easier for her because, for the first time in his life, Hugo was writing not in French but in English, and against all traditions it was proving itself the language of love. It was difficult for other reasons, though, the main one being

522

the fact that she knew the characters inside out. Most of them. One, she thought perhaps she didn't know at all. Maybe that was because she still hadn't opened Joel's notebook. Instead, she had given it to Hugo, and he had read it, once, twice, three times over. Then he had begun to write. It had started as an exercise, to see if he still had it in him, just as one might walk a little farther than usual, or climb a flight of stairs. Hadley caught him one day. She saw him sitting straight as a gun at a table by the window, his hands flying over the keys of the typewriter, staccato shots ringing out.

"You're writing," she said.

"Is that all right?" he asked.

And she nodded. She sank into the chair opposite and watched him, her chin resting in the flat of her hand. He got to the end of the page and handed it to her.

"A terrible liberty," he said. "I'd change everything, of course, all the details that don't matter. But all the things that do . . . I'd write them just as they happened. If you'll let me."

"Hadley," she said slowly. She tried it for the first time and found herself pleased with the name. *"'Hadley.'"* She read on.

"Or, I'll abandon it. Just say the word, and it's gone. I only know that I want to write again. *You* make me want to write again. You always did. And then you gave me your professor's notebook. It wasn't written for me, it wasn't written for anyone else except you, and yet, *ma chérie,* you refused to read it. A man pours out his heart, his broken, weak-willed heart, but his heart nonetheless, and you ignore it. And I see what that does to you, the strength that takes, and I know that I want to write it. I want to write all of it. Not the crime, not the mystery, but you, the green girl, who desired nothing more than to come to Lausanne and fall in love."

"Fall in love? Oh, but I did, Hugo. Don't you see? In all the ways you could possibly think of."

A slip of a smile crossed his face.

"Hadley, for most of my life, I've done a very good impression of someone who is living. Only now, at the final stretch, have I discovered my own deception. I never had a Kristina, you see. I never had a Joel."

"But you do have me," she said.

He raised his glass of lemon water to her. She lifted her cognac in reply.

"It's all for you, you know, the writing," he said.

"That's not true. I can see just by looking at you that that's not true."

"No," he said, setting down his glass. He ran his fingers over his typewriter keys in light caress. His eyes gleamed like treacle. "No, I suppose it isn't, not entirely."

There never were any more words from Joel. No envelope bearing a Swiss prison stamp. She'd visited him just once, at eleven o'clock on a Thursday morning. Outside, thick January snow had been falling on everything, rendering it perfect, a soft, unquestioning blanket. Inside, Hadley had held his eye, and it was Joel who had looked away first. He'd been crumpled and drawn and had refused his own bail. He wanted everything that was coming to him and more, he had told her.

"I came to say goodbye."

"You're not leaving Lausanne?" he said. "Because of me?"

"No," she said, "I'm not leaving. Not yet, anyway, not until I have to."

"I didn't think you'd come. I never expected you to."

"I nearly didn't."

She had practiced what she'd wanted to say to him. She had tried to say it in front of the mirror in her room, with her pale, angry face staring back at her. Too often she'd been lost in tears, her words cracking and breaking, her reflection streaming and blurred. Faced with him again, she knew she couldn't, and shouldn't, remember it all.

"Joel, I want you to know that for a little while you were the best thing I knew. And then you were the very worst. I guess somehow that should equal things out, but I don't know if it does. Does it make you disappear? Should it?"

Her voice was softer than in any of her rehearsals, its hard edge lost.

"I'll be as good as gone," he said. "I deserve to be."

"No, you won't," she said.

"Hadley . . ."

"I have to go now. I'm going to say good-bye."

"Did you read the things I wrote? Is that why you came?"

"No. I gave it to Hugo."

"To Hugo?"

"He needs it more than I do. I'll read it one day, but only when I'm hard as a stone, when all this feels like someone else's story. That's when I'll read it."

Looking at him, she thought suddenly of her first night in Lausanne. Before she knew who he was, before she'd met Kristina. A voice from the dark, friendly, inquiring and rumbling with just-kept laughter. *Take it easy,* he'd said, and all the way home she'd hugged the phrase to her, like a secret shared.

"Before we went to Geneva that time," she said, standing up, "you gave me two conditions. Now it's my turn. I want you to make me a promise. Two promises."

"Hadley, say it. Anything."

"The first. Please don't try and contact me. Ever."

"I wrecked everything, Hadley. I'd never hope for anything from you, I . . ."

"And the second," she said, her voice breaking but holding, just about holding, "the second is that one day, when I'm older, when I've lived a lot more, and loved a lot more, and my hair is as gray as Hugo Bézier's, I want to hear about you again. I want to hear something good about Joel Wilson. I want to know that this wasn't the end of your life, too."

Behind the glass he stood up, and for the briefest moment they were mirrored. He tried to speak and failed. She walked from the room, her arms stiff by her sides.

Later, she thought about him. She couldn't not; she always would. Joel lying on a hard bunk, staring at a blank ceiling, his hands knotted and resting on his chest.

527

Was it justice? Nothing felt right. But then the picture faded and in its place stood Kristina. Smiling her cat-smile, laughing with a flash of pink tongue. Such stories she spun, and every one was true.

At L'Institut Vaudois, Joel's classes were taken over by an Englishman named Paul Draper, who also taught Canadian Literature that same semester. He had a spiky beard like a medieval merchant and wore battered brogues. He had a problem saying his *r*'s, and he talked quickly, his words falling over one another. In the end, the note-taking students didn't try to keep up. They left the lecture hall talking about coffee and cigarettes or that night's plans, not the things they had learned as once they used to. Nor what Hemingway had meant when he said that the world would break you, just as it breaks everyone, but sometimes you ended up stronger for it. Paul Draper didn't make them think like that.

As to Jacques, Hadley never heard from him again. He'd come and gone, a ghost in shined shoes, a Genevan city slicker with a bandaged marriage and a private grief. Everything Kristina had said about him was true. And everything she hadn't was true also. Sometimes she thought of Kristina's parents, northeast of Lausanne, far away in Copenhagen. Hadley wanted to send a card, but she wasn't sure what she would have said. Perhaps that the days were warmer, that winter was at last beginning to feel as if it was behind them. But it wasn't, was it? Not for them. Then one day, Hadley received a parcel with a Danish postmark. The note inside simply said, *She meant this for you, we found it in her things.* There was a book, written in French, and it was called *L'Adieu aux armes.* Slipped inside the cover was a card without an envelope. *Happy Birthday, dear Hadley,* Kristina had written messily, as though on the fast-moving train from Geneva to Lausanne, *Sorry I've been a pain. I'll try not to be. You said this was your favourite book, but I bet you haven't read it in French. Here's to all the fun we're going to have, tonight, and for all our time here. Love from me xx*

Hadley looked again at the cover of the book, her eyes blurring. It showed a man and woman embracing, and there was something ineffably sad in their posture; it felt like goodbye.

Chase and Jenny, Bruno and Loretta, sometimes with Luca, too, continued to thread their way through the Lausanne year. Helena, the not-so-new girl, made a wide and easy gaggle of friends. She drew them from her French language classes and the shelter where she served hot meals to the homeless on a Saturday and where she was once serenaded on a three-stringed guitar by an old railway worker and his French love song. As Helena laughed and clapped, a woman with stringy plaits caught her eye for a moment and grinned, rolled her eyes, then ambled outside for a cigarette. Helena's good humor proved infectious wherever she was, whomever she was with, which was often, but not always, Hadley.

Hadley had planted a small garden on the slope below Les Ormes, and now that it was spring, it was blooming. Sunshine-faced daisies and potted palm trees, head-turning hydrangeas and elegant lilies. She'd started off on her own, kneeling on the damp grass and inexpertly stabbing the soil with a trowel that still bore its price tag. Luca was lounging on Loretta's balcony and saw her. He called out an offer of assistance, and despite Hadley's resistance, he joined her. Everyone came down in the end. Jenny and Chase, Bruno and Loretta, Helena. Other students who were passing, whose names they didn't yet know but soon would, they all came and helped turn the soil, clear patches of nettles, shuttle pans of water from the kitchens. Hadley didn't make a plaque, there was no official naming ceremony, but everyone knew it was a garden for Kristina. She saved the best until last, a row of leggy sunflowers that turned their heads to look out over the city. Hadley stood beside one, knowing that by summer it would have outgrown her. She wiped her hands on her jeans. Chase handed her a bottle of beer.

Hadley's mum and dad and little brother, Sam, took a leap of their own. They visited for a week in the full blush of a Swiss spring, as the flowers along the lakeside popped pink, and the steamships to Montreux passed on the hour. They ate buttered croissants and drank coffee; they peered out over the carpeted city from the top of the cathedral and bought a hard slab of cheese from the market on the square. They took a bus to the L'Institut Vaudois, and Hadley showed them the view from the library, the silver band of lake and sky full of mountains. Her mum said, "How you manage to concentrate on your studies, I'll never know." They passed Caroline Dubois as they walked on campus, exchanged a *bonjour* and a smile, and her dad said, "They're a charming sort, the professors here. Nothing like I imagined." And Hadley held her breath. She thought of Joel Wilson, spinning on his heel at the front of the class, blasting passion, and how she had felt, for the first time, as though the top of her head had come clean off, and she'd dissolved, tiny stars fizzing in the ether. He had taken so much away, but he had given her that. That feeling that didn't belong anywhere on earth, where there were fears and blizzards and dark nights and consequences and loathing and shame and pretending that things were all right when they weren't, not even close.

Hugo wrote all through the spring, and Hadley let him. She saw how it charged him, and so the story changed hands. It became his, not hers, to do with whatever he wanted, to stay tucked forever in a drawer, or passed into the light of day. When she read it, it was almost as though it had all happened to someone else. Everything that mattered was in there but rendered differently, painted in a shifted palette. Except the writing in Joel's notebook, he refused to change a word of that. So Joel's words became the notable omission. Hadley let Hugo take just one thing from it, and that was because it was Hemingway who said it first, even though he was talking about Paris. "There is never any end to Lausanne." Joel had said it in his very first lecture, appropriating his hero's words and addressing the room of green-tipped students. Yet how prophetic a statement it had been. In the notebook Joel had written that his days were marked forever, that there was a stain on his soul that no amount of rubbing could shift. That there would never be a morning when he would wake up and think about anything other than what he had done, and what he had not. He could never leave Lausanne, he'd written, all he wished for Hadley was that she could, and forget everything that had been. *Except perhaps one thing. One true thing.* And as Hadley finally found the heart to read Joel's words, she knew that he was right, although she'd never said it back to him. In among all the sad things, love in the past tense was surely one of them.

Joel had been right about another thing, too.

One early May morning she opened her eyes, and the very first thing that hit her was, pure and simply, the quality of light. It was that particular brightness she had grown so used to throughout the winter months. She went to the window and opened the blinds. Outside, the spring day was just beginning, spry blue, with great peals of sunshine, yet all of Lausanne was dusted with snow. It would be gone again by midmorning, the last fall of the winter, surely, for she could already hear the drip, drip, drip from the rooftops. She pushed open her balcony door and stood looking out over her city. Soon she would be in the thick of it, trailing footprints in the white. Hadley turned from the view and went in search of coffee and toast. She left the doors and windows wide-open; the light streamed in, and against the walls, the shadows started to shift.

Meanwhile, in a hotel by the shore, an ageless man sat writing. His fingers danced over the keys of his typewriter, his heart pulled in all the directions he'd forgotten, and others he'd never known at all.

ACKNOWLEDGMENTS

Thank you to my earliest readers, my friend Kate and my husband, Robin. You braved my messy first draft and our kitchen table sessions set me on the right path. Without your well-timed help, I'm not sure I would have stayed sane.

Thank you to my editors and agent, Erika, Leah and Rowan. This book is better because of you, and for that I'm forever grateful. The last months of writing, with your words and wisdom filling my sails, proved to be the most enjoyable of all. Thank you.

Thank you to my dear family, the Halls and the Etheringtons, and brilliant friends for always cheering me on. Sonya, Jo and Aisling, while Hadley's year is not *our* year, I hope I've written something of our joy into the story. Special thanks to my parents and sister, Szilvia, Alwyn and Emese, for reading early drafts and always being unfailingly enthusiastic in your support. I couldn't ask for more.

And again, Robin. Thank you for everything, always.

Finally, this book began with a place. I was lucky enough to have lived in Lausanne for a year as a student, and even luckier to be able to put it in a novel and share it with you now. I hope I've done its beauty justice. Of all the books that talk of Lausanne, *A Farewell to Arms* and *A Moveable Feast* by Ernest Hemingway, and *The Paris Wife* by Paula McLain, were particularly important to the writing of this one.

■ ■ ■ ■

THE SWISS AFFAIR

EMYLIA HALL
READER'S GUIDE

■ ■ ■ ■

QUESTIONS FOR DISCUSSION

1. When Hadley arrives in Lausanne, the world she finds herself in appears to be perfect: stylish, elegant, a place of privilege and pleasure-seekers. To what extent is this veneer broken down throughout the course of the novel?

2. Love is everywhere in *The Swiss Affair*, from slow-building crushes, to illicit liaisons, to platonic but no less wistful attachment. How is the idea of love explored? Do any of the characters experience what you would consider to be "true love"?

3. When Hadley first meets Joel, Kristina and even Hugo, they each make a striking impression on her. Talk about the value of first impressions and what makes each character appealing to Hadley. Is she too

easily impressed, or is her critical aware-
ness sound?

4. To what extent does sorrow play its part
in bringing the story's characters together,
or driving them apart? Is Hadley justified
in her judgment of the attitude of her Les
Ormes friends toward her grief?

5. The lines between generations blur in *The
Swiss Affair,* as Hadley falls for a man
twice her age and often chooses the company of the elderly Hugo Bézier over her
contemporaries at Les Ormes. Is age a factor, in friendship and romance? Does it
make a difference to the characters in *The
Swiss Affair?*

6. How does Hadley's character grow
throughout the novel? Compare when she
first arrives in Lausanne with her expecta-
tions and her outlook at the end. What are
your hopes for her?

7. In *The Swiss Affair* we're presented with
a writer who doesn't write. How important
is Hugo's renewed appetite for story in
driving the narrative? Are his motives
mixed? If they are, does that affect how

you view his friendship with Hadley?

8. Issues of truth, lies and the masking of feeling are key in *The Swiss Affair*. Think of Kristina's patchy accounts of Jacques, Hadley's growing affection for her tutor, Hugo's disgruntlement, Joel's secrets. How would earlier honesty from every character potentially have changed the story's outcome?

9. The work of Ernest Hemingway is important to *The Swiss Affair*. Talk about the numerous Hemingway references in the novel and how they relate to the story.

A CONVERSATION WITH EMYLIA HALL

The Swiss Affair is the story of a young woman's coming of age and journey of self-discovery during a year abroad. What was your inspiration for Hadley's story, and how, if at all, do you relate to her?

Like Hadley, I spent my second year of university in Lausanne, Switzerland, and it was this experience that provided the initial inspiration for the novel. It really was a golden year. My French improved hugely, I made great friends, I learned to snowboard in the nearby mountains and I fell in love — not with a boy but with a city, and that love has endured. I also discovered Ernest Hemingway while studying literature in Lausanne, starting with A Farewell to Arms, *a story that ends in the Swiss city. For me, the author, and where I first read his work, will be forever entwined. I always wanted to write a story set in Lausanne, a*

543

desire to capture that glorious time, but I wanted an unexpected darkness amid the seeming perfection. That's where Hadley's story and mine differ; her year abroad is extraordinarily sad, as well as extraordinarily happy. One thing Hadley and I do share is an affinity with the lovely French phrase "il faut profiter" — we both enjoy luxuriating in a moment, and making the most of an experience.

In your first novel, *The Book of Summers*, you chose Hungary as the backdrop for the novel. In *The Swiss Affair*, it's the Swiss city of Lausanne. What is it about these foreign locales that inspires you, and why did you choose Lausanne specifically for this novel?

I love traveling almost more than anything — it's the sense of anticipation in the buildup to a trip, the quality of experience as you're living it and the longing that so often follows when it's all over. For me, spending time abroad has always represented freedom and possibility. There's something thrilling about being able to slip sideways into a different existence, where everything feels new and undiscovered. I'm fascinated by the way that people behave when they travel, the emotions that the act of relocation engender, and I think

544

that's a subject I'll return to again and again in my writing. There's also pleasure in desk-bound travel; when I write I can go anywhere, and for me, that's part of the magic of it. Lausanne is an important city in my own history, and writing it into a novel is a wonderful way of tapping my memories, while enjoying all the liberties of fiction.

In the novel, Hadley befriends a cast of international students and gets involved with an American professor. What were some of the challenges of writing characters who come from places unfamiliar to you?

My experience of living in Switzerland was similar to Hadley's in that I found myself part of an expat crowd. Our student residence was brilliantly cosmopolitan, which I enjoyed, so the cast of characters in The Swiss Affair *was always going to be diverse. The challenge came in portraying nuance through language. Early on I realized that it would be tiresome to read dialogue written in stilted English, however accurate a representation that might have been. Instead, I tried to convey distinction with small phrases here and there, and certain gestures. That said, most of the international students I encoun-*

tered in Lausanne spoke excellent English, putting my own language skills to shame, so it felt entirely natural to write characters like Kristina and Hugo, people who are intelligent, well traveled, with a fluent and even idiomatic command of English. When it came to the American Joel Wilson, I had some help from my U.S. editor!

Hadley's character makes an enormous transformation over the course of the novel, from someone who is perhaps a bit naive to someone who is forced to confront and adapt to the cruelties of life. Did you have her journey entirely mapped out from the start? How did she surprise you along the way?

I broadly planned Hadley's journey from the start, in that I wanted her year abroad to be hugely transformative; full of immense happiness, challenge and the inevitable sadness of existence. She arrives wide-eyed and full of expectation — not extraordinarily naive, but just as any fresh-faced girl arriving in a new country might be — and then throughout the course of her stay she cultivates new relationships, her resolve is tested, her emotions stretched, and she has to decide what really matters in the face of some huge questions. I had a strong sense of her early on. She always felt like a fully formed person to me, never just a "character," and as such she behaved largely as I expected. There is, however, a moment late on in the novel when she's in an incredibly difficult position and manages to be quite steely. I'd finished writing the dialogue, but then it felt as though there was more that she wanted to say, so I revisited it. She ends up displaying more compassion than I'd originally intended, and that felt right. It was Hadley's voice in my head saying, "Wait, I'm not done yet. Let me say this one thing." And to me it was a real moment of grace. During the creative process the most surprising character was Hugo Bézier. His role in the novel increased throughout its writing as, quite simply, he demanded more page time, and I was happy to give it to him. I love those sorts of surprises when writing, and it's why a sense of fluidity is so important. I plan . . . but only to a point. I do believe that, in the end, the nature of the novel takes its own course.

As with **The Book of Summers**, identity is an important theme in **The Swiss Affair**. What message about identity do

you hope readers take away from the novel?

Our experiences make us who we are. The Hadley who leaves for Lausanne is a different girl to the Hadley who will return after the book's end. While her essential qualities will remain unchanged, she'll be looking at the world with altered eyes. Change is essential, and even through difficult experiences we can draw some comfort from what we've learned. As a result of adversity, Hadley makes meaningful connections with people she might otherwise never have encountered, and that's all part of her journey. Being open to life's possibilities, and the people around us, is what I hope readers will take away.

What was your greatest challenge in writing *The Swiss Affair*? Your greatest pleasure?

Not everybody in the book behaves nobly — each has their own set of motivations that, at times, outweigh all else — but I really wanted every character to be largely likable, or at least deserving of sympathy, so I had to keep stepping back from them and appraising them objectively. When you spend a lot of time in a story, it's easy to feel a sort of unconditional affection toward your cast, motherly, almost. The reader's view was always my sense-check. As to my greatest pleasure . . . Where to begin? I tremendously value a sense of place in writing (and reading), and I loved revisiting Lausanne and Switzerland in this way, taking to the city streets and the snow-swept mountains. Writing the dynamics between the characters also excited me, especially the Hadley-and-Joel and Hadley-and-Hugo scenes — a curious sort of triangle whose tips don't quite meet. And the figure of Ernest Hemingway loomed always at the edges of my writing. I took huge pleasure in channeling aspects of his work — the books that Hadley was studying, the interests of Joel — while also dotting my story with references that perhaps only an enthusiast would spot.

Can you describe your writing process? Do you write the scenes consecutively or do you jump around? Do you have a schedule or a routine? A lucky charm?

I always, always write consecutively. The only time I'd consider jumping forward would be if I was describing a setting or place. But if it's people . . . never. I think that's because I have faith in the natural process of character development. That's not to say I don't go back and forth in the editing process, but at the first draft stage I write as "naturally" as possible. I like to experience events as they unfold, just as the characters do. I write best in the mornings, aided by several cups of coffee always in my same bright orange Santa Fe mug, bought from a Five and Dime store on my honeymoon in New Mexico. That mug is the closest thing I have to a charm. If it broke I think I'd have to get on the first flight out to replace it.

Can you tell us something about what you're working on now?

I'm enjoying writing some short fiction, while playing with ideas for my next novel. I love this time in a new book's creation; the story tantalizes, and while its details are as yet unknown, a really strong sense of its heart can still exist. It's exciting, and the possibilities feel endless.